D0629242

overexposed

also by susan shapiro

overexposed

∾

Susan Shapiro

Thomas Dunne Books
St. Martin's Press
New York

This is a work of fiction. All of the characters, organizations, and events portrayed in this novel are either products of the author's imagination or are used fictitiously.

THOMAS DUNNE BOOKS.
An imprint of St. Martin's Press.

OVEREXPOSED. Copyright © 2010 by Susan Shapiro. All rights reserved. Printed in the United States of America. For information, address St. Martin's Press, 175 Fifth Avenue, New York, N.Y. 10010.

Short sections of this book appeared in slightly different forms in *The New York Times*, *New Woman*, *The Forward*, and the *Jewish News*.

www.thomasdunnebooks.com
www.stmartins.com

Book design by Rich Arnold

Library of Congress Cataloging-in-Publication Data available on request.

ISBN 978-0-312-58157-2

First Edition: August 2010

10 9 8 7 6 5 4 3 2 1

To Ryan Fischer-Harbage, Katie
Gilligan, Barb Burg

& in memory of Emma Segal

overexposed

prologue

I spent years cutting myself out of photographs.

All through elementary school I'd sneak down the steps of our huge white house in Highland Park, hiding my mother's sewing scissors in my pocket. Sitting on the basement floor, I'd turn the pages of her albums and carefully lop off my early faces. I removed myself from boisterous Solomon family reunions, garish weddings filled with hordes of out-of-town Jewish relatives eating heart-shaped chopped liver, and the series of my kiddie birthday parties held at the circus, bowling alley, and doll infirmary.

Late one night my mother stormed in and caught me, demanding to know why I kept ruining her memories.

"I don't belong here," I told her. "Besides, I look hideous."

"You're crazy." She seized the evidence and turned her perfect face toward the stairs, shrieking, "You were always so pretty and happy!"

It was an ongoing argument between us. She insisted my childhood was filled with joyous Kodak moments, that I loved being the only girl, posing between my kid brothers and showing off the frilly, pastel dresses she favored. But two decades later I can still feel those lacy collars scratching my neck and the pink leather shoes with tight straps strangling my big feet, leaving marks that hurt for days. No wonder I wound up in black sweats, oversize T-shirts, and worn sneakers...on the other side of the camera.

My life really began the fall morning I joined my junior high's yearbook staff as a photographer. Skipping all my classes, I couldn't stop secretly snapping candids of my teachers, classmates, and enemies. Ironically, being a picture freak, my most antisocial fetish, made me popular. Soon everybody I knew in suburban Illinois was striking poses before my lens, begging for portraits of themselves, praising my clever eye.

When I turned fourteen, envious of the elaborate bar mitzvah thrown for my brother Ben, the exalted oldest Solomon son, I coerced my father into building me a darkroom in our downstairs walk-in closet. Working alone in that dim, cramped hovel was the most at home I'd ever been. In the middle of the night, under the orange glow of the safe-light, I'd get stoned and pore over all the head shots I'd taken, people collecting.

At fifteen, I got a camera tattoo on my ankle and lost my virginity on the darkroom floor to a Deadhead named Derek, surrounded by strips of negatives and toxic chemicals. For my Sweet Sixteen Mom gave me a thick gold ring and a set of Chanel No. 5 perfume and body lotion, but I preferred the acid smell of fixer and stop bath on my fingers.

Right after high school graduation, I grabbed my Rebel K2 lightweight Canon—with retractable flash—and fled to college in the big city. Landing my first job at a hot glossy, I bumped into Elizabeth Mann, who became the most vivid person I ever captured. How unsettling to view my vexing friend now, replacing me in the plastic-covered sheets of my family's album, stealing my position, my mother's Russian Rose lipstick, and the antique white wedding gown that was promised to me.

part
one

chapter one
new vision
August 9, 2000

We met the day I replaced her.

I was sitting at my newly assigned desk after hours, still psyched out of my mind to be an art assistant at *Vision* magazine, when she ran in, startling me. She was a tall, gangly brunette, older than I was. Taking off her raincoat, she draped it across a chair, along with her leather handbag, as if she owned the place. She was wearing a V-neck ash-colored sweater and gray pants. There was a rip on the bottom of her pant leg, and her flats were caked with mud.

"Jane's gone already?" she asked after my coworker.

"Left a half hour ago," I said.

I couldn't tell if she was a hotshot editor from upstairs or just a peon like me.

"Damn. She said she'd loan me twenty bucks." Her eyes were red; she'd been crying. "Nobody fucking warned me the unemployment checks take six weeks to start. I have to get to Boston." She was half talking to me, half mumbling to herself. Then she picked up the phone, dialed, and said, "Right, like Dad can check himself in. There's a train at seven. Call me back here, at 555-1394. I'll wait." She hung up, then looked me up and down as if just noticing I was there. "You must be Rachel."

I didn't recognize her from anywhere. "I'm sorry…"

"I'm Elizabeth Mann."

So this was the notorious hotheaded Elizabeth everyone couldn't stop talking about all day! I'd been dying to meet her. Obviously the father she'd just mentioned was the famous *Life* photographer William Mann. Why couldn't he check *himself* into a Boston hotel? Was it the Four Seasons or the Ritz Carlton? Jane said Elizabeth was launching her own career as a shutterbug with an upcoming solo exhibit. Aside from getting Cindy Sherman to sign her book *Untitled Film Stills* at Barnes & Noble, I'd never spoken to a famous female photographer before.

I stared up at Elizabeth. She had an oval face and a slender Roman nose, with limp, shoulder-length chestnut hair the same shade as mine. My hair was longer and feathered on the sides with Cleopatra bangs; hers was parted down the middle. She was plainer than I'd pictured. No makeup or color in her cheeks. She looked about my weight—size eight on a good day. Taller than me, even without heels.

"I bought your father's book for my brother," I blurted out. "It's incredible."

"Which one?"

Oh no. How many were there? I felt stupid. "*Blind Streets.*"

"Everybody gets that one." Her dark blue eyes seemed to take in everything. Weariest eyes I'd ever seen.

"Jane said you're showing at a Soho gallery. What an achievement. That's like my life's dream. Congratulations."

"They're only doing it as a favor to Dad," she said.

I was taken aback by her humility. Or was it bitterness? "I'm sure that's not true." When she didn't say anything else, I added, "Well, it's great to meet you. An honor." Maybe she'd critique my work. Or help me figure out how to get *my* prints into a gallery. "Please call me Ricky."

"Rachel's a fine name. Biblical." She sat down in Jane's chair. "Why ruin it?"

What business of hers was my nickname?

I wanted to know why she'd really wound up leaving *Vision*, the most prestigious magazine resurrection in Condé Nast history. Elizabeth's abrupt defection on Friday had thrown the top brass into a tizzy, according to Jane, leading Elizabeth to pick my résumé out of the slush pile and offer me up as a last-minute replacement. Had she been fired? It would be shortsighted of her to give up such a cool gig. Yet I admired her independence. I bet she was a true artist, sick of being a subservient assistant. She couldn't be swayed by materialistic limitations or masthead hierarchies.

Or was there a man in the picture?

"Change your mind and want your old job back?" I joked. I prayed she didn't. How could I compete with her pedigree?

"Nope. Now it belongs to little twenty-four-year-old Rachel Solomon in her new designer suit," she said, distracted, drumming her fingers on the desk, watching the phone.

How did she know my age? From my résumé? I wondered if Elizabeth had spoken to Jane, my mousy coworker, about me. Now I felt paranoid, trying to remember everything I'd spilled about fighting with my crazy intrusive family and the sick love triangles I was constantly dissecting with my shrink.

"So how old are you?" I wanted to know.

"I'm a twenty-nine-year-old spinster," Elizabeth said with a smirk.

What a weird, sexist term. Though she was dressed kind of like an old maid, in earth tones and baggy fabric. Or she was so antichic she was chic, in that WASPy "I have a life, I can't be bothered with frills" kind of way. I feared I was trying too hard, coming off like a suburban wannabe.

"What was it like, being at the relaunch of such a famous old rag?" I asked.

"Fashion people are inane and tawdry." She reached over to finger the sleeve of my blouse. "Is this silk? Where'd you get it?"

"Saks." I stopped before divulging that my mom had it sent from the branch in Highland Park, along with the pumps and a stash of Givenchy panty hose: $14 each, ten pairs. That was the paradox of planet Solomon. I couldn't afford a taxi from my Village apartment share to the real Saks, but I had $140 worth of my mother's fancy hosiery. "I heard you grew up in the Village. Lucky you. My folks are originally from New York," I said. "I was switched at birth. I should have grown up here."

"Nothing wrong with being a Midwest doctor's daughter," she said. "Wish I had two older brothers."

"I have two *younger* brothers," I corrected. This must have been the reason Jane had asked me so many questions all day. I bet Jane was Elizabeth's lunch date and spy, gathering a dossier on the new girl who'd taken Elizabeth's desk. "What else have you heard about me?"

"Jewish photojournalism grad who thinks she's the next Diane Arbus."

Ouch. Nothing like reducing my religion, degree, art, and naked ambition to a cultural stereotype. Well, better to resemble Arbus than one of her subjects. If I shot Elizabeth, I'd give her bangs to shorten her long face, put blush on her cheeks to highlight her decent bone structure, and pencil in the gap in her left eyebrow. Then again, my well-groomed childhood girlfriends aspired to be dental hygienists, nurses, or brides. I longed to be a bitter screwed-up urbanite showing candids at a chic Soho gallery, just like Elizabeth.

"You don't have any siblings?" I asked.

"I have an older sister I'm trying to reach right now." With that she picked the phone, dialed, and left another message. "It's me. I have to catch this damn train to get him in by ten. I'll wait five more minutes."

Get him in where? I gathered that Elizabeth had come back here because she was broke with nowhere else to go. She looked even lonelier than I was. I'd taken out some cash to split a bag of Jamaican weed with my best friend and roommate, Nicky, but that could wait since our stash wasn't depleted yet. Ten bucks would be enough for the subway home and the dinner I planned to eat by myself at Dojo. I handed Elizabeth twenty-five dollars, five more than Jane was going to give her.

Without looking at me, she stashed it in her pocket. "I'll pay you back next Thursday."

"Whenever."

"That's right," Elizabeth said. "You're a rich girl."

"The job pays three hundred a week before taxes," I said. I didn't want her to know my father was helping with my rent.

"Oh, yeah, Jane said you're playing suffering artist."

This chick sure had balls. But I'd detested the fakers in Jewburbia who'd fawn, "Hello, gorgeous" and "That's so fabulous" to my face, then trash me behind my back. Even when it stung, I preferred raw honesty.

"Well, for a little hamster, Jane sure has a big mouth," I said, pulling a pack of Marlboros from my purse and lighting one, getting lipstick on the filter, slowly sucking in.

"Little hamster." Elizabeth chuckled. Her whole face softened when she laughed, making me feel as if I'd won a prize. She stole a piece of Juicy Fruit from Jane's desk drawer, then reached over to the ashtray and put out my cigarette, the way my brother Ben did.

"I can't believe the daughter of an oncologist is a smoker," she said.

Were there any details I hadn't told Jane? I had to stop giving everything away.

"Jane's not so bad," Elizabeth said. "Her father's a drunk, like mine. She thinks that's why we keep screwing the wrong men. Not that I go in for all that Freudian garbage." She paused, obviously assuming I did.

What? Her famous father was a drunk?

"I bet you left a trail of broken hearts in the heartlands," she said.

Wait, *she* screwed idiots too?

"I met that cute staff writer Peter Heller at lunch today. What's his story?" I asked, betting Elizabeth would spill the real deal about everyone around here.

"So Heller found you already." She seemed amused.

"He asked to see my work."

"That means he wants to fuck you."

"He said I had a good eye."

"Means he wants to fuck you soon," she said.

She'd trashed him too fast; I sensed a subtext. "Did you ever go out with him?"

She shook her head. "Let's see what you showed him."

I hesitated, feeling a little intimidated.

"You ask the opinion of the office Lothario, but not me?" she challenged.

I didn't want her to think I was one of those annoying girly girls who only lit up when a penis walked into the room. Reaching under the desk, I pulled out the grad school portfolio I carried with me everywhere and turned to the last photo. It was a close-up of an innocent-looking girl in an NYU T-shirt, afternoon light falling across her face, the Delancey Street sign in the background. I'd caught the girl locking eyes with a six-foot male Marilyn Monroe impersonator just as Marilyn winked at her. My parents had met on Delancey Street.

"It's called 'Culture Shock,'" I explained. "You don't like it?"

"Downtown street scenes." Elizabeth rolled her eyes. "How original."

"Hey, I just gave you twenty-five bucks. Can't you fake it?" I asked. "Look at the student's expression when she sees Marilyn." I pointed. "It's like she's not sure if the two of them are allies or archrivals or doppelgängers."

"You learn all that crap at NYU?"

"If you think so highly of NYU, why did you recommend they hire me?"

"I hate entitled Upper East Side Ivy League snobs nailing the coveted positions here. Wanted to discover a humble hayseed. Wish I grew up in Illinois."

"You can have it."

She impatiently paged through my portfolio, making me nervous. She turned back to the final shot of Marilyn and the student. "This one isn't terrible," she finally declared.

She almost liked me.

"Could be timely. Don't NYU classes start next week? You have an eight by ten?"

"Sure." Wired about my new gig, I couldn't sleep last night. So I got stoned and printed ten in my bathroom at four A.M. I pulled a smaller version from the side pocket.

"Drop it off with the photo editor at the *Post*." She jotted down the editor's name and address on a piece of scrap paper. "Say Elizabeth Mann thought this might be timely, since NYU's term is about to start."

"Really? Are you sure? I hear they started using digital."

"Film's okay."

"Not a contact sheet?"

"Just leave the print." She turned it around. "Write your name and address on the back."

When the phone rang, Elizabeth picked up. "Finally. Thank God. Yeah, meet me at Penn Station. I know, but he won't go to the hospital unless we take him...."

Oh, it wasn't a hotel, it was a hospital. I wondered if my father or brother Ben could help diagnose the problem over the phone, or prescribe something. Trying not to eavesdrop, I wrote my info neatly on the back of the photograph. "Listen, thanks so much for your help with...," I started to say. But when I looked up she was gone.

Two days later, Ruth Lott, the *New York Post*'s photo editor, called to say they were using my photograph to illustrate a story on the overflow of out-of-town NYU students this term.

"Oh my God! Where's Elizabeth's number?" I asked Jane as I rushed through the company Rolodex.

"Congratulations on selling your first picture," said Jane.

Had she been listening in on my phone conversation with the *Post* editor?

"I can't believe they're buying it. I just wanted to tell Elizabeth..."

"She already knows," Jane said. "You get two hundred fifty dollars for the cover of Friday's arts section. You can pick up early copies at the office at eleven P.M. Thursday night."

I looked at her, confused.

"The editor's a protégée of William Mann's," she explained.

So I had only made my first sale because of dropping the Mann name. Was this Elizabeth's way of paying me back? "Wow. I really owe her big-time."

"You might regret saying that," said Jane.

chapter two
the disease game

September 29, 2000

When I was a little girl, I'd stand at the doorway of my father's den, pretending I had chest pains and needed him to save me. He'd swoop me up in his huge arms, then touch me with the silver tip of his stethoscope to hear me inside. "Your heart is perfect," he'd say in his deep doctor voice, making everything better. Two decades later I still longed for his approval, his magic medicine.

Since the first night of Rosh Hashanah fell on Saturday and my mother had sent me a free plane ticket, I flew to Illinois for the weekend. Mom picked me up on Friday night at O'Hare. She looked happy I was home for the Jewish holidays; ever since I'd finished my MFA over the summer, she'd been hounding me to give her the date I was moving back. The answer was never! Tonight I was breaking the news that I'd taken the job at *Vision* magazine and planned to stay in New York forever.

During the hour drive to our house, it was hard for me not to give away the news. But I waited until dinner. We gravitated to our old seats at the oblong oak table, which seated seven though there were only five in the family. I always thought Mom left room for her mother and father, who'd both died when she was little. My father reigned at the head. I sat to his right, closest to the door.

"Disease?" asked my brother Ben, sitting across from me, trying to initiate the sick game they'd shoved in my face my entire life.

"Do it later," I insisted. I was the firstborn of the three Solomon kids, fourteen months Ben's senior. I had just flown six hundred miles. I was ready to make my announcement.

"Okay." My father cleared his throat. "Sixty-year-old fat lady with mitral endocarditis, blood growing strep bovis."

"Colon cancer," Ben jumped in.

"You're faster than your old man already." My father forked string beans onto his plate. "Seventy-eight-year-old cachectic Malaysian male with pneumonia and hemoptysis."

"Listen, can we not do this while we're eating tonight?" I asked. I couldn't wait to see the reaction on my father's face when I told him I'd landed my first real job. It was important I tell him in person. He'd be as proud of me as he was of my brothers.

"Just coughing up blood," said Danny. He was fifteen months younger than Ben. We were all too close in age, fiercely competitive since birth.

"Tuberculosis?" Ben asked.

"AFB negative," my father said.

"Pulmonary embolism," Danny offered.

"Bingo," my father said. "Pass the salad."

My mother passed it. She looked pretty in a purple satin dress, her hair redder and pouffy—she'd been to the beauty salon. As usual, the light was too bright; I turned the dimmer switch on the wall so it was a little darker. To help her, I took out the soda and heated the garlic bread in the microwave. I placed it on the lazy Susan by the lamb chops, pasta, and pizza. Instead of disappointing anyone, my mother chose to serve everything. She loaded a platter with turkey, offered it to my father. He grabbed the bigger leg with his hand.

"Go back to the Lower East Side," she told him.

"What did I do?" He looked at Ben and Danny.

"Try silverware," she said. "And you know Rachel hates the game."

I'd always hated their games: insect dissections, lab experiments, and animal amputations left in the refrigerator. Plus the actual human skeleton, assembled like a jigsaw puzzle on the kitchen floor. Or the rats, rabbits, and tarantulas skittering around. By the time I was ten I was eating alone upstairs, homesick in my own room.

"What's wrong with the game?" asked Ben. Since he'd started medical school, he'd become even more myopic, a parody of my dad.

"She can't win," said Danny. He was also premed, following in Ben's footsteps; they were turning into my father before my eyes.

Ben and Danny had my mother's red hair and freckles and my dad's thick glasses. I was the dark one, and the only girl. My mother, with her pathological insistence on finding good in all tragedy, claimed I'd won the gene lottery: I got her perfect eyesight and my father's bunionless feet. But Danny was right about our ongoing sibling battle over who was the favored child. With no penis, bris, bar mitzvah, interest in cooking brisket, or premed cred, I couldn't compete.

"Then again, that's assuming she wants to win," Danny added. What no one else knew was that he also took pictures, which he'd develop in my darkroom at four in the morning. Everyone else slept soundly; we were the two insomniacs. But I was sworn to secrecy.

Taking advantage of the lull in gross-sounding symptoms, I cleared my throat. "So I have news to share. I've been offered a full-time position on the staff of *Vision* magazine."

"Mazel tov, honey." My mother draped her arm around my shoulder. "Are you going to take it?"

"Yes! Of course! I already started."

"Isn't that a really old magazine?" asked Ben.

"They've relaunched it," I said.

"You know, *Vision* was *the* magazine between January 1913 and December 1936," Danny said. Reading several newspapers a day and memorizing every fact in the encyclopedia was how he'd learned to keep up with us. By five he was reciting pages from *Professional Guide to Diseases*, the easiest way in our house to get Dad's applause.

I turned to my father, who didn't say anything. When I'd started at NYU, he'd yelled, "You're doing this to spite me!" Landing a real job in his old city meant I was going to stay. He hated my being in New York. I knew he'd try to stop me.

"This calls for a celebration," my mother said, taking champagne from the refrigerator. Moët, the expensive stuff. She often kept a bottle chilled, ready for good news. She uncorked it, an expert bartender, though the Solomons were eaters, not drinkers. She lined up five crystal glasses, filling each halfway.

"I was lucky," I said. "This woman Elizabeth quit at the last minute. Can you believe someone would throw that kind of a job away? Though she's a photographer too, with her own show at a Soho gallery."

"You can still go to law school," Dad said. "I'll pay for it. We need a lawyer on our side."

I glared at him, stunned.

"Paging Dr. Solomon," Danny said. "She doesn't want to be a lawyer."

"This guy Powers at U of C admissions owes me one." My father bit into a sour pickle. "His wife had a double mastectomy, and some bozo wanted to do the reconstruction before—"

"She's not going to law school in Chicago." My mother cut him off.

"She's going to be a tattoo freak in the East Village, which is really just the Lower East Side; the Realtors are lying. You know, Leah, they'll never let her in a Jewish cemetery." A decade later, Dad still wasn't over the tiny body art on my ankle. I would have gotten a nose and lip ring too if I wasn't so freaked out by needles.

"She told you. She's going to be a photographer in New York." Mom wiped his chin with a napkin.

"Yeah, you fit in so well there," Ben said. "What's that picture of yours you sent from that tabloid? A homeless transvestite?" He picked off the pepperoni from his pizza, put it on the side of his plate.

"You have any clothes that aren't black? I'm just curious," added Danny, eating Ben's pepperoni.

I sneered at Danny the traitor, wondering if my brothers got meaner and more conservative every month to please my father. Or maybe they found my decision to stay East threatening. After all, I was deserting them too. They were stuck here, pleasing my parents on a daily basis. They couldn't leave or make their own mark or break everything that needed to be broken, like I did.

"They're right." My father nodded. "It's a dirty, scummy, terrible place."

Looking out the window, I noticed my brothers' cars parked in the driveway. Ben had an ostentatious royal blue Camaro. Danny drove my father's old beige Lincoln, as if he didn't think he deserved a car of his own. Before my exodus east, I'd sold the ugly lime green Cutlass my father had bought me, the only model in the lot I didn't have to wait a month to order. I called it my Escapemobile.

"Bravo, Rachel, honey," said my mother, passing around the champagne until everyone had some. "Way to go!" She clinked her glass against mine.

"So what's your official title?" Ben put his glass down. "Secretary or receptionist?"

"I'm an assistant in the photography department. I work directly with the art director," I lied. Ben didn't have to know I spent my days Xeroxing and fetching people coffee for three hundred dollars a week, a third taken out of my paycheck for taxes.

"*The* assistant?" Ben wanted to know. "Or *an* assistant?"

"Who cares? It's incredibly hard to break in and get a job there," I said. "You wouldn't believe how many résumés they get a week."

"They were the first to publish Eugène Atget and Walker Evans, if I recall correctly," said Danny, holding up his champagne, then downing it in one gulp.

"Thank you." At least somebody here understood what a prestigious place I'd miraculously gotten my foot in the door of.

"What's your salary?" asked Ben, once again managing to zero in on my weakest spot.

"What does it matter, you materialistic slob?" I snapped. I preferred Diet Coke to Moët, but I sipped my champagne anyway.

Ben spooned more mashed potatoes onto his plate. "Where's the—"

My mother pointed to the gravy, as if her game was guessing what her men wanted to eat. My game was now getting the hell out of here again.

"Forty-year-old man with pneumaturia?" Ben asked.

"Vesicular necrosis?" my father tried.

I stared at the yellow and red lithograph on the wall, Chagall's *Lovers and Flowers*. My mother filled her kitchen with long-stemmed pink and red roses, their faces so fat they looked like they had Down syndrome. They were overblooming in different-sized Lalique vases on the marble counter. It looked like a funeral parlor in here.

"Sigmoid diverticulitis," Danny guessed.

"Righto!" Ben told him.

"Boy, you're good," my father fawned. "Did you hear Daniel aced his MCATS? He scored in the ninety-ninth percentile."

"That's great, Danny," I said, finishing my champagne, pouring myself more.

"It just means peeing air," he told me.

My mother patted my arm. "They don't mean to exclude us."

Of course they did. She'd been encouraging the Jewish Male Doctor God Disorder since my brothers were born. At the stove she filled a platter with French fries, held them before my father like a reward. He took a few, blew her a kiss.

"Saks is open till nine," she told me.

"I can't," I said. "I have to make some work calls."

The phone rang, and my father picked it up. "When? Where? Okay." He hung up. "Dr. Davis croaked. Leah, where's the gravy?"

My mother pointed, then said, "We're very proud of you, Rachel. Aren't we, Joe?"

"She prefers Ricky now," Danny said.

"Poor Davis," Ben said. "He had it in the pancreas?"

"Can we not talk about death for ten minutes?" my mother asked, taking the mostly eaten lamb chops from Danny's plate. She preferred to chew on the bones.

"Any of that shrimp left?" Danny asked her.

She nodded, brought him a plate of shrimp. He ate five in a row. He was eating a lot tonight. My father, Ben, and Danny were all exactly six feet tall. I bet Danny weighed the most now. For years he'd been the smallest of the Solomon men. Was this his way of finally getting to be big?

"Sad book you sent me," Danny said. "*Blind Streets.*"

"You like it?" I asked about the Mann photography book I'd given Danny, which depicted sharecroppers in Mississippi during the Depression. "That woman I replaced is Elizabeth Mann, his daughter. I actually just met her at the magazine."

"I know her father's work well. He's an amazing documentary photographer," Danny said. "Even darker than his mentor, Walker Evans. Literally darker. In fact, I just read an article where they asked Mann why he didn't use brighter lights—"

"I read it too—in *Artforum*!" I jumped in. "Mann answered, 'Because the light misleads.'"

"You know, he's a famous manic-depressive," Danny added.

"On medication?" Ben leapt in. "Lithium or MAO inhibitors? I always thought it was dumb to put manic-depressives on a drug where they'd die if they drink a glass of wine."

I finished Ben's champagne. "I hear antidepressants help you sleep."

"Don't take them. You don't need them," said Ben. "You're neurotic, not psychotic."

"That's a compliment." Danny giggled the way he used to when I was upset, making him seem more like twelve than twenty.

"So this guy's on the table for a subdural hematoma," said Ben.

"Blood clot in the head," Danny chirped.

"They drilled a hole on the wrong side ...," Ben went on.

"This is disgusting," I said, unable to stop picturing the damn drilling.

"His head was bandaged," Danny explained. "They drill to drain the blood."

"So the doctor goes, 'Hey, where's the nose?'" Ben was smiling.

"Who was it?" My father chuckled. "That asshole Steiner?"

"Joseph, watch your language," scolded my mother.

"CAT scan was backward," Danny clarified.

"Then Steiner took one look at the mess and said, 'Get me a valium.'" Ben laughed loudly; they all did. From the hysteria, I gathered that was the punch line.

"You're not eating." My mother pushed the salad toward me. "I got your Star Deli tuna. You want some now? And that Kraft Caesar dressing you like."

"I'm good," I told her. "Thanks."

"Forty-year-old flatulent female with four children?" Ben was relentless.

"Jaundice and fever?" Danny asked. Ben nodded.

"Hepatitis?" my father threw out.

"Acute cholecystisis," Danny said. He spoke their language in his doctor voice. He was one of them now too; I'd lost him. "It's classic," he whispered to me. "Just a hot gall bladder."

"I saw in the paper that Saks is having a sale on women's suits." My mother looked at me. "We'll get you a new outfit for services tomorrow."

"I'm not going to services," I said. "I have to finish some prints for my new project."

She put the soda away, then pruned the leaves of yet another monster bouquet by the window. I could tell I'd hurt her feelings.

I took all the plates and glasses to the sink. "I could use some low black shoes I can walk in," I caved, picturing Elizabeth's flats. "Let's take a ride." I hated shopping, but I liked being driven in my mom's silver Cadillac; it made me feel safe.

"Aren't you going to say anything about my job?" I asked my father.

"I'll pay your rent till your birthday. Then you need to get real," he said, grabbing the *New York Times* from the counter, and marching down to his den.

He thought my magazine gig was a lark that wouldn't last. That meant I had five months to make a thousand more a month or I was out in the cold. I finished Dad's champagne too, demoralized, the way visiting home always wound up making me feel.

"Give me five minutes," my mother said, oblivious to my father's threat.

I headed upstairs, a little tipsy. I took a jacket from my closet and put it on, enraged that my brothers had a free ride with tuition, rent, cars, and endless expenses paid for while I was getting cut off 'cause I hadn't picked the career my father wanted.

Fuck him. I was going to be twenty-five in January. Dr. C— who used a sliding scale and charged me only twenty dollars a session—said I was getting too old to depend on my father to subsidize my life anyway. I was determined to make more money fast, if only to spite him. I lit a cigarette.

"Stop smoking," Ben yelled. "Nicotine's more addictive than heroin. Are you trying to kill yourself?"

"Oh, yeah, thanks for your care package," I said. It was the only thing my brother Ben had ever sent me in the big city: X-rays of a tumorous lung.

chapter three

lady in red

October 5, 2000

Going out with my first new girlfriend in Manhattan felt like embarking on a love affair—without the sex and agony. Elizabeth was my Svengali, playing the role of an older, more successful date, completely in control. After she'd called and we'd had two lunch dates near the office, she suggested we get together at night. We made plans to go to a photo exhibit by a friend of hers at Parsons. She was coming by at seven to pick me up.

All day I'd tried on different artsy black outfits to wear. When Elizabeth was a half hour late, I feared she wouldn't show. Finally the doorman buzzed and she breezed into my place, wearing black jeans and a black sweater. She'd stolen my color scheme! It was quite an improvement over her usual schoolmarm beiges, grays, and browns. She looked sleek. I'd looked up our palettes in a fashion book. Intense colors were the most flattering for extremists like us, it said. We were both "Women of Winter."

"Nice apartment. What an impressive building," she said as she walked in. "Sixty-nine Fifth Avenue. Good address."

"My mother likes the Fifth Avenue, my boyfriends like the sixty-nine," I quipped.

"Try telling guys you live at 107th and Broadway. Not exactly an aphrodisiac," she said. She walked the length of my living room to the window, then she walked back to the door. "This room must be six hundred square feet. It's larger than my whole apartment. Where's your roommate, Nicky? She's your best friend? The one traveling around the world for MTV? I want to meet her."

"Nicky's at work, editing a segment about female genital mutilation in Africa."

"So every Jewish girl from the suburbs wants to be an artiste," she said, looking at the futon. "At least I have a real bed. Why don't you buy a frame? You think sex on the floor makes you bohemian?" She slapped the pillow. "In your high-rise with a doorman."

"I pay fifty dollars less than you a month."

"How do you know?" she asked.

"Jane." Since I'd fixed Jane up with my college pal Andy Arnoff, a budding real estate mogul, she told me everything.

"For a little hamster, Jane has a big mouth," Elizabeth said, and we both laughed.

"Nice chair. Where'd you get it?" she asked.

I followed her around my apartment, wondering why she cared about furnishings when I had so many important things to ask her. "Do you miss working with Jane?" I was flattered that Elizabeth wanted me for her date and not Jane, her best friend, who was going out to a fancy dinner with Andy anyway.

"No," she said without hesitation.

"You know, you never told me what happened with your father in Boston," I said.

"Oh, he fell down drunk and broke his hip. My sister and I had to get him to the hospital."

"I'm sorry." But now that I had her attention, I might as well take advantage of it. "You never really told me the reason you quit *Vision*."

"It was stupid. Dick asked my opinion of the new front of the magazine section. I said, 'I thought we were pretending we're for people with brains. Why use the same slick untalented poseurs who work for your other rags?' He said, 'If you don't like it, why don't you leave?' So I did."

It took me a minute to realize that "Dick" was the editor in chief, Richard Lesser, my boss's boss, whom I'd never even met. "Couldn't you just apologize?" I asked.

"For telling the truth? I was sick of the whole superficial scene anyway. The lies and back-stabbing. That insipid magazine company, filled with pretty girls from rich families biding their time before they land husbands."

Yes, what a stupid goal, husband-hunting, I was about to say. But she finished her sentence with "I couldn't compete."

"Why not?" I asked. I found her vulnerability surprising; it certainly knocked the edge off her arrogance.

She ignored my question. Feeling the fabric on the navy couches, she said, "These are classy. Where did you get them?"

Why did she care about the fabric? "From my mother's friend Lois's store. I think Mom wants to make sure there's enough room for my brothers to sleep here. Even though I moved east to get away from them."

"Wish I had your brothers," she said once again, sitting down, draping her arm along the top of the couch. "There hasn't been a male child in my family for half a century. There were barely any men around anywhere. My dad left home when I was three."

She got up, walked through the kitchen, and declared, "This is twice the size of mine."

She was so competitive about everything, just like my brother Ben. Growing up, he hated sharing a bedroom with Danny. They divided it with train tracks and little green army men. Stepping on the other's side meant war. The battle raged constantly, since Ben was on the side with the door.

Elizabeth picked up my purple candle. "I have candles too. Mine are longer." She put it down. "Where did you get that Baccarat bowl?"

"From my mother," I said.

"Wish my mother knew what Baccarat was." She sat down on the couch again. "Jane's going out with Andy for a fourth time. I invited her to come tonight, but she had no interest."

"He'll eat her for breakfast and still be hungry," I said, heartbroken that I hadn't been Elizabeth's first choice after all.

"Don't underestimate Jane; she's a smart cookie."

I feared she was implying Jane was a smarter cookie than me.

Elizabeth stood up, went into Nicky's room, then the bathroom. Finishing her tour, she scanned the space one more time, as if deciding whether or not she was going to move in.

I found my copy of *Blind Streets* and handed it to her. She took it, delighted, and turned her father's book over as if she'd never seen the oversized hardcover before. She read Walker Evans's praise: "'The force of William Mann's work comes from tension between the excruciating pain he witnesses and the empathic eye he sees it with. These brutal, brilliant images implode from lyric restraint.' Evans wrote that in 1974," she said. "Right before he died."

"Wow. What a blurb to have on your back cover," I fawned.

"It never sold much. It's not fair."

"It's *not* fair," I repeated, though the reason seemed ludicrously obvious. Taking back the book, I turned through Mann's images of sick, poor, and lonely people in the rural South. In one photograph, a dead baby boy lay in a field, flies buzzing around his eyes. In the next, a young veteran in a torn soldier's uniform who had lost his arm was carrying a mutt that had lost its leg. The pictures were too explicit and bleak for a commercial audience, one more tragic than the next. Each page made you want to cry in a different way. Mann might have been a genius, but the guy never saw a hopeful frame in his life.

I put diet soda and popcorn out on the end table. Elizabeth grabbed two handfuls of popcorn, as if she hadn't eaten in days. I lit a cigarette.

"If your father is a cancer specialist, why doesn't he tell you to quit?" she asked.

"He's smoked on and off for forty years."

"What an ignorant habit." She shook her head. "My father smokes too."

"Is he still sick?" I asked.

"He's always sick," she said. "Manic depression enhanced by chain-smoking and booze binges."

"That must be so hard for you." I blew smoke toward the window. "Did your dad always want to be a photographer?"

"No. He wanted to be a doctor."

"Really? Are you kidding? Why?"

"Why? To have a good life. To be a normal person." She looked amazed that I even had to ask, then ate more popcorn, dropping some on the floor, which got on my nerves. "His entire life is a disaster."

"It is not." I put the kernels in the ashtray.

"His mother deserted him when he was a baby. His father was a crazy drunk too. He had no luck from the day he was born."

"But he overcame his past."

"No, he didn't," Elizabeth insisted. "He's a complete wreck."

"But his work was in *Life* magazine for ten years," I reminded her. "And didn't you tell me he published four books?" I'd take alcoholism and depression if I could get even one hardcover collection of my photographs out of the deal.

"For all the good it did him. The magazine's dead, three of the books are out of print, and now he's poor, sick, and alone," she said.

"I'm sorry." I put my hand on hers. She stood up abruptly. I'd clearly crossed a line. She was someone not used to being comforted. Fidgety, she continued to inspect my apartment.

She went to the closet, stepped inside. "Hey! A walk-in! How many jackets do you have?" Was she counting? "Fourteen!" she called. I went into the closet with her, pulled down a red silk Donna Karan blazer my mother had sent me, though I never wore red.

"This would look good on you," I said. "Try it on."

She put it on and went to the bathroom mirror. Coming up behind her, I caught us together. We were cut from the same mold: tall sturdy girls with big shoulders and dark hair. We could almost be sisters. I sat on the counter. She took Rose Petal blush from my makeup bag.

"Show me how you do blush. Yours looks so natural," she said, inspecting my cheeks carefully. "I think I put mine on too low."

Surprised by how enrapt she seemed about makeup, I picked up the tiny brush, ran its bristles against the soft powder, and swept it across her left cheek, along the bone. I turned her face to the right, brushing her other cheek with rose powder, then lined her eyebrows with brown pencil, the way my mother used to color me.

"Shut your eyes. Lightly," I instructed, painting mascara on her top and bottom lashes. Her eyes were sultry; I thought she should bring them out more. I tried a dab of gray shadow in the corners. Then I pulled out a comb and tried to untangle her limp hair. We needed Ricardo, my mother's hairdresser, who had magic hands. He could fix anything.

"This is fun. Is this an Illinois thing?" she asked.

"Nicky and I have been doing makeovers on each other since we were kids. In junior high she plucked out half my eyebrow." I plugged in the curling iron; maybe that would help.

"Is she good-looking?"

"She's gorgeous," I said. "Guys always fall all over Nicky." I pointed to a photograph on the wicker shelf of me and Nicky at a dorm party during our freshman year of college.

"You're both so pretty." Elizabeth kept staring. "Is Nicole another doctor's daughter?"

What was this girl's hatred of nicknames? "Yeah, but her parents are divorced."

"There are divorced people in Highland Park?" Elizabeth joked.

"No. Only happy intact Jewish families are allowed to live there."

It occurred to me that Nicky was tall with big feet and sturdy shoulders too. Though she wasn't Jewish or Midwestern, Elizabeth fit my emotional type: sharp-edged, hungry, fiercely candid—even when she shouldn't be.

"I don't know any happy intact families," she admitted. "My parents, aunts, uncles, and sister all split up right after they had kids. The only woman I know who's still married to her first husband is my friend Hope Maxwell."

"The famous photographer?" My mouth opened.

"When we were kids staying at my dad's place in the Village and he'd forget to feed us, she'd always come over with fish sticks and French fries. She's like my fake mother."

"Oh my God, I can't believe you know Hope Maxwell! She's my hero. You have to introduce me. She lives nearby?" I kicked myself for not knowing that such a stellar artist lived in my very neighborhood. "How old is she?"

"She's fifty, I think."

"Really?" I didn't know Hope Maxwell was that old—my mother's age. I'd pictured someone younger. "How long has she been married?"

"She tells people twenty-nine years. But she left him for a decade."

It figured this was Elizabeth's dream couple. "What did she do during that decade?"

"She took pictures all over the world and had passionate affairs with foreigners. Then she came home and she and Stanley got back together." Hope's marriage seemed to impress Elizabeth, though I couldn't tell which part: its longevity, its destruction, or its resurrection.

"She was good friends with your father?" I picked up the now hot curling iron, stood beside her. I took a section of her hair and curled it, continuing with one clump at a time until the bottom was wavy.

"She was a colleague of my dad's at *Life*," she said. "She took care of him."

"Her last book got amazing reviews. Do you like Hope's work? Tell me more about her."

"Tell me more about that guy you're fixing me up with, Eliot Panzer the doctor. Is he as cute as your friend Andy?" she asked, dabbing my mother's Opium perfume behind her ears. "This smells really nice."

"Rich Republican." I didn't add that he was the type I'd fled the suburbs to get away from. The only right-wingers I could stomach were my father and brothers, and that was because I didn't have a choice. "But he can't make it tonight; he's on call. He's doing his residency in urology or something boring like that," I said.

"I don't think being a urologist is boring," she said, handing me back my mother's perfume. I sprayed it down my sweater. "Take Peter Heller, who manages to be a staff writer at the best endowed magazine in the country and still can't pay his rent. Now that's boring."

"Peter's going to Milan for his next story, on Italo Calvino," I told her. "He'll be gone for two months. He asked if I want to stay at his place. He has a better computer and printer and a big-screen TV he said I can use."

"He needs you to feed his cats," she said. "Have you slept with him yet?"

I didn't recall mentioning Peter's cats. "No. But we're having dinner again on Friday. I like the idea of staying at his place, sleeping with his stuff," I said. "It's a nice metaphor."

"You don't need any metaphors. And you have your own place," she said.

I watched as she carefully adjusted the collar of the red blazer. Red definitely suited her. I wished my mother would stop sending me all these dumb bright-colored clothes I never wore.

"Let me take your picture." I went for my old Canon on the living room table.

"I hate posing." She emerged from the bathroom, hands deep in pockets. "I never come out well." Jane had told me that Elizabeth used to love posing for her father.

"Shut up and smile." The flash went off. "Don't move." I took a few more.

I shot everyone I knew, it was an initiation ritual. I had more photographs of my family than my mother did. I'd taken pictures of every guy I'd ever slept with, and every friend I'd cared about or lost. It was time to add Elizabeth Mann to my collection.

"You can keep the blazer," I said.

She looked startled; she was obviously not used to getting presents.

"I owe you for your *Post* connection. The photo editor bought three more pictures. All downtown street scenes," I emphasized, since she'd been so sarcastic on the topic. "Do you want to see my latest clips?"

"This feels really soft." Elizabeth ran her hand down the silky sleeve of the jacket, pleased. She seemed more into my clothes than into my photographs. "Which jacket are you wearing tonight?" she wanted to know.

I pulled out the black version.

"It looks better in black," she said. "On you."

Anything not hers would look better, she had that kind of personality.

"You need a shrink," I said.

"I don't believe in shrinks."

My family didn't either. But I found that antitherapy zealots were always the ones most desperately in need of being shrunk.

"Why doesn't that shock me?" I asked, taking a few more pictures. "Maybe my doorman will take one of us together on the way out."

"Enough. Don't take any more," she protested, yet she gave me a half smile while continuing to vamp.

"There's an Indian tribe that believes photographs steal your soul."

"You can have my soul," Elizabeth said. "If I get your hair."

chapter four
present tense

November 21, 2000

Singing along to Nicky's cool new Macy Gray CD, I lit a purple candle, filling my living room with its lilac scent. I rolled the last of my Jamaican pot into a slender joint and puffed slowly, blowing smoke out the open screenless window. Since I'd just flown to the Midwest to see my family for Rosh Hashanah, I had the perfect excuse not to go home again for the goyish Pilgrim fest. I was jazzed to have the whole week to myself in New York. No disease games, no food orgy, no football. I French inhaled, swaying to the edgy rhythm. Nicky had been suckered back to her family's Highland Park insanity for Thanksgiving; she'd already left. I had better plans.

I blew out the sweet-tasting smoke and continued to work on "Present Tense," the new photo series I was submitting to *New York Arts* magazine's photography contest. I had twenty-four hours to make the deadline. The first prize would snare me a three-page spread and a thousand-dollar prize—exactly what I needed to tell Dad to take his rent supplement and shove it. It felt destined. Especially since my project chronicled the ridiculously superficial gifts a hypothetical Midwestern mother sent her daughter in the big city: a Dustbuster, two huge navy couches, yellow pot holders. The latest was a hot pink angora sweater that shed.

Spreading the sweater out on the wooden floor, I placed little specks of pink around it, like fairy dust. I considered posing with each object, mirroring my favorite stills from Cindy Sherman's riveting downtown show of self-portraits, which I'd seen eleven times. Or maybe I would juxtapose a collage of my mother's face, using images I'd stolen from her old albums before I'd left.

Shooting away with my Pentax K1000, I was making sure the pink fuzz wouldn't bleed when I heard a knock on the door.

I ignored it. My doorman was supposed to buzz me first, so I could have him tell people I was busy working, go away. I recalled the advice Elizabeth passed on from her father: shoot from the heart, not the hip. Clicking fast and furious, I was starting to feel what he meant. But then my doorbell rang. Who was rude enough to stop by without calling at ten o'clock on a Tuesday night? I put the joint in the ashtray and went to get rid of whoever it was. They must have the wrong apartment. I hadn't ordered anything. Through the peephole I spied red hair. Two heads of it. Oh no, it couldn't be! Another present from my mother: Dumb and Dumber. I opened the door, half stoned and shocked. My brother Ben, wearing my father's old blue scrubs, bear-hugged me, then walked the length of the apartment.

"Hey, Sis. You can smell that wacky tobaccy from the hall."

Well, what was he doing in *my* hall, anyway? He should be in his own hall, seven hundred miles away.

Ben found what he was looking for—the joint—and took a deep puff. "Big-city stuff. Not bad." Then he handed me a shop-

ping bag containing magnesium citrate for constipation, Lo-
motil pills for diarrhea, samples of Midol, and Band-Aids, my
father's idea of a care package.

"Great pad," said Danny, trailing behind Ben. He was in his
University of Chicago sweatshirt, a Bears cap, and my father's
old green scrubs. Danny tossed a duffel bag on the couch, put
out the purple candle with his fingers, like Tarzan. "Very swank.
Love the doorman."

"What's all this sistah soul shit? You're white," Ben said,
ejecting my wispy CD and sticking in the *Best of Willie Nelson*
he'd brought, blasting "On the Road Again."

"Could there be anything more cracker than your good ole
boy twang?" I turned off his country, trying not to flip out. "You
know, you can't just barge in here without calling," I said, shutting the door after them, still stunned they'd showed up without being invited. Who does that?

"We told you we'd be visiting," said Danny, dropping his
backpack on the floor.

"Come on, you like Willie, admit it." Ben put his Southern
noise on again.

"Saying 'We'll be visiting soon' is different from 'See you
Tuesday,'" I whimpered, hoping this wasn't true. They didn't
really think they were going to crash with me, did they? "You
can't stay here and ruin my week. I have serious work to do! Go
find a hotel."

"We just drove ten hours straight," Ben said quietly, obviously hurt by my reaction.

I looked into his brown eyes, then into Danny's. All the Solomons had big intense brown puppy-dog eyes like mine. God
damn. It wasn't fair. They were making me feel guilty for wanting to get rid of them.

"Where's your TV?" Ben asked, walking around, opening
drawers and closets. He went to Nicky's room, but she didn't have
a TV either.

"Stay out of my roommate's stuff!"

"Why? Where's Nicky now?" Ben asked. "Peru or Afghanistan?"

"Believe it or not, she's in Highland Park for the holiday," Danny said. "Mom bumped into Dr. Hart at the club. That's how she learned you'd have room for us."

I knew it! This was my mother's fault, Mrs. Family Circus—the more family in your face, the better. She'd grown up in a Lower East Side tenement so crowded she slept in the same bed with her brothers Max and Izzy, and Izzy's three cats. To her, this was a good memory.

"Too bad Nicky's not here," Ben said. He'd had a crush on her since high school. But every guy who'd ever met Nicky had a crush on her. Plus Ben had secretly lusted after all my girlfriends over the years. "Remember when she was shooting that documentary in the fish cannery in Alaska?"

"Yeah. Her father called her from their club and said, 'I had sole almondine today and thought of you,'" I recalled, laughing.

"You're making me hungry. Where's your food?" Danny rattled around the tiny kitchen. I followed him. He looked different than when I'd seen him just eight weeks before. He was back dating the older woman he'd met at the science lab at school. Now he was wearing contact lenses and had grown a thin red mustache. He had started a beard too, my mother had reported. But then she'd shown him a picture of her great-uncle Tudras, a mystic rabbi from Minsk, famous for his long auburn beard. So Danny shaved. He kept the mustache, but his new theme seemed obvious: I'm not Ben.

"Don't you look debonair?" I said.

"Simon Legree," Ben said, pulling on Danny's mustache.

Danny swatted him away, then unpacked the care package from Mom: two cans of chicken soup, two bottles of Kraft Caesar dressing, Vernors soda, Sanders hot fudge, and a hot pink scarf to go with Tinker Bell's hot pink sweater. "Turkey dinner from Second Avenue Deli will be here Thursday," Danny said. "Nine A.M."

"Who gets deliveries at nine A.M.?" I shrieked as the phone rang.

"I hear you have visitors," my mother said merrily, as if this were a wonderful surprise.

"Why didn't you warn me?" I asked, wanting to kill her.

"So you have visitors," said my father, on the other extension. "What's up? How are you feeling?" My dad and I communicated best when there was something physically wrong with me that he could fix over the phone.

"I feel fine."

"Make sure to call Uncle Max and Uncle Izzy to say happy Thanksgiving," my mother sang. "You could visit them in Fair Lawn since the boys have a car."

My own brothers weren't enough headache, now I needed her brothers too.

"You could even stay over there," she went on.

She adored my uncle Max, her oldest brother. She'd been an orphan, so Max had became a father to her. But she forgot that we weren't the same person, and that I had intentionally moved far away from her jurisdiction to avoid overeating lox and bagels with hordes of her relatives. I was the only person on the planet who had picked New York City for peace and quiet.

"Okay. Bye, Mom," I said, handing the phone to Ben.

"How's she going to survive a holiday without feeding you?" I asked Danny. "How long are you guys staying anyway?"

"We're leaving at eight Saturday morning," Ben said after he hung up.

"Why does everything have to happen so early?" I asked. I remembered the pink sweater and the photographs of my mother on the floor. I quickly stuffed them into a box in the closet with the rest of the project I was dying to get back to.

"Let's go out to eat," Ben said. "We're starving."

"Let's order in." I pulled out a menu from Sammy's Noodle Shop, picked up the telephone, and ordered what they liked: General Tso's chicken, shrimp with broccoli, egg rolls, and scallion pancakes. Like my mother, I found that serving everything for dinner was easier.

"Why don't you have a TV?" Ben was still circling the place, as if there had to be one hiding somewhere. "Is this an artsy liberal thing?"

"I would rather read or work than be plugged in to mindless inanity," I said.

Danny nodded assuredly. "It's an artsy liberal thing."

"How long will the food take?" Ben unpacked a thick anatomy textbook and a stethoscope from his bag. Second year of medical school and he was already Doctorman, ready to save patients at a single bound.

"Twenty minutes," I said. "Nicky and her boyfriend play 'Beat the Chinaman.' They order in and try to have sex before the food arrives."

"I'd play that with Nicky," Ben said.

"In your dreams," said Danny, who was shy with girls. "And saying 'Chinaman' is racist."

"You're right," I agreed. "I'm sorry." For somebody who called himself a libertarian, Danny sometimes seemed more left-wing than me.

When the food came, we sat on the floor, eating from the cartons. Ben pulled my paperback of Sylvia Plath's *Ariel* from the shelf. "Is this by that schizophrenic poet who put her head in the oven?" he asked.

"There's no indication that Plath was schizoid," Danny said. "Manic depression triggered by her father's early death is my guess." He dipped an egg roll in duck sauce.

"Suicidal tendencies are genetic," Ben said, eating the chicken with his fingers, like it was caramel corn.

"Her husband dumping her in England with two kids didn't help," I reminded them.

"Oh good, blame the guy, like you always do," said Ben.

He got up to continue his inspection of my desk. Did he think there might be a small TV set hiding under it? He smoked more of the joint. Pulling a silver instrument from his duffel bag, he used it as a roach clip. I stared at him as he sucked in smoke from his weird fork thing.

"Hemostat. Clamps off blood vessels," Danny explained. "To stop hemorrhages."

Ben hit the joint a few times, held it up. Danny shook his head. I wondered if he'd ever tried toking before. Having degenerate older siblings like me and Ben had probably scared him straight.

"Finish it," I told Ben.

At midnight I pulled out extra blankets and pillows. Ben claimed my futon on the living room floor. Danny crashed on one of the navy blue couches from my mother's friend Lois Niss's furniture store in Chicago, Niss's Nest. I sought refuge in the bedroom, which had Nicky's African mask on the wall and a six-foot Amnesty International poster taped to the ceiling. I listened to Macy Gray with headphones; she lulled me to sleep.

On Wednesday morning I was happy to use work as an excuse to escape taking my brothers to New York tourist spots. But they insisted we have lunch together, so I had them meet me at the cheap coffee shop right across from my midtown office.

"We checked out Tompkins Square Park," said Ben, eating a cheeseburger. "Found a few bizarre specimens down there."

"Was that guy transsexual?" Danny poured ketchup on his fries.

"Hermaphrodite," Ben diagnosed.

"Ambiguous genitalia," Danny said. "He had marked gyneco-mastia, obvious exogenous estrogen."

"The East Village is your oyster," I said, finishing my chef salad.

"I've got a friend at Bellevue Hospital," Ben said. "Might go check him out."

"Working there or living there?" I grabbed Ben's tomato slice.

"I'm going to the Thanksgiving Day Parade at nine tomor-row," Danny told me. "Want to come?"

"Nobody who lives in Manhattan goes anywhere at nine on a holiday morning," I said as I stole the last few fries from his plate.

"Just watch your wallet this time." Ben poked Danny in the stomach.

"At least I'm not hung up on a guitar player in Washington Square Park." Danny twisted Ben's arm. "Say chicken."

"But she was seriously cute," said Ben, squirming. "Ouch. Screw you. Chicken." Danny let go.

I didn't ask what they'd been doing all morning. As long as they were alive to tell the story, I didn't really care.

Getting up to put on my coat, I glanced out the window and noticed Elizabeth crossing the street and waved to her. What was she doing here again? Probably on her way home from having lunch with Jane. Aside from the two of us, she didn't appear to have any other friends she hung out with. She was wearing a black peacoat, striding quickly with long steps, a real urbanite. Accord-ing to Jane, William Mann had accepted a professorship at Em-ory and moved to Atlanta and Elizabeth hardly ever saw her mother, who lived in Westchester. So I imagined that Elizabeth was spending the holiday weekend in the city, alone, working on her photography. I was envious.

While we were standing in line at the register to pay, Elizabeth came into the restaurant. I was nervous she might be condescending toward my hick brothers. But she looked delighted.

"Oh, the Midwest doctors are here! I always wished I had brothers. Your sister is lucky to have you. She's a very well-protected woman," she gushed.

"Yeah, you're lucky to have us," Danny said.

"Why is she taking you to a tacky diner?" Elizabeth asked. "She should be cooking for you."

"Ha-ha," I responded to her dumb joke. Everybody knew I couldn't boil water and had no intention of learning.

"I'm serious. They came all this way to see you and you're feeding them this cheap crap?" She crossed her arms.

"Don't tell me." I rolled my eyes. "Feminist WASP loses her job and becomes a *balabusta*."

"I didn't lose my job, I walked out. And I never called myself a feminist. I hate that seventies women's movement rhetoric," she said. "And what's a *balabusta*?"

"An overfeeding Jewish mother," Danny said.

"I wish my mom was as generous and warm as yours," she told him. "The last time I visited my mother's house in Rye she asked me why I was eating so much and told me I should pay for my own food."

How did she know anything about my mother's food, anyway? Oh yeah, I recalled doing a parody of Mom feeding her men cows during the disease game the last time we got together.

Elizabeth waved good-bye and left. On the walk to the subway Ben asked, "So who's your hot friend?"

Of all the adjectives I'd have used to describe Elizabeth—brilliant, erudite, eccentric, world-weary, sardonic—"hot" was not one of them.

"So when are you gonna cook for us?" Danny threw in.

"You know the expression 'When hell freezes over'?" I asked. "Longer than that."

————

At six o'clock that night, I came home from work. Danny was sitting in front of a thirty-inch television set, watching a *Law & Order* rerun.

"You *bought* a TV?" I stared at the huge ugly thing on the table. "How are you going to get it home?"

"It's for you. We got a great deal at 47th Street Photo." Danny said, turning to the news. "We already got your super to hook up the cable."

How much was this going to cost me monthly? How dare they order cable for me without asking! That was so typical of my family—they just took over and made decisions that affected my life as if I wasn't the one living it. I was about to lose it, but Danny smiled at me proudly, as if he and Ben had just given me this generous present they thought I'd love.

"To remember us," he added quietly.

"How could I ever forget you?" I messed up Danny's hair. "So where's your ringleader?"

"He'll be back for Thanksgiving dinner tomorrow."

"Don't tell me, Ben went to Bellevue?" I asked.

"Nope." Danny flicked the station. "He has a hot date."

The word "hot" echoed in my mind. "With whom?" I asked, nervous. He couldn't possibly have hooked up with Elizabeth, could he?

"With the guitar girl he met in the park," Danny said, to my relief.

Late Saturday night I called my parents. "Did they get home okay?" I asked, flipping through channels, a great way to avoid commercials. I'd never had my own remote control before; it was kind of fun.

"They sure did," my father said.

On TV Gilda Radner was doing Roseanne Roseannadanna on an old *Saturday Night Live* rerun.

"We wound up having a nice mellow Thanksgiving," I said. "Thanks for the Second Avenue Deli tray."

"Yeah, Ben brought a little something home with him," said Dad.

"Those pickles from Gus's that mom likes?" I flicked to a weather channel. A storm watch for Manhattan. Illinois was fifty degrees and sunny.

"The clap," my father said.

"What?" I turned the sound down. Ben got an STD in five days in New York? "Are you kidding?"

"Nope," he said.

He must have gotten it from the girl in Washington Square Park on Wednesday night. Who knew you could get infected so fast. Where did big randy Ben think he was visiting, the sixties? "Is he okay?"

"Yeah. I gave him a shot of Rocephin. Ben will try anything once." My father chuckled before he hung up. If I ever brought home anything sexually transmitted, there'd be an intervention with our Illinois synagogue's sisterhood.

I ordered in Chinese food again, and when it came, I gave the delivery guy twelve dollars. He handed me my General Tso's chicken and a Federal Express package the doorman must have asked him to bring up. Pink and purple place mats from my mother, with the note "The boys said you don't have any." I took out my camera to add them to my "Present Tense" series, but I was out of film, and I'd missed the deadline anyway. I put the food carton on one of the horrible place mats and flipped through channels on my new TV, trying not to cry. My kid brothers had destroyed my entire week of work. And now I missed them.

chapter five
dispossession

December 9, 2000

"I'm totally psyched to meet your friend Hope Maxwell," I told Elizabeth. "She knows I'm coming, right?"

"I'm looking forward to meeting your friend Eliot," she countered. "Are you sure he's meeting us here?"

I nodded. "Just make sure you introduce me around. I'm a little nervous." I lit a cigarette, forgetting I hadn't put out my other one.

Okay, so I was a *lot* nervous to connect with Elizabeth's father's famous photography crew—but I was very flattered that she thought I could fit in and not embarrass her. As we walked into the lobby of Hope's fancy prewar building on lower Fifth Avenue, the doorman smiled at Elizabeth, waving us past. I followed her into the elevator, holding the tulips and small box of cannoli I'd insisted on buying on the way. "Never visit somebody's home empty-handed," my mother had long ago indoctrinated me.

"Why would you be nervous?" she asked. "You're brilliant socially."

Elizabeth always managed to give me such backhanded compliments. I wanted her to think I was brilliant artistically, intellectually, psychologically. Who wanted to be brilliant socially? Paris Hilton?

"I get insecure when I don't know anyone." I let her hold the flowers so it looked like she had brought a gift too.

"It's just a bunch of boring old artsy types," she said.

Indeed, when we opened the door, we saw several dozen aging artists milling around Hope's living room, drinks in their hands. We hung our coats in the closet, put the flowers and cannoli in the kitchen, and then I looked around. Copies of Hope's photography book *Dispossession* were displayed on the mantel by the fireplace.

"Elizabeth, hello. Hello, dear," said a tall, slim, older woman, coming right over, shaking Elizabeth's hand. No huggers in this crowd. "I'm Hope," she told me. "Welcome. We're pleased Elizabeth brought you." She shook my hand also.

"Hello. Me too. It's such an honor to meet you," I gushed, staring.

Hope must have been six feet tall. She was wearing a long cobalt blue dress that matched her eyes, with a lovely silver broach. She was elegant with her high forehead, salt-and-pepper hair in a bun, and regal posture. You could tell she'd once been a real knockout. I suddenly wondered if Hope had ever slept with Elizabeth's father. Jane said that everyone had.

"Look who's here. Hello, dear." A man came right up and shook Elizabeth's hand.

"Meet Rachel," Elizabeth said to him. "Her dad is a doctor. Rachel, this is Stanley Maxwell. Hope's husband. He's a doctor too."

Did that mean Hope had taken his last name? I was surprised and a little disappointed, thinking that a feminist crusader, one of the rare women high up in our profession, should proudly keep her own surname.

"What kind of doctor is your father?" asked Stanley, who was also tall and thin. He looked sort of British in his beige corduroy suit and bow tie.

"Oncologist," I said, but who wanted to talk about medicine at a book party in the Village? More important, was Annie Leibovitz really going to make an appearance? Hope ordered Elizabeth a scotch from the bartender and asked if I wanted one. I shook my head, requesting diet soda. Elizabeth gave me a horrified look.

"Okay, wine. Red wine," I relented, and Stanley soon handed me a tall glass full.

"So I hear you're shooting an upcoming cover for *Vision*," I told Hope.

"I hear they're sacking Richard already," she told Elizabeth.

"I'm not surprised. He has no idea what he's doing," Elizabeth said. "He's totally over his head."

Hey, they were talking about Richard Lesser, my editor in chief. He was getting fired? Oh my Lord! When? What did that mean for me and for *Vision*? I wondered if they were pulling the plug on the whole magazine.

"Is there a problem with Richard?" I asked, hoping it wasn't tacky to probe for the inside scoop on my boss in the middle of a party.

"I spoke to your father last week," Hope told Elizabeth.

"How bad was he?" Elizabeth scrunched up her face, as if she didn't really want to hear.

"He was raging again." Hope shook her head. "I told him, 'Billy, insanity is no excuse for bad behavior.'"

They were speaking in the tone reserved for adorers of William. Apparently Hope and Stanley had been "Billy's" closest comrades during his decade at *Life* magazine, the most productive time of his life, from what Elizabeth said. The only photograph of him she'd shown me was of William, Hope, and Stanley at Cedar Tavern, their old haunt. It was taken in the seventies, when her father was still dashing.

I looked around, feeling too young, inexperienced, dressed wrong in black jeans. I should have worn a skirt, like Elizabeth. I took down a copy of *Dispossession* and paged through the oversize grainy photographs. There was a homeless African-American woman sleeping in the subway with her three children, a Navajo field-worker with bleeding palms, an Indonesian teenage girl behind bars in a rundown prison. They were quite stirring. Hope and William Mann seemed to be locked in a contest to find the most pained human faces on the planet. Elizabeth came over.

"Impressive book," I fawned.

"The old lefties always confuse art with social work," she said.

"Who's that woman with huge glasses near the bookshelves?"

"Bette Tyler," she told me.

"Oh wow. I just saw her series of old film directors in *The New Yorker*. They're really good."

"More glorification of the cult of celebrity," Elizabeth said into my ear. "Just what the world needs."

"Elizabeth, sweetie." Bette Tyler rushed over to her. "Hello." She kissed both her cheeks. "How is our beloved Billy goat?"

"He's the same old pathetic wreck," Elizabeth said. "How are you?"

"Off to Cannes tomorrow. For what your father would call 'commercial shit.'"

"While he's phoning me at four in the morning, petrified that his medical coverage might be canceled after all the false alarms," Elizabeth conceded.

Bette moved closer to Elizabeth. "Is it being canceled? If he needs me..."

"No, we're okay. My sister took care of it," she said. "Thanks."

I kept glancing between them, hoping Elizabeth would remember to introduce me, but she didn't.

"I'm Ricky Solomon," I finally interjected. "I work for *Vision*. I loved your film director spread, found it stunningly original."

She smiled, not the least interested, and turned back to Elizabeth. "I heard Harvard let him go again."

"It's amazing they took him back to begin with," Elizabeth said.

"Where will he go now?"

"He's at Emory; he had an offer there."

"Where's that?" she asked. "Atlanta?"

Elizabeth nodded. "He loved your new introduction to *Blind Streets*. He's using it for all the foreign editions."

"Those deserving of praise rarely get it." Tyler kissed both of Elizabeth's cheeks before she left.

I looked around some more. "Who's that?" I pointed to a lanky guy in platform shoes near the bar.

"Devan Forrest," she said.

I was thrilled to be in such close proximity to Forrest, an icon known for splashy portraits of musicians. "I'm a big fan," I said. "I loved your photos of Bob Dylan in *Rolling Stone*."

"Do you have a cigarette?" he asked.

I held out my pack and he took three. "They aren't for me." Then he walked away.

"Hey! Devan Forrest bummed my cigarettes!" I whispered to Elizabeth.

"I wish you'd quit that disgusting habit already. Why don't you listen to your brothers?" she asked. "When they were visiting, you should have invited me to hang out with you guys."

"Next time they come to New York," I promised. But I couldn't even picture it. What would she have to say to my small-town brothers or vice versa? I doubted they'd have anything in common.

"You didn't tell me your older brother was a hunk," she added.

I was about to vomit when I noticed Eliot walk in. "That's him. That's Eliot." I nudged Elizabeth. She stood up straight, brushed her hair back, on male alert. I introduced them, and she took his coat.

"Sorry I'm late," he said. "We had an emergency."

I didn't want to imagine what an emergency in urology could mean.

"I've been on call for thirty hours straight," Eliot bragged.

"Which hospital?" Elizabeth asked, intrigued.

"New York-Presbyterian," he said.

"Prestigious hospital," Elizabeth mooned, beaming at the hapless Eliot.

While I enjoyed the company of females, Elizabeth clearly preferred being around men. Or maybe it was just me she appeared to be ignoring.

"Yes, actually, it was my first choice," Eliot said.

"I'm not surprised," Elizabeth said. "Isn't that one of the city's best hospitals?"

Bored by their conversation, I sneaked to the bathroom and called Peter on my cell phone.

"Hey, you want to pick me up here?" I asked him.

"I have to pack for Italy," he said.

"You want company?" I asked.

"Sure, baby. Why don't you stop by later?"

I assumed this was Peter's code for having sex. We'd had lunch, drinks, dinner, and had gone to three foreign movies at Film Forum, but we hadn't consummated our relationship. I was determined not to keep jumping into relationships that turned into sick twisted triangles. I wasn't sure if sleeping with him for the first time the night before he left for two months was really sexy or really stupid, but I agreed to go over to his place after the party.

Back in the living room, Elizabeth and Eliot were talking

with Hope. Trying to fit in, I awkwardly sidled up next to them and turned to Hope again. "I heard you're curating ICP's Izis Bidermanas retrospective next month."

"More experimental foreign shit," Elizabeth jumped in.

I worried that she'd insulted Hope. At the same time I couldn't help but be awed by Elizabeth's confidence in her own opinions, especially in this intimidating crowd.

"Not everyone can shoot like William, now can they, Lizzie?" Hope laughed.

Lizzie. Aha! She did have a nickname.

When Eliot went to the bathroom, Elizabeth finally said, "Rachel takes pictures too."

"Oh really?" Hope asked. "What are you working on?"

"I've actually been having a lot of luck with humorous street scenes."

"That's good, dear." She patted my shoulder. "We could use a little humor around here."

"You won't believe it. I complimented Devan Forrest on his Bob Dylan shoot. But I looked it up and they were Bette Tyler's photos! Forrest must think I'm a moron. Why didn't he correct me?" I asked Elizabeth over the phone the next day, during our slo-mo recap of the evening.

"Everyone was drunk. He probably thought they were his," she said. "I have to hand it to you, Eliot Panzer is a real gentleman. We went to Knickerbockers for a late dinner. I wasn't sure whether to get the shrimp or the pasta, so he ordered both. And he treated, along with paying for my cab home."

"Sounds almost healthy," I said. "Did you let him in?"

"I just let him out," she said. "Ten minutes ago."

"Tell me you're kidding."

"You're such a prude," she mumbled.

"You should go slower."

"Like you and Peter?" she asked. "Seventeen dates before you go to bed? What if the sex is lousy and you wasted all that time?"

"Weirdest thing happened on my way home. I was supposed to go over to his place," I admitted. "But when I called at midnight to say I was on my way, he didn't pick up his phone or call me back. You know Peter. What does that mean?"

"It means he doesn't want you to stay at his place while he's in Milan," she said.

"Why not?"

"Because I told him it was a really bad idea."

"You what? When?" I was stunned and confused. I had just set her up with a new relationship, while she was ruining mine. Why the hell should she care if I stayed at Peter's? Unless...

"Elizabeth, I thought you told me you never went out with Peter."

"We never went out. We went in."

"For how long?"

"Four years."

"Four years!" I yelled. "Why didn't you tell me? When did it end?"

"I think last night," she said.

chapter six
breaking up is hard to do
January 26, 2001

After a month I still couldn't believe Elizabeth had sucked me into another sick love triangle. When she begged me to have lunch I relented—only to let her know how mad I was and how I was putting an end to all this twisted triangulating. It figured she'd be late—on my birthday; the worst birthday of my life, no less. Not that I'd told her. Since I'd decided to end our friendship, my personal life was no longer any of her business. And I was probably going to have to leave New York, so I'd lose touch with her anyway.

Sitting at the Village Den this rainy Saturday, I chain-smoked and held my camera up to the window. Everybody was carrying something odd. An old man with a gray beard lugged a tuba. A woman with a purple scarf held an easel with both arms, like a dance partner. Two teenagers transported a stuffed antique chair they'd probably found on a street corner. They all seemed to be checking each other out. I liked the idea of watching people who were people-watching. But the dim light would ruin any shot. I put my camera down. I hadn't taken a single frame in four weeks.

"You don't look so hot," Elizabeth said, finally slipping into the booth. She was wearing black jeans and her black peacoat— my old uniform.

I looked at myself in the mirror behind the counter. My hair was stringy from the gray Old Navy hoodie I'd been wearing. My face was pale.

"Did you come here to insult me?" I asked. "You're late."

She took off her coat and scanned the dive. I flagged the waiter for a diet soda refill.

"I wanted to make sure you were okay," she said. "What happened to your apartment?"

"The sublet turned out to be illegal. When the landlord heard, he made us leave. I didn't have enough money for a new security deposit. Nicky's VH1 producer found her a place in the East Village, where I've been crashing."

"My studio is tiny, but you can stay with me if you want," she said.

"Thanks." I was surprised by her offer. But maybe this was a trick to keep me stuck in another psychotic trio where she'd be sleeping at Peter's place when I was at her place. Yuck. No way was I playing third wheel any longer.

"It's a two-thousand-square-foot loft, so I'm good," I said, feeling anything but.

"I hate diners. How can you eat this junk? My dad used to take us to diners."

I loved diners. "In this neighborhood?"

"Yeah. We'd take the train from Rye and meet him at his apartment on West Tenth." She scanned the menu.

"I thought you grew up in the Village." I was confused.

"I grew up in a small house an hour away. My mom paid the thirty-year mortgage herself, on a teacher's salary. We only stayed with Dad one weekend a month."

"I can't believe you didn't like coming here. What kid wouldn't like the Village?"

"It's not like you coming to the Village," she said. "At six I was a caretaker for a drunk father. We'd stay with his shady friends in dark places with mice, rats, and roaches. I never knew if he'd collapse or forget me and my sister somewhere."

Odd, my father had bad memories of being down and out in this area too. "My dad grew up poor on the Lower East Side. When he refused to visit New York, I told him, 'You're afraid of your ghosts.' He said, 'If you had my ghosts, you'd fear them too.'"

"Right," she jumped in. "He has reasons not to come back. You should listen and leave him alone." Typical Elizabeth—taking the man's side when she didn't even know the man.

"Listen, you made me look like a total idiot with Peter," I blurted out. "That's the opposite of the way a friend should treat you."

"I'm sorry," she said. "We've been off and on for years. It was never exclusive."

I chewed on my ice. "Why didn't you just tell me?"

"I didn't want to broadcast that I was fucking him. And I didn't want you pathetically babysitting his cats and waiting for him to call like I used to," she said.

"What you getting already?" the waiter asked. His name tag said Louie.

Elizabeth looked at the menu. "Hamburger, fries, and a Coke."

"Another diet soda for me, Louie." After three he'd give me free refills.

"Why don't they just hook you up to the machine intravenously?" she said. "Rachel, you have to eat something. Get some soup. She'll have some chicken soup. A bowl."

"You auditioning to be a Jewish mother?" I asked. "The real one keeps calling."

"Why don't you visit your family for a few weeks?" she asked.

"Because I have a job."

"Xeroxing and getting magazine idiots coffee?" she asked.

"Screw you." I lit a cigarette, French inhaled, and blew smoke rings in the air. Full circles. I was getting better at it. "Just what I need now, my family to make everything worse. I'm afraid they'll make me move back home."

"I wish I had your family to move home to." She was still staring at the menu. "I changed my mind," she called out to Louie. "I'll have a cheeseburger instead."

I looked at the sticky tabletop, then dipped my napkin in the water, wiped it off. The busboy brought a basket of bread. Elizabeth smeared butter on a roll.

"Jane said you're having a party tonight," she said. "The big twenty-five. Can I crash?"

"I just told friends to meet me at Cedar Tavern. Everyone's buying their own drinks."

"Can I bring a date?" she asked.

Red flares went up. "I already invited Peter."

"I'm totally finished with Peter. I swear," she said.

So why had she ruined my relationship if they were really over? It didn't make sense.

"I invited Eliot too," I added.

"He didn't call me back. I met a new guy—Barry Green, an LA TV producer. He's neurotic and Jewish, like you."

"You know, Jews don't find anti-Semitism all that charming," I said.

"Oh, don't be silly. My sister married a Jew."

"You're already marrying Barry?" Sounded like she was even more fucked up about men than I was.

"I might if he wasn't impotent," she said. "We tried four times. He couldn't do it."

"Really?" Hearing of her new guy's sexual dysfunction made me feel better. "This older theater producer I used to see had that problem because he was on Prozac."

"I wouldn't date a guy on antidepressants," she sniffed.

"Is that because your dad was depressed?" I asked, but she didn't answer. I lit another cigarette.

"Your dad's an oncologist and you smoke. My dad got emphysema from cigarettes. Can't your smart brother who sends you X-rays of cancerous lungs talk sense into you?"

Why wouldn't she get off of my brother? "Ben guzzles six-packs of beer and eats whole steaks like a hog."

"A real man," she said. "Can't wait to meet your parents."

"They don't get east very often. You'll have to fly to Illinois."

"I can't afford plane fare. I'm totally broke. I walked here because I lost my last subway token. That's why I was late."

Her life was so much tougher than mine, it was hard to stay mad at her. I slipped her a ten and two subway tokens.

"Thanks." She put them in her purse. "You're the most generous person I know."

"I am not."

"You are, Rachel." She looked down, like she was embarrassed. "You're the type who makes things happen. You're one of the magic people."

I was? The way she said it made me almost believe it.

When our food came, she crammed a bunch of fries in her mouth, as if she were starving. Didn't she have enough money to eat? Then she lifted the bun, looking disappointed. "I should have just gotten the regular burger," she said.

"So switch it." The Solomon tribe always knew what they wanted to eat. I never understood somebody who couldn't decide what to put in their mouth.

"That's okay." She tentatively took a bite.

"Jane said you finished putting together a series of portraits." I tried the chicken soup, but it was too hot. "Can I see them?"

"I'm getting them to Dad's agent, Joris, on Monday," she said. "Let's see what he says."

I didn't know any photographers big enough to have agents.

"I'm afraid he'll just compare my work to Dad's and I'll come up short," she admitted.

"Everyone's aesthetic is derivative at first, then you develop your own visual presence." I tried to be reassuring.

"Where'd you learn that crap? NYU?"

I had a theory that whenever Elizabeth felt close to me, she'd be insulting purposely, to ruin the moment.

"I brought you a present for your birthday." She handed me a package from her knapsack. It was a first edition hardcover Diane Arbus, which the late photographer had signed. I was shocked. "This is incredible. She's my idol." I opened to the introduction. "Hey, this is where she says my favorite line: 'A photograph is a secret about a secret.'"

"Yeah, yeah." Elizabeth smiled. Was this why she'd wanted to have lunch today?

"Don't tell me—Arbus and your father were friends?"

"They both assisted Lisette Model in the sixties," she said. "Dad gave me a bunch of signed copies. I had an extra. I don't like Arbus so much."

"Thanks. Wow." I ran my hands over the black-and-white picture of the melancholy twin girls on the cover, Elizabeth's discard suddenly my treasure.

That night she waltzed into my party, in a black dress and gray eye shadow. Her guy, Barry Green, was balding on top with long graying hair on the sides.

"I've heard nice things about you," I said, putting my hand out to shake. He ignored it.

"I hear the Highland Park Jewish mafia might come tonight," he said.

"Yeah, the whole club," I confirmed, leading them to a back table. "What do you do?"

"Masturbate," he answered.

"Is that supposed to be funny?" I asked him, ordering a double vodka and Diet Coke.

"And what do you do?" he asked me.

I'd assumed Elizabeth had told him. "I work at *Vision*."

"Oh yeah, you're the new assistant vice gopher," he said. "Cubicle number three, right?"

Oh good, an arrogant, condescending male, like my dad and brother Ben. Just what I needed tonight. When my drink came, I downed it fast and ordered two more.

"Happy birthday. You look great," said Jane, giving me tulips. Jane was growing on me.

Nicky came in and handed me a package. Opening it, I found a thick birthday joint the size of a cigar and a black velvet scarf wrapped in tissue paper.

"Aren't we chic?" I put it around my neck. "It's beautiful, Nicky."

"So you're the other half of Ricky and Nicky?" Elizabeth asked. Hearing our old high school nicknames out of context was disconcerting.

"'Ricky and Nicky' sounds like a Vegas act," Barry jumped in. "Or Texas twins in *Penthouse* muff shots."

Had Elizabeth brought Barry to insult my roommate and embarrass me at my own party? I was mortified. I'd felt so close to her that afternoon. But now I feared it was a setup. As more guests came, the more vodka and Diet Cokes I downed, the angrier I became. I wished Barry would go back to LA where he belonged and take Elizabeth with him.

Confused and dizzy, I surveyed my guests. Andy, who'd stopped calling Jane, sat across from her. Eliot the urologist talked with Jane to avoid Elizabeth. There was an empty seat for Peter, who didn't show. Barry flirted with Nicky, which pissed off Elizabeth. Though the table was oblong, my whole fucking life was a triangle.

I walked outside to smoke a cigarette. Standing on the sidewalk, I recklessly lit my birthday joint instead. Andy followed me. It was cold and snowing, and I'd forgotten my coat. He took off his and wrapped it around my shoulders. I'd been madly in lust with his roommate, Lance, all through undergrad. When I'd found out Lance had been secretly screwing my redheaded suite mate Tina for six months at the same time he'd been sleeping with me, Andy was the one who'd come over to scrape me off the floor.

"What's wrong, Ricky?"

I handed him the joint. He shook his head, so I smoked it alone. Andy, who was tall and thin with dark curly hair, looked cute. He'd be a great catch if I hadn't been psychotically entwined with his best buddy for four years.

"If you're upset about that new guy who didn't show up, he's not worth it," he said, guessing the reason for my mood.

"I was so psyched to escape my family. But I have no money, no boyfriend, and now no apartment. I've never not had a place to live," I told him. I hated sounding so pathetic on my big birthday.

"You have a good job."

"Getting people coffee. And I fear my editor in chief is on the way out."

"Listen, what you're doing is very brave, trying to make it in the art world in a new city." He put his arm around me. "Come on. You've been through worse than this. Remember that night freshman year when you ate those bad mushrooms and walked in on Lance and Tina in the shower?"

"Don't remind me!"

"Didn't your shrink say the reason you lost it and started throwing all your negatives into the shower was 'cause her hair was the same shade as your mother's?"

"Stop it!" I couldn't help but crack up at the sick memory, punching his shoulder.

Through the window, the scene inside the restaurant looked more fun. At parties I usually thought of who wasn't there. I went through a mental list of everyone I wished had come: Peter, whom I should have been over, and big-shouldered Lance, whom I couldn't believe I actually missed. My brothers, who'd called to sing "Happy Birthday" on my answering machine. My mom, who'd sent a basket of candy and flowers. My father, who hadn't even bothered to get on the phone when she'd called or to sign his name to the card.

"Ricky, do you ever question why we're always single?" Andy asked.

"Me and you?"

"Yeah. I mean, most people from college are paired up already." He looked gloomy, as if this had been weighing on him. "But nobody from our inner circle. Why do you think we're all still on our own?"

"We're the most emotionally damaged," I joked.

I wondered if people from broken homes, like Elizabeth, felt the need to rectify it, whereas those like me, with too much family closeness, need to be alone longer to combat the early claustrophobia.

"Maybe it's 'cause we're so ambitious. And the more you want in life, the harder it is to get?" I ventured. "Or that we're not team players. We don't follow rules or need to be validated by someone else."

He smiled, pleased with my self-serving rationalization. "We march to our own drummers?" he asked.

"Or we could just be selfish assholes," I added.

"Hey look, that creepy guy Barry, with the Donald Trump comb-over, is kissing Nicky," Andy said, pointing to their table.

Barry kissing Nicky? I couldn't believe it, and I marched

inside. I looked for Elizabeth, but I didn't see her. Somebody handed me a cell phone. It was Peter on the line.

"Sorry. I can't make it, hon. Zelda's sick. She's flipping out," Peter said.

"Well, why don't you just marry that stupid cat!" I yelled, slamming the phone shut. I walked back outside, heading to Peter's Tribeca place to tell him off.

"Ricky? Where are you going?" Nicky asked.

"Why'd you kiss Barry? He's with Elizabeth."

"Really? I thought he was alone." As I tripped on the curb, she grabbed my head. "Ricky, you're a bit wobbly."

"Yeah, I might be a little zoned," I admitted. "Can you get me home?"

We took a cab to Nicky's apartment on Seventh Street, where I was staying.

"There's this big lawsuit 'cause my boss bought the building and is trying to get rid of the rent-controlled tenants so she can combine four apartments," Nicky said. "When I came home from work the other day, this crowd was chanting 'Kill yuppie scum.' I joined in until I realized I was the yuppie scum. The police had to escort me in through the back."

"Kill yuppie scum," I chanted. It seemed hysterical. "On my twenty-fifth birthday I'm broke, drunk, and stood up for a fat cat named Zelda." I laughed so hard tears came to my eyes.

The next day I woke up on one of the blue couches my mother had sent, which I'd crammed into Nicky's living room. I was still in black jeans, my sweater twisted around me. I tried to remember the party. "How bad was it?" I asked Nicky, my head pounding.

"Want some coffee?" She avoided the question.

I shook my head. "You're not going to go out with Barry?"

"No," she said. "I was just having fun. I wouldn't have touched him if I'd had any idea he came with your girlfriend. What a scumbag."

"Good." Seeing Nicky fooling around with that loser had totally creeped me out, especially since she and I usually agreed on people.

"So what did you think of Elizabeth? Could you tell how smart she is?"

"I could tell how sad she is," Nicky said. "Diet soda?"

I nodded and she handed me one. "She was the one who helped me land my first byline. And she gave me this amazing Diane Arbus book. I don't really get why she was so rude to me at my own party."

"Don't expect anything from unhappy people," Nicky advised. "They need all their energy to keep going. They don't have much to give."

When her cell phone rang, she picked up, then handed the phone to me. It was Jane. A bad connection; I could barely hear. I looked at the clock. Four P.M. "Have you seen Elizabeth?" Jane asked. "There's a problem...."

"I know. Barry kissed Nicky. It's disgusting! But Nicky didn't know he came with Elizabeth and she isn't into him."

"No, you don't understand. There's been a fire," Jane said. I could hear a siren in the background. "I'm outside Elizabeth's apartment on Broadway."

"A fire? Is she in there?"

"No. She never came home last night. I tried calling."

"Oh no," I said. "She just put together all her slides for the agent."

"I don't know where she is." Jane sounded desperate.

I heard more sirens and screaming. "Don't go anywhere. I'm on my way."

I hopped on the train, feeling petty for being upset with her. Overall, she had actually been quite a good friend to me. She'd picked me as her *Vision* replacement, helped me sell my first photos, introduced me to the majestic Hope, and steered me away from Peter, the loser, who wasn't even an interesting kind of bad news. Not to mention giving me the beautiful signed hardcover Arbus, my favorite book ever.

At Broadway and 107th Street there were police cars, fire engines, and a roadblock set up. Elizabeth's high-rise was still standing and the fire was out, though smoke seeped through a lower floor. A photographer shot the scene. I was so freaked, I'd forgotten my camera. Some photojournalist I was. Jane ran over.

"Four people were taken to the hospital—all males," she said. "No sign of Elizabeth. I called her mother, and her sister. They haven't heard from her. Where else would she go?"

The smell of smoke made me nauseous. I counted floors to find her studio. The brick was charred, the windows busted. Her level looked completely destroyed.

"I think her place got it the worst. What a fluke," Jane said.

But it was no fluke. During my party, when I was angry with Barry, I feared I'd inadvertently put a curse on both of them. Elizabeth had called me "one of the magic people." Now I feared she was right, but it was black magic. Indeed, my mother had once warned me that in the old country, her female relatives were known witches.

"I feel so guilty I was mad at her," I confessed. "Especially after she asked if I wanted to stay with her. And brought me that extra copy she had of the Arbus book."

"Extra copy?" Jane said. "It's a signed first edition. You have no idea how hard it was to get her father to part with it."

Two days later the phone woke me in the middle of the night.

"Ricky, it's me."

"Elizabeth!" I bolted up on the couch. "Thank God you're okay! Where are you?"

"I'm in LA," she said.

"LA? What are you doing there?"

"Chilling out for a while," she said.

"Jane and I went to your apartment. What the hell happened?"

"This stupid fire started downstairs at the laundry. My place was totaled."

"What time is it?" I turned on the light in Nicky's living room.

"It's one A.M. here," she said. "Must be four in New York."

"But you're okay? What happened to you after my party?" I asked, lighting a cigarette.

"I left with Barry. We drove to Long Island and stayed with his parents. When I got back to my apartment Sunday, I didn't have one. The fire trucks were there. The police wouldn't let me in. So Barry charged me a plane ticket and they bumped me to first class. Weather's great here. It's seventy-five and sunny."

I sucked in smoke, coughed, then took a sip of the warm diet soda I'd left on Nicky's table, trying to make sense of what Elizabeth had said. "You're with Barry?"

"He got this big pilot deal for a sitcom, *Barry's World*. He's acting and producing. I've been hanging out poolside at the Chateau Marmont, where he's staying."

My relief that she was okay switched to bafflement. "You're still with Barry?" I couldn't wrap my head around it.

"Yes, I know he flirted with Nicky at the party," she said. "Don't be so provincial."

Provincial? Nobody had ever called me that before. With my tattoo, in Highland Park I was downright radical. "Well, since he had his tongue down Nicky's throat and you said he can't get it up anyway, I assumed you were finished with him."

"So what?" she asked. "That doesn't fit into your neat little Midwest rule book?"

"Didn't John Belushi OD at the Chateau Marmont?" I changed the subject.

"Dad just accepted an offer to teach at USC. They're going to pay for a two-bedroom in Santa Monica, right on the beach. So I think I'm going to stay here. With him."

"What? Isn't he at Emory?" It was an eerie time of the morning, with blue light coming in through the curtains. I wanted to go home, but I didn't have one. Elizabeth didn't either, but she seemed happy about it. "You sound pretty good for someone whose place and work just went up in smoke."

"I hated that scummy little apartment and the fake photography scene," she said. "The city was too hard for me. I'm too thin-skinned. You can handle it. I couldn't compete."

But she was the smartest, strongest woman I'd ever met. If she couldn't make it—with her brains, talent, famous father, and connections—where did that leave me?

"You should see my dad's place here," she said. "There's a pool and sauna on the roof. I haven't lived with him since I was four."

I looked out the window—another snowy, freezing day in the east. I wished I was in California. "What are you going to do out there?"

"Think I'll join Gold's Gym."

"With your life," I said. "One day in LA and you already sound like an airhead."

"You're not exactly the CEO of your own company," she said. "You're getting three hundred dollars a week to be a peon."

"Well, Ruth Lott wants me to do more work for the *Post*. And the photo editor from *Allure* just called."

"Now, that'll win you a Pulitzer," she said.

Her insult stung. But I remembered that years of her work had just gone up in flames. "Do you have copies of your slides?" I asked.

"Forget about my photography!" she shouted. "I can't do it anymore. Don't bring it up again. It's your dream, not mine!"

———

Two weeks later, when I got the mail, I found a tape Elizabeth had sent of the pilot of *Barry's World* and I put it in Nicky's VCR to watch. Barry—played by the real Barry—was a cynical TV producer who lived with Terry, his neurotic loser brother, part of the reason he couldn't marry his long-suffering girlfriend, Elena.

"You can't go to the baseball game with Terry tonight," Elena argued. "It's my friend Ricky's birthday party."

"I don't want to celebrate your friend Ricky's twenty-fifth birthday," Barry yelled.

My birthday party was on national television! I moved closer to the TV and turned up the volume.

"She'll kill me if we don't show up," the Elena character said. "She's really depressed because she just got fired and evicted from her apartment, *and* her boyfriend dumped her."

Wait a second. I hadn't been fired, and Peter hadn't dumped me. I'd dumped him after I found out he'd been screwing Elizabeth. Why hadn't Barry stuck that one in there?

"I don't like Ricky," Barry continued. "*You* don't even like Ricky."

What did that mean? Had Elizabeth said that to Barry?

"We have to go to make sure she doesn't kill herself," added Elena.

That was a joke? I was depressed, but I wasn't ever suicidal! How dare she tell him I was suicidal!

"I'm not going," said Barry, pantomiming hanging himself with his tie. Cut to Barry, Terry, and Elena entering a restaurant and saying hello to Ricky, a hyper, neurotic—but thankfully very cute and thin—woman.

"How's the birthday girl?" Elena asked.

"All men are pond scum," Ricky told Elena.

"Not all men!" I screamed at the set. "Just Barry the bald pig TV producer!"

"Oh, honey; there's great guys out there. You just have to find the right one, like I did," Elena crowed. Cut to Barry, picking up the woman to his right. Cut to hours later, when a very wasted Ricky was crying hysterically, falling down on the floor as the laugh track roared.

Humiliated, I got stoned by myself, feeling like curling up in a fetal position and bawling in real life. But then I noticed an envelope in the stack of mail with my father's messy handwriting. I opened it to find a check for six thousand dollars—enough for six more months of New York rent—and on an index card he'd scrawled, "Happy birthday to my only girl."

part
two

chapter seven
roofhampton
August 5, 2001

"I'm back!" Elizabeth announced over the phone. "I'm coming over."

I was shocked. For the last six months, in her sporadic e-mails and rambling phone messages, she'd raved about her life in LA. I was dying to know why she'd just returned to New York and was on her way downtown to see me. I also wondered why she'd asked if my new studio apartment had roof access. My West Village high-rise did have a beautiful paved roof. In fact, I'd just taken a splashy series of portraits of downtown designers posing on their rooftops for *Paper* magazine. And in their last issue they'd also published "Present Tense," my six-page series of the off-base gifts my suburban mother sent me, under the headline "Er, thanks for the pink angora, Mom." I couldn't wait to show Elizabeth.

After we hung up, I rushed to my files and pulled out all the clips. I couldn't decide which of the tear sheets would impress Elizabeth most. I desperately wanted her to see how far I'd come. My recent bylines would prove to her that I was no longer a novice, the green kid from Illinois she saw me as. I was an official photographer. In the time she'd been gone, I was getting to be known as a serious professional, almost on her level.

She was late, as usual. At the door, I went to hug her, but she recoiled. Then she air-kissed me. Was that a West Coast greeting?

"Whoa. You look good," I said, inspecting her. Her hair was cut shorter, right below her ears, and the sides seemed sun-streaked. She was tan, and her yellow midriff top definitely showed she'd lost weight. Since when did Elizabeth wear yellow and flaunt her belly button in public? She'd somehow shaved years off of her appearance since she'd left. She looked younger than me. I led her inside. She didn't mention how I looked. Instead, she glanced around my place and said, "What a big studio. Must be eight hundred square feet." She went to the TV my brothers had bought me, turned it on, then off again.

"So, they fixed up your old apartment for you?" I asked.

"It wasn't my choice. The lawyer agreed not to sue if they'd renovate and give it back to me at the same rent."

"How did the renovation go?"

"Good. They replaced everything. It's half the size of yours, but they painted it white and put in a new kitchen and bathroom." She put her hand over the air-conditioning vent. "You have central air?" I nodded. She picked up the silver-framed picture of my family on the shelf and stared at it. "And aside from renovating the place they're paying me forty thousand dollars in damages."

"That's a lot of money."

"Well, not as much as my trainer, Fernando, got from flake insurance."

She had a trainer? Named Fernando? "What's flake insurance?"

"Flood and quake," she said, as if I was dumb not to know.

I put my *Paper* magazine tear sheets on the table, hoping she'd pick them up, but she went to the window. I wanted to show her my makeshift darkroom and how I was organizing all my slides and contact sheets, but she seemed in a hurry.

"Come on," she said. "It's sunny."

"Did you see my *Paper* magazine spread?"

"Yeah. Not bad." She sounded bored and unconvincing. "Come on. *Hasta la pasta.*"

I shrugged. Was that LA slang for *hasta la vista*?

"What are we waiting for?" she asked. "Let's go to your roof."

"Really? You want to sunbathe?"

"Yes. I told you. That's why I'm here."

I thought she'd come to catch up. Not to mention my fantasy that she'd be wowed by how far my work had progressed and would help me figure out my next step. Dejected, I went to the bathroom and changed into my black one-piece, donning my denim shirt as a cover-up. When I came out, I retrieved the two plastic deck chairs the last tenant had left in the closet.

"I don't need a chair," she said.

I put hers back and gathered towels, newspapers, diet soda, and last year's sunscreen from the bathroom. We took the elevator up to the roof, where I spread out my chair, sat down, and rubbed on the SPF-30 lotion. Elizabeth took off her jeans and shirt to reveal a turquoise Day-Glo thong bikini. She put one of my towels on the cement next to me and sat down.

"You're so thin," I said.

"I weigh 130. Solid as a rock." She made a muscle and showed me her arm. "Feel."

I obliged, impressed at how hard her body was. She had a flat stomach, steel thighs, and a dark California tan all over. Had she sunbathed nude? I weighed about the same. But I'd been such a workaholic lately I hadn't been out in the sun or done much exercise all summer. I felt soft, pale, and flabby.

"Fernando had me working out four hours every day, running and using weight machines. I just bought a used bicycle. I rode forty-five miles at my mom's in Westchester yesterday." She stood up and did stretches, reaching her arms into the air, then pulling her leg from behind like a pretzel. She pulled a half-liter bottle of Evian water from her bag and drank it all in one long gulp. "I really wanted to stay in LA." She straightened the sides of the towel. "But Dad lost his job just as my old landlord called and said they'd completely renovated the building and were legally obligated to give me back my studio for six hundred a month. How much are you paying?"

"Got a great deal for eleven hundred."

"You can afford that?"

I nodded. "The photography work has been really steady lately," I said, not clarifying further. I was proud to be paying my own rent now. Elizabeth didn't have to know that most of the money was coming from an ongoing advertising assignment I'd gotten to shoot babies in Pampers.

"Just freelance newspaper and magazine work?" She sounded skeptical.

"Well, different kinds of gigs," I admitted.

"Advertising? Direct marketing?" she asked.

"A bit. But I'm making more money on my own than I was as a full-time employee at *Vision*."

"I'm so glad you're gone from that tacky taco stand," she said.

"Me too," I echoed, though we both knew I hadn't had a choice. When Richard was fired six months before, they axed his whole regime, me included. "My name's really getting around as a freelancer. If I could just get paid on time."

"I thought your father gave you enough money for six months' rent for your birthday," she said.

I forgot I'd told her. Damn, she could always locate my Achilles heel and throw it back in my face at the worst time, just like my brother Ben.

"That ran out last month," I informed her curtly. "But I'm cool on my own."

"My dad was supposed to be helping me. But after USC fired him, he went on a bender again, getting drunk every day."

"Oh shit. I didn't know," I said. "I'm sorry."

"He's got an offer at a third-rate college in Indiana. My stepsister Jenna's flying him there next week."

"You have a stepsister?"

"From his third marriage," she said casually. "Jenna is twenty. Pretty sweet, but I've always been my dad's favorite."

"You never told me about Jenna."

"Yes I did. You weren't listening."

"You only told me about your older sister, Michelle," I argued. "You never mentioned Jenna."

I believed sibling order determined your entire personality. That's why I was bossy with a strong sense of entitlement, typical oldest child. I'd thought that being the second daughter of divorced parents explained how someone as smart as Elizabeth could be so unsure of herself. But maybe having a younger sister in the mix changed everything, even if they hadn't grown up together. No wonder she'd felt so lost and nervous about her father's affection. She was actually a middle child who'd been usurped by a sibling, like I'd been by Ben.

"I told you about Jenna before," she repeated.

"You didn't," I insisted. "How could a Freudian forget major details about somebody's family?"

Dave and his boyfriend Ken from the eighth floor came up. They spread out a blanket and unpacked a pitcher of margaritas, a CD player, and classical CDs. Elizabeth got up from the towel and walked by them. Why was she showing off her body? Dave and Ken had eyes only for each other. Itchy and already burning, I lathered on tons more sunscreen.

"Do you have the *Post*?" she asked.

I took it out of my beach bag and handed it to her.

"Did you check out the TV section?" She turned to it. "*Barry's World* is the number two sitcom in the country."

"I still think that was a really mean parody of my birthday party," I said.

"I didn't write it."

"I thought you said TV was an ignorant medium that appealed to the lowest common denominator," I quoted her back to herself.

"Oh, lighten up," said the darkest, most intense woman I'd ever met.

Sherry, the single mother from 8D, emerged from the elevator and sat down on a bench. She was holding a pack of Marlboros and a Walkman.

"Can I bum one?" I asked. I'd forgotten mine downstairs.

"Sure." She handed me one and lit it. "Freedom! My mother's taking the baby all day. Thank God it's sunny," Sherry said, plugging in her earphones.

"She has a two-month-old daughter. Never got married," I whispered to Elizabeth.

"I could do that," Elizabeth boasted.

What? She'd never mentioned anything about kids before. The only woman on the planet I knew who seemed less likely to have a baby than me was Elizabeth. I couldn't even imagine it. I puffed on the Marlboro and sipped my diet soda through a straw.

"Nobody smokes cigarettes in LA," she sniffed.

"So you and Barry are still happening?" I asked.

"I wish. We're just friends now. He started sleeping with his old girlfriend Dee. I guess he gets it up with her," she said. "Probably because Dee's prettier."

Some things stayed the same, like Elizabeth's insecurity about her looks. That's what all the exercise was about, something she could control. She sprayed tanning lotion on her back and legs, then stood up. Did she have *shpilkes* or was she showing off her body again? As if Sherry from 8D cared about her muscular thighs.

"I think they're getting engaged," Elizabeth added.

"So do you think it would be cool if I sent Hope some of my latest work?" I ventured.

She didn't answer. She'd turned facedown on her towel. Soon she was standing on her head. Blood rushed to her face.

"What are you doing?"

"Yoga. To stay flexible." She came down, sat with her feet on her thighs, pushing them toward her stomach. "Dee's rich, Jewish, and pretty, like you. Barry's known her since high school. He talked about her like she was the one who got away."

Her father had lost his job and free apartment and Barry the jerk was in love with someone else. It was becoming more clear why she'd left her beloved LA and didn't want to help me plan my latest work strategy. She pulled a joint from my bag, lit it with my lighter, and sucked in, toking alone, something we still had in common. Only Elizabeth would invent a health regimen that included dope.

"I just applied to nursing school," she threw out.

"You what?" My cigarette dropped from my mouth. I picked it up from the ground.

"I applied to Columbia nursing school. Figured the settlement money would pay for it."

"You're going to nursing school?" I was still stunned she was back in New York. Now she was becoming a nurse? With the Marlboro in one hand, I reached for the joint with the other. She hit it three times before handing it over.

"Why are you shocked? I took a nursing class at USC, and I aced it."

"Nursing?" I puffed in the weed. "Since when?"

"Since I was an eighteen-year-old science major at Harvard. I was thinking about applying to nursing school when Dad got me the magazine job. All my old credits will transfer. I might try their anesthesiology program."

I'd never known Elizabeth was interested in that field; the thought totally depressed me. "Is this just to marry a doctor?"

"No. But what would be wrong with that? Your mother did it."

"My mother did not choose a husband with a good profession to snag a meal ticket. In fact, she met my dad when she was fifteen and wound up putting him through medical school," I spat, annoyed that Elizabeth had brought my family history into her inane argument, and inaccurately at that. "What about photography? You've definitely decided to give it up? Like, for good?"

I'd just assumed she'd needed a break to recover from losing the magazine job and her pictures in the fire. I could envision somebody not wanting to submit work for a while. But I couldn't imagine a true photographer giving it up. I certainly never could. It would be the equivalent of cutting out my own heart.

"I can't do commercial junk like you do," she said.

I tried to ignore her insult. She had to denigrate the whole profession in order to leave it, I told myself. "What about that big agent you mentioned, Joris?" I asked.

"I have nothing to show him. I'm going to be a nurse."

I handed the joint back to her. "Is this because Jane decided to go to law school?"

"Maybe," Elizabeth said. "When she applied for loans I thought she was crazy, but in three years she'll be making over a hundred thousand a year."

"But she'll be a lawyer."

"And I'll be a nurse."

"Is this so you can take care of your father when he's sick?" I asked, determined to get to the bottom of it. There had to be another reason.

"Don't start in with the psychobabble again. If I get accepted, I'm going," she said. "I can work three days a week and make forty thousand. You can't talk me out of it."

"I'm not trying to," I said. The dope was making me too tired and spacey to keep arguing anyway.

"I hate the Manhattan art scene. It's pretentious, cold, and fickle. Look what it did to my father. It's a horrible life."

It didn't have to be a terrible life if you weren't a flaky old drunk, I didn't say. Or a gold digger on the prowl for high-paid doctors.

"If I keep up my current pace of three assignments a week I'll gross forty grand freelancing this year," I said, pleased with the thought, pretending to forget that two-thirds of it would likely be from diaper ads. I waited for her reaction. There was none. I drifted off. When I opened my eyes she was doing one-handed push-ups on the ground, grunting, "Ninety-eight, ninety-nine, one hundred."

Was she on coke? If so, why wasn't she offering me any? "Isn't it too hot to do that?"

She stood up, put on her jeans and shirt, and said, "I have to go."

I didn't want her to leave before I had a chance to get her eyes on my new work. I put on my shirt and folded the chair, and we took the elevator back downstairs. "Are you okay here? Do you need anything?" I asked. "Clothes? Books?"

"No thanks."

I went to my closet, pulled out a long-sleeved red blouse, and gave it to her. "You like red. It's a good color on you."

"I took some candids of you," she mumbled before going into the bathroom to try on the blouse.

"What? You shot me? When?" I never knew she'd secretly taken pictures of me. Why hadn't she ever shown them to me?

"When you weren't paying attention." She emerged in jeans and the blouse, which meant she liked it. "They were good shots," she said. "Not that you could take a bad picture with those high cheekbones of yours. It's a shame all my contact sheets went up in flames."

So she could compliment my cheekbones, but not my photographs. I knew better than to try to hug her. "I'm sorry about the fire," I said. "Doesn't it feel good to be back, with everything renovated?"

"Didn't have a choice." She shrugged. "Are you going home over the summer?"

"I'm flying there next week for my father's sixtieth birthday party," I said. "It's a big surprise."

"You're so lucky to have such great parents," she said, sounding wistful. "Can I take you up on your offer to visit Highland Park?"

I'd forgotten that last April, for her thirtieth birthday, when Northwest had a seventy-five-dollar special on round-trip airfare, I'd invited her to visit my family with me and booked us two cheap tickets. That was before our falling-out. But since then she'd barely returned my calls and e-mails. I wasn't sure the offer was still good. We'd barely reconnected, and now I didn't think I wanted to spend my only vacation with Elizabeth. What would she do in Illinois, anyway? The Solomons wouldn't know what to make of her. *I* barely knew what to make of her.

"I can talk to your father and brothers about medicine. Do they still do that disease game at dinner?"

"My shrink outlawed it in my presence," I said.

"I could play it without you," she offered cheerfully.

Why would I invite her home as my guest to participate in a despised childhood ritual that excluded me? Then again, Elizabeth and her father still knew every photo editor and agent in the country, and I was sure she'd relent and help me. Especially if we were spending time together in my old haunts. I wondered what she'd make of the old darkroom my dad had made out of the basement closet. I bet she'd totally get it.

"Okay. Let's do it," I agreed, slipping my best tear sheets in an envelope and handing it to her. "I put together some of my recent magazine clips for you. I'd love to hear who you think I should send them to."

She stood in front of the mirror in the foyer, brushing her hair, ignoring me. "My hair is still too thin. I got a perm in LA and it was thick for two weeks, then it went limp again. It'll never be thick like yours."

I walked her to the elevator. Back in my apartment, I noticed that she'd left my work on the table, next to an empty Evian bottle, which I threw in the garbage.

chapter eight
heart to heart
August 11, 2001

At O'Hare airport, I threw my black bags into the backseat of my father's Lincoln. As he pulled out of the waiting zone I said, "Happy birthday" casually, so he wouldn't be suspicious. I stared at him. He looked rested and tan, though his hair was almost all gray now, which made him seem old. I hadn't visited in almost a year, the longest we'd ever gone without seeing each other in my whole life. I was determined not to screw this up or get embroiled in an upsetting family drama, like I had last time.

"Flight was twenty minutes ahead of schedule," he said.

"Cool. Glad you were early." I fumbled for a cigarette, which I lit with his car lighter. "Ever notice that the airline schedules the flight for two hours when it's only an hour and a half?" I asked.

"Yeah, then they give themselves a big award for always being on time." He chuckled.

I inhaled, flicking ashes out the window. "So Mom said to meet her at the club?" I awkwardly threw out.

The plan was to get there at seven o'clock; everyone would be waiting. I actually felt special to be the one delivering him to his surprise party. Since it was a forty-five-minute drive, I'd envisioned we'd have time for a tête-à-tête, to reconcile, sure that by now he'd forgiven me for not moving back to Illinois to go to law school. I'd made sure to include two zoom lenses and ten extra rolls of film in the bottom of my camera bag to capture this special night for my parents. I hoped he wouldn't figure out why it was heavier than usual today.

"Did you get the latest clips I sent?" I couldn't help but ask.

"Smoking is a stupid habit," was all he said.

Oh yeah; according to Ben, he'd quit again. He couldn't even give me credit for my major career leap. So much for our big reconciliation. I flipped through the radio stations, stopping at an Eminem song about wearing disguises because his split personality was having an identity crisis. I could relate.

"What is that crap?" Dad asked, turning off the radio. "Hey, listen to this." He stuck in a CD that made loud rub-dub noises. "Heart murmurs," he said. "This is systolic." He fast-forwarded to another muffled rub-dub set. "This is diastolic." He smiled, pleased with himself.

Was he kidding? For a second I was afraid he knew about the party, but he seemed oblivious, driving seventy-five miles an hour on the highway, lost as usual in his own head. "You really listen to this while you're driving?"

"Have to keep up," he said, nodding.

No wonder my relationships with guys were always such a disaster. How could they not be when the most important man in my life treated me like a total stranger, with no idea of who I really was.

Finally he broke the silence by saying, "Your mother said

you have a friend coming to visit. Not another idiot with a tattoo and a nose ring?"

I'd brought home Derek ten years ago and my father still wasn't over it. "No. A girlfriend."

"A girlfriend? You're not—"

"No. Not a lover," I cut him off. "Just a friend I met at the magazine."

"Oh." He looked relieved.

"Elizabeth," I added.

"Yeah, you mentioned her. She's a photographer too?" he asked.

That implied he was acknowledging what I did for a living, maybe for the first time. Okay, we were making progress. "Well, actually, now she's going to nursing school. At Columbia."

"Really?" He looked amazed that a New York friend of mine would go into that field. Little did he know that I was more stunned than he was. "It's a top-notch school."

"She's trying a specialty. Anesthetics, I think."

"Columbia has a grade-A anesthesiology program," he said with intense interest.

I felt like I'd scored points for being close to someone with a career he approved of. "So I've heard."

"Does your shoulder still hurt?"

Weeks ago I'd mentioned it was sore from lugging around too much equipment. My dad was always concerned if I was hurt—physically, at least. "No. It's okay now."

"Want to go home first to drop off your stuff?"

"No," I answered too fast. That would ruin everything. "I didn't eat on the plane. Let's just get to the club. I'm starving."

"Good evening, Dr. Solomon," the valet said, taking his car keys. The doorman opened the door for us. I threw my camera bag over my shoulder and led my father to the dining room, which was dark and quiet. Then the lights went on and everyone yelled,

"Surprise!" He looked shocked. I feared he was upset because he hated parties. But then he shook his head and laughed and gave my mother a big hug.

"Happy birthday, Joseph." She kissed him on the lips.

"Hey." Ben punched my arm. "Good job."

"Plane was twenty minutes early," Danny said. "I called."

"They schedule the flight for two hours so they can say they're always on time," added Ben.

I pulled out my camera and started shooting. I took pictures of the room, which my mother had decorated with bandages, Band-Aids, and stethoscopes. Plastic doctor bags filled with candy and balloons served as centerpieces for the oblong table. Waiters served hors d'oeuvres, and bartenders made everyone mixed drinks. I snatched a bunch of little pigs in blankets as they went by. I hadn't had them since my brothers' bar mitzvahs. I still wasn't over the fact that my parents had never thrown me a bat mitzvah, but I tried not to focus on what was missing tonight. As I joined my brothers in the corner, I couldn't help but notice that although we were in our twenties, we were all mateless on a Saturday evening. Danny had an older girlfriend, Kim, and Ben was rumored to be screwing his way through his half-female medical school class. Yet none of us had brought a date. We were eternally stuck together as a trio, the same as we'd been as kids.

"I'm getting the old man a drink." Ben headed for the bar.

"He's already on his second black Russian," Danny said.

"Then he could use a refill." Ben ordered two more, handed one to my father, then shook hands with some of Dad's doctor friends. I snapped a picture I planned to title "Ben the Physician, Networking Already."

When everyone sat down, I gravitated to a table with my brothers. One at a time, my father's colleagues stood up and made silly speeches. Dr. Neiman, a cardiac surgeon, handed my father a leather-bound book.

"*The Principles and Practice of Medicine* by Sir William Osler,"

Danny whispered to me. "Very important. 1901. Bet it's a first edition."

Dr. Niss, a thoracic specialist who was married to my mother's friend Lois, gave my father a framed caricature of seventeenth-century French physicians called "Gens du Médicine." Pediatric neurosurgeon Dr. Galway contributed a plastic naked woman. Dr. Siskin, a podiatrist, brought out a big cage with a sheet over it and said, "Here's a young chick for an old cock." My father uncovered it. Inside was a live chicken, squawking and ruffling its feathers. I took a picture.

"Siskin's always been an asshole," Danny said.

My brothers presented Dad with a sculpture of a monkey posed like Rodin's *The Thinker*, contemplating a human skull. It was pretty ugly. But it made a good picture, the three Solomon men in dark suits and silver glasses.

"I bet you picked that out," I told Ben. Of the three of us, Ben had the worst taste. He liked things big, blunt, and ostentatious.

"And we ordered him a wide-screen TV, seventy-one inches," Ben added. "Should be delivered tomorrow."

What was his goal in life? To outfit the entire world with TV sets?

Next my father opened my mother's gift, a black Italian leather jacket. He tried it on. It reminded me of the photograph I'd seen of him as a teenager on the Lower East Side, a cigarette dangling from his lips as if he were a gangster. I realized my mother must have wanted him to look like he did when she'd first laid eyes on him.

I'd gotten my father his own black Olympus camera, the kind I sometimes used for fun. I wanted to teach him how to use it, hoping it would give us something in common. He blew me a kiss, held it up, and pointed it at me, though there was no film in it yet. But I feared he didn't really like it. I drank a glass of white wine, then asked the waiter for a refill and downed another.

I felt tipsy as the waiters served a three-course meal, the main course a choice between steak and fish. I was the only one in the family to pick the latter, laughing that I was always a fish out of water. As we finished eating, my father went to the microphone, tapped on it awkwardly. "I'd like to say a few words to my family, friends, and colleagues..."

"Dad must be really drunk." Ben nudged me.

"We save lives every day," my father said. "Well, there's someone who saved my life. That's my beautiful bride, Leah. I'm so lucky to have her. She's the most wonderful wife ever."

"He thinks it's the Gettysburg Address." Danny giggled.

"He's shit-faced," my mother said, laughing.

"Watch your language," I teased. Every once in a while she surprised us all by swearing.

"I met Leah when she was only fourteen, on Clinton Street. I couldn't have done anything without her," he said. "Our kids are here tonight—Rachel, Benjamin, and Daniel, who I love." He turned to us and pointed.

"Shouldn't it be *whom*?" Danny asked, uncomfortable with my father's rare display of emotion.

"At least he got the order right," Ben smirked.

"I'm very proud of them," my father continued. "No matter what they decide to be. They don't want to get married yet. I don't know what the hell they're waiting for...."

Inappropriate and intrusive. Now I felt like I was home.

"My marriage is the best thing that's happened to me, and I hope they are just as happy someday," my father said.

My mother stood up to hug him as everyone applauded. But I was hurt, pretty certain that my father's clause "no matter what they decide to be" had been directed at me. After going through stages of trying to talk me into medical school, like my brothers, then business school, then law school, he at least hoped I'd marry a doctor, lawyer, or businessman. Being a single photographer in New York, the city he couldn't stand, was what my old-fashioned Yiddish relatives would detest and label "a triple *shanda*."

"Okay. Enough blubbering!" Danny yelled. "Where's the dessert?"

I shot my mother cutting the cake, which was shaped like a human heart. When I finished the roll, I went to sneak outside for a cigarette. I bumped into my father coming out of the men's room, with a drink in his hand.

"Nice party." His words sounded slurred.

"Are you okay?" I'd never seen him drunk before. I was a bit wobbly myself.

"You pulled one over on me," he said as we walked outside together. He took a cigar from his pocket, and I followed him, taking out a cigarette.

"From Davie," he said, lighting it. "Not much of a gastroenterologist, but a helluva nice guy."

We sat on a bench outside, near the valet stand. I smoked one of my More Menthol Lights, a new brand, which looked like skinny cigars, while he puffed on his real one. The only smokers in the family, I imagined we were bonded by our method of self-destruction. He hadn't really ever quit cigarettes. He'd merely switched to cigars, which he was probably inhaling.

"Nice speech," I said. "Did you get the clips of my latest work I sent you?"

"You're going to stay in New York, aren't you?" he asked.

"Dad, it's going better now. I know you don't understand why I love the city, but..."

"Your old man understands more than you think." He stared at the rows of parked cars. "I went to NYU too, you know."

I didn't know. "You always told me you went to City College." I was astounded to learn this revised history.

"For three years, then I transferred to NYU for the last two terms."

"You went to my school?" I asked.

"It was in University Heights back then," he said. "The Bronx."

"NYU was in the Bronx?" I couldn't picture NYU anywhere but the Village.

"My friends Lefty and Bubel went to Vietnam. Lefty never came back. My father didn't want to pay for my college; he wanted me to work for him."

"At the furniture store," I said. I remembered the grainy photograph my father had shown me once of my grandpa Jake, holding out the "Solomon & Son Furniture" sign in front of his storefront on Norfolk Street. He never forgave my father for choosing medicine.

"I was lucky there was a war. That's how my mother convinced my dad to pay for school. She said I would be a dead soldier if he didn't."

I'd always loved my grandmother Hannah, who'd died when I was in high school. She was as sweet as Grandpa Jake was bitter.

"You were premed from the start?" I asked him.

"At first I wasn't sure. I liked to take pictures too."

"You wanted to be a photographer?" Now I was truly flabbergasted.

"They put some of my pictures in the school newspaper, *The Heightsman*." He lit the cigar again, puffed a few times to get it going. "Second year I switched to chemistry."

"Why did you switch?"

"It was your uncle Melech's idea. The whole idiot family had meetings once a month to decide who could go to the bathroom. I got good grades in science, so Melech decreed I should be a doctor. Your grandfather was pissed off. That's probably why I did it." He puffed, but the cigar was out. I lit it for him quickly, afraid he'd stop talking.

"Why was Grandpa always pissed off?" He hardly ever talked about his father, who had died when I was in college.

"He had a lousy life. His mother abandoned him in Poland when she had a chance to come to the United States. She didn't send for him until he was six, and that ruined him. If you don't have your mother's love, you have nothing."

What about your father's love? I didn't ask. My worst fear was that by moving back to his old city against his advice, I had somehow ruined our connection forever.

"Grandma Hannah loved you, right?" I asked.

"My mother? I was her favorite. She was so proud when I got into medical school."

"Did Mom want you to be a doctor?"

"Well, she was in high school when I met her and I lied and told her I was already in medical school. I kept it up for a few years."

"You lied to Mom about being in grad school when you were an undergraduate?" My mouth opened.

"Yeah. I told her I was older. When she found out she broke up with me. I almost lost her."

Wow. I never knew. For my father, in vodka veritas, apparently.

"I had to leave New York to get away from my family, if I was going to be anything," he added.

Just like me! "So why the hell didn't you ever tell me any of this before?" I asked.

"I was afraid I'd be a bad influence," he said, and we both laughed.

The next night, my father was reading a batch of EKGs in his den. I'd always liked his electrocardiograms, which, he'd said, graphically recorded internal fluctuations. As a kid I thought they were paper Slinkys. "Good talk at the party," I said.

"What talk?" His expression was blank, as if he didn't remember a word of it. Then his eyes turned downward again, to the hearts he could decipher.

chapter nine
road trips

August 13, 2001

"Where's Elizabeth?" my mother asked, tying her sneakers. She met me at the end of the driveway. She looked young in her green skirt and sweatshirt. Her hair was messy, red bangs in her eyes.

"She's asleep," I told her.

"For the night?" Mom sounded confused. "But it's only seven thirty."

"She gets up early."

"I figured that out when she woke me up at five this morning. The burglar alarm went off. You didn't hear it?"

"No." I hadn't gone to sleep until three A.M., so I was totally out of it.

"Who exercises for four hours a day?" my mother asked. "Of all your girlfriends, this one is the wackiest."

I'd asked my mom to take a power walk with me, as I did every night I was in Highland Park for my ten-day vacation that August. I needed the exercise and escape from being inside the gilded cage of my old house. I would have rather been with Nicky, who was filming a music video in Paris. But now that I wasn't dependent on my father's money, I couldn't afford the airfare. As much as I adored Manhattan, I was burned out from working hundred-hour weeks, and my shrink and editors were away most of the month anyway. Since my mother had sent the plane ticket home for my father's party, I'd decided to stay an extra week. I feared I'd gain weight from all of her overfeeding. But if we speed walked for an hour a day, I'd at least burn off some of the calories and not completely blimp out during the trip.

It was one mile around the block, and if we kept moving fast we could keep up our four-miles-in-sixty-minutes pace and get a chance to talk and catch up. At 7:30 P.M. it was still light outside, with a nice breeze. I thought Elizabeth might join us, but she wanted to run, not walk, and only before dawn. Heaven forbid she alter her exercise schedule, even on vacation. *My* vacation. She'd arrived the day before and within twenty-four hours had already made me regret that I'd invited her here.

Mom waved at Mr. Jennings, who was mowing his lawn next door. Most of my friends had moved away, like me. Across the street the new neighbors, a blond couple in their twenties, tossed a football with their two boys, the wife pregnant again. I felt very single, alone, and tired all of a sudden, afraid I could be wasting years chasing a fantasy career that would never really crystallize. Instead of being a famous photographer like Diane Arbus or Cindy Sherman, I'd be stuck doing advertising drek.

"You worked with Elizabeth at *Vision?*" my mother asked.

"Sort of," I said. "I took her job. She was the one who hooked me up with that *Post* editor who loves my work."

"How old is she?"

"Thirty-one; she's five years older than me."

"She'd be prettier with makeup," Mom said. "She's the one with the father who drinks?"

I nodded, feeling like I should defend Elizabeth since I was the one who'd invited her here. But that was when I knew she couldn't afford the ticket and I longed for her companionship.

"Is that why she has a chip on her shoulder?" she asked.

"Her dad left her mom when she was little," I said. "She grew up poor."

"I grew up poor too. But I was always polite and neat. Did you see what she did to Ben's room? She's a cyclone."

I laughed, thinking better his room than mine. I'd kill her if she woke me up at 5:00 A.M.

"Look!" My mother pointed to the geese by the lake. I counted eight waddling around. I forgot how lovely the summer was here, breezier than in Manhattan.

"I thought you hated the geese."

"No, it's your father who hates them because they go to the bathroom in the pool. That's why he got that blown-up alligator toy. But the geese figured out it won't bite. Now he's getting a plastic shark."

"Dad versus the elements," I said. "He loved the party Saturday night. I think he's been much more emotional since Grandpa died."

"Your grandfather Jake was a piece of work. He told your father not to marry me. 'Vat do you vant from an orphan girl?'" she said, imitating my grandfather's Yiddish accent.

"He trashed you for being orphaned?" My mouth opened. "Like it was your fault."

"I know. My mother died when I was four," she said. "I barely even remember her, but I know that she loved me." She looked at the ground, kicked a stone. "My stepmother, she was another story."

"You had a stepmother?" I asked.

"For two years."

"You never told me." My dad had never told me he'd gone to NYU or wanted to take pictures, and now this. I wondered what other weird family secrets would surface during this visit.

She started walking faster, so I hurried to keep up. It seemed shocking that she'd never told me about her stepmother. Elizabeth had kept her stepsister quiet too. Did they think I couldn't handle the truth about their stepfamilies?

"Just for a year, when I was nine. But when my father got sick, she divorced him. He died a few months later. I hated her."

"What was her name?"

"I don't remember." I knew that she had truly forgotten. Mom only remembered good things. "She'd put a crust of challah and leftover pea soup on the stove for my dinner. She never sat with me while I ate."

"What a bitch!" I put my arm around her.

"Then I went to live with my brother Izzy and his three cats." This story I knew by heart, how the cats smelled up the tenement and ruined the couches. "Uncle Max wouldn't come upstairs; he hated Izzy's cats." She smiled. "We're both so blessed to have brothers."

"So you've told me," I said, not entirely convinced.

Three kids on bicycles flew by. The last girl turned to wave to my mother. The neighborhood kids called her "the candy lady" since she'd started her own party-planning business in our basement, which was now filled with goody baskets, different-colored table assignment tags, and sample centerpieces from "Sam's Bar Mitzvah Casino Getaway" and "Lolly and Frank's Sixtieth Anniversary Extravaganza."

Since August was a quiet month for parties, I was glad to have her to myself. Dad worked late at the hospital, Danny had just started medical school, and Ben was already hell-bent on becoming a swashbuckling surgeon. They'd both moved out on their own, so I could pretend I was the only child I'd always wanted to be, with both of my parents' undivided attention. If Elizabeth would just leave, everything would be perfect.

"Danny's coming over for dinner tonight," my mother said. She liked the occasions when my brothers visited, her excuse for keeping too much food in the freezer just in case.

"Where's Ben living?"

"A town called Zion, where he's the only Jew," my mother quipped.

"How far is it?"

"About a half hour from here and from school. He said he was sick of living like a student but Chicago was too expensive. So he got a great deal on a house in a new development. It's big, looks like a hunting lodge."

How could my kid brother afford to buy a house already? With his bar mitzvah money he'd invested? I knew it was superficial, but I felt eternally slighted that our conservative temple—and my parents—hadn't encouraged me to get bat mitzvahed. My brothers both got twenty grand in gifts for their "today I become a man" ceremonies, and Dad had helped Ben and Danny buy stocks with all that gelt. Who needed those investments now—two future Illinois doctors or a freelance photographer who couldn't afford her New York rent?

"Dad helped him get a mortgage. We saw that he stopped partying and was really buckling down. He was top of his med school class last year, and he got a summer job working for the head of surgery at Northwest Memorial. They published a paper together. Dad's so proud of him." She beamed.

We kept walking. At the corner, she paused. "Are you okay? Your father's worried about you." That meant she was worried. "No job. No boyfriend. You're freelance everything."

"I have two magazine spreads out in the fall." I tried to sound convincingly upbeat.

"Did you ever meet that TV director Nicky was fixing you up with? Matthew Wald?"

"He called, but I haven't gotten back to him." Strange that my mother knew the name of a blind date I hadn't even met yet. I'd mentioned him only once.

"What about that writer from the magazine, Peter? Whatever happened to him?"

"He's okay. We stayed friends."

"Elizabeth said your problem is that you only date losers," my mother said.

"When did she tell you that?" I asked. How dare Elizabeth talk to my mother behind my back! When the hell had they gotten so chummy, anyway? It must have been early in the morning, after Elizabeth's run, when I was still asleep. "Elizabeth has worse taste in men than I do," I added, outraged, about to tell her how Elizabeth had ruined any chance I'd had of a relationship with Peter by forgetting to tell me they'd spent four years as fuck buddies.

Enraged, I stomped past the house where I grew up. The gray brick had faded, and two of the numbers from the address had fallen off. But the flowers and shrubs neatly lining the lawn were colorful, my mother's fetish for bright pastels still flourishing.

"Your father will be home soon," she said. "I should fix dinner."

"Let's walk one more mile. Come on." I took her hand. "Don't worry. Elizabeth's leaving in two days, I promise," I said, consoling myself.

"My patient was this angry old hairy guy who needed heart medication, Digoxin, but I wasn't supposed to give it to him unless his pulse was higher than sixty," Elizabeth said.

One summer extension class that involved three hours in an LA ER and already she was Nurse Hathaway. "Do we have to talk about this at nine A.M.?" I asked.

"Or if his PR interval was less than two hundred," Danny said, opening the front door for us. Since when was he such a gentleman?

"How did you know?" she asked. "I couldn't hear through the stethoscope. He was screaming. I thought I was going to kill him."

"Congestive heart failure is nasty," Danny said, like it was his patient now.

Elizabeth threw her suitcase in the back and jumped in the front seat of Danny's Lincoln, chipper and awake in tight jeans and a turquoise top, buzzing from the endorphins she got from running and sharing medical disasters. It was midday for her. We were on our way to check out Ben's new house in Zion before she flew back to New York.

"He was a monster," she said. "But he lived."

"The monsters always live," Danny said, cheerful too, basking in her attention, which was making me ill.

"Is Ben even up at this hour?" I crawled into the backseat, disgusted by the McDonald's bags, soda cans, country music CDs, and maps. "Do you live back here?"

"Daniel's been studying organic chem for eight hours straight. Give him a break," Elizabeth said as I waded through more of his junk on the floor: copies of the *New England Journal of Medicine*, bandages, and three quarters, which I slipped into my pocket.

How did she know what Danny was studying?

"I saw a twenty-four-year-old with cervical cancer," she told Danny. "She really freaked me out."

"I once saw a twenty-two-year-old patient with it at Rush when I was making rounds with my father," he countered.

As Danny merged onto the highway I noted that, unlike me, he was a serene driver. He chatted up Elizabeth as if they were going to a party. She was always so lit up around men. I bet it was a doctor/nurse thing, although he wasn't a doctor yet and she'd only been a part-time nursing student for ten minutes.

"She had jaundice, Cheyne-Stokes…," Danny said, as if I wasn't even there.

"That's just what happened to mine!" Elizabeth said. "Her lungs filled up with fluid."

"Can you turn on the radio?" I asked.

He turned on a country station, where a woman was crooning, "Gosh dernit, Hal, I'm pregnant again." I put my finger down my throat, then reached forward, right between the two of them, to change the station. I sang along to En Vogue's "My Lovin' (You're Never Gonna Get It)," lighting a cigarette.

"You're not allowed to smoke in here," Danny scolded.

"You're not allowed to talk about diseases before noon." I blew smoke in his direction.

We drove farther away from Highland Park, an exciting metropolis compared to the farms and barren land we were passing. There were even a few cows.

"Did she bleed through the nose and mouth when she died?" Elizabeth asked.

"Death ain't pretty," Danny said, flipping back to country.

"Can you imagine dying at that age?" Elizabeth shook her head.

"I can't handle this femme whining," he complained.

"Please. Anything but country." I reached forward, turning the dial to a station playing Bob Dylan's "Tangled Up in Blue," afraid that if my stupid friend didn't stop flirting with my baby brother I was going to smash her in the head.

"Well, this macho mumbling isn't any better," Elizabeth commented. "She has the weirdest taste in music."

"I do not. I like all music except for country."

"Dylan's her favorite since her boyfriend Derek took her to a Dylan concert when she was sixteen," he said. "Even though he slept with all her friends."

"He did not. Derek only slept with Jenny Lynn. And he was a Deadhead. It was Lance who took me to Dylan freshman year of college." It irritated me to hear my first love bungled and trivialized for Elizabeth's sake. "And Lance didn't get the tickets, I did."

"How did your parents handle Derek?" Elizabeth asked him, as if I wasn't there.

"We all hated Derek from the start. My dad blamed him for her tattoo. They hated him so much they sent her to New York to get away from him. They hated Lance too."

"Wrong! They hated Derek, but nobody hated Lance. You invited Lance to your graduation party even though we'd broken up," I clarified, flicking my ashes out the window.

"Once when Lance called, Ben said, 'Ricky doesn't want you to call her anymore,' and hung up." Danny laughed.

"What happened?" Elizabeth asked.

"That wasn't Lance." I turned off the radio. "He hung up on Derek three years earlier."

"She brought it up at dinner. Dad agreed we should get rid of Lance."

"That was Derek. Everyone liked Lance until he fucked Tina in the shower!" I yelled. "You were all sadists. Even my shrink says so."

Chez Benjamin was a huge white house just like my parents' but with green siding. It was the kind of house where a married couple with four kids would live. Ben's black lab, Spock, ran out, jumping on me as we got out of the car. Elizabeth petted him, and he rolled over so she could give him a good scratch.

"I thought you hated dogs."

"I hate dogs in the city," she said, still scratching his stomach. "Oh, this big guy needs attention, don't you, Spock?"

Ben came out and hugged me. "Hey, Elizabeth, welcome to the Midwest," he said. "You're looking good. I hear you're up to seven miles."

"Eight yesterday. Great house you got here." Elizabeth lit up. "It's huge."

"Come on. I'll give you a tour," Ben said. His monster dog joined us, licking Elizabeth's hand as we walked indoors.

There was wood paneling, with green carpets, flowered wall-paper, and beige leather couches. The couple who'd first lived in the house had four kids, Ben confirmed, and moved when the husband was transferred. He offered Danny and Elizabeth beers and they took them—at ten thirty in the morning. I had diet soda. I saw Dad's human heart paperweight on Ben's desk. I used to have nightmares about that paperweight.

"I need to lie down for a few minutes." I went up to Ben's bedroom. I had to admit it was comfortable, with a king-size bed and a down comforter.

"It's the middle of the night for her," Danny joked behind me.

"Hey, sleepyhead, get up." Ben shook me. "Your friend has a plane to catch."

"What?" I opened my eyes.

"Come on. It's three o'clock," he said. "Danny's going to drop Elizabeth off at the airport. I have to get to back to work." He sat on the side of the bed. "You like my new house?"

"Yeah, your house is great. Sorry I fell asleep. I was developing pictures in my old darkroom all night," I said. "What did you guys do?"

"I showed them around and we grabbed a bite at the hospital. Elizabeth loves cafeterias."

That liar. She'd told me she hated diners and cafeterias and had even refused to eat at the old Automat when her dad once took her there.

I looked at Ben. Though he was only twenty-five, his hair was thinning and his glasses were thicker than Dad's. Still he had the same shit-eating grin he'd had a kid.

"Are you okay?" he asked. "Do you need money?"

"I'm fine, Joseph Solomon the Second."

"I'm going to be a surgeon, I decided," he said.

"Are you ever coming back to visit me in New York?"

"When I graduate, I'll come and stay at a fancy uptown hotel. And I'll take you out on the town." He messed up my hair.

"This is a nice house. You did good," I said. "We're proud of you."

"Love you," Ben mumbled, then walked downstairs.

"Love you too," I said, vaguely aware that it was much easier to argue than to feel close to him.

chapter ten
trick and treat

October 31, 2001

"Ricky, quick, catch the three blond gay Osama bin Ladens. To your left," Matthew Wald said.

"Thanks." Nicky had been right about this blind date—he was smart, tall, and he did have good hair and a decent eye. "Oh no, where's my bag?"

"I have it," he said.

After making sure my black bag—which contained my life (ten rolls of film, batteries, Vivitar 283 flash, other camera, latest clips, and extra cigarettes)—was indeed over his shoulder, I sprinted down the block. Cradling my new Nikon F3, I chased the bin Laden triplets and snapped them. Then I became enamored with a chorus line of dancing skeletons. Matthew zigzagged after me through the crowd, trying to shield me from the drizzle with his big umbrella.

"Fun first date," he said.

It really was.

Instead of canceling the Halloween parade after terrorists struck Lower Manhattan six weeks earlier, the organizers argued that the annual antic event would give the city a much-needed emotional release. But was it my imagination or did the air still smell like death? The health commissioner assured the public that we didn't need air masks, but I wasn't so sure. Racing ahead and flashing my press pass at the police patrol, I left Matthew outside the roped-off area to join scores of photographers and film crews capturing the elaborate floats and costumes coming down Fifth Avenue—a political and campy pop culture array. I chose a wide angle with the flash, focused the lens to five feet, and snapped away. I shot a trio of black-bearded Chers, a walking shower stall next to George Bush, a bar of soap, Madonna, and Saddam Hussein riding a green missile. I struggled to get closer, pushing elbows out of my face.

"What good is sitting alone in your room?" sang two male Liza Minnellis in boas and fishnet stockings as Superman and Spider-Man groped each other. A TV news cameraman jumped in front of me, ruining my angle. I darted around him for an unobstructed view of the Conehead family and a six-person caterpillar. I shot like mad, finishing three extra rolls just in case some of the shots didn't turn out because of the weird lighting. When I was done I looked for Matthew but couldn't find him. If he didn't have my bag I would have given up and rushed home to make my deadline. All my love affairs ended in disaster anyway.

Matthew and I had been ambivalent about meeting; we'd been e-mailing and playing phone tag for months. But living this close to such heartless terrorism made me feel vulnerable and alone. As a workaholic who loved what I did, I'd always made fun of Elizabeth's obsession with finding a husband. Yet now sleeping solo every night felt cold and not as appealing. As did the recent downtown rage: hooking up with an ex for trauma sex. Matthew's old-fashioned desire for a real dinner date suddenly seemed charming, and I agreed to meet him on Wednesday night at seven, not remembering it was Halloween.

The minute I committed to our date, the *Village Voice* photo editor called. Since their staff guy was sick, she begged me to cover the parade for five hundred dollars, a mint for the *Voice*. Problem was, the parade started Wednesday night at 7:00 P.M., they usually went to press Tuesday but were publishing late to get it in, and I didn't do digital. When the editor offered to scan negatives or hard copies, I couldn't say no. I was sick of doing diaper ads and getting a hundred dollars for head shots from the dailies. This could be my chance.

I tried to cancel with Matthew, but I kind of dug that he wouldn't let me and kept insisting on coming to help. I thought I'd look hip and wore my black leather jacket, picturing myself like Diane Arbus. But I'd never worked outside in such a whirlwind before. It started to drizzle, and I was sweating and freezing at the same time, my hair a stringy mess. I left the crush of press to look for Matthew, wading through the mix of drag queens, bridge-and-tunnel teens, and perplexed-looking foreign tourists in ridiculous costumes. Most of them seemed drunk or stoned. I was feeling stressed and nervous about my big assignment and big date and wished I was high too.

Matthew saw me and waved. He was about six foot two, the tallest guy I'd ever gone out with, if you considered this going out. But he looked to be in his late thirties, too old for me. He came over and tried to shield me with his umbrella, getting his clothes and hair soaking wet. How chivalrous. Or was it masochistic? I took a Kleenex from my pocket and wiped his lenses. They were thick, like my father's and brothers' glasses.

"You have my bag?" I checked again.

"Got it." He turned to show it was still around his shoulder.

It was hard to trust a male stranger I'd just met to protect something so important to me. Still, I had to hand it to Nicky,

Matthew came off very self-assured and sexy. Maybe Elizabeth's dictum that Jewish men made good husbands wasn't as absurd as I'd pretended.

Police stopped the chaotic throngs of people on Tenth Street. I was desperate to get home, but there was no way they were letting anyone cross Fifth Avenue yet. "Bet you're not used to running after Liza Minnelli and high-heeled blond terrorists," I shouted above the noise.

"I've seen a few nuts in my day," he said. "I shot the Church Lady, Linda Richman, the Coneheads."

"That's right. Nicky said you're a director for *Saturday Night Live*."

"I used to be."

"The original Coneheads?" I asked.

"No, the movie. I was on the show after its heyday, before its resurrection. I hit the only ten years when they didn't win an Emmy."

"Cool job." Television gigs didn't really do it for me, but Elizabeth—who often bragged about Barry's TV money—would be impressed. I tried to snake my way farther down the avenue, but the crowd was too thick. Two male Dolly Partons and a female Three Stooges crammed in next to us. My fingers kept checking the film rolls in my pocket, making sure they were safe.

A wind gust made me shiver, and Matthew took off his scarf and wrapped it around my neck. The gentlemanly gesture melted me.

"I forgot, how do you know Nicky again?" I hoped he wasn't into her like every other male on the planet, and only dating me for a vicarious thrill.

"She was working on this MTV documentary about AIDS," he said, adding, "with my ex- girlfriend, Alice."

Not a good sign that he was already throwing around his old girlfriend's name. I recalled Elizabeth's advice: "Listen to what a guy says about his exes, because that's how he could soon be talking about you." But her relationships with men were even more screwed up than mine.

"When did you and Alice split up?" I tested.

"Four months ago, but we stayed friends."

So he was calling me one minute after they'd broken up?

"Though this week she hates me," he continued.

"You still talk to her a lot?" I jumped in too fast. I'd just met him; it was none of my business. Instinctively, I reached in my pocket for a cigarette.

"Do you really have to smoke?" asked the male vampire standing behind us. He wore a black cape, fangs, a miniskirt, and high heels.

"A transsexual on acid is telling you to put out your cigarette," Matthew said, grinning.

I laughed as he moved us away from Vampira, appreciating that he was defending my right to smoke.

"Why does Alice hate you?" I couldn't help but ask.

"I fixed her up with a guy friend last week and it was a disaster."

"Alice still works in TV?"

"No, she went back to school. To become a shrink."

"Don't tell me," I said. "You hate therapy."

"Don't tell me," he said. "You're in therapy and think that entitles you to overanalyze everyone."

"It's interesting that you fixed up your ex. Out of guilt?"

He shrugged, not noticing the line of Lolitas checking him out. He was pretty cute.

"So why was Alice's blind date such a disaster?"

"She said everything went wrong from the first second," he reported. "I thought Alice was exaggerating. But Barry said it was the worst date of his life. And he's a comedy writer whose bad dates make up most of his material."

"Not Barry Green?" I asked.

"Yes. The one who created the sitcom *Barry's World*."

"I know him! He trashed my twenty-fifth birthday on his dumb show," I said, vaguely aware that I was showing off about being humiliated on TV's top-rated comedy. I threw my cigarette on the ground and stomped out the butt. "I hate Barry," I added.

"So does Alice," Matthew said. "I thought he was successful, smart, funny."

I feared Matthew's friendship with Barry was a bad sign. Well, he was too old for me, anyway. Elizabeth could keep the older men.

"He's been off and on with his girlfriend, Dee," Matthew said. "When I heard they were off again, I thought it could be good timing."

Dee! That was the woman Elizabeth saw as her archnemesis for Barry's affection. She was going to totally dig that my date knew Barry and the latest on his love life and demand a full report when I got home. Though we barely got along in Illinois, ever since her jaunt to my hometown, she was calling and e-mailing every day. A hot Barry scoop would definitely make me eclipse Jane in the best friend battle.

"Dee. Is she the one he pined after at Long Island High?" I asked.

"Yes, Dee's the one who got away," he said. "How did you know?"

"My friend Elizabeth used to go out with him."

"Elizabeth?" Matthew shook his head. "I don't remember that name."

"Elizabeth Mann. Barry based the Elena character on her."

"Barry said Elena was a composite of a few women."

"No, it was Elizabeth," I insisted. "Barry did a whole episode about meeting her father, William Mann."

"*Blind Streets*, of course," Matthew said. "Barry's a lifelong fan of his work. So am I. It's one of the things that bonded us at first."

"You two are close friends?" Uh-oh. Now I wanted to take my bag back. His deep bond with someone I despised meant our date was headed south.

"Not close enough that he'd hire me for his hit show. Not that I'm bitter," Matthew joked. "Look." He pointed to a row of male Marilyn Monroes blowing kisses from the last float. "That reminds me of a picture I clipped from the *Post*," he said. "A cute NYU student was checking out a Marilyn Monroe impersonator on the corner, and..."

"Nicky told you to say that."

"Say what?" he asked.

"I took that picture," I told him. "It was my first published photo."

"I didn't know. Really. I taped it to my wall," he said. "You'll have to come over and see it."

Instead of "Come up and see my etchings," this was "Come up and see your own work on my wall." Nice trick. I guessed he was lying about Nicky not telling him.

Sensing my disbelief, he said, "I never checked the photo credit. I promise."

After the tail of the parade turned, the police finally let us cross. Part of the mass exodus west, we headed down Ninth Street, and came to a stop at my building on Horatio Street. I took my bag back from his shoulder and gave him a quick peck on the cheek. "Thanks for your help. I'm on deadline, so..."

He pulled me in for a hug, then asked, "How about dinner Friday night?"

"Great," I said, breaking away, preoccupied. "Call me."

I rushed upstairs to my makeshift darkroom, set up in my bathroom for just such freelance emergencies. The enlarger was on top of the toilet, three trays of chemicals in the shower stall. I went to work on developing all the Halloween rolls. By one thirty in the morning I was using my blow-dryer to dry off the six negative strips hanging on my shower door.

While I was impatiently inspecting the first roll for anything hip and juicy I might have missed, a short, stout old man
caught my eye. He was wearing a black suit with a knitted yar-
mulke, had a long white beard, and was holding up a salami. At
first I thought he was a prankster dressed as an old Jew. Then I
remembered he was left over from the shots I'd taken the day
before on the Lower East Side. He'd posed very proudly for me,
calling himself "the Last Kosher Butcher of Broome Street." As
I'd left he'd called out, "Don't forget me, *sheyne meydl*," which I
knew meant "pretty girl" in Yiddish, 'cause when I was little it
was my Uncle Max's nickname for me. I wasn't sure whether the
butcher was flirting or pleading. While I was there, I printed
him out. Then I couldn't help noticing the one-eyed waitress at
Ratner's deli right next to him. Funny how they were left over
on the roll, two real, compelling people I felt I'd somehow met
before lurking amid the kooky young strangers in silly costumes I was taking only for the money.

It was just past two, under the eerie shade of the safe-light,
when I saw that I'd also accidentally caught Matthew Wald in
the corner of the last frame. He looked handsome, his big soul-
ful brown eyes staring right at me, like he knew me.

Reeking of fixer and stop bath, which Nicky used to complain smelled like vinegar, I hopped into a taxi at 5:00 A.M.
The streets were still loud and packed with crowds of drunk
dressed-up kids showing off their fantasy alter egos. I dropped
off my contact sheets and eight rough 8×10 black-and-white
Halloween prints at the *Voice*. At the last second, I'd stuck in my
friends the old butcher and one-eyed waitress, just to show the
editor my range, that I wasn't all fast razzle-dazzle hipster, in
case she ever had anything more serious in mind.

Back home, I crept under my futon's covers and slept the
entire day. I woke up to check my messages and heard the photo
editor say she'd chosen my dancing skeleton shot for their cover
story, which they were titling "Downtown Unmasked." Yes! In

celebration, I smoked a joint and two cigarettes, ate an Almond Joy, and promptly went back to sleep; I loved freelancing.

"How was it?" Elizabeth's call the next morning woke me up.

"Fantastic! They're using my picture on the *Voice* cover," I said, all turned around but happy. "I can get an early copy at midnight. And check this out—the editor might also use the Lower East Side shots of old Jews I took for this downtown gentrification series they're doing next month. Oh, and she's upping my fee to six hundred 'cause it's the cover."

"Not the assignment. The guy," Elizabeth said. "How was he?"

"Nice. Tall. Lives near you on the Upper West Side. Used to direct *Saturday Night Live*."

"Oh, he has a big TV job," she said, buoyant.

I knew she would like the sound of him. "Your favorite category—artist guys who sold out," I replied. Too bad he seemed still hung up on his ex-girlfriend.

"You didn't sleep with him?" she asked.

"You're calling to see if I got laid?"

"No. I have news," she said. "We just found out that the International Center for Photography is giving Dad the Ernst Haas Award for best documentary photography."

"Wow. That's a big deal," I said.

"It certainly is," she said. "Dad's publisher is flying him in from Indiana. You have to come to the award ceremony with me. It's next Friday night. Can you make it?"

"Sure." I wondered whether she'd singled me out or if she had also invited Jane.

"They think this will get some heat on Dad for the new edition of *Blind Streets*."

"Get some heat on?"

"Barry's LA slang," she admitted.

"Matthew knows him. They worked on a sketch show together."

"Really? What did he say?" She predictably perked right up.

"He knows Dee and thought it was off again," I reported. "The world keeps getting smaller."

"Everybody knows Barry now; he's famous," she sniffed, adding, "Bring Matthew to the ceremony."

"It's too soon. I barely know him." I wasn't sure if Matthew's knowing Barry was a good thing. Or, after the Peter Heller mess, if I trusted Elizabeth to meet my new potential guy. Our relationships with men were already too twisted; I'd made a vow to keep our social lives as separate as possible.

"I like the sound of this one. Tall, knows Barry, has an excellent job in television," she said. "Oh, can I borrow something to wear? I'll be downtown tomorrow."

"Sure," I said. "Are you okay about your father coming to town?"

"Of course. I can't wait to see him."

"You said he's been sick. I thought maybe this might be rough for you...."

"Don't psychoanalyze me," she snapped. "You're always wrong."

When Elizabeth dropped by on Thursday, her face was black-and-blue, her lip and left eye swollen. Shocked, I put my arm around her and led her inside.

"I fell off my bike. Hit a speed bump. Smashed my face on the sidewalk." She was shaking. "Help me hide it with makeup."

"I don't think makeup's a good idea." I put my hand on her shoulder, but she stood up and started pacing. "Do you want to go to a doctor? Or the hospital?"

"No. It's just bruises. I'm fine," she said, sounding very not fine.

"Want me to get some Tylenol?" I asked.

"No."

I was freaked out and needed to do something. I went to the bathroom and took out a bottle of extra-strength Tylenol anyway. I also grabbed a box of Band-Aids, a towel, and rubbing alcohol. No, that would hurt too much. "Do you want me to call my dad or my brother Ben?" I finally asked.

"Yes, let's call Benjamin. Good idea," she said, calming down.

"Shouldn't we put cold water on it? Or ice? You're the nurse," I said. "Which?"

"I don't know. Let's see what Benjamin says."

"Everyone calls him Ben." I dialed his number but there was no answer.

"Too bad," she said.

I went to the kitchen to make her tea. I wet the towel and came back out and wiped the blood away with cold water, not alcohol. Then I tried my brother's home phone. "So you have no anxiety about your father coming?" I couldn't stop myself from asking.

"No anxiety at all," she said, laughing, though it obviously hurt to move her face.

It was clear that Elizabeth's dad's problems had always caused her pain. I saw her black-and-blue marks as an external symbol of the damage he'd caused. Compared to him, my dad suddenly seemed like a miracle. He was a healthy, sober, strong man, still in love with my mother, proudly providing for his family. I wished I could help Elizabeth, but there didn't seem to be anything I could do to make her bruises go away. I couldn't exactly get her a good father.

"Ben. It's me." I was relieved he'd picked up, and quickly gave him the recap.

"Jeez," he said. "Did she hit her head? Dizzy? Have a concussion?"

"No. But her face is really banged up. What should she do?"

"She should go to the emergency room," he said.

"What's he saying?" Elizabeth asked.

"You should go to the emergency room."

"That's stupid. I don't need an emergency room!" she yelled at me, then took the phone. "Benjamin, hi." She switched to a soft, girly voice that made me cringe. "How's everything in Zion? How's your dog? I know," she said. "Okay. Right. You're right."

I'd actually forgotten how much time they'd spent together when they met over the summer. As they kept chatting, I started to feel like a third wheel in my own apartment. I went to the stack of photos on my desk and starting filing.

"Thanks. Okay. Great," she said, then laughed and finally hung up the phone. Nearly a half hour had passed.

"What did he say?" I asked.

"Extra-strength Tylenol and cold compresses," she said. "It's so great to have a doctor around."

"That's exactly what I suggested!"

"What a sweet, nurturing brother you have."

Ben, sweet and nurturing? Were we talking about the same guy?

After Elizabeth left, I called Matthew. I wanted to tell him the good news about my *Voice* cover. Since we were having dinner on Friday anyway and he was a fan of William Mann's, I decided to ask him to accompany me to Elizabeth's father's event. I was casual, not wanting to make it sound like a big dressed-up date, more like a business connection to thank him for helping me land the cover photo.

"I can't do it tomorrow night," he said. "I was about to call you to cancel."

His rejection stung, but I tried to be cool. "What's up?"

"I just took a job in LA," he said. "I'm going to direct *Barry's World*. Barry called with an offer. I'm leaving tomorrow morning."

Bad enough that the only mensch I'd met in a long time was leaving, but he was rejecting me to go work with Elizabeth's jerky ex.

"What are you doing tonight?" he asked. "Want to come say good-bye?"

When he lived three miles away from me, I was playing hard to get. But now that he was putting three thousand miles between us, I felt closer to him.

"We can go out for dinner. Or order in."

Well, he wasn't spending his last night in New York with his ex, Alice. Maybe he really did like me. "Sure. What time?"

"Can you come by late? How's nine thirty?" he asked.

Or maybe not. Had I just switched from potential girlfriend to a last-minute booty call?

"I have to warn you in advance," he said. "Packing everything so fast, my place is a pigsty."

I spent the rest of the day mooning in my bathroom/ darkroom, making Matthew a good-bye present. I juxtaposed the frame of him from my Halloween contact sheets with a flattering shot of me facing the other way. I pasted a collage of parade scenes underneath. With our images together, we seemed to be standing on the heads of the crowd, staring into each other's eyes. I carefully put the collage in an envelope and slipped it in my briefcase, which I carried with me on the crosstown bus, then uptown to his apartment on Columbus Avenue and Ninetieth Street. I was nervous as he buzzed me in. He apologized for being so disorganized. He wasn't kidding. Books and magazines were strewn around the floor, comics and videocassettes covered all the tables, and two suitcases were open on the couch.

"I can't believe you're leaving tomorrow," I said, putting my briefcase on the floor.

I went to hug him but instead he planted a wet kiss right on my lips. Then he pushed me down on the couch. He slipped his big hands under my shirt and started taking it off. I started helping him.

"Want to stay over tonight?" he asked, unbuttoning his shirt while I was making progress getting mine off. Knowing he was leaving town made him much bolder. I had to admit there was something to Elizabeth's preference for aggressive men.

I remembered the gift I'd brought and put my hand out to stop him. "I have a present for you, something I made." I reached over to my briefcase and pulled out the envelope.

"Thanks." He took it and started to open it.

"Wait," I said, suddenly petrified that my present was way too sentimental, and that I'd look like a lovesick teenager. "You can either open it now or I can stay over—but I can't handle both in the same night."

He sat up, looking at the present, then at me. Then he looked at the present again. "Is this a test?"

"No. Not at all," I told him. But if he just wanted to screw me, I was out of there.

"I want to see what you're giving me."

"Okay," I said, glad he'd aced the answer. "Open it."

I watched as he took out the collage of us finding each other above the misty crowd. He ran his fingers over it. He looked a little embarrassed.

"Do you like it?" I asked.

"I love it." He put his arm around me, still inspecting my present, as if there were important secrets hidden there. "These two are my favorite costumes. I don't remember seeing them." He pointed to the kosher butcher and the one-eyed Ratner's waitress I'd hidden in the corner.

"They're real! Old Jews I shot on the Lower East Side the day before," I told him. "The *Voice* editor might use them for an upcoming series."

"Very compelling little guy. Like there's wisdom in his eyes," he said.

"Right! I thought the same thing." I laid my head on Matthew's shoulder, feeling like I belonged there, like we were two odd-shaped puzzle pieces that were meant to fit together.

He stroked my hair in a gentle way that made me purr.

"I know we just met, but I feel like I finally found you. What if going to LA is a mistake?"

"Don't be an idiot," I said. "It's the highest-rated show in the country."

"That's what my agent said."

"You told your agent you didn't want to go?"

"Yes. I told him I just met someone very special. Thank you for making me this beautiful present," he said shyly, walking me to the door, giving me a peck on the forehead.

Then I jumped him.

chapter eleven
blind streets

November 9, 2001

I was a half hour early on Friday night but there was already a swanky crowd gathering at the midtown Hilton, where William Mann was being feted. Confident silver-haired men in tuxedos strode inside, elegant mates in long gowns on their arms. Boy, was I underdressed. Why had I chosen a short black skirt, a GAP sweater, black pumps, and my peacoat? The beaded shawl my mother had sent didn't spruce up the outfit as I'd hoped. I wanted to rush downtown to change. But it was Elizabeth's big night too; I had to stay.

While puffing on a cigarette at the corner of Sixth Avenue, I saw her friend Hope Maxwell standing by herself near the door. She was wearing a beige silk blouse and a floor-length black skirt with flats, managing the right combination of artsy and glitz that I'd missed. I put out my smoke and went to greet her, wondering if she'd remember me.

"Ricky. Hi, honey. How are you?" Hope said.

I was touched that she knew who I was, and used a term of endearment and my nickname. "Great to see you. Where's Stanley?" I asked.

"He's coming from work," she said. "Should be here any minute."

"I'm meeting Elizabeth. But she's always late."

"It's genetic. Her father's always late too, if he shows up at all," she said. "Elizabeth showed me your *Village Voice* photograph. Very arresting."

"Thank you." I couldn't believe that not only had Elizabeth showed Hope my latest work but that Hope liked it and found it "very arresting." That was a compliment, right? Did she mean striking? Or trying too hard to get attention? Damn, I wished I didn't always feel the need to decode everything. I should just learn to take a fucking compliment.

"And the cover too." She patted me on the shoulder and said, "Mazel tov."

Did non-Jews say mazel tov?

Sensing my confusion, she said, "You didn't know I was a Yid, did you?"

"No. Hope Maxwell sounds..."

"I worked under my maiden name, Hannah Resnick, when I started out in the fifties," she said. "But my agent suggested I try Hope and take Stanley's last name for my Cairo book."

I didn't know she had a Cairo book. I made a note to buy it at Barnes & Noble on the way home. "So is William Mann really Billy Manikowsky?" I joked.

"Nope. He's the real deal. A white Anglo-Saxon Protestant lush," she said. A group of tall, slim young women in all black slinked in. The chic factor was overwhelming. "He hasn't been back in New York in more than a decade," Hope added. "This is historic."

When Stanley arrived, he walked up to his wife and gave her a kiss on her cheek.

"Do you remember Ricky, Lizzie's friend?" she asked him. "I was just telling her that William hasn't been back here in more than a decade."

"The last time was December 1990," Stanley said. "His Soho show when he got drunk, fell down, and broke his arm."

He escorted us inside and upstairs to the second-floor auditorium, where the award ceremony was being held. I excused myself to look for the ladies' room. Elizabeth was in front of the mirror, dabbing concealer under her eyes to cover up the faded bruises.

"I was waiting outside for you. I bumped into Hope. Thanks for showing her my *Voice* cover." In a swirl of gratitude, I went to hug her, but she straightened her back, extremely uncomfortable with my show of affection. I stepped back and said, "You look pretty," inspecting the black knee-length dress of mine she'd borrowed, which was cinched at the waist and flattering on her tall, slim figure.

"No, *you* look pretty," she said. "I look pathetic." She put more beige cream on her face. It looked caked on and blotchy.

"Gently." I rubbed it in softly.

"Where's Matthew?" she asked. "I thought you were bringing him."

"Matthew went to LA because your creepy ex-boyfriend Barry just hired him to be the new director of his stupid sitcom."

"Did you sleep with him before he left?" she asked.

"Why do you assume we slept together?"

Elizabeth gave me a look. "How was it?"

"It was fine, considering he now lives in another state."

"Well, it's great that Barry hired him," she said.

"Great for whom?" I brushed her hair back behind her ears.

"For you. You'll love LA. You could move there."

"You're the one with the LA fantasy," I said. "I have a business here. Plus I barely even know him."

"Matthew will make so much money he'll send you plane tickets." She put on my lipstick. The color was a little too pink for her. "Barry will make him rich and famous."

Having overlapping lovers working together weirded me out. Did she think I wanted a sugar daddy to send me airline tickets, like she did? First she screwed up my relationship with Peter, now she was too pleased that Matthew had been called to a different coast. She seemed determined to worm her way into my inner circle of men, and I was determined to stop it.

"Did you make Barry hire Matthew?" I had to ask.

"I wish I had that much power over Barry," she said. "I heard he's back with Dee. Engaged. She looks pregnant. Either that or she's just fat. Barry's brother hates Barry too."

"You know Barry's brother?" I asked. "The real one who Barry based the character on?"

She nodded. "Yeah. Terry will be here tonight, but Barry couldn't fly in." She brushed on powdered blush, but the color was too dark. I took out mine. It had a lighter pink base. "They hate each other."

"Terry hates his own brother? Why?" I pulled a Kleenex from my purse and wiped the burgundy powder off; she never got blush right. I brushed my lighter shade up her cheeks.

"Terry wanted to play himself on the show, but Barry said no." She patted down the dress, which on closer inspection looked too plain. "His brother can't act at all, but now Barry's drowning in Jewish guilt that he turned him down."

"Hey, you never told me Hope was Jewish." Taking off the black beaded shawl my mother had given me, I wrapped it around Elizabeth's shoulders, covering a little bruise. "There, that's better." I lit a cigarette.

"It's beautiful," she cooed in a way that let me know I'd probably never get the shawl back. I missed it already. "Thank you," she said. "You're such a good friend."

"You are too. I'm honored you invited me tonight. And showed my *Voice* cover to Hope." I flicked my ashes into the sink. "She said it was very arresting. That's good?"

She nodded.

"Really? Would she lie just to be nice?"

"She'll lie about anything but photography," Elizabeth said. "Did you see the ICP bigwigs here? Dad's finally getting his due. It's about time," she said. "I have to find him."

She walked out quickly, shooting me a look that said: Do not follow. One minute I was her best buddy, the next she didn't want to be seen with me. I'd never met someone so socially schizophrenic before. Leaning by the sink, I finished my cigarette. Then I puffed up my hair and put on more lipstick in a last attempt to look chicer, guessing that Elizabeth's erratic trust issues came from being the daughter of an alcoholic who'd never been able to take care of her. So what was my excuse?

As I made my way toward the auditorium, Hope and Stanley walked down the aisle to the first row slowly and silently, staring ahead with perfect posture, as if a sacred ritual were about to take place. Jane came over to me, looking stylish in a black suit and heels.

"The attorney at law," I said. "What's going on?"

"I'm buying an apartment in the Village," Jane announced.

"Congratulations," I said as we stood in the back, watching everyone take their seats. I pretended to be happy for her, but really I was mortified that she could afford to buy a whole downtown apartment while I was working thousands of hours but could barely pay my rent.

"What's shaking, guys?" Peter asked, coming to join us. Even he was dressed appropriately tonight, in a black suit and a gray turtleneck. He tapped me on the head, as if I were his kid sister. "So I have a secret," he said. "I left *Vision*."

"Really? Why?" I asked.

"Because the new editor was running even fewer of my pieces than Richard did. Don't repeat this, but I think *Vision* is going bust." Peter shook his head. "I'm becoming editor of the arts and entertainment section of *Newsday*. Higher salary, full benefits, my own office."

I couldn't afford health insurance, and my office was half of my bathroom and half of my living room, where I slept on a futon. "Fantastic. I'm happy for you," I lied, ready to shoot myself.

Betsy, who'd been *Vision*'s long-suffering receptionist, showed up with a group of people from the office. When they took their seats in the back row, Jane and I followed.

"How's it going?" Jane asked Betsy.

"Good. I just got a job as a fact-checker at *The New Yorker*," Betsy said.

The New Yorker! Jeez, I didn't even rate a rejection slip from their photo editor, who just ignored all of my submissions. I suddenly realized that nobody had come to see William Mann get an award. They'd come to show off. All of my former coworkers were thriving, doing way better than me. I was jealous.

By seven o'clock every seat in the auditorium was filled, and a few people were standing in the back. So where was William the Conqueror? We walked over to Elizabeth, who was standing with her sister, Michelle, a look-alike older, blond version of her.

"I called the airport. His plane landed at five o'clock," Elizabeth told us, biting her nail.

"But he hasn't checked into the hotel yet." Michelle bit her nail too.

"Maybe there was traffic?" I asked.

We stood there nervously, checking our watches, avoiding one another's eyes.

"He's twenty minutes late. Should I tell them to start without him?" Elizabeth asked, flustered and sweating. "I'll call the hotel again." She ran out the door.

"He probably just had trouble getting a cab from the airport," Jane offered.

"We hired a car to pick him up," Michelle said.

The room was now packed with hundreds of dressed-up literati and glitterati, all eager for the great lensman to arrive.

"My, my," said Hope. She came to join us, patting Michelle on the shoulder.

Finally someone ran in, and a hush came over the room. But we turned around to see that it was Elizabeth, not William Mann. "Oh my God," she said as she rushed over to us, crying. "Joris just called to say Dad's at NYU hospital. They met him on the runway with an ambulance."

"It'll be okay, Lizzie," Hope said, stroking her hair, taking charge of the situation, as one sensed she'd done hundreds of times before. "Stanley and I will accept the plaque in William's honor. We'll let everyone know there's been a little change of plan." They worked their way to the stage.

"I have to go." Elizabeth grabbed her purse and ran outside, accidentally dropping my mother's beaded shawl. I picked it up from the ground.

Jane looked at me. I looked at Jane. Then we sprinted after Elizabeth, all three of us jumping into a taxi to NYU hospital to find out what the hell had happened to our guest of honor.

"He didn't take his medication, passed out on the plane, and needed an emergency operation for a pancreatic abscess." Jane repeated what the doctors had told her. After waiting three and a half hours with a frantic Elizabeth and her sister, I was feeling shaky myself. Hospitals made me queasy. Elizabeth said there was nothing we could do anyway and told us we should leave.

By the time I got home, there was a long message from Elizabeth. "Dad's out of surgery. He made it," she said. "Michelle's having a fit because his insurance won't pay for a private room. My mother won't come in from Rye to see him. Can you come back tomorrow morning? Visiting hours start at eight A.M. I could use a friend."

Eight in the morning? Shit! Was there anywhere I'd less rather be at that early time than a hospital? But I left her a voice mail saying I'd be there. In the morning, when I found William Mann's room on the eighth floor, there were four women surrounding the patient, who was in a blue hospital robe, propped up by pillows. He looked gruff, like Ernest Hemingway in photographs I'd seen. Along with Elizabeth and Michelle, Jane stood by his bed on the right. Hope was on the left side, holding his hand, laughing at some story he was telling about a despised photo editor.

"That son of a bitch kept cropping me," he said, coughing. "Lizzie, get me another drink."

"Pepsi, Daddy? Or Seven-Up?" Elizabeth asked meekly, like a little girl.

"Water's better," said Michelle, who had a softer voice than her sister. She was the more maternal Mann, with two young daughters. "Sugar isn't good for you."

"He's a wormy maggot who feeds off of true talent," Mann continued. "He had this sad little wife, a skinny girl from Connecticut, but he couldn't get it up with a crowbar." William looked big, tired, and hairy, with gray whiskers everywhere—on his chin, nose, and ears. He had huge white eyebrows. Aside from the IV, he didn't look very sick. He seemed to be enjoying himself heartily, coughing and swearing, putting on a show for his female audience.

"Hi." I nodded to Elizabeth, handing her yellow tulips. She put them in a plastic vase. I waited for her to introduce me to her father, but she didn't. When there was a lull in the conversation, I inched closer to him and said, "It's an honor to meet you, Mr. Mann. I'm Rachel. I hope you're feeling a little better."

He looked at me blankly, then went back to his story. "So I

met his wife, this broken little bird, at a party. I planted one right on her kisser. I tongued her. She turned red. Then she smiled. She loved it! It was the biggest thrill of her life. I still don't know if she ever told him." He laughed so hard he coughed up phlegm, which Elizabeth wiped away. I tried not to look at the IV in his hand; needles and bags of blood spooked me. I was getting dizzy.

"Liz, where's my drink?" he grumbled.

"Come with me to get him another soda." Elizabeth took my arm, and I followed her down the hall. "Get this, get that. He's making me crazy," she said as we walked down the white corridor. We passed two patients in wheelchairs. One held a rolling IV stand with cloudy fluid in the sack. I took a few deep breaths.

"His liver's shot," she said.

"I'm sorry."

"Advanced emphysema, and I caught him sneaking a cigarette in the bathroom. He's a fucking mess."

"I'm sorry that I didn't really get a chance to talk to him."

"He doesn't know you from Adam." She led me to the soda machine.

"Well, he knows we're friends," I said.

"No, he doesn't."

"Well, who does he think I am? A nurse wearing all black? The grim reaper?" I joked.

"I said you were another *Vision* wannabe," she snapped, suddenly sounding as if she barely knew me. Then why did I have to wake up at 7:00 A.M. to be there for her?

I stared at Elizabeth, stunned, trying to decide whether I was more shattered by her callous denial of what I thought was a close, important relationship or angry that she'd told her father I was a "wannabe." My photographs had appeared on the cover of the *Village Voice*, in the *Washington Post*, and in the *New York Times*. How could she describe me like that to her father?

She was more condescending about my work than my haughty brother Ben was. And Elizabeth and I weren't even related!

I was no longer the needy Midwest naïf she could boss around and trash. I was not going to take her abuse anymore. Between my hurt, exhaustion, and nausea, I lost it. "I have to go," I said abruptly, the way she always did. I ran to the elevator in tears, getting in the first one that stopped.

The elevator went to the tenth floor, then down to the basement, and I wound up lost in the south corridor for half an hour before I fought my way out a side door and ran to the subway. On the way home I buried myself in the *New York Times* crossword puzzle, trying not to cry, vowing that it was the last time I would ever do Elizabeth a favor. I certainly was never going to visit her father again.

At home I lit a joint, though it was before noon. Then I went back to sleep. When I woke up I saw that I had missed a call from Matthew.

"I'm on the ABC lot. We're shooting two episodes back-to-back today; it's a zoo on the set," he said, adding, "I have frequent flier miles if you ever want to come visit...."

That was just the escape I'd been waiting for. Before listening to the end of his message, I called him at work, but he didn't answer, so I left a message for him at home, saying, "I'd love to visit LA. I miss you." The longer he was gone, the closer I felt to him.

That night Jane left a message saying they'd had to take William Mann into surgery again, this time for an emergency tracheotomy. I was sure he'd be fine. What did my brother say? The monsters always live. I didn't pick up the phone.

The next day, Mann's picture was on the front page of the *New York Times*. The headline read AWARD-WINNING PHOTOGRAPHER WILLIAM MANN DIES AT SIXTY-ONE. The obit listed his ten years at *Life* magazine, four books, twelve awards (including the one from the ICP that Hope had just accepted for him), four wives, and three daughters, and the nine universities where he had taught. The list of colleges was alphabetical, not chronological, and they didn't say he'd been fired from each one, so it looked impressive. In reality his life was sadder than the subjects he photographed.

I called and left a message for Elizabeth, saying I was sorry. That afternoon I put a condolence card in the mail.

Within a week, Jane and Peter mentioned that they'd received written invitations to Mann's memorial. So had Betsy and Hope. I didn't hear from Elizabeth. She obviously didn't want me there. I tried to be mature and empathetic, but I found myself feeling offended that I hadn't been invited, insulted all over again. Then, two days before the service, she called.

"What a horrible life he had," she said. She seemed unaware that anything bad had transpired between us. Had I misread everything? "I keep hearing Dad's voice." She imitated him. "'Baby, it's okay. Don't worry about me.' It's like he's still talking to me. He was smoking in the hospital. Can you believe it? The fire alarm went off twice."

"Did you put 'lifelong smoker' in his obit?" I asked.

"Of course I did," she said. "He died of emphysema."

"I thought he died of liver disease."

"He died of a lousy life," she said. "He's being cremated. Michelle wants his ashes. I thought he'd left us some money, but the lawyer said he was in debt. He never came out of the second surgery, but they're still billing us for it because his insurance doesn't cover an out-of-network doctor. His agent, Joris, said maybe he could push the publisher to reissue his book, which could cover it. Jane's helping us figure out his estate. I called my mother, but she said if she had any money, she wouldn't spend it burying him. She said, 'I buried him thirty years ago.' You're coming to the memorial service, aren't you?"

"I didn't think you wanted me there," I told her honestly.

"It's this Friday morning at nine thirty," she said.

"I didn't get an invitation."

"It's been crazy."

"You didn't forget to invite Jane, Peter, or Hope." The second the words fell from my mouth, I heard how horribly petty I sounded. The first time I decided to stand up for myself was the absolute wrong time.

"Hold on, that's Joris," she said as her call waiting clicked. When she came back, she said, "He found some negatives for a new book that might be salvageable. See you at the service."

I was sorry that she'd lost the most important man in her life. I knew I should forget my stupid pride and be there for her. But I had reached my limit of being there for Elizabeth. She would have hundreds of people around who'd known and adored her father, whom he'd cherished in return. She didn't need me. And I didn't need to hypocritically attend a memorial service for someone I didn't know just because it would be a Who's Who of American photojournalism.

When my mother used to call me selfish, I answered: "Better selfish than selfless." My mother took care of a lot of people in her life. I was now going to choose to take care of myself—by taking Matthew up on his offer for a free ticket to California. I called the airlines and booked a flight to LA on Friday. I left him a message. In the middle of it, he picked up.

"You're flying here Friday afternoon?" He was taken aback. "You don't have to work?"

"Nope. I just have William Mann's memorial, which I'm skipping."

"I was sorry to hear about Mann. Barry's wrecked about it. He's taking the red-eye tomorrow to attend."

Barry was flying all the way in to comfort Elizabeth? That was nice of the jerk. Even less reason she'd need me there. "I'll be sure to wave to him from the plane window," I said.

chapter twelve
la dreaming

November 14, 2001

"Do you always dress like you're going to a funeral?" Matthew asked when he met me at the gate at LAX airport.

Had he only just noticed? He sounded like my brothers, bemused that urban women wore black clothes. But did that mean he didn't like how I looked in my dark ensemble?

"I'm skipping the funeral, remember?" I said, trying not to feel guilty, wondering why he didn't kiss me or put his arm around me. I suddenly feared he might be sleeping with the perfect-looking size-two actress playing the Elizabeth character on his show. "Thanks for coming to pick me up."

"No problem." He took my carry-on bag and dutifully put it on his shoulder.

"Glad you're off work tomorrow."

"It's rare we get one day off, let alone a whole long weekend.

Lucky for us Barry's in New York until Monday," he said, leading me to his car.

I was dying to check out his California residence, but he insisted on driving directly to dinner. He'd made reservations at Shutters on the Beach in Santa Monica. During the forty-minute drive, I felt paranoid, as if there was a sinister reason he didn't want me to see the apartment he'd rented. I imagined he was secretly living with another woman, or already having an affair with somebody who lived in his building. Or his place here was dingier than his Manhattan pad and he was embarrassed for me to see it.

As we drove by the lovely, foggy, palm tree–laced streets, he pointed out his favorite bagel shop, used-bookstore, deli, sushi joint, and comic book emporium. Then he turned into a charming little cul-de-sac at Pico Boulevard, where the valets were parking cars. Matthew stopped, threw the guy his key, and opened the door for me.

He led me through the spacious, dimly lit lobby. Beautiful people, casually dressed in jeans and khakis, sat in clusters, on stuffed leather chairs and big couches, in front of crackling fires in fireplaces in every corner. In an elegant bar area waiters brought drinks right to your semi-private table. The walls and high ceilings were painted ivory and sky blue, as if the place had been decorated to lull neurotics. I felt right at home.

We were led to a table outside on the balcony, facing the ocean. I lit a cigarette. It was still warm out at seven o'clock, about to get dark. I hoped I wasn't becoming like Elizabeth, wanting a West Coast man to take care of me. Still, I could see why she'd loved LA. The mix of natural beauty of the sand and light blue water with the modern white architecture made it feel unreal; the whole city looked like the Gothic set of *Sunset Boulevard*. Matthew looked cute and off-season in jeans, a heavy gray wool sweater under a T-shirt, and army boots. Too many clothes. I had the urge to unlayer him.

"We've been shooting fifteen days straight," he said. "I can't believe we're finally getting a break."

"So it's good timing I'm here now." I tossed my hair back behind my ear and took off my blazer. I hadn't worn a bra, but he didn't seem to notice.

"Want some wine?" he asked. I nodded, and he ordered a bottle of Pinot Grigio.

"You want to go to Disneyland while you're here?" he asked. I shook my head.

"Thank God," he said. "Want to see a sitcom being shot?"

"No, thanks." Why was he treating me like a kid sister? Offering me a plane ticket had seemed like a bold, rugged gesture. But now that I was really here in the flesh, he didn't seem to know what to do with me, offering me the standard tourist destinations.

"This is a better setting than the Halloween parade," I said, looking out at the view. I'd recently lost six pounds on what I called the "new lover diet," unable to eat due to the fear of somebody seeing me naked for the first time. (We'd been half dressed on the floor under the covers with the lights out the first time.) But all of a sudden I felt insecure. He wouldn't have flown me out to LA if he wasn't interested, would he?

"It's nice here, isn't it?" Matthew asked.

I nodded, though I couldn't help but wonder if this chic outdoor restaurant was where he brought all his women.

The waiter came with the wine, poured us some, and left the rest of the bottle on ice. Matthew lifted his glass and said, "I'm so glad you're here."

"You are?" I asked, clinking my glass against his. Was he really? "Me too." I drank quickly, then poured myself more.

"I have ten copies of your *Voice* cover," he told me, sipping his wine.

"I framed that picture of you," I admitted, then regretted saying it. Humiliating enough that I'd made him that corny collage before he left and I was chasing him all the way to the West Coast. I filled his glass. He drank the wine quickly but made no moves on me.

"Are you hungry?" he asked. "They have great seafood pasta here. Let's get menus."

I looked out at the water. The waves were getting more turbulent with each gust of wind. "Why don't you want me to see your place?" I asked.

"I thought we'd stay here tonight," he said. "I wanted someplace romantic."

"At the restaurant?" I asked. Or did he mean on the beach? I was confused.

"It's a famous inn. I thought you knew." He pointed to a white brick building behind us, which I'd missed. He took a key from his pocket. "I wanted a place as beautiful as you."

Wow. Great line. Did he mean it? I downed the rest of my wine, then moved my chair closer to his, putting my hand on his leg. I kissed him on the lips.

"Why don't we get room service?" I whispered, all drunk and tingly.

He summoned the waiter and signed the check quickly. Then he led me up six small white stairs, into an elevator and then down a long hall to an ocean-side room on the third floor. A sliding door opened to a small wooden balcony, and the ocean hummed in the background. I dimmed the lights and pressed the button on the CD player by the bed. Matthew lit the vanilla-scented candle in the glass container that said "Bliss." Everything about the place was an aphrodisiac. I lay on the soft white fancy cotton sheets of the king-size bed, feeling like I was tripping on magic mushrooms.

"Come here," I said.

He sat down on the edge of the bed, opening the top drawer of the night table. "Here's the menu for room service."

I wanted him to fuck me, not feed me. I pushed him down

on the bed and fell into his arms, kissing his ears and licking the back of his neck. Finally he stirred, like a bear that had just woken up, grabbing me as if he owned me, tearing off my T-shirt and jeans. Blissful and jet-legged, I pulled his hair, rubbing my body against his. I was tipsy, my mind half swimming in that tangy ocean breeze, half slow-dancing back and forth, feeling lost in his gigantic arms. When I came, I heard a siren and rap music blaring in the distance. Then he moaned and I felt the floor move. It was like standing over a subway grating when the train was coming. But they didn't have subways in LA.

"I love you," he whispered for the first time.

Holy moly! Did he really? "Me too," I mumbled, scared that he was the type who always said "I love you" after sex, just to make the girl feel better. Or perhaps I was more scared that he wasn't the type.

There was a knock on the door. "Are you okay?" a woman's voice asked.

Matthew bolted up, put on his robe, and went to the door. When he came back he said, "There was an earthquake."

"That was an earthquake?" I asked. "Just now? I've always wanted to know what being in an earthquake felt like. I can't believe I missed it."

"She said it registered a 5.6," Matthew reported.

"You come, say I love you, and the world blasts apart." I smiled, looking for my clothes on the floor.

"We don't have to date," he said. "We've already played out our whole relationship."

"Is it dangerous?" I asked, smirking.

"Me or the earthquake?" He smiled.

"Well, if anybody asks how it was, I can honestly say the earth moved," I said. I was only scared of neurotic minutia; natural disasters didn't really phase me.

"Bet you say that to all the guys," Matthew said, getting dressed.

It turned out Shutters had "an earthquake special." If you

were staying at the inn when a quake occurred, or an aftershock that registered more than four points on the one-to-ten Richter scale, you got a free rain check (check?) for another night. Since he was worried about his apartment, Matthew and I drove back to his place in Westwood, off Wilshire Boulevard. Aside from ambulances, police cars, and more traffic, we didn't see any sign of wreckage on the highway home.

When he let me into his apartment, I was shocked. Not by the damage, which seemed minimal, but by the size of his new place. It must have been two thousand square feet. Compared to our tiny New York hovels, it seemed like a mansion. There were lots of windows, wall-to-wall carpeting, a sunken living room, an eat-in kitchen, and two big terraces.

It had definitely been hit by the quake. Books and CDs were on the floor. All the paintings hung lopsided on the walls. He surveyed the room.

"It's like *The Cabinet of Dr. Caligari* in here," I said.

"That's my favorite movie!" he said.

"Not *The Sorrow and the Pity*?" I joked.

"Don't tell me, your favorite is *Annie Hall*." He rolled his eyes.

I stuck out my tongue, but I was psyched he'd caught the reference.

"There could still be some aftershocks, but it doesn't look too bad. I was here for the 6.7 quake. All the food was flung out of the refrigerator and freezer; glasses flew from the cabinets and shattered." He walked around, unplugging the computer, clock, answering machine, and DVD player, then plugging them back in. "This is how Jews fix things," he teased. "Plug, unplug. Then we call for help."

The phone rang. "Will you get it?" he asked.

His letting me pick up his phone was an important sign. It showed that he wasn't expecting another woman's call during an emergency. Right?

I picked it up and said, "Matthew Wald's residence."

"Are you okay?" my mother asked. "It was a 5.6."

"How do you know how big the earthquake is?" I asked.

"Who is it?" Matthew wanted to know.

"My mother in Illinois," I told him, embarrassed. "I'm sorry. I gave her your phone number before I left. In case of emergency."

"It was on CNN," she told me.

"We weren't here, Mom. We were at this really chic seaside hotel called Shutters."

He looked at me horrified, as if I'd just told my mother we'd had sex, which I sort of had.

"Did the earth move?" she joked.

"Ha-ha." But it had. The call waiting clicked. "That's his other line. We're fine. Gotta go, Mom."

"Don't screw this one up," she added. "You're not getting any younger."

With that I clicked to the person waiting and said, "Hello?"

"Hello. This is Matty's mother in Westchester," she said. "Who is this?"

Matty! So that was his nickname. "Mrs. Wald. Hi," I said. "This is Matty's friend, Rachel Solomon." I used the given name I hated to score points for being a nice Jewish girl. "Glad to meet you."

Matthew made a face with his eyes bugging out of his head.

"Call me Laura," she said. "He told me all about you. You're the photographer with the picture on the cover of the *Village Voice*. Are you okay? It was a 5.6."

"How do you know?"

"CNN," she said.

Ah, the favorite station of Jewish mothers everywhere.

"We were spending the night at this chic little hotel," I told her.

"I know. He told me. Shutters. I tried calling there but they said you left," she said. "Did the earth shake?"

"You told your mother you were taking me to Shutters?" I asked, handing him the phone. While they spoke, I went into his bedroom. More books were on the floor, with CDs and Kleenex boxes. All the wall hangings were crooked. I liked it better this way—a little off, tilted, like a Picasso painting. The skewed angle fit my mood. Everything seemed surreal and different now that I was staying here with Matthew. On the nightstand there was a framed picture of a dark-haired girl who looked a little like me. I feared it was his old girlfriend Alice. Bad sign that he still had her picture on display.

I turned on the TV to CNN, which kept flashing the number 5.6. Then I turned it off and checked my answering machine.

"Who's that?" I asked when he got off the phone, pointing to the picture of the girl.

"That's Shelley, my sister."

"Oh, she's really cute," I said, relieved. Then, quickly changing tracks, "Good news. My editor friend at *Newsday* asked if I'd shoot Barry's brother, Terry, for the cover of their arts section."

"I hope you'll say no," he said.

"Why?"

"You know what that story is about, don't you?" he asked. "Barry's brother is going around saying that Barry stole his identity for his TV show without giving him any money or credit for it."

"Did he?" I wouldn't put it past Barry.

"No. He cast an actor to play a fictional brother character named Terry," he said. "You have to turn the assignment down or Barry will kill me."

"So Barry is now dictating which assignments I take?" I asked, thinking how bizarre it was to be arguing over Elizabeth's ex, as if even long-distance she was still setting up triangles I kept getting stuck in. How had she become so omnipresent in my life? I made a mental note to once and for all get her out of it.

"Well, if you want to be my girlfriend ...," he started to say.

"Am I your girlfriend?" I jumped in too quickly.

"Not if you shoot Barry's brother."

"Barry doesn't know I'm your girlfriend, does he?" I liked saying the word again, not telling Matthew that he'd just convinced me to turn down the assignment.

"I already told him," Matthew confessed.

"You already told him I'm your girlfriend?" I cooed. "That's so sweet. But you know I'm not a big fan of Barry's. He trashed my birthday party and then hurt my friend Elizabeth."

"Just don't get me fired," he begged.

If Matthew got fired he'd be back in New York with me.

"Barry already half hates me because I have all of my hair," he said.

"You do have great hair." I unbuttoned his shirt and rested my head on his big shoulders, twisting strands of his long curly chest hair around my fingers. Between the flight, wine, hot sex, and earthquake, I was feeling groggy, about to lose consciousness. When the phone rang again, we let the machine get it. I was afraid it was another female relative but the voice on the machine was male.

"Matty. Are you there? It's Barry calling. I'm in New York."

Matthew and I sat up.

"William Mann's service depressed the hell out of me," Barry said. "I didn't know Terry would be there. You wouldn't believe the lies he's telling the press about me. That I'm this horrible mean brother who won't throw him a crumb."

We watched the phone machine, as if it were a television set.

"At least I missed the earthquake. CNN says it was a 5.6. A guard on the lot said nobody was hurt but the office is a total mess. Listen, I'm coming back on the early flight tomorrow," he said. "Meet me at the office tomorrow morning. We need to get right back to work on the new episode. Thanks. You're a pal."

"Does Barry know I'm here?" I asked.

"I didn't tell him," Matthew said. "But I bet Elizabeth did. Why?"

"There goes the honeymoon," I said.

part
three

chapter thirteen
the setup
July 18, 2002

A summer later, when Ben graduated medical school early and was accepted to a top surgery program in Illinois, he booked a room at the Plaza—of all the glitzy uptown New York clichés. Still, I felt honored that he chose to spend his last free five days celebrating in my city with me. I left a message for him at the hotel, but his plane was late. I was anxiously waiting to hear from him when Elizabeth called.

"This guy with stomach cancer was spitting up black," she said. She'd been sharing stories from the twelve-hour shifts she was working at Bellevue.

"Black? That's disgusting."

"It's blood," she explained. "It turns black in the digestive tract."

"Glad I just ate lunch." I was becoming resigned to her daily calls filled with grisly medical mishaps. It reminded me of home.

"Oh, I caught your shots in today's Arts and Leisure section," she threw in. "I knew they were yours before I saw your name. It's hard to be distinctive in the *Times*."

"Thanks," I said, psyched that she'd called me distinctive. "I tried your friend Greely. Good call."

Aside from her annoying oversharing of medical grossness, we'd been getting along better than ever, hanging out often in between both of our work jags. I wasn't sure if she was atoning for her past insults or just too tired to be condescending. But with Nicky traveling around the world and barely checking in, and Elizabeth taking my photography seriously and hooking me up with her luminary business links, Elizabeth was becoming my closest confidante, like the older sister I'd always wanted.

"Did you send your slides to Joris yet?" she asked.

"No, I'm still putting the series together." I didn't admit I was as afraid of getting rejected by her father's famous agent as she was before her apartment had been destroyed. On some level I actually believed her fear had caused the fire, but of course she'd rejected that theory.

"What are you doing this weekend?" she asked. "I'm having dinner with Chip Saturday night. You want to come?" She'd been mentioning that we should meet each other's boyfriends for months now. But she and I were finally clicking. I feared bringing more men into the picture would risk our closeness.

"He sounds too old and sick for you," I told her.

"How can a liberal Jewish girl in the Village be so superficial and closed-off?" she asked. "Chip happens to be the nicest man I've met in years."

"What kind of sixty-year-old guy still goes by the nickname Chip? He's old enough to be your father. He *is* your father. That's why you like him."

"Will you ever lose the psychobabble, or is this a permanent affliction?" she asked in an amused tone, like she was resigned to my obsessive overanalysis.

After all the fame, divorces, alcoholism, and death that her clan had been through, it astounded me that nobody had ever tried therapy. They were as narrow-minded about exploring the psyche as my family, as if something was wrong with you if you saw a shrink. I thought there was something wrong with people who *didn't* see shrinks.

"Come on," I chided her. "Chip's sixty with back problems and arthritis. You obviously want to nurse him back to health 'cause you couldn't save your father."

"You don't know anything about my dad," she snapped. I guessed it still bothered her that I'd skipped town on his funeral, though she never brought up the subject directly. "Just leave him out of this, Okay, Ricky?"

"Okay." I lit a cigarette. "But he *is* your father's age."

"Chip's not my father's age. he's fifty-eight. I want you to meet him," she said. "And stop smoking already. It's disgusting."

She could always hear me puffing over the phone. "I can't. My brother Ben's coming in. He has a week off before his surgery program starts."

"Wow. Benjamin's going into surgery. Just like he said. A man who goes after and gets what he wants. That's so impressive. Tell him congratulations for me."

"His name is Ben," I said, annoyed that she'd finally accepted my nickname but refused to use his. "I'm throwing him a party tomorrow night at my place, to introduce him to some girls." My mother was worried that Ben was dating a yokel from Zion with four kids; she wasn't even divorced from her ex-con husband yet. I need to set up Ben with someone single and smart, but nobody good came to mind.

"Can I bring Chip so you can meet him?" Elizabeth asked.

"Sure," I said. That would be a good way to get it over with so we wouldn't need a whole double date.

I could hear someone yelling at her.

"That's the head nurse. Gotta go," she said, and hung up.

A minute later the phone rang again.

"Barry's in his psycho mood today," Matthew said. "I can't take it. I'm thinking of flying to New York for the weekend."

For the entire year we'd been dating long-distance, he constantly called, e-mailed, and texted complaints about Barry. Yet since *Barry's World* was an international hit, he couldn't leave the job or LA.

"My brother's coming to town, so let's all hang out." I'd been dying for Matthew to meet somebody from my family. He made excuses to avoid coming to my parents' house in Highland Park. I bet meeting Ben in the Big Apple would be less threatening. "I'm inviting people over Friday to introduce him to some women. Saturday he wants to see *Les Miz* on Broadway. Will you come?"

"You're kidding," said Matthew. He used to direct Off Broadway and hated the commercial crap that made it onto the big stage these days.

"Ben's from the Midwest," I reminded him. "Please come. For me."

"Okay. I'll live through *Les Miz*. For you. How long has it been around? A decade?" Matthew asked.

"Thanks. I'll get three tickets for Saturday night."

"Get four," Matthew said. "Bring one of your girlfriends for your brother. It's on me. Let's have a late dinner afterward."

"Cool. I'll make a reservation for four."

But who would I bring for Ben? Nicky was shooting a documentary in Prague. Betsy and Jane were too old. My single girlfriends from NYU were artsy downtown snobs like me— preferring midnight performance art in East Village basements. How would I find a female who would appreciate a free ticket and dinner, someone old-fashioned enough to dig suburban-seeming Saturday evening plans. I could ask Elizabeth if she knew anybody, but her girlfriends were all her age—too old for Ben.

On Friday I ran out to get beer, booze, and food for my big

bash. I was jazzed; I hadn't had a party since my twenty-fifth birthday, which started with Barry being an asshole and ended with Elizabeth's apartment going up in flames. This soiree would be better. (It couldn't be worse.)

I put on a sexy black V-neck sundress and heels. Then I rushed around, putting Motown CDs into the shuffle of my player, arranging cheese and crudités on trays, making ice, opening all the windows and turning on the standing fan, hoping there would be a nice breeze so people wouldn't sweat. Dozens of my cronies and even a few new female doctors and nurses I found through Eliot the urologist started showing up right around eight. I got stoned, feeling psyched that my party was pretty happening. By the time Ben arrived at nine, the bash was already brewing.

"Brother Number One!" I said, kissing him as he walked in. He bear-hugged me back.

"Hey, Benjamin. Congratulations," Elizabeth said with a little wave. She looked awkward tonight, wearing a long wool cardigan over her turtleneck and jeans though she had to be hot since I didn't have air-conditioning.

"Hey, Elizabeth," he said. "Nice to see you."

"Dr. Solomon," Matthew said, shaking Ben's hand. "So great to finally meet you."

"Likewise." Ben patted Matthew on the shoulder. "I saw your credit when I was watching *Saturday Night Live* reruns. How could you leave such a great job?"

"I got a little too old to do coke and crash on my office couch," Matthew quipped, though unlike me and Ben he'd never been a drinker or a druggie.

Watching them speak, I saw that Ben and Matthew were both husky, wearing blue jeans, blazers with shirts untucked, and silver-rimmed glasses. Had I just noticed that?

"Ricky's still a party girl." Ben jabbed my side. "Some things never change."

"Says the original party animal. I bought Jack Daniel's, your favorite." I pointed to the drinks on the counter of my kitchenette. He made his way there, hitting the joint Peter handed him, shaking hands with Jane, and high-fiving my college pals Andy and Eliot at the doorway. I suddenly felt really happy and proud of my brother. After all these years of antagonism we were finally connecting.

"What happened to Chip?" I asked Elizabeth. "I thought you were bringing him."

"He's sick," she said sheepishly, looking sweaty and uncomfortable. Did it bother her that I was right about Chip's being too old and infirm for her? Or was she nervous to bump into two of her exes, Eliot and Peter? I thought they were ancient history.

When Matthew walked by, I stopped to introduce them. "So this is my love," I said boldly, putting my arm around him, feeling no pain.

"We're finally in the same city," she commented.

We would have all been in the same city a long time ago if your idiot balding ex hadn't stolen him away from me, I didn't say.

"Heard a lot about you," Matthew told her. "You know, I've been a fan of your father's work since I was a kid."

"Which work?" Elizabeth gave the William Mann test, as she often did when somebody claimed to be an admirer of her dad's.

"Well, *Blind Streets* is his masterpiece, but I've always had a soft spot for his India book, *Death and Agony*. I know it's out of print, but I comb used-bookstores for it. I have three copies, one a first edition."

"You do?" She beamed. He'd aced it! Elizabeth looked like a different person when she smiled, years younger. She took off her sweater, getting her arm stuck in its sleeve. Matthew reached out to help her. "How has it been, working for Barry? I think he's a genius."

Leave it to Elizabeth to bite the hand untangling her.

"It's nice working *with* him," Matthew said pointedly.

"You know Barry's wife, Dee, I heard." She never could let go of a Barry connection. He'd ruined my last party. What was she bringing him into this one for?

"I've met her a few times," Matthew said.

"Need another drink?" I wished Elizabeth would change the subject and stop trying to worm the latest Barry scoop from my beau.

"What does Dee look like? I heard she's not as good-looking as she used to be. Do you think she's still pretty?" Elizabeth demanded, a bitch with a bone.

He looked over at me, then at her. "Dark hair. Thin. Though she just had a baby."

Elizabeth winced. Barry obviously hadn't been in touch with her lately. "Boy or girl?"

"A little girl."

"At least it's not a boy. Barry couldn't handle a boy. He's not athletic or anything." I waited for her to mention Barry's legendary impotence.

Luckily right then Ben returned with the Jack Daniel's and took a swig from the bottle. He passed it to Matthew, who usually didn't drink hard stuff. But for the special occasion of meeting my bro, he obliged with a big gulp. I tried a sip but it tasted horrible, so I chased it with Diet Coke. Ben handed the bottle to Elizabeth, who took a long gulp like a pro.

"Go for it," said Ben, impressed with a woman who could drink. (My mother and I got plastered from one glass of wine.) He pulled a Johnny Cash CD from the pocket of his jacket and put it in my player.

"You can take the good ole boy out of middle America," I

teased, not admitting that I actually liked Johnny Cash and had stolen one of Ben's greatest hits CDs when I'd moved.

"Remember that loser you dated who used to follow the Grateful Dead all over the country?" he asked me.

"Remember the only Jewish girl you ever dated in college? The one who turned out to be a stripper?" I asked, vaguely recalling that he'd really liked her and was shocked to find out her sideline.

"Okay, let's not ruin Benjamin's celebration," said Elizabeth.

Nothing could ruin my celebration for Ben tonight, not even her. We were rocking. I brought over Connie, the cute blond twenty-two-year-old nursing student I'd picked up for him while in line at NYU's bookstore. They chatted in the middle of the room; they seemed to be hitting it off. But then Elizabeth walked over and handed Ben another Jack Daniel's, in a glass with ice. Peter joined them, flirting with Connie. Elizabeth nodded a few times but didn't jump into the conversation. Peter's hitting on fresh meat was typical. But Elizabeth so polite and demure? Now, that was unusual.

"What else are you doing while you're in New York?" she asked Ben.

"We're going to *Les Miz* tomorrow night," he said.

"I've always wanted to see it," she told him.

"Great, we have an extra ticket. You'll come with us," Ben offered before I could jump in to tell him I was hoping to ask the cute blond Connie.

"Sure, I'd love to," Elizabeth accepted.

I was surprised, since she'd mentioned plans with Chip. She wasn't bringing her boyfriend, was she? Did she know it was just one extra ticket?

"I want to go to Orso for dinner beforehand, at about five." Ben continued planning the train wreck of an evening I now wanted to get out of.

Five? Who ate at five? *Alter cockers* in Florida? Matthew and I preferred dining *after* the theater, at eleven. And I didn't want Italian; I was on a diet. I'd been thinking Japanese.

"I love Orso," Elizabeth said. "They had the most amazing pumpkin pasta last time I was there."

When had she gone to Orso? Were we now buying her dinner too, along with a theater ticket? So much for Ben's rendezvous with Connie the nurse. Elizabeth was almost seven years Ben's senior, too old to be his date. Oh, well, so it would be a platonic foursome. On the bright side, they were already friends and could talk about diseases all night. At least that way I wouldn't have to hear about disgusting bodily functions. They could keep it to themselves.

On Saturday night Elizabeth wore a knee-length silky blue dress with matching heels and a lot of makeup. Ben was in a pin-striped suit that was too big on him. They looked like little kids playing dress up. Matthew and I, casual in jeans, T-shirts, and cotton blazers, made small talk, but we were hungover from the party the night before and didn't love the early-bird special at Orso. Elizabeth gave us all a headache asking first for the pumpkin ravioli and then for whole wheat pasta (which they didn't have) and sending back her steamed vegetables because she insisted they'd been sautéed.

"A little butter isn't going to hurt you." Ben rolled his eyes.

"You have no idea how much butter and oil they use." She defended her anal diet.

"So why the fuck did you want Italian?" I snapped. "We could have had Japanese, which is much healthier."

"I like Japanese. I just had some good shrimp tempura," Ben said.

"Might as well eat KFC," said Elizabeth, who'd suddenly become the food police.

"You trash-talking KFC? I loves me some Kentucky Fried

drumsticks," Matthew squawked in a Southern hick accent, obviously trying to chill us all out.

At least Ben insisted on treating. But *Les Miz* was the expected Broadway schmaltz. Matthew and I hoped nobody we knew would see us there.

When we walked out of the theater Ben said, "God, that was so great."

"You have the worst taste. That was total drek." I stuck out my tongue.

"What are you talking about? It's the longest-running Broadway musical."

"Right. That proves it's drek," Elizabeth agreed with me.

"It's based on a book by Victor Hugo," Ben argued, showing us the program notes.

"Yeah, and Baudelaire thought it was tasteless and inept a hundred years ago," Elizabeth added.

"You New Yorkers are such jaded snobs," Ben sniffed.

A homeless man stopped us on Broadway at Forty-seventh Street, asking for money. Ben and Elizabeth brushed right past. Matthew stopped, as he usually did. He took out a ten-dollar bill for the guy, who said, "God bless you, sir," and made a run for it, as if Matthew might change his mind. Ben and Elizabeth laughed.

"Another bleeding-heart liberal." Ben put his arm around Matthew. "You're perfect for my sister."

"Yeah, you're perfect for Ricky," Elizabeth chimed in.

They were laughing that he'd given money to charity? "You made a donation to that 9/11 fund," I told her. "Even when you were totally broke."

"That's the complete opposite," she insisted. "That was for the families of firemen who died doing their job, protecting us. Not for bums on the street."

"Well, you would treat a patient who couldn't afford to pay, right?" Matthew asked Ben. "Even if he was homeless or a drunk or a drug addict."

"That's not the same thing," Ben argued.

"He's only a Republican when it comes to his wallet," I said.

"Who paid for dinner and the show, you limousine liberal?" Ben punched my arm.

I punched him back, anxious to end this dismal double date and get home to my own bed—with Matthew in it. I looked for a cab, but there were none in sight, so we decided to take the subway downtown. Ben offered to put Elizabeth in a taxi uptown. We waved good-bye on the street.

"They didn't seem to like each other at all," Matthew commented as we walked down the stairs of the Times Square subway station.

"I know. The only time they bonded was when they were making fun of our politics." I shrugged.

"Listen, I have a ton of work. Would you mind if I stayed at my place tonight?" Matthew asked.

"Not at all," I lied.

Luckily he called me on Sunday to have brunch at Veselka, an East Village Ukrainian dive I liked. I left a message to see if Ben wanted to join us, but he didn't return my call. In fact, my brother didn't make contact again for three days. Although he'd said he wanted to see friends and explore the city on his own, I was getting worried. It turned out I had good reason to be. On Tuesday night, they finally called. "They" as in Ben and Elizabeth, who'd apparently been holed up at the Plaza together since we'd left them on the street Saturday night.

"There's nothing wimpy or confused about your brother," Elizabeth whispered into the phone, giggling.

"Hey, thanks, Ricky. I loved the play," I could hear Ben yelling in the background while Johnny Cash's "I Walk the Line" was playing. "Best play I ever saw."

"We did it seven times the first night," Elizabeth cooed.

What? Oh my God! Yuck! No way! Shit! Now I'd never be able to get the hideous picture of Ben and Elizabeth in bed together out of my head. How completely uncool and intrusive of him to hook up with my New York friend. Couldn't my brother ever keep it in his goddamn pants? And was it Elizabeth's goal to worm her way into the middle of every single male relationship in my life?

"How did I not see this one coming?" I called Matthew, back in LA, to ask him.

"Well, maybe it's a good thing for both of them," was his lame response.

"A good thing? How could it possibly be a good thing? The only question is who's going to fuck over whom worse! I'll probably have to scrape her off the floor, and it's going to ruin our friendship—not to even mention all my important work connections," I yelled, trying not to freak out. But I was haunted by the picture of my brother and Elizabeth having sex, which revolted me. It probably didn't help to realize that Matthew and I had barely touched each other all weekend.

Every time Ben came to New York, something terrible happened. First an STD, now Elizabeth!

When she called back later she said, "Jesus, I can't get over how amazing your kid brother is. Did I tell you we went to Bellevue and he met my boss? She was really impressed. How could she not be?"

"Yeah, don't you have to go to work?" I asked.

"And when we were walking up Fifth Avenue, we stopped at Bergdorf's and he bought me a black leather jacket and—"

"He bought you a leather jacket?" I was appalled. "You let him buy you a jacket already? What is he, your sugar daddy?"

"We ordered in butterscotch ice cream sundaes from room

service. I wished I'd ordered the brownie, so Benjamin called back and ordered me the brownie too. We stayed up all night, talking about medicine and politics. We agree on everything. I'm going to Illinois next week and—"

"Next week? What about your steady boyfriend, Chip, the nicest guy you've met in years, remember? And your job? Don't you have to be at work? Ben has to work! He'll be working at the hospital a hundred hours a week! This is way too quick! You're going to get hurt again and blame it on me!" I screamed, but she wasn't listening.

"We went to the Oak Room. Then I took him shopping at Saks. We're getting him better glasses; I hate those thick frames he wears. He has sensuous eyes," she said. "And he has your small lips. I noticed when I was kissing him."

chapter fourteen
rules of engagement
September 3, 2002

The minute I landed at my parents' house for Labor Day week-end and checked my phone messages, I knew my dream trip would be a disaster. First Matthew—the mellow male I'd invited to accompany me—left a message saying he had to go back to LA for an important interview and needed to cancel our big week together. Then Elizabeth—the female headache I hadn't invited and didn't particularly want to hang out with right now—informed my machine that she and Ben were taking us all out to dinner Saturday night at Ben's country club, which I hated.

In the last six weeks, she'd been spending more time at my brother's house in Zion, while her ex-squeeze had unceremoni-ously axed Matthew from *Barry's World*. So as she was ecstatically being wined and dined by my brother, my boyfriend was cata-tonic, desperately flying coach back and forth on the red-eye for sitcom meetings even though it was off-season and nobody was hiring. Great way to start my annual vacation, the only time I could afford to take off since my jaunt here a summer earlier, which—I couldn't help but recall—had also been marred by Queen Elizabeth.

To make matters worse, my mother was even more taken aback by Ben and Elizabeth's lightning-fast romance than I was.

"Does she love him?" she asked as we power walked around the neighborhood.

"I don't know. Maybe it's just a fling. Her relationships don't usually last that long."

"Let's go in." She turned toward the lawn, though we'd only done one lap around the block.

"One more time." I steered her past our house. Through the window we saw my father in his den, watching the large-screen television my brothers had picked out for his big birthday last year.

"Dad seems to like his fancy TV," I commented. "They already got him a computer that shows videos and plays music, a laser printer, and a loaded cell phone with a camera. What's next? His own robot?"

"All Danny's idea. He's always been a technology nut. I think that's why he wants to be a radiologist, because he likes machines better than people."

"That's true. He gets to sit alone, analyzing X-rays all day." They looked like the negatives of my photographs; it was something I could relate to.

"Ben always liked nature," my mother said. "He chased raccoons, put bees and wasps in jars."

"Putting a WASP in a jar," I said. "Good metaphor for domesticating Elizabeth."

"Your brother Ben never does anything small."

"He's in his big career stage. So maybe he needs a big house, a big jeep, and a big woman," I joked.

"He bought her a big diamond bracelet." My mother shook her head.

"I heard."

"Well, Kim heard too. The four of them double-dated last weekend."

Like Elizabeth, Danny's girlfriend, Kim, was tall, smart, edgy, from a divorced home, not Jewish. Though unlike the lapsed Protestant Elizabeth, Kim was a lapsed Catholic. They both worked in science, too, Kim as a lab technician, so they could talk about cells or protozoans, or whatever it was that science people talked about. And they liked younger men. Coincidentally, both Kim and Elizabeth were six years older than their partners. Growing up with two little brothers, I never could see the attraction to younger guys.

"I bet Elizabeth and Kim hit it off," I said.

"They hate each other." My mother was near tears. Aha, that was why she was so upset. She could never handle any family unrest. I put my arm around her.

"So what? They don't have to hang out," I said, once again extremely glad I lived in New York.

"Kim is a hardworking girl. Elizabeth told her she wants to quit her job and go to the gym every day." My mother threw up her arms.

"She was probably talking hypothetically. Or kidding around," I said, fearing that she wasn't.

"Kim asked Elizabeth if she aspired to be a gold digger who worked out for a living."

"Kim didn't really say that?" I asked. I knew there was a reason I liked Kim.

"She did." My mother shook her head. "Kim likes her work."

"But she doesn't really have a choice. She has a lot of student loans to pay back. Danny never really saved money or invested in the stock market, like Ben did."

"How long have Danny and Kim been going out?" I asked.

"More than two years," she said. "They're really in love. They're very sweet together."

Had it really been two years already? Where the hell had I been? Freelancing for peanuts and entangled in my own long-term off-and-on relationship, avoiding the Highland Park branch as much as possible. Now I knew why.

"The girls are fighting, and Danny and Ben aren't speaking. We can't even all have dinner together. We have to see Danny and Kim on Friday night and Elizabeth and Ben on Saturday. You'll come to both dinners, right?" She was manipulating me into a weekend of being the only single person in the room. "I just want peace," she said. "I want Danny and Ben to stay close."

"Ben and Danny were like twins growing up," I said. "It figures they'd like the same kind of woman. Elizabeth and Kim are older, smart, strong women, like us." I tried to sound convincing. A flock of geese stood on the man-made beach. By the water were four white swans, cleaning themselves.

"They keep shitting all over the neighborhood," she said. "They shit green."

"You're in a good mood, Mom," I said sarcastically.

She kicked a branch on the ground, walked ahead of me. I caught up. "What's with Matthew?" she asked.

"He wasn't rehired for Barry's show," I reluctantly admitted.

"Barry is the one who used to date Elizabeth?" she asked.

"Yeah. So now Matthew's interviewing to direct some sitcom pilots."

"Is that good or bad?" my mom wanted to know.

"Good, 'cause he's getting back out there. Bad 'cause out there means he'll probably stay in LA."

"Doesn't sound good," she said.

Later I left another phone message for Matthew, desperately attempting to convince him to fly to Highland Park for just

Saturday or Sunday. But even the new outgoing message on his machine sounded inconsolable. I curled up under the pink covers of my old bed and took a nap to avoid thinking. When I opened my eyes, Kim was standing over me.

"Are you ready for a sister-in-law?" she asked. I was startled as she sat down and lit a cigarette. Danny didn't know she smoked, so Kim lit up only in my room.

"Oh no. Don't tell me Elizabeth got Ben to propose?" I sat up and stole one of her cigarettes.

"No, I'm not talking about your friend, the JAP wannabe," Kim shot back, lighting mine. "I'm talking about me. I'm making an honest man out of Danny."

I was dazed and still didn't get it. Until she showed me the ring on her finger, a small diamond on a thin gold band. "Isn't it beautiful? Can you believe it?"

I couldn't. Kim was thirty. But my littlest brother Danny was barely twenty-four. Who got married at age twenty-four these days? People I knew in New York couldn't do it until their late thirties—if at all.

"Well, congratulations." I gave her a hug, then stared at her. Kim was very pretty, with reddish-brown hair and big brown eyes. She looked a little like my mother. Had I just noticed that? Everyone was starting to look alike around here. Kim wore makeup and pastel colors, dressing in a more feminine way than Elizabeth, perhaps another reason why they didn't get along.

"We're going to do it soon," Kim said. "November sixth. Just a small dinner. I won't make you wear a pink bridesmaid dress, I promise. Though I do want to wear a white gown. Nothing pouffy," she said. "Aren't you happy for us?"

"Of course I'm happy for you," I said, despondent at the thought of being a bridesmaid—in any color dress—for my baby brother while being single.

I'd been dating Matthew exclusively for almost a year, but he didn't even feel obligated to return my phone calls. I was the oldest of the Solomon offspring, and the only girl. I should have been the first one to walk down the aisle. The third child's getting married first threw everything out of whack. When Kim left, I called Matthew one more time. Again nobody answered.

The next night was Dinner Number One, at Ben's country club, a ten-minute drive from his house. It seemed like it was in *Shnipashuk*, a Yiddish word I thought my mother made up, which roughly translated to "God's country." Elizabeth uncharacteristically greeted me with a hug the minute I got there, then she embraced my mother and father too. Uh-oh. I lit a cigarette, wondering what was up. Before we could announce Kim and Danny's big news, Elizabeth jumped in.

"Guess what?" she said. "We're getting married."

She stuck out her finger, showing off a thick gold band with a solitaire diamond the size of a pea in the middle. Elizabeth and Kim both had instant rings on their fingers. I couldn't believe that my twenty-four- and twenty-five-year-old siblings were both ready to tie the knot without me! I thought only hillbillies, Mormons, and Orthodox Jews got married so young. I was left out, mixed up, and *farklempt*. I wondered when my little brothers had surpassed me to learn about engagement rituals, and then actually felt offended that they hadn't come to me for the immature advice I would have given them: I'm the oldest, and I'm supposed to go first! Don't do it before me.

We all stared at Elizabeth's ring, which looked familiar. How odd—it was just like the one adorning my mother's finger. Had she seen Mom's ring and asked my brother to get her the exact duplicate? I guessed that was Ben's idea of what bling a doctor's wife should wear. My mother, obviously noticing the similarity too, put her hand below the table.

"Mazel tov!" my father said. "Danny and Kim are getting

married too! They told us last night." He was elated, completely unaware of all the multilayered traumas brewing. "That's very, very good news!" He told the waiter to bring a bottle of champagne.

"We're doing it soon. In October," Elizabeth said.

"*This* October?" my mother asked, looking pale and petrified. She took a sip of water. "How can you plan anything so quickly? Why don't you take a little time and ..."

"My mother's going to plan it," Elizabeth said. "She wants it in Rye."

"We want October," Ben reiterated.

My mother gave me a horrified glare that shouted: "This is all your fault. Danny and Kim will be shattered. I'm blaming you that our whole family is falling apart. This is causing a rift that will destroy it forever." But what could I do? "Do something," her eyes were screaming at me. "She's *your* friend."

My mother turned to my father, looking like she was about to have a nervous breakdown.

"October isn't good," I blurted out. "Kim and Danny are getting married on November second. They announced it yesterday. Why don't you let him go first?"

Elizabeth looked at Ben with pleading eyes.

"I called Danny and told him I was proposing," Ben said. "That's why they're getting married now. Kim would have killed Danny if Elizabeth got a ring first." So it was a conspiracy between Danny and Ben, the two redheads. Or another battle in the Solomon siblings' lifelong rivalry. Either way, surely Elizabeth was to blame. She'd barged in like the infantry, causing all kinds of explosions and chain reactions.

"Come on. Danny and Kim have been together for two years," I said, identifying with the poorer, longer-suffering woman. "You two have been together for, what, like two months?"

"So what?" Ben said. "What does the amount of time we've

been together have to do with anything? There's not a rule that whoever is together the longest gets hitched first."

"Yeah. There's no rule about that," Elizabeth echoed.

I looked at my brother and moved in closer to him. With my teeth clenched, I said, "Listen, Dr. Benjamin Scott Solomon. You were the firstborn son. You bullied me and Danny your whole life, got your first-choice med school, your first-choice internship, every woman you ever wanted, and just wasted tons of money at the Plaza, of all the tacky freaking hotels in the world, to sleep with *my* New York girlfriend. Now it's Danny's turn to go first for once in his life. Can't you just let him win?"

The waiter came back and uncorked the champagne, pouring us glasses.

Ben looked at me. "Okay."

"We can do it the Saturday night *after* Danny and Kim. So they can go first," said Elizabeth, instantly bouncing back, as if she'd had a Hallmark calendar and a backup plan in her head all along.

What was her hurry? I had to ask myself. Elizabeth barely knew Ben except through me, and I suddenly felt like I didn't know either of them. But looking at Elizabeth, I saw that she was radiant. She'd had a lousy life, and she deserved a break. I just didn't know that break was going to be Ben. I sipped the champagne. My first famous Manhattan friend, confidante, and mentor, Elizabeth Mann, the tall aspiring shutterbug with acerbic wit and a genius father, was giving it all up to be the wife of my Illinois kid brother.

"November thirteenth it is," I said, as if giving my permission.

Everyone looked at my mother.

"Danny and Kim will do it November second, then Ben and Elizabeth on November ninth," decreed the bright red–haired Solomon matriarch, looking dazed but plastering on a fake smile for the rest of the night.

I remember when I was four, my mother barged into my bedroom, saw my Barbie dolls and my brothers' G.I. Joes and little green army men strewn all over my pink carpet, and screamed, "No man is going to marry such a slob." She'd basically been bugging all of us to get married and procreate since we were born. But now that two of her offspring were actually doing it two weekends in a row, she looked like she was going to cry. "We can't fight," she said. "Families take care of each other."

We lifted our glasses and toasted, though nobody felt much like drinking. Except for Elizabeth, who had four glasses of Dom Pérignon, then took twenty minutes to order, finally choosing the lobster special, the most expensive thing on the menu.

chapter fifteen
the wedding dance
November 2, 2002

"Why's he posing Uncle Max and Aunt Sally by the door?" I asked my mother, sneering at Kim and Danny's wedding photographer. "It's freezing and the light sucks."

"Why? I don't know why," my mother said, teeth clenched. "I didn't plan the wedding. Nobody asked me to plan anything."

I understood her hurt. Although I saw myself as a professional who didn't have time to document every boring family event for free, I nonetheless felt slighted that Kim and Danny had hired somebody else to take pictures without even running it by me.

I checked my watch. It was 6:30 P.M. on the first Saturday night in November, in the back room of the Highland Park restaurant. The intimate French dinner for thirty people was supposed to begin at seven. I hoped small would mean less turmoil.

I'd been in a tizzy since Matthew and I had landed in the Midwest just in time for a snowstorm.

"Your father and Matthew seem to be hitting it off at least." Mom pointed to the bar area, where the two most important men in my life were having a beer, eating peanuts, and chatting amiably, oblivious to all the under-the-surface chaos brewing.

"You look pretty," I told her. She'd abandoned her jolly pastels to wear a black dress. I wished I was in my usual ebony uniform, but she'd sent me a gray silk number that I'd dumbly decided to don to please her. I'd put on five pounds, so gray silk was not the way to go, which I unfortunately didn't realize until I'd passed a mirror a few minutes earlier. Not to mention the black stiletto heels I could barely walk in.

"Where are Ben and Elizabeth? It figures they'd be late," said Kim, carrying the train of her long white dress.

"See? Kim and Elizabeth can't stand each other," my mother mumbled under her breath, sounding near tears. "This is how it's going to be for the rest of my life."

"Don't worry. I'm sure they'll wind up close," I lied, remembering again why I'd moved to New York.

I thought we were all subconsciously traumatized that Danny, the youngest, was the first to get married. I'd pictured us winding up like the siblings in *The Accidental Tourist*, who grew old and demented together in their childhood home. I was going to be the one alphabetizing soup cans in the pantry. It was as if Danny was now breaking the secret single Solomon sibling code.

Ben and Elizabeth rushed in holding hands, reminding me that I'd soon be the only solo player left in our clan.

"Sorry, there was horrible traffic. It's really coming down out there. They're saying four inches," Ben said, rushing their wraps to the coat check.

"Luckily Ben's a great driver," said Elizabeth cheerfully.

She was in a red dress. I remembered the similarly colored

blazer I'd given her two years before. I was the one who'd told her red was her color. This suddenly seemed significant, as if my telling her that being a siren would attract a man meant it was my fault that the one she'd snared was my brother.

"Where is everyone?" Kim asked, dragging my father and Ben down the hallway, where they were taking group pictures. "They shot my family; now they want the men."

"If I had her family I'd shoot them too," Elizabeth told me when Kim was out of earshot. "I know you usually stay at your parents' house when you come to town. But you can come back and stay with us if you want."

Staying at Ben's big suburban house would be an even worse hell than staying at my parents' big suburban house, but it was a nice surprise that she offered. "Thanks," I said.

"Are you okay?" she asked.

I shook my head.

"I figured you wouldn't bring any pot on the plane, so I saved a joint for you," she said quietly, slipping it into my purse. "It's the last of my good New York stuff."

Fantastic! Exactly what the doctor ordered.

"Hey, girls. What's shaking?" asked Aunt Sally. In a pink glitter top and spandex pants with tortoiseshell glasses, Sally was your average sixty-four-year-old housewife dressed as a trailer-park teen.

"Have you met Elizabeth?" I asked her.

"Are you kidding? We're already bosom buddies." Sally put her arm around Elizabeth. "She said your guy Matthew is that tall commitment-phobe over there. He's no spring chicken; what's he waiting for?"

Needing a quick exit, I went to the coat check, switched to the black Nikes I'd left in my camera bag, and put on my black parka. Pulling the hood over my face so nobody would recognize me, I sneaked outside to the end of the parking lot to smoke Elizabeth's joint alone in the snow. When I returned, I dried myself off and switched back to my heels just in time for the ceremony to begin.

"Where did you go? I was looking for you," Matthew asked, sitting to my right.

"Emergency work call," I lied, recalling Dr. C's advice to not let on how much being the single sister at both of my kid brothers' weddings was freaking me out.

"You reek of dope," said Elizabeth, sitting to my left.

She reached in her purse, dabbed perfume behind my ears, and handed me her packet of Listerine Breath Strips. I took five and let them all dissolve in my mouth as Judge Meyer Katz performed the sacred rites. My relatives and family friends all smiled and nodded, pretending that having a Jewish judge made the intermarriage more kosher. The short civil ceremony was interrupted with emergency calls on my father's, Dr. Radlow's, and Dr. Niss's cell phones.

"How impressive, a room full of doctors," Elizabeth whispered to me.

"How disgusting, a room full of doctors," I whispered to Matthew.

After Kim and Danny said their vows, they smashed a glass on the floor. The Solomon contingent let out a collective "Mazel tov."

Danny and Kim's comrades made their way to table four. My parents' friends were seated at three. At the second table, Matthew and I were parked next to my parents, Ben, Elizabeth, Uncle Max, and Aunt Sally. Kim and Danny sat at the head table, along with Kim's siblings, mother, stepfather, real father, and his wife, all in from Toledo, Ohio. The seating arrangement disturbed me. I thought Danny and Kim should be seated with the Solomons. I had a tall glass of wine, but neither the strong joint nor the alcohol mellowed me in the least; just the opposite. I was tense and paranoid about losing Danny forever.

"Can't you switch it around so you can sit with us?" I asked the groom.

"No," he said. "Just leave the seating arrangement alone."

"Will you ask Kim?"

He nodded, then came back and whispered, "Kim said you should take your Prozac and ruin your friend's wedding next week, not hers."

What a sarcastic, snide, mean, bitchy, flamingly obnoxious thing to say to a new relative at her wedding! I knew there was a reason I liked her.

All through the Caesar salad, onion soup, and braised chicken with butternut squash, I stared at Danny at the Toledo table. He was so busy with medical school, I hardly saw him anymore. He'd been married for ten minutes and I already missed him terribly. My entire childhood I couldn't wait to get rid of my brothers, and now they had no use for me. I felt replaced, rejected, and alone. It was my mother's curse; we were all too connected, the whole clan's guts and hearts and fears overlapping. I ran to the bathroom, sobbing. Mascara was running down my face. My nose was red. Elizabeth came in and stood behind me in the mirror.

"Jeez, you're a wreck tonight. Did you smoke that whole joint by yourself?" She handed me a Kleenex.

I nodded, blowing my nose. "I hate this dress my mother sent. Why didn't I wear black?"

"You happen to look very classy in gray," she reassured me, wiping away the makeup smudged under my eyes. "But if you don't want that dress, I'll take it. Your mother has such great taste."

"I'm having an off night."

"I know. Your two younger brothers getting married before you isn't fair."

"It's not?" I asked.

"No. It sucks." She took out the makeup bag and hairbrush

from my purse and started untangling the back of my hair. "I hated when my sister Michelle got married, and she's four years older than I am. It felt like I was being deserted."

"Me too." I sniffled.

"Then she got divorced and I wished she'd stayed married."

"Sorry." Was she saying Kim and Danny would get divorced too? She was right, that would be worse.

"And it's stupid that we couldn't get married first just because Daniel and Kim have been dating longer," she added, brushing my straightened hair behind my ears.

"At least you only have to wait a week."

"I bet you'll be next," she promised, taking out my foundation and rubbing some around my face to get rid of the blotches on my tear-streaked, pale skin. "Your old Rabbi Levin will marry you and Matthew and your parents will be so happy."

"They don't care about religion," I said as she dabbed a dash of concealer on my chin.

"Sure they do. This is killing them. Why do you think they wanted Jewish judges for both weddings? So they could pretend they're plainclothes rabbis." She laughed, taking out my blush and brushing a bit of color around my face. "I would kill for your high cheekbones."

I sucked them in exaggeratedly, vamping in the mirror. "It just all happened so fast."

"Next weekend will be worse." She pulled out my black eyebrow pencil and drew a line over my thin brows. "My family is WASP city."

"My mother wanted to plan the reception."

"The bride's mother gets to plan the wedding. So she'll plan yours." She added a little mascara to my top lashes, then inspected her creation.

"Matthew's looking for jobs in LA. I offered to move out there but he said he's not ready to live together." I started crying again.

"If you cry you're going to look like a clown in all the pictures," she warned.

"Sorry." I took a deep breath, then lit a cigarette.

"Why would he come to your brothers' weddings if he wasn't going to marry you?"

"Sadism," I guessed.

"He's such a handsome guy. Brainy with big shoulders, my favorite type. Just like the Solomon men. They all love him. He fits right in," she said. "He'll come around. I'm sure he'll want you in California with him."

She led me back to our table, where dessert was being served.

"You have such a nice family," Matthew said in my ear. "And your friends are so warm. Everyone looks so happy for Kim and Danny."

Were we at the same event? "What are you talking about? Everyone's psychotic. I can't believe all the doctors picked up their cell phones in the middle of the ceremony."

"They had emergencies," Matthew defended them. "Someone was sick."

"Someone's always sick," I said, about to lose it. I didn't want to be here in the freezing Midwest, with two married little brothers and a long-distance boyfriend who couldn't even commit to living in sin.

"How is it a nightmare?" Matthew asked.

"My mother's insulted that Kim didn't let her bring candy or centerpieces. Ben and Elizabeth resent that they couldn't be first to tie the knot. Kim and her whole Toledo clan are pissed that I wanted Danny to switch tables. And I'm flipping out that I'm the only one not getting married," I couldn't help but blurt. "You're the only one having a good time, because nobody here is related to you."

"At least the food's great." He ignored my analysis, taking a bite out of his chocolate soufflé.

"I hate French food. Do you know that Kim, Danny, and all their friends are going to Hooligan's later?"

"Yeah, I heard that's their hangout," he said.

"So she's going to sit on a barstool in her wedding dress, drinking beer?" I picked the ice out of Matthew's water and chewed on it.

"Ben and Elizabeth's wedding next week will be easier," he promised.

"It'll be like death," I said.

"Your brothers look happy," Matthew told me. "You should be happy for them."

I knew I was being a rotten sport. But since when was Matthew Mr. Happy Wedding? The only reason he was meeting my parents was that Barry had fired him and he hadn't landed another job in LA before my brother's wedding. I finished my wine, then drank his.

Maybe it made sense that Danny, the youngest, went first. He often said he'd benefited from having me and Ben, with our huge type A stubborn personalities, come before him. Aside from his obsession for reciting facts nobody else cared about, Danny seemed comparatively well-adjusted, the most flexible and easygoing of the three of us. I thought he'd tricked the gene pool and managed to avoid the demons that plagued the rest of the Solomon clan. But Kim fit right in, with her nicotine addiction, impatience, and sarcasm. Elizabeth had a theory that people married their dark side. Wait—didn't Elizabeth used to be *my* dark side?

When she and Ben landed in New York for their weekend wedding extravaganza, Ben called from the hotel in Rye, where out-of-towners were staying. We went over the schedule. Everything sounded okay. Until he started complaining that Elizabeth's mother had chosen flute music for the Saturday evening reception.

"Flute music?" I asked.

"For when we walk down the aisle," Ben explained.

"Just flute music? That's the only music you've got?" I was pissed that I'd have to travel an hour to the Rye Women's Club, also Elizabeth's mother's choice, where there'd be no real music or dancing the whole night. There were a hundred guests coming. What would we do after dinner—stare at each other? They'd planned the wedding in such a hurry, maybe they'd forgotten. I didn't know what to get them, and music suddenly seemed an inspired gift. Plus it would also be a present for my mother; she loved to dance. And boy could she use a horah about now.

"Can I get you a DJ?" I asked my brother.

"I'll ask Elizabeth," he said. When he came back to the phone he told me, "Sure, a DJ would be great. But can you find one on such short notice?"

"No problem," I said, wondering where the fuck I was going to find a music man to schlep all the way to Rye at the last second.

Determined to save the Solomons from a flute-filled, danceless evening, I turned to Craigslist and made a bunch of phone calls. Finally I located Wild Bob, who agreed to play five hours of music for five hundred dollars in Rye on Saturday night—if I brought him the cash before midnight. I ran to the ATM, emptied my checking account, and took a cab to Wild Bob's Washington Heights apartment. Wild Bob himself came to the door. He was a short, friendly Latino guy with a mustache and gold chains around his neck. He handed me a list of the most requested wedding songs. When he promised he'd throw in a Jewish medley that included a long horah, he had me. I signed a one-page contract, gave him all my money, and we shook on it. I was proud of myself for being such a great big sister to Ben and great friend to Elizabeth.

Saturday night, mirroring my state of mind, there was a rainstorm, with fallen trees and flooding on the highways. Matthew rented a car too small for him; his head hit the roof. Though he'd driven so well in LA, in New York he drove like a half-blind old lady. He didn't know how to work the wind-shield wipers and had to pull over three times. When we found the white brick building, which looked like a small-town li-brary, he dropped me off in front to go park the car so I wouldn't get wet. But a gust of wind blew my umbrella inside out and my black velvet dress and hair were damp by the time I walked in the door. The first person I saw was Mom, in the foyer, pacing. My mother and I were eternally early for everything.

"We've got to stop meeting like this," I told her, taking off my coat.

"You look like a drowned rat. Go dry off," she admonished. "Can you believe Elizabeth's not here yet and it's five thirty? The ceremony starts at six. Will you take pictures for me? This photo-grapher doesn't look too sharp."

"I'm on it. I brought my Canon," I told her, determined to be a better sport tonight than I'd been at Solomon Wedding One a week earlier. After all, I'd introduced the happy couple. I'd al-ready taken responsibility for the entertainment; now I was all set to preserve this historical event in celluloid too.

"I would have made the ceremony start at seven thirty. But nobody asks me to plan anything." Despite her hurt feelings, she looked regal in her shiny green satin dress, her hair still pouffed despite the rain.

I gave the coats and my camera bag to the coat check lady and went to the bathroom to dry off my calf-length frock. In the strategically flattering light of the Saks dressing room, it had looked sleek and slenderizing. But now that it was all wet and clingy, I saw that it made my hips and behind look huge. Why in God's name had I chosen velvet? I tried to tell myself I was being overly self-conscious. And my high heels helped me look elongated—though I could barely walk in them. Coming back out, I found Matthew and my father in the pale pink room where the ceremony was to take place, standing next to my New Jersey relatives.

"Nobody marries Jews anymore," said Uncle Max, who planted a kiss on my cheek.

"Elizabeth is great. Very smart," I reassured him. "You know she was my friend first, right?"

"Your guy seems nice. He's a Yid, isn't he?" Max asked as if he weren't right there.

"I can recite the haftorah from my bar mitzvah as proof," Matthew offered.

"Is he over his fear of commitment yet?" Aunt Sally asked me.

"The Solomons need some Jewish grandkids. When are you going to tie the knot already, Rachela? You're not getting any younger," said Uncle Izzy.

I was only fucking twenty-six!

"You putting on some weight?" Aunt Sally asked.

"Rachel, I think it's your DJ," Matthew called. "Unless some more of your relatives just arrived in a white van that says 'Wild Bob's Musical Jungle.'"

I teetered to the door and waved to Wild Bob, who was in a cheap white tux. So were two of his homies, who unloaded the equipment in the pouring rain. As I shook Wild Bob's hand, Elizabeth flew by in a running suit and sneakers. Then came Elizabeth's mother, Pamela, a tall white-haired matron in a knee-length navy dress, a blazer, and a gold cross necklace, looking like she was going to church. Pamela was followed by Michelle, Elizabeth's sister, and Michelle's two young daughters.

"Sorry. We're always late," said the last, littlest one as the five Mann females all dashed through the doorway.

"It's genetic," Michelle added.

"Is everything okay?" I followed Elizabeth up the side staircase. "The judge and the photographer are here, though I'll take a few rolls of the party too." She'd been so understanding about my breakdown at Danny and Kim's wedding last weekend, I felt indebted to her. "Need help with anything?" I asked as she rushed into the changing room in back, undressing behind a screen.

She'd planned the wedding so quickly she'd decided against having bridesmaids. Still, I stood right outside, getting into self-appointed maid-of-honor mode, feeling like a VIP. "Are you okay in there? Anything I can do?"

She flung her jeans out and said, "Mom doesn't want music."

"What?" I folded the jeans neatly. "Do you need something?"

"My mom doesn't want music." She threw out her shirt, bra, socks. "Cancel it."

"What? You're kidding, aren't you? I can't cancel the music now."

"Where are my hose?" she asked. "Are they on the hanger?"

I handed them to her.

"Get rid of the music," she called. "Where's my bra?"

I slipped her the white lace bra. "I can't," I said. "I paid Wild Bob in cash from my own pocket and it's not refundable. He drove an hour in this storm. It's a miracle he made it. Everyone wants music. My mother wants music."

"My mother doesn't want music." She grabbed the brassiere.

For two strong, independent women who'd both left home at eighteen, our maternal figures were suddenly looming everywhere. I handed her the huge gray zippered bag that was protecting her gown. "Elizabeth, look, you're a little emotional now, and..."

"You're ruining my wedding!" she yelled, snatching the garment bag from my hands before I could unzip it for her.

Ruining her wedding? I was her matchmaker, dress maid, music booker, free backup shutterbug, and psychiatrist-on-call, currently running a group seminar for my *mishpokhe* on how to cope with intermarriage. I was saving her wedding, which wouldn't be happening at all if it wasn't for me! What game were we playing now—Dueling Mothers?

Leaning on the radiator, I took a deep breath. Elizabeth was the bride. It was *her* day, I reminded myself. The bride got everything exactly the way she wanted it; those were the rules. Then again, this particular Protestant bride was barging into *my* big loud tribe of Jews, who—she didn't even know—had a long history of plotzing if they couldn't horah. She'd already agreed to the music; I'd asked my brother for permission before I spent all of my money on Wild Bob. And anyway, since when was I obligated to be tactful with Elizabeth Mann, my big-city mentor in incivility?

She could get herself into her own damn white dress, I thought, marching downstairs to find the groom. Ben was mingling with guests in the foyer. He looked dignified in his tuxedo, a rose in his lapel. He'd lost thirty pounds since the summer. Elizabeth had him working out on the StairMaster and the rowing machine. She'd even bought them matching mountain bikes.

"You look handsome," I said, trying to be calm and helpful on this important occasion. But within seconds I breathlessly blurted out my side of the music dilemma. "...And now that Wild Bob miraculously fought the storm from the city to finally arrive—"

Ben put his hand on my shoulder to stop me. "Don't worry, Sis," he said, smiling and jovial, man of the hour. "Elizabeth is just nervous. Everything's fine. The music's fine. Thanks for getting it for us. What a great present."

At that moment I wanted to marry him myself.

On an inappropriate roll, I told my mother that Elizabeth's mother didn't want the DJ. She looked at me in disbelief. Abandoning all protocol herself, Mom threw down the gauntlet, declaring: "The music stays."

During the ceremony, Mom sat to my right and Matthew to my left. When I turned to watch Elizabeth walk down the aisle, I gasped, shocked to see her wearing my mother's antique wedding dress. It had been in storage all these years, so I'd never actually laid eyes on the gown itself. I only recognized it from my parents' beautiful framed wedding photograph in the foyer of our Highland Park house.

Why had I not known it would be on Elizabeth's body tonight? I should have been consulted on such an important family decision! I felt betrayed and heartbroken in so many ways I could barely breathe.

"I can't believe you didn't save your wedding dress for me," I whispered to my mother, holding back tears.

"You said you'd rather die than don that disgusting symbol of sexist white patriarchal society," Mom whispered back. "And that if you ever got married—which you weren't going to—you'd only do it wearing black leather."

Oh, yeah. That sounded like me.

"It cost a fortune to have it refitted for her. But I told her it's yours next if you ever change your mind," she added, patting my hand.

"We are gathered here today to unite Dr. Benjamin Solomon and Miss Elizabeth Mann in holy matrimony," said Judge Marvin Cohen. "Now, some people might think a storm during a wedding ceremony is a bad omen. But I hear it means lots of kids are coming."

Judge Cohen appeared to be an overly friendly, frustrated stand-up comic who'd sprinkle bad jokes through the ceremony. After the DJ-versus-flute music fiasco, just what I wasn't in the mood for.

"Elizabeth Mann and Ben Solomon's union is a case of opposites attract," the judge continued. "Especially since Benjamin majored in beer pong at Northwestern while Elizabeth was a Phi Beta Kappa at Harvard."

Don't tell me that Elizabeth had told our judge about my brother's underwhelming undergraduate career! When she went to college, he was in junior high school. She was robbing the cradle, I wanted to stand up and scream. She was at Harvard only because her famous father was teaching there before he got thrown out for being a drunk. What little career she'd had post-college, she couldn't wait to throw away. On the other hand, my brother had woken up, stopped partying, gone to medical school, and was becoming a surgeon. Dr. Ben Solomon was going into a profession where he would be saving lives daily. He was living the American dream and enhancing the Solomon legacy, a legacy of which I was all of a sudden shockingly proud and protective. Jeez, when the hell had that transformation happened? I was the only one allowed to trash him in public, not Elizabeth— and especially not on their big day.

"Everyone thinks he's a comedian," Matthew said in my ear.

I kept muttering to myself during the thankfully short, secular vow exchange. After the service, my brother stomped on a glass and everyone from our side yelled "Mazel tov!" and clapped. Then we were led to a quiet room filled with pictures of white-haired Westchester ladies that looked like a library decorated by Laura Ashley. On the way I bumped into Danny, who'd rebelled against the black-tie dress code by wearing a tux with a black T-shirt and no tie. Who would have thought he'd turn out to be the rebel of the family? He nuzzled the neck of his new wife, Kim, her nose sunburned from their six-day honeymoon in Aruba, clearly proud they'd wed first.

Wild Bob tested the microphone, which screeched. Elizabeth rushed up to me in the long lacey antique white dress. She looked stunning, the most beautiful she'd ever looked, as she hissed, "No music during dinner."

"Music during dessert," I countered.

She stormed away in a huff, mumbling how she'd never speak to me again. She'd obviously forgotten that she'd seated me right next to her at the head table. During the salad course she sneered at me and whispered to Ben, as if she desperately wanted him on her side.

I was too emotionally traumatized to fight. He's already yours, I wanted to tell her. You won. I concede defeat.

The waiter said the choice of entrée was salmon or steak. Matthew and Ben chose steak. I picked salmon, though I had no appetite. Elizabeth looked confused about which to order, and had the waiter come back twice. Finally, the third time the waiter asked, she conferred with Ben. Then she smiled and proudly proclaimed: "I'll have both." She was the only bride I'd ever seen eat at her own wedding—attacking both dinners with gusto. No frail, frilly anorexic for Ben. It made me remember what I liked about her in the first place. I went to the coat check to get my cameras. I couldn't help it; I had to capture her all made-up and glamorous in that gorgeous gown, fork and knife drawn, joyously eating from both plates.

After they cut the cake, Elizabeth nixed the idea of a first romantic slow dance. Instead I signaled Wild Bob to go straight to the fast stuff. Soon Lil' Kim's version of "Lady Marmalade" was blasting from the speakers. Jane, Ruth, Peter, Richard, Hope, and Stanley all got up to dance together in one big group. In the corner of the room I saw Elizabeth's mother stand up, throw her hands over her head, and run outside.

"She's going to faint," Matthew said.

"Don't worry," I told him. "There're doctors in the room."

For the next hour, Wild Bob spun songs by Usher, Jay Z, JLo, Beyonce, Mary J. Bilge, and Lenny Kravitz. Soon the room was rocking out. I took off my uncomfortable heels and joined the dancers barefoot. At one point, Danny and Kim glided by us. "Not a bad party for a nursing home," she quipped.

When Wild Bob put on Ludacris's "What's Your Fantasy," Uncle Izzy led his 350-pound bride, my aunt Ida, in the twist. "This is the guy who can't commit after sleeping with you for more than a year already?" Izzy asked loudly.

Matthew waved.

"You're next, we all hope," said Aunt Sally. When Uncle Max sat down, she did the bump with our family hairdresser, Ricardo, whom my mother had flown in for the occasion.

Wild Bob played Madonna's remix of "Like a Virgin," and I was pleased to see Elizabeth and Ben trot out onto the dance floor. I was sure it meant I'd won the music round, but Elizabeth still wouldn't look at me. To make myself feel better, I decided that she couldn't be emotionally connected to me and Ben at the same time. So tonight she needed to choose him.

With Ben and Elizabeth on board with the dancing, I nodded to Wild Bob, who launched into the horah. My mother jumped to attention. She took my father by both hands, and they made a circle. All of the sitting Solomon relatives now took to their feet. "Can't wait to dance at your wedding. Hurry up already," Uncle Melech said to me as he breezed by. Uncle Izzy, Aunt Ida, and cousin Eve jumped up, kicking and singing. Everyone held hands and went around, making circles within circles. I caught Pamela Mann peering in at us, then running out again.

"What if she doesn't hate music as much as she hates Jews?" I asked.

"It's almost over. You look beautiful." Matthew patted my knee.

While Wild Bob continued the Hebrew medley, Ben's friends commenced with the ancient rite of lifting the bride and groom up on chairs. Aunt Sally handed Elizabeth a white scarf, showing her the custom of waving the *shmate* in the air until the groom could grab onto the other end. They bounced up and down in their raised chairs, bonded by the silky white fabric, which Ben caught hold of. Everyone gathered around, applauding, and Elizabeth looked absolutely delighted by the attention. Try doing that to flute music, honey.

"I hope she doesn't fall off there," said Elizabeth's niece Katie, an eight-year-old cutie I'd met at the rehearsal dinner the night before, as she sidled up to me on the edge of the dance floor.

"What an idiotic custom," I told her, shaking my head. I wondered if any brides or grooms had ever died that way. Or broken bones, or fractured anything. "That's a pretty dress you have on."

"We got it at the mall yesterday. I wanted a black dress like yours, but Mom said black was too morbid for a wedding."

"I hate weddings," I admitted.

"'Cause you're not married?" Katie asked, pulling on the bow at her waist.

"Is it that obvious?" I laughed. What Elizabeth's side lacked in social grace they obviously made up for with candor. "Probably just sour grapes."

"You're funny." Katie stared at me like she'd just discovered a fascinating alien. "Where are you from, anyway?"

"I was born in Illinois," I said. "But now I live in New York."

"My aunt Lizzie lived in New York, but now she's moving to Illinois," she said.

It took me a second to remember that Aunt Lizzie was Katie's name for Elizabeth, the not-so-blushing bride. "Yeah, I know. Ben's my brother. I introduced them."

Katie glanced at the Nikon and Canon in my hands, and at the flash hanging around my neck. "Lizzie used to take pictures," she added.

I nodded, aiming my lens at Elizabeth as she was being lifted up and down on her chair in the center of the crowd. She was laughing in the air, regal and triumphant as Queen Esther, my entire loud kooky clan clapping and swirling around her. The flash went off three times.

Then Katie turned to me and said, "So you guys just switched lives?"

I looked at the kid. Wow. She was right; we had. I'd replaced Elizabeth as an assistant at *Vision* magazine and was taking her place as an up-and-coming shutterbug on the Manhattan photography scene. Now she was wearing the traditional dress meant for me, filling my role with the Solomons in Illinois. I stared up at my friend, her face lit with joy. I'd never seen her laughing and smiling so much. She'd never been this happy. I did want her to be happy. How wonderful that something I'd done had made such a difference. "You're one of the magic people," she'd told me.

Putting down the camera, I grabbed three glasses of champagne from the passing waiter's tray and downed them. With the additional Moët seeping into my bloodstream, the switching-lives story became more mystical as it wound around my mind. Tonight was changing the course of everything. Elizabeth was moving west to marry a doctor like my father while I was following in her father's footsteps back East. I couldn't help but wonder who'd gotten the better deal as I aimed my camera one last time at the woman of the hour.

When Wild Bob spun a bunch of James Brown songs, my parents' friends—the Radlows, the Adlers, and the Siskins—all got down and boogied. My mother grabbed Matthew to dance with her. Uncle Melech, an eighty-two-year-old widower, took Pamela Mann's hand. She was flustered at first as he led her to the dance floor. Then she took off her blazer and started twisting and shaking, looking delighted.

"Hey, guys," Kim said as she and Danny sidled in next to us. "Three Rusty Nails and Mother Superior can shake it." She pointed at Pamela Mann, who was now doing a combination of the bump and the tango with Uncle Melech, who tapped his knee to her hip, then dipped her.

"Oh my God, we might actually be having fun," I told Danny.

Then the music stopped. In the middle of a song. I worried that the storm had caused a blackout, or that someone had tripped on the plug. But out stepped another white-haired Rye lady named Bunny. Where had she come from? Didn't any of these women believe in hair dye? Bunny held the plug in her hand.

"The Women's Club closes at nine," Bunny announced to all the guests halted in mid-dance moves. "It is now nine thirty-three."

"You're closing the club at nine o'clock on Saturday night in the middle of my brother's wedding?" I yelled toward the stage, about to bash Bunny's face in.

"The club closes at nine," Bunny repeated. "It's a Rye city ordinance."

"Let's just go," Matthew said, shuffling me to the coatroom to calm down.

"Why? She's wrong!"

"I know. But we don't really want to fight with a Westchester psycho-WASP named Bunny, do we?"

"No," I agreed. "Let's get out of here. Plus, if Uncle Izzy asks when I'm getting married one more time, I'm going to pull that rug off his head."

"Your relatives are supposed to insult and demean you," he said. "That's their job."

His voice and his arm around my shoulder made me feel better. But I didn't want him to protect me from my family. I wanted him to be part of the family I needed protection from. "You're coming to the brunch with me tomorrow, aren't you?" I asked.

"Ricky, there's something I have to talk to you about," he said, turning me to face him.

I looked at him anxiously, my heart racing. Was he reading my mind? Now that we'd survived two weddings together, the timing couldn't have been better for him to finally offer his hand.

"I got an offer today for a Fox pilot," he reported.

"In LA?" I managed to eke out, and he nodded. "When are you leaving?"

"On Monday."

It wasn't the news I'd hoped for. Yet it wouldn't be so horrible to move to California for a while, like Elizabeth. "I could freelance on the West Coast for now," I offered. "If we get a two-bedroom, I could set up a darkroom there."

He looked down at the floor, avoiding my eyes. "Ricky, listen, you're a really great girl. But I'm not sure how the job is going to pan out yet. I'm not ready to live together or make a commitment."

I was a really great girl? Holy shit. I'd been monogamous for thirteen months, assuming our link was leading to something special. If not marriage this minute, than at least shacking up. But this guy really couldn't even commit to living in sin!

"You don't expect me to hang on and do long-distance indefinitely?" I blurted out.

"No. I don't expect that," he said even more noncommittally. "I'll get our coats."

I went back to the table, trying not to burst into tears, searching for my camera bag, which was lurking under a chair. I slung it over my shoulder. With all the extra flashes and film, the bag felt heavier than usual. I tottered toward the door, sure the damn heels had given me a blister. Before we took off for good, I surveyed the happy wedding scene one last time, knowing I'd never return here. Elizabeth had nailed the love of her life on the night I lost mine.

chapter sixteen
second chance
November 30, 2002

I was staring at the latest draft of my ten-page letter to Matthew, who hadn't called, e-mailed, or texted in three weeks, when the doorman buzzed to say I had a package. I imagined red roses from LA, with the urgent confession: "I can't live without you. I'm moving back to New York so we can elope." Instead I found Hanukkah presents from my mother, sent from her favorite Highland Park clothing boutique, Marlene's Designs.

Inside were two sweaters. One was a purple cardigan with pink trim, the other a turquoise pullover. Instead of giving me her cherished wedding gown, she was overcompensating by gifting her old-maid daughter with Jewburban rainbow gear. Deciding I would rather pay my phone and electric bill next month than own two more hideously colored sweaters from Mrs. Sunshine, I called Marlene's Designs in Highland Park.

Marlene's assistant put me on hold for eight minutes, then said, "Sorry, hon. Return policy is five days."

I went to my closet and examined all the clothes my mother had sent me since I'd moved to New York. Each had its own bad memory. I took out the red satin blouse with bow I'd worn for my interview at *Interview*, with the beige Armani skirt suit Mom had mailed. I had thought I looked sophisticated. The editor in chief—who was wearing camouflage pants and army boots—thought I was a salesperson and sent me down to advertising.

I held up the gray potato sack dress my mother had sent for Ben and Elizabeth's rehearsal dinner. It was bad enough being single and broke, watching Elizabeth win everything: the ring, the wedding, a successful doctor husband, my oldest brother. But I had to do it looking like the Goodyear blimp on stilts.

I removed two Donna Karan dresses, a purple Betsey Johnson blazer, a cotton sundress with a bolero jacket, the hot pink angora sweater that shed, a fox coat, and the full-length seal fur she'd given me for my last birthday.

"People who wear dead animals are emotionally depraved," I'd told her. "Animal activists spray-painted three women in fur outside Bergdorf's last week."

"Fur's back in," she said. "And since when do you go uptown?"

"Face it," I screamed. "I'm just a schlump! The only thing I'll ever wear is jeans and black sweaters."

I laid everything out—this wardrobe of another woman, the daughter my mother always wanted. It was time to get rid of her. I Googled the address for the Upper East Side resale shop called Second Chance.

"Good-bye, fox and seal," I told the hideous pelts.

"Elizabeth would die for those," I imagined my mother saying.

"So give them to her!" I planned to tell her. "You already gave her your bridal gown and your blessing."

"She has a good husband to take care of her," Mom would tell me. "You're the one who can barely afford your rent and can't even keep a long-distance boyfriend."

"Wearing a pastel blouse with a bow and four-inch heels is going to bring him back? I can't even walk in these shoes! How do you expect me to get to the subway?"

"We couldn't wait to get out of the Lower East Side!" she'd yell back. "You moved there to spite us."

"I should have been born here!" I retorted.

I continued the screaming match with myself as I put on my jeans, a Gap sweater, and black cowboy boots. I collected the fancy clothes into a big hanging suitcase and sat on it to zip it up. I kicked it downstairs and out the door, trying to hail a cab on the corner. No dice. I schlepped the suitcase to Seventh Avenue, feeling as desperate as an immigrant pawning family heirlooms. Finally, a cab. When I reached the shop, I lugged the suitcase up the stairs. The saleswoman was heavy, with short red hair. She reminded me of Aunt Ida.

I spread my clothes on the counter, as instructed. Ida II inspected the stash, checking hems, turning sleeves inside out, making two piles. She held up the beige Armani.

"The top is size six, the bottom size eight," she said.

"The pieces were sold separately," I explained.

"How many women do you know who wear a size eight bottom and a size six top?" she asked.

"Thousands," I said.

She put the two Karan dresses to the side. "These are fine."

The Karans were okay, thank God.

She went through the sweaters and stopped at the two my mother had just sent. "We'll definitely take these." She folded them neatly, as if she planned to take them home with her. Then she stared at the seal and said, "This really isn't our favorite fur." She checked the label. "Well, maybe."

I was sure selling all the clothes would bring me thousands.

Yet she discreetly wrote a number on a card she slipped me that said $240. My heart sank, but the amount would at least cover the phone and electric bills. Then she said, "It's on consignment. When we sell it, we'll send you a check. If it doesn't sell in four months, you have two days to retrieve it or we throw it out."

I tried to look on the bright side. My mother's taste would never threaten my closet again. I'd taken control of my own space. I'd have more room for my camera equipment, prints, and old negatives. Mission accomplished.

"And these items we won't be needing." Ida pointed to the second pile, more than half the stuff.

"Half price?" I asked. She shook her head.

I repacked my rejected garments and lugged the half-full suitcase down the creaky stairs, taking the subway home. In my apartment, I spread the hanging suitcase on the floor so the clothes I would never wear wouldn't wrinkle. It looked like a dead body. I turned off the light and sank into the couch, shutting my eyes. In a day dream I wasn't wearing anything and Matthew was whispering, "You look so beautiful."

When the phone rang, I jumped up, sure it was him calling from LA. Rushing to grab it, I tripped over the suitcase and fell. The answering machine picked up.

"Honey, it's me," Mom's voice said. "Marlene's assistant didn't realize you were my daughter. I explained it. She'll extend the return policy for a week and send you cash. The sweaters were two hundred and fifty dollars each, so mail them back right away. Sorry they weren't your style. I bought the same ones for Elizabeth and they looked great on her."

chapter seventeen
playing doctor
January 17, 2003

One hour after I informed Mom it was definitely over with Matthew, she left a message that her friend Lois had given my number to Abram Silver, a thirty-five-year-old Chicago neurosurgeon visiting New York for a conference. He sounded too old, too conservative, and too Midwest for me. But I felt so rejected and lonely, I figured I'd go out with him once, just in case I decided to get a lobotomy, marry a Jewish doctor, move back to Highland Park, have 2.3 children, and become the daughter my mother always wanted after all. "What do you have to lose that you haven't lost already?" she asked.

I told Abram to meet me at the White Horse Tavern, keeping my expectations low. So I was pleasantly stunned to find a good-looking guy with a nice build, about five foot ten. His hair was too short and he was nerdy, but he had sexy blue eyes with long lashes and a kind half smile. He seemed overdressed in a cashmere blazer and khakis.

"I hope this place isn't too dingy," I said, leading him through the packed, woodsy, rowdy bar to a table in the back. I suddenly wished I'd worn something hotter than blue jeans and my Old Navy black sweater.

"No, what a fun scene." He nodded in approval. "I read that Dylan Thomas drank himself to death here."

I was impressed that he knew about the White Horse. Danny said the neurosurgeons he knew were intensely reclusive odd-balls. That came from doing so many long operations on patients who were severely disabled, paralyzed, or in vegetative states. But so far Abram Silver didn't appear to be too odd. What was I missing? When the waitress came, I asked for wine and a salad. Abram ordered a beer and a hamburger, which I liked; he seemed to be a regular guy like my brothers. He spoke with a slight Slavic accent I hadn't detected during our very brief phone con-versation.

"So Lois told me you're a photographer in the Village," he said.

I nodded. "Where are you from? Chicago?"

"I was born in Russia. But after my father died when I was eight, we moved to Chicago, where my mother had relatives."

"I'm sorry about your dad," I said. "That must have been some culture shock."

"Yes, I barely spoke English. I was originally Avraham Silvo-novitz, but my third-grade science teacher couldn't pronounce it. I think I became a doctor to spite him."

"My father and brother are doctors."

"Really?" He lit up.

Since the thought of falling for a nice Jewish physician from Illinois was so thoroughly ridiculous, I decided to be honest, to freak him out now and get it over with. "I've always detested doctors," I added. "Except shrinks."

"You should talk to your shrink about that." He grinned.

"I already have. Come on, admit it. Most doctors are closed-off myopic egomaniacs. Last time I was home my father diagnosed all the pictures in my Diane Arbus book, saying, 'I don't call pictures of sick people art.'"

He laughed heartily. "Good one! Though I happen to love Arbus. Middle-class rebellion, that stubborn insistence on seeing the ugly."

A neurosurgeon versed in Arbus? I tried to hide my shock. Tell me what's wrong with you now, I wanted to ask. What's your fatal flaw? Why couldn't I see it? "Lois said you're going through a divorce," I said. "That must be hard." I shouldn't like him too much, since he could wind up back with his wife.

"Yes, bad breakup." He nodded.

I pulled out a cigarette, assuming a doctor like my brothers would tell me to put it out. Instead he lit it for me. I noticed he had long, graceful, slender fingers, thinner than mine. This guy was full of surprises. "Don't I get the whole saga? How your wife didn't understand you and stopped sleeping with you?"

"Big-city women are pushy and obnoxious, no?" He hit my arm playfully.

"Midwest men are conservative and evasive, yes?" I winked.

"What do you want me to reveal?"

"What's your ex's name?" I finished my wine and signaled the waitress for another. "Where did you meet her?"

"I met Caroline at Yale. We'd both just started medical school. We were so busy, we never saw each other, so we decided to get married."

"How old were you?"

"Twenty-four."

Married young, like my brothers. Bad sign, as if he was too insecure to be alone. He took my cigarette from the ashtray and hit it. Good sign, as if he didn't mind his mouth on my saliva. When the salad and hamburger arrived, he asked for a side order of fries and another Heineken. Alcohol, fried food, and cigarettes—another item in the plus category.

After we finished eating, I asked, "So how'd you screw up your marriage?"

"We were fine during our residency at New Haven hospital. Then we had two kids, a boy and a girl. I offered to get full-time help, but Caroline completely gave up medicine. She began cooking and baking, hounding me to make more money. I was bringing in two hundred thousand a year; that wasn't enough for her. She stayed home all day, wearing sweatpants and an apron. Total regression."

Great sign, since I was a serious apronless working woman and planned to stay that way.

"And yes, you're right," he added. "She didn't understand me and stopped sleeping with me. We turned out to be completely incompatible."

"Why do men always figure this out *after* they have children?" I asked.

"Oh, because we're all swine. Or stupid, immature little boys. Look, I feel guilty about it. But I also feel very free," he said. "I had to be so serious so early. Now I want to chill out, have some fun."

"Does fun consist of sleeping with tons of women?" Was I next on his list?

"Thousands. I have a whole harem," he teased.

"When did you split up?" I stole a few fries, dipping them in his ketchup.

"A year and a half ago. It's been hectic. The divorce isn't final yet. I've been living with my mom since I left," he said.

"Living with your mother? Don't tell me—she cooks your favorite foods, does your laundry, and thinks you're God. I bet she understands you."

"Are you always such a bitch?" He smirked. "Lois said you just had your own breakup. Let's hear your pathetic story."

"We went out for a while but it was long-distance. He was basically a nice guy," I said, attempting evasiveness for once, putting out my cigarette.

"Did he break your heart?" he wanted to know.

"Nothing so dramatic," I lied.

"How long have you been smoking?" he asked.

"I know, it's a terrible habit. I should quit." I lit another one. "My father's an oncologist."

"What's his name?"

"Joseph Solomon."

"Not *the* Joe Solomon who's Rush Hospital's chief of medicine?"

I nodded.

"I know your father. I work for him!" he said. "He's the funniest guy around. He's a riot!"

Abram's knowing my father felt strange. But the fact that he found Dad hilarious really floored me. "You think he's funny?"

"You're Joe Solomon's daughter. Too wild. What a great guy." He shook his head. "Now that you mention it, I can see the family resemblance."

I finished my wine, buzzed and a bit creeped out.

"What are you doing tomorrow night?" he asked. "Want to go out again?"

Was it my imagination or was he more animated now that he knew who my dad was? "You're still a married father of two," I said. "Who lives in Chicago."

"My kids are in New Haven with Caroline now. I'm thinking about moving east to be closer to them."

"Really?" I tried not to sound excited by the prospect. He wasn't doing it, he was merely thinking about it. I barely knew the guy. I hated doctors. And geography had just ruined one relationship. I didn't want to make the same romantic mistake all over again. I should at least aim for a different kind of mistake.

"Well, I need to get out of Highland Park. It's suffocating. Everyone knows everyone. It's too much," he said. "I have relatives in New York who are affiliated with Mount Sinai. One of my cousins, Nachamah, keeps telling me that I belong here."

"When will you be officially divorced?" I asked.

"It should be final in a few months. Come on, you have to see me tomorrow night. Let's go to the theater. Or Soho. Or Chinatown."

"Was your father a doctor too?"

"Yes. Why?" he asked.

"Just wondering."

We made a second date for the next night. But from the way his eyes lit up at the mention of my dad, I wondered if Abram didn't want a new wife, but a physician father to replace the one he'd lost. I couldn't help but fear that I'd somehow managed to create another triangle.

Ever since she and Ben had returned from their honeymoon, Elizabeth was my best pal again, e-mailing and leaving long cheerful phone messages, as if our emotional turbulence at her wedding could be excused as temporary bridal insanity. I was sure that she would encourage my connection with a Midwest surgeon, following in her footsteps. But when I phoned to share the scoop on Abram, she said, "He's thirty-five years old and lives with his mother."

"I know. But that's because his father died and he's going through a rough divorce. It's only been a year and a half."

"He's thirty-five years old and lives with his mother," she repeated.

"But he's a doctor, like Ben," I retorted.

"My husband was living in his own house when he was twenty-four," she reminded me.

"How did it go with Abram Silver?" my mother asked when she called an hour later.

"He's thirty-five years old and lives with his mother."

"I know," she said. "Elizabeth told me."

"He is cute," I admitted.

"Maybe taking care of his widowed mom means he's a mensch," she offered.

It might have been sweet if taking care of his mother wasn't juxtaposed with deserting his wife and kids. Then again, unlike Matthew, at least Abram could get himself a wife and kids, even if he didn't stay with them.

"Oh, Abram knows Dad from the hospital," I threw in.

"You like a doctor who works at Rush?" she asked, sounding stunned. "If I tell your father, he'll go into cardiac arrest."

For our second date I told Abram to meet me at my apartment. I wore a tight knee-length black skirt, hose, and high heels this time. I knew I was in trouble when I put on hose for a guy. He showed up with a bunch of purple lilacs. How did he know I liked lilacs? I put them in a vase and turned on a mellow Norah Jones CD.

"Nice music," he said. "You're more traditional than you let on."

"I don't have a traditional bone in my body!" What was he talking about? I'd always had a postmodern, avant-garde, radical sensibility. Anti-establishment. Anti-religion. I handed him a Heineken (which I'd picked up for him at the Korean deli), poured myself wine, and draped myself over the arm of one of the blue couches Lois had sent—along with the neurosurgeon to sit on them. Abram sat on the other end, too far away.

"I meant it as a compliment." He'd seemed so interested the night before, but now he already needed space.

"Do you have pictures of your kids?" I asked.

He handed me two from his wallet. They were professionally taken, a little too posed. But the kids were adorable. He also showed me a picture of his mother. Then he absentmindedly left his wallet on the cushion next to him.

"You're already putting your mom and kids between us." I pointed.

He looked at the photos beside him, then at me, and said, "So we both like to stick our fingers in other people's heads."

After two more fun yet confusing New York dates where we kissed passionately but kept all our clothes on, Abram returned to Chicago. My mother sent me a plane ticket for my twenty-seventh birthday, so I flew home for the weekend. On Saturday Abram drove up my parents' driveway in a red Jaguar with the windows wide open, playing the Norah Jones CD I'd bought him and holding a dozen roses. What a sweepingly romantic gesture.

As I went to find a vase for the flowers, my father rushed upstairs from his den to shake Abram's hand and—from what I could gather—get an update on a patient they'd shared.

"Ependymoma?" Dad asked.

"Choroid plexus papilloma," Abram answered.

"Better. What's Pressner saying?"

"We should wait for the tumor to declare itself." Abram rolled his eyes as if this was the dumbest thing he'd ever heard. "Right. A thirty-eight-year-old needs seizures and intracranial pressure like he needs a hole in the head."

My father laughed at this apparent brain cancer joke, then said, "You're going in?"

Abram nodded a definitive yes. "You kidding? Monday morning it's out."

"Good man," my father said, patting him on the back, adding, "Have a nice time, kids," before bouncing back downstairs to his den.

After that incomprehensible medical chatter, Abram and I were off, cruising around my old neighborhood. It was liberating to be out of New York, speeding down the highway with the roof down and the wind tangling my hair. Unable to turn off the fast-forward button in my brain, I couldn't help but find humor in the potential scene. How bizarre would it be to end up wed to a neurosurgeon who drove a red Jaguar convertible and worked with my father?

"What a cool car," I heard myself saying, suddenly morphing into a materialistic air brain.

"I know. I bought it for myself after the divorce. I always wanted a red Jaguar," he said. "Where do you want to go?"

"It's forty degrees." I turned the music lower. "You should put the top up. I'm freezing."

At the light, I gave him a deep, juicy kiss that made my feet tingle. Or maybe it was frostbite. I put my hand on his leg. He had skinny thighs. Could I really sleep with a man who had smaller thighs than I did? Matthew had big guy thighs, which made mine seem thinner. I recalled Elizabeth's funny rule about a man's size: "If his pants are too small for me, he's not getting into mine." Another reason she fell for Ben.

"Want to go to the Water Tower? They have a dessert at the deli there called The Last Time Ever I Saw My Waist. Four Seasons? Road trip to the Motown Museum in Ohio? I'm up for anything," he said. "Your birthday, your call."

"Let's go see my brother," I surprised myself by blurting out. It was a very odd field trip, dropping in on Ben and Elizabeth, who lived a half hour away. But I was only home for a few days, and all of a sudden I felt a strong urge to check in on the newlyweds.

"Shouldn't we be alone?" Abram asked.

"If we're alone, we'll have sex and then I'll freak out, realize we're doomed, get weird, and ruin everything," I told him matter-of-factly.

"Okay. So let's go see Ben and Elizabeth," he said, getting it. I pointed, and he turned down the highway toward Zion. "You want to call to let them know we're stopping by and make sure they're home?"

"Sure," I said, taking out my cell. Elizabeth answered and sounded pleased with the idea.

"So what's your brother like?" Abram asked.

"Ben's loud, confident, warm. You'll love him."

"You said Elizabeth was one of your best friends?" he asked.

"Used to be," I said. "Before she married my brother in my mom's wedding dress and became the daughter my mother always wanted."

"No mixed feelings about their marriage?" He laughed.

He seemed almost as perceptive as my kind of head doctor.

When we arrived at Ben and Elizabeth's house, there was a mezuzah by the door, a little oblong parchment inscribed with a passage from Deuteronomy that religious Jews put on their doorjambs to ward away evil spirits. Since when had Ben turned kosher? I was even more disoriented when he answered the bell wearing beige khakis and a V-neck sweater straight out of the J.Crew catalogue.

"Hey, Mr. Prep!" I said.

"Hey, Sis." He hugged me. "Happy birthday."

"This is Dr. Abram Silver." I hadn't told Ben I was bringing company. I thought he'd be pleased to see me on a date with a doctor for the first time ever. "Want to party with us?"

"I can't," Ben said. "I'm on call."

Elizabeth waltzed out, looking like a Stepford Wife in a cutesy beige smock dress. I'd forgotten this was beige and blue territory.

"Hi, Ricky!" She looked cheerful and amused to see me.

"This is Abram," I said.

"Oh, you brought the neurosurgeon?" she asked, smiling. "Come on in."

Their house looked chaotic, with boxes and suitcases everywhere. Two dogs ran to greet us; they'd gotten another black Lab. The huge StairMaster machine was in the middle of the foyer. No Christmas residue, but I noted a menorah on the shelf.

"Where'd you get that?" I asked.

"Your mother. She showed me how to light the candles and say the prayers," Elizabeth told me.

It was an unusual ritual for somebody I'd secretly feared was borderline anti-Semitic, but I kept my mouth closed. I took out one of the joints Abram had brought for my birthday weekend.

"I quit," she said. "But you go ahead."

So I did. She poured us wine. We drank it but she didn't. Marriage had obviously sobered both of them up. Ben checked his beeper, then said, "We can grab a bite at the club."

I hated country clubs, but theirs wasn't far away and I was starving, so we drove there in Ben's SUV.

"Want some dope for later?" I asked Ben as we walked toward the club's entrance.

"Keep your voice down!" He grabbed my arm, enraged. I pulled my arm away and punched him.

"What the hell's wrong with you?" I asked him.

"How old are you—sixteen?" Ben asked me.

"How old are you? Sixty? Listen, you hypocrite, who are you talking to? I was the first one to ever get you—"

"I know," he cut me off, speaking with his teeth clenched. "But this is a small town. Everyone knows each other and talks."

"Since when do you drive a gray SUV?" I asked Ben.

"You'd prefer I drive a red Jaguar?" he asked condescendingly.

I walked away from him and put my arm in Abram's. "Ben and Elizabeth used to be fun," I told him. "I swear."

At the club it suddenly seemed like they were playing the parents and I'd become their troubled teenager. I ordered a bottle of wine, deciding to become a lush in my old age. Elizabeth and I chose chef salads; Ben and Abram ordered steak.

"So where did you do your training?" My brother began his cross-examination.

"New Haven Hospital," Abram answered.

"I met their chief of medicine at a conference. Sam Margolick. You know him?"

"Sure, I know him. Great guy. He's actually my ex-father-in-law," Abram said buoyantly.

"You're divorced?" Ben asked.

"Well, it isn't quite final yet. Sam's daughter, Caroline, and I were residents together."

"I see." Ben stabbed a pat of butter and spread it on a roll. "So you visited Ricky in New York, I heard."

"Yes, I love New York. I always have such a great time there. When I got back to my hotel last Thursday night, I had a nightcap at the bar," Abram started telling a story. "And this heavy young girl came up to me and—"

"Go to bars a lot?" Ben interrupted.

Abram had aced the hurdle of my father. My oldest brother was a different story altogether. Ben was now looking at him with the expression Dad used to greet my dates in high school, when he'd come to the door in his underwear, smoking an eight-inch cigar.

"She was eighteen and really overweight. She asked me to dance. I felt bad for her," Abram said. "I figured I'd dance once. But then I realized no guy had ever paid attention to her before. So we wound up dancing for an hour—"

"You make a habit out of picking up fat teenage girls?" Ben finished the roll and took another.

"Hey, chill out," I said. "Abram was a husband and father for thirteen years. He's getting divorced. He's allowed to go to a bar." But I also was wondering what the hell Abram was doing picking up fat teenage girls, let alone telling my brother and his brand-new wife about the experience.

"You have kids?" Ben asked.

Oblivious to the third degree, Abram happily pulled out pictures of his kids. "This is my little Shelley," he said. "She's six. My son, Gary, is eight."

"They're really cute," said Elizabeth, finishing a glass of Chablis, then switching to water. Since when did she stop at one drink?

Ben stared at the pictures. "I just read a study that said divorces have a negative effect on kids' health."

"Oh, my parents divorced when I was four and I turned out okay," Elizabeth said.

"Yeah, your family is the picture of health," I couldn't help but mumble.

"That's why I stole your family," she said.

When she went to the ladies' room, I followed, worried about leaving my new guy alone with Ben. But Abram was still in his upbeat divorced mode, everything rolling off him. Walking through the dining room, Elizabeth waved to several older couples having dinner.

"Nice to see you, Mrs. Solomon," someone said. I turned around, looking for my mother. Until I realized they were addressing my sister-in-law.

"You changed your name?" I asked from the stall next to hers.

"I always felt haunted by Mann since everybody knew my father. I prefer my married name now," she said.

I was about to ask why she always had to define herself by men when I flashed to the byline Ricky Silver, which had a nice ring to it. "What do you think of Abram?" I really wanted her to like him.

"He's charming. Nice build," she answered.

"I know. He works out. He's fast, thin, up for anything. And for a medical doctor he seems pretty psychoanalytic."

"So he's the anti-Matthew," she said as we washed our hands next to each other.

Exactly! I'd forgotten how well she knew me. "Plus Abram is capable of having a wife."

"Maybe a few of them," she joked.

At the mirror she pulled out Russian Rose lipstick, I bet from my mother. "Here, you could use some color." She drew a line around my lips. "Good. Now rub it in."

As we drove out of the subdivision, Abram turned up the music.

"Your brother and Elizabeth are great," he said.

"Dr. and Mrs. Republican?" We turned onto a dirt road leading back to the highway. It was ten o'clock. I wondered if my parents were back from their club yet.

"They just got married. They're in the newlywed phase," he argued. "Give them a break."

"You're pretty romantic about marriage for someone who's going through a bad divorce," I said.

"Ben's a young husband who is about to be a doctor," Abram continued. "He's very pleased with himself. He should be."

"He was acting like a condescending asshole," I insisted. "He insulted you all night."

"Ah, he's just protecting his sister. My divorce is a threat to his stability. He's excited about taking care of his wife and kids."

"He doesn't have any kids," I said.

"Look, Ben is right. I'm a thirty-five-year-old father of two. Why am I hanging out in bars and driving a sports car? It is a little crazy," he said at the light, looking at me and winking.

By the time we got back to Highland Park, it was ten thirty.

I was sure my parents were still awake and would want to hang out with us, but I didn't feel up to double-dating with them just yet. I told Abram to pull up in the church parking lot by my house, where we made out passionately. "Want to get crazy?" I asked, putting my hand on his little thigh.

"I do, but I can't. I have to get home," Abram said. "Mother waits up."

Back in New York on Sunday night, I came home to find the light on my answering machine blinking. I secretly hoped it was a Happy Birthday message from Matthew, or at least Abram, saying he already missed me. But it was a message from another man, a more important one: Joris Brecker. He said he loved the slides I'd sent him four months earlier. When I hadn't heard back, I'd assumed I'd embarrassed myself and never followed up. But it turned out he'd shown my downtown street portraits to the owner of the Lacey Jones Gallery in Soho. If I could do more prints, enlarge them, and frame them better, I could have my own show there in the fall! I danced a little jig, punching my arms up in the air and shouting, "Yes!"

Then I called Joris back and left a jubilant message on his machine letting him know that of course I could enlarge and reframe my portraits. I phoned my mother and left a screaming message for her. I tried Nicky, but her voice mail wasn't working. Jane didn't pick up either. Neither did Matthew. Why wasn't anybody home when I had such amazing news? I called Ben to tell him, but Elizabeth answered. I kept forgetting she would now be there all the time. She was family too, and all this was happening because she'd introduced me to her father's agent.

"Joris got me a solo show at the Lacey Jones Gallery!" I blurted out. "They want thirty-six portraits. Can you believe it?"

"I know, Joris told me." She sounded kind of withdrawn. Was she jealous? Since she was the one who'd hooked me up, I wondered if I should offer to share the show with her. Elizabeth had sworn that she'd given up her photography to marry Ben and move to Illinois, but I didn't really believe it. "Oh, your dad says Abram is an excellent doctor. One of the best neurosurgeons in the Midwest."

"You already knew about my show?" I said, almost incredulous.

She didn't say anything.

"You're okay with Joris handling me?"

"Yes, it's great," she said. "I'm just not feeling well."

"What's wrong?" I asked, guessing that my success was affecting her the way her wedding had depressed me.

"Morning sickness," she blurted. "I'm pregnant."

That I wasn't prepared for.

"That's fantastic. Congratulations." I sat down on my bed, pulled out a fat joint, and lit it, looking for more words, but I was shocked silent. A normal person would be thrilled in this situation. I really wanted to be happy for her and Ben, but I felt like I'd just been sucker punched. Was it because she'd stolen my thunder? I recalled the Gore Vidal quote, "Every time a friend succeeds I die a little." But I didn't want to be like that! And Elizabeth was no longer a friend. She was my family.

"I hope it's a boy," she said. "There hasn't been a boy in my family for decades."

That was why she was no longer toking and had had only one glass of wine. Abram had made a reference to Ben's "wife and kids." How had he picked up on it when I'd completely missed it? "So when are you due?"

"October."

"Joris said they were thinking about having the show at the end of September," I told her.

"That might be cutting it too close," she said.

I looked at a calendar. "I could ask for a date right after Labor Day," I offered. "But could you fly then?"

"Sure. It's only an hour-and-a-half flight. The beginning of September would be much better. I'll be fat, but I'll definitely be at your first show," Elizabeth promised. "You know I wouldn't miss it for the world."

chapter eighteen
pearls of wisdom
June 18, 2003

Attending Elizabeth's baby shower and my old classmate Arlene's wedding on the same weekend was my idea of double suburban death. Especially since Arlene's reception was at my former synagogue, where I'd bump into a bunch of married yentas who'd been giving me headaches since high school. Yet I had a sudden idea that might make an Illinois weekend trek into JAP territory more tolerable: I called Abram to be my date.

We'd been e-mailing, and he gave good phone. Yet since he seemed more friendly than sensual, I'd been endlessly analyzing our sexlessness with my court of advisers. Mom thought he was just being a gentleman. Nicky—e-mailing from a shoot in London—declared him psycho. Jane said, "Jerk secretly sleeping with someone else." Andy guessed he was "gun-shy from his bad divorce." Elizabeth said, "He's thirty-five years old and lives with his mother."

I worried that inviting him as my escort to the wedding would make it too obvious I was crazy about him, but he took it in stride.

"Sounds like a plan," he said without hesitation. "I'm in."

"We're all close from the old neighborhood, so my parents are invited too," I threw out, trying to sound casual.

"I would be honored to double-date with your parents," Abram answered. "But the next day is my birthday."

"Oh, you're probably too busy," I tried to backtrack.

"My mother is giving a little family brunch in my honor on Sunday. Will you come?" he asked. "It would mean a lot to me. Really."

"Sure." I envisioned surprising him with a birthday present—myself in a hotel room at the Water Tower for a few hours late Saturday night. I'd jump his bones before meeting Mommie Dearest, then zoom back to the Big Apple before she could check my nice Jewish girl cred too carefully. Since everything was happening for me now—in work and in love—I was ready to handle watching my whole family fawn over the new Solomon growing inside my sister-in-law.

Elizabeth's shower was scheduled for Friday afternoon at two o'clock. (The ladies who lunched obviously didn't work.) Since my mother was busy being the big host, I arranged for a car to pick me up at O'Hare and take me right to the country club, where the luncheon was being held. The nice black pants and black blouse I wore on the plane weren't too wrinkled. When we landed, I tried to dress it up with makeup and jewelry. I expected my mother to call me a schlep.

As I walked into the Highland Hills club, I greeted the New Jersey contingent of Yids—all staying at my parents' house, in the den and in my brothers' old bedrooms, thankfully not mine.

I quickly stashed my duffel bag in the coat check room, taking out the large, triple-wrapped present I'd brought. My mother brought candy baskets with her to parties; my contribution was sour.

"Oh good, honey. You made it early," my mother said.

"Hi, Mom." I kissed her on the cheek.

"You look pretty." She kissed me back.

No insults about my attire. I was almost insulted she hadn't noticed. "I brought you something." I handed her the bag.

She opened it to find a jar of sour dills. "Gus's Pickles on Essex Street. God, this brings back memories." She showed them to Uncle Max.

"Regular or sour?" Max asked.

"Sour," I said.

"Good, *sheyne meydl*. The sours are the best!" Uncle Max patted me on the back for acing the Solomon pickle test. As if I hadn't heard them rave about Gus's my entire life. "The kosher butcher, knish baker, and pickle guys have been there fifty years. That's who you should be taking pictures of, Rachela," Max told me. "All the old Jews still left on the Lower East Side."

"I know, I did. I took your advice," I told him. "Don't you remember I sent you the pictures of the butcher and Ratner's waitress that the *Village Voice* ran?"

"I don't mean in that gay commie rag," he said.

I decided to let his sweet "*sheyne meydl*" cancel out his redneck politics and homophobia.

"I'm using some of the shots for my Soho show." I'd feared the leftover Jews would be too cliché and old-fashioned for such a hip gallery. But Joris said he'd let me hang a few in the back of the room, just to make Uncle Max happy.

"In my day, Broome Street wasn't called Soho. It's the Lower East Side," Max said. "The Realtors are lying."

Decked out in a chic Armani suit and diamonds, my mother

looked both ways, pulled a pickle from the jar, and sank her teeth into it. She then handed it to Max, who finished it in two bites, wiping his lips.

"They always had the best pickles," Max said.

"So Uncle Max, my opening is September eighth. You and Sally will come to the city, right?" I asked him.

"Isn't that right before the high holy days?"

"Seven days before Yom Kippur," I said. "Why does it matter? You're not Orthodox."

"At least he goes to shul," my mother said, piercing me with her laser eyes.

"You don't go to services for the high holidays?" Max shot me another guilt ray. "Since when?"

"Since forever," my mother tattled. "Don't you remember, she quit Hebrew school to work on her junior high yearbook? She even refused to have a bat mitzvah."

"What are you talking about? I didn't refuse!" I argued. "You and Dad didn't care about me getting bat mitzvahed. You were too busy planning huge galas for Ben and Danny."

"How could you get bat mitzvahed when you and Nicky called Rabbi Weiner a sexist pig and walked out on his class in seventh grade?" she asked.

Oh yeah. I recalled the clash over our petition to renounce the *mikve*, the women's cleansing bath that implied females were unclean after menstruation.

"Of course we cared," my mother added. "It broke our hearts."

I once joked to Nicky I was going to make a mockumentary about my and my mother's conflicted views of my childhood, *Rashomon with Rugelach*.

Walking down the hall, I bumped into Elizabeth, who was wearing a black knee-length dress, black hose, and pearls. Her hair was swept up. She looked classy and thin except for her protruding stomach. She surprised me with a big hug and said, "Thanks for flying in."

I hugged her back, then checked out her prim, high-necked silk dress. "Very chic."

"Your mother bought it for me. She did my makeup too. The hair is Ricardo. You were right—he has magic hands." She showed me her French braid in the back. "He can even fix my mousy hair." More than halfway through her pregnancy, she looked like one of the ladies who lunched. I fingered the pearls around her neck.

"From Ben," she said. "He can't wait to be a father. He gave me the necklace last week, with an e. e. cummings poem."

"Since when does Ben know who e. e. cummings is?" I asked. "Which poem?"

"'I like my body when it is with your body,'" she said, blushing.

Out of thousands of cummings's poems, my brother had chosen one that had deeper meaning if the woman was pregnant. I'd never thought of it that way.

"You don't know everything about Ben," she said.

Apparently I didn't.

"She's carrying the latest member of the Solomon tribe," Aunt Sally piped in, putting her arm around Elizabeth.

Sally was wearing a purple skirt and a glitter top, her hair in a high bouffant. She was Uncle Max's second wife. I'd seen pictures of his first wife, whom my mother called a "cold, classic raven-haired beauty," who'd died when he was in his fifties. When Max turned sixty-three I was surprised that he married Sally, a loud, flamboyant blonde with a Queens accent who loved discos and Atlantic City. Though everyone had met at the wedding weekends, I worried Elizabeth would clash when spending more time with the Solomons' brazen New Jersey sect. But she and Sally held hands and walked inside.

"Hey, Joe, did you see Gus's pickles?" Izzy asked my father when he walked in.

"Regular or sour?" my father asked, grabbing one.

It was an all-girl lunch. But God forbid my mother ever turn away a hungry man. So while the women baby-showered in the back room, she insisted Uncle Max and Uncle Izzy have lunch in the front room with my father. Ben and Danny were too busy working to come. I was actually hurt that my workaholic dad had left the hospital early for such a froufrou occasion. When he was younger, hospital emergencies had kept him from most of my school events and birthday parties. My mother once let slip that he'd missed my actual birth—at his own hospital! He'd apparently hurried in a few minutes after I'd appeared, just in time to pose with Mom and me for my first picture.

When they weren't looking, I snapped a few shots of the patriarchs in the front room while they ate, smoked cigars, and conversed seriously, as if participating in an ancient tribal ritual. Then I turned my film to the female brigade: Jane, Betsy, Elizabeth's mother, her sister Michelle, and Michelle's daughters, who had all driven in from New York to be with Elizabeth for this special occasion. Aunt Sally, Aunt Ida, and cousin Eve walked in with my sister-in-law Kim and we gathered in the back room, where the girl-power shower was being held. Alas, the room wasn't ready yet. The harried waitress asked us to give her fifteen minutes to set it up. Mom offered to show the Westchester and Jersey troops around the club. I declined the tour, went out to sneak a cigarette instead.

When I came back, I noticed Aunt Sally and Elizabeth sipping sodas at a small table in the bar area, sitting side by side. I slinked over to eavesdrop on their intense-looking tête-a-tête.

"Well, I never called him Max, mind you. I always called him Mr. Goodman." Sally was telling the story of how she'd met my uncle. "This was the nineteen fifties, remember. I was a divorced single mother working as a receptionist. He was my boss, tall and handsome and much older than I was. I knew he was a widower. I was scared of him. When he walked in the first day he looked at me and said, 'Who the hell is that?' and I started crying."

"That wasn't nice of him," Elizabeth said. "He was a little gruff around the edges. Like Ben."

Glad they were getting along, I sat down at the table too and ordered a diet soda.

"How long did you know him before it caught fire?" Elizabeth wanted to know.

"I worked for him for a decade and we barely spoke. I'm alone, he's alone," Sally said. "One night he says, 'I have theater tickets. Want to go?' I called my mother and said, "Mommy, Mr. Goodman wants to go to the theater. What should I do?' She says, 'Hurry. Get a new dress!' I didn't have any money. I borrowed a blue dress from my friend Lorraine. The show was Cole Porter. It seemed magical."

"Ben took me to the theater on our first date too!" Elizabeth piped in. "What a romantic first date. It did seem like magic."

Interesting that she'd wiped out the memory that I was the one who set up the double date. It made me sad that less than a year later she and Ben were thriving but Matthew was history. I couldn't help but feel that Elizabeth had done something right while I'd screwed up my love life again. Maybe I should stop chasing after liberal artist types. I bet men with normal jobs, like Ben and Max, were more the marrying type.

"Afterward, we went to dinner and he tells me, 'Look, I'm no spring chicken. I've been alone ten years,'" Sally continued. "He says 'I have a nice house in Fair Lawn and you and your son could move in if you want.' I was shocked and said, 'Why, Mr. Goodman, I couldn't ever do that.' And he says 'I mean, only if you want to get married.' He went by the book. I was so stunned I said, 'Yes, Mr. Goodman.' I couldn't believe it."

"I didn't have anything—two pairs of ripped underwear," Sally continued. "I was living with my mother and son in a one-bedroom in Bayside. I couldn't believe someone like Mr. Goodman would even take me to dinner."

"I know. Everything in your world changes," Elizabeth said with a tear in the corner of her eye. She took Sally's hand.

"One *good man* to take care of me." Sally emphasized the wordplay. "And since then he has. He was my *bashert*, which means my destiny. He gave me a new life."

I wanted my *bashert* too. Elizabeth and Sally both moved to their men's cities and into their houses. I wondered if I'd have to relocate to Illinois, like Elizabeth, to land Abram. Was that the sacrifice I'd have to make to get married? Was it worth it?

"A new life." Elizabeth nodded again.

I was stunned that Elizabeth was identifying with Sally's story. Was that how she felt about Ben? That he was a good man who had given her a new life? I was touched that she saw my brother as her hero. She'd never told me that before. Fearing she was a gold digger, I was pleasantly relieved to hear how much she really loved him, after all.

"Mr. Goodman knew what I'd been through," Sally added. "When we went to Sears after we were married, he insisted on buying me twenty pairs of panties. Just to have extra and not worry. He understood. This doesn't make sense, but he even made the past better."

"I know, I know," Elizabeth told her. "When I used to go out to dinner with my father as a kid, he never had enough money. So I was afraid to order. Because anything I chose on the menu could be wrong and embarrass him. For our first dinner date, Ben took me to this fancy French restaurant. I choked when ordering. I thought he'd tease me when I didn't know whether to get the veal or the fish. But Ben said, 'Let's get both and share,' and ordered a whole bunch of appetizers and four desserts."

"Max was the same way. Now, that's a real man," Sally said. "And I bet you enjoyed that meal the best."

"Yes!" Elizabeth raised her voice, nodding enthusiastically.

"See, they know where you come from, so they make you feel at ease," Sally told me.

So that was why Elizabeth never knew what food she should order at restaurants. I felt like a mean shrew for judging her flaky and making fun of that trait. With my penchant for psychoanalysis, how had I missed that one? See, true love did exist in the world, and it would heal your past pain. I had to stop being so cynical.

My mother arrived, carrying two candy trays, and led us all to the back room. I took a picture of Elizabeth with mom, the chocolate centerpieces, and Aunt Sally, who'd never told me that story. Then again, I'd never asked.

After lunch, we sat around while Elizabeth unwrapped her presents. There was a playpen, several crib toys, and baby clothes. Then she held up a pink Victoria's Secret box. Inside was a low-cut red silk teddy.

"That's from me," Sally yelled out. "So you'll be a red-hot mama."

"It's gorgeous." Elizabeth held it up against her. Underneath were hand-embroidered baby pajamas.

"Something for the baby too," Sally said.

Elizabeth held up the gift from my mother, a set of nursing bras with a check inside the cleavage. Sensing my discomfort, she whispered that Elizabeth had requested the special bras, which kind of creeped me out. I just wanted to know how much the check was for.

"This is from my sister-in-law Ricky, a photographer who flew in all the way from New York," Elizabeth said when she got to my present—a large black cashmere sweat suit from Saks, with a drawstring waist. "It's perfect. Thank you. We're all going to Ricky's big opening in Soho at September eighth, at the Lacey Jones Gallery," she announced.

I smiled at her, thinking what a total bitch I'd been. I'd been so envious of the attention paid to her wedding and pregnancy. Yet she didn't begrudge me acclaim for my show in the least. She was so content she was no longer competitive. If Nicky's adage was true and unhappy people had nothing to give, then those getting what they wanted could obviously afford to be generous.

Walking out to the parking lot later, everyone helped carry the presents to Elizabeth's car.

"Did you know that I used to take pictures too, Ricky?" Uncle Max asked me. "I was the oldest, like you. We're the historians."

"That's right, he was always taking pictures," Izzy confirmed. "Annoyed the hell out of me. Whenever you weren't looking. In the morning. When I had food in my mouth. Snap. Snap. I once almost bashed his camera."

"Yeah, and now who comes over and always wants to steal my copies?" Max asked his younger brother.

"Rachel, when are you getting married already?" Ida asked.

"Shut up. She has a big double date with that Jewish surgeon of hers tomorrow night," said Cousin Eve.

"So Ricky, you finally got the sister you've always wanted," Sally called out.

I glanced over and noticed Elizabeth walking slowly between Sally and Ida, holding their arms. I'd never been a big fan of having ladylike grace, but the way Elizabeth treated my relatives got to me. She'd looked beyond their loud exteriors and saw how kind and good they were underneath. She was helpful, charming, enhancing a family event in ways I'd never imagined Elizabeth could do.

After hugging and kissing everyone good-bye, I went over to her. "Thanks for being so sweet to the New Jersey gang."

"Thanks for that great sweat suit. Though I know you really flew in to see Abram," Elizabeth teased.

Was she right? Uh-oh. If so, would that wreck my *bashert* karma?

"Have you slept with him yet?" she asked.

Some things never changed. I was actually relieved.

"I might surprise him with a hotel room," I confided, all of a sudden seeing a connection between the *Les Miz* foursome that brought Elizabeth and Ben together and this big double date with my parents. Maybe if a man saw you with your family, he'd want to join the gang?

"You can always move back here and be like me and your mom after all," she said.

God forbid was the first thought that came to my mind. But maybe for someone as great as Abram I would consider it. Elizabeth certainly liked it better here.

"His mother is giving him a birthday brunch on Sunday he invited me to," I told her. "But don't tell anyone."

"I just don't get why he's still living with his mother after a year and a half," she said. "Oh. Hey." She put her hand on her belly. "The baby's kicking. Feel." She put my hand there, and I could feel the thrusting. "We found out it's a boy," she whispered. "He'll be a Solomon, really related to you. He'll have your blood."

chapter nineteen
tying the knot
June 28, 2003

"So what are you wearing to Arlene's wedding tonight?" my mother asked on Saturday afternoon. We were on our way to pick up her dry cleaning and exchange duplicate diaper bags Elizabeth had received at her shower.

"My black dress with the eyelet sleeves."

"Oh no. Not that *shmate?*" Mom shrieked. "It's four years old. Did you roll it up like last time? I'm sure it's all wrinkled."

"Who cares?" I opened my window halfway and lit a cigarette.

"Stop smoking." She put her window down all the way. "What time is Abram coming?"

"Not till eight thirty.

"Don't smoke in front of him."

"He's already seen me smoke," I said.

"You can't wear that dress." I noticed she was suddenly driving faster. I looked at the dashboard. She was going seventy-five miles per hour in a fifty-five zone. My mother cut across three lanes and got on the highway.

"Becoming a speed freak in your old age?" I asked. "Where are we going?"

"To the mall to get you a new black dress for tonight," she said.

"You know, I'm not even sleeping with him yet." I inhaled deeply, blew the smoke out the window.

"I know. Elizabeth told me," she said. "Is that good or bad?"

"I don't know," I admitted. I flipped through the radio stations.

"Buying his mother the house and moving in because she's afraid to live alone is being a good son," my mother argued.

"He'll be thirty-six tomorrow. And he left his wife and kids in another house," I reminded her.

"I heard that she had an affair on him." My mother turned off the radio. "Besides, your father said Abram is a brilliant neurosurgeon."

"Dad would pay him to marry me," I said matter-of-factly.

"He would not." She rolled her eyes.

"Dad told me he would."

"He was kidding." My mother veered into the mall's huge parking lot.

"He wasn't kidding." I tossed my half-smoked cigarette out the window. I didn't tell her I was meeting Abram's mother at his birthday party on Sunday, fearing she'd send an engagement announcement to *The Jewish News*.

Walking into Neiman Marcus, she looked snazzy in her mint green knee-length skirt and blouse. Her shoes and handbag were mint too. The only thing that wasn't mint was her red hair and the purple and red Hermès scarf around her neck. She led me right to evening wear and waved at the woman behind the counter, another well-coiffed woman in her fifties.

"Anne, this is my daughter, Rachel."

"The photographer from New York?" Anne asked, taking in my cheap Lee jeans, black Gap sweater, and cowboy boots. "This is nice," she said, pinpointing the one semi-expensive object on my body—a slender uneven gold heart pendant on a long black cord. I didn't usually like jewelry, but I'd splurged by spending a hundred dollars on this one-of-a-kind hand-made piece by an Israeli artist I'd met at a street fair. I bought it for myself to celebrate my upcoming show. It seemed unobtrusive and a bit edgy, with the heart's jagged rim. Somehow it just fit me.

"I used to wear it on my sleeve; now I wear it around my neck," I said, but Anne didn't get the joke.

"She needs a dress for a wedding tonight," my mother instructed.

"It has to be black," I said emphatically.

"Size six, low cut, has to be black," my mother said.

"Or size eight, depending on the fit," I threw out.

Hearing the seriousness in Mom's voice, Anne went right to work, first bringing out a tiny beaded mini that would barely cover my upper thighs.

"Too Madonna," I said.

"I thought you liked Madonna," Mom said.

I'd liked Madonna when she wore ripped clothes, slept with everyone in sight, and published photographs of herself having orgies. Not the mommy incarnation. But I just shook my head as Anne brought out a very low-cut strapless silk with sequins and a boa attached.

"A boa?" I said. "What's your Yiddish word—*farputzed*?"

"Arlene's wedding is black-tie. Everyone will be *farputzed*," my mother said. "It's three hundred people, very fancy."

"It's not me," I said, shaking my head. "It's Céline Dion in Vegas."

"So? She's happily married *and* she makes millions. Just try it on," my mother ordered.

"Okay. Okay."

In the dressing room I threw off my clothes and slipped the sequined number over my head, where it got stuck somewhere between my shoulder and elbow, tangling with my necklace. Just then my mother walked in.

"Take off your knee socks," she said, helping to untangle me. "There's a hole in the left one."

For the next three hours, she marched me through Ann Taylor, Lord & Taylor, Marshall Fields, Nicole Miller, Saks, and Bebe in a frenzy, pulling out one overdone black garment after another that I wouldn't be seen dead in. I tried on black boas, sequins, strapless, minis, midis, and maxis, with fringe on the bottom, taffeta on the sleeves, and slits up the sides. When Mom handed me a short, tight, tiny satin Armani with a price tag that said $3,800, I realized what we were really doing here. We were looking for the dress that would bring Dr. Abram to his knees. Literally. Instead of being satiated by two family weddings in a row and Elizabeth's pregnancy, my mother was hungry for more. The wedding and baby shower she was dying to plan were for her only daughter.

Though I hated to disappoint her, I always flunked shopping and was too exhausted to continue. It was hard enough trying to leave my sardonic big-city side at the door for a baby shower and a Jewish wedding in my hometown on the same weekend. I couldn't handle feeling uncomfortable in an ill-fitting, overdone outfit. I'd just tried to sell the frilly clothes she'd bought me to Second Chance and didn't need any more crammed into my minuscule Manhattan closet. To Mom's chagrin, I decided to stick with the four-year-old dress with eyelet sleeves that I already had. We drove back home in silence.

Abram arrived at my parents' house a little early, around eight. My father greeted him at the door, and within seconds the two of them were cursing the high cost of malpractice insurance—their stance was "no money without malice proven."

They went down to my dad's den while upstairs my mother tried to spruce up my black dress with her black velvet shawl and diamond jewelry. I liked how my gold heart looked better, but I'd forgotten where I'd left it.

"We should have bought the Armani." She brushed my bangs out of my eyes like she had when I was a little girl. Then she applied her Russian Rose lipstick to my lips.

"I'll go get Abram," I said. I went downstairs and caught him standing over an anatomy text, next to my father. They were the same height, in matching tuxedos. They both had thick short hair, though my father's was now gray. Had I noticed they looked so much alike before? My God, they could have been father and son.

"Let's take separate cars," I said.

Ever since Nicky and I quit Hebrew school in a huff, I'd avoided my old conservative temple as if it were the eleventh Passover plague. I hadn't been there in more than a decade. My memories of being a fat, nerdy, awkward, artsy militant misfit were so torturous that I'd been afraid to go back and mingle with all the normal happy neighborhood kids I'd left behind. But Abram's confidence and pride at being by my side seemed to rub off on me. I felt fine as he took me by the arm and led me through the thick doors and the hallway filled with ancient artifacts until we reached the shul, where the wedding service was taking place. I wasn't claustrophobic at all this time; in fact, I was downright bouncy and psyched to be there as I walked down the aisle, staring up at the colorful, impressive stained glass framing the bimah. Why the extreme change?

As a third-wave feminist who'd spent years on the couch, I wanted to think facing down my demons and becoming an acclaimed big-city photographer had defanged my past. Yet as I smiled at old classmates seated in the back rows, pleased to see them checking out Abram, I realized it was more likely my good mood was based on the shallow feat of landing a good-looking, successful neurosurgeon date. Oy vey. I hoped my envy over Elizabeth's marriage to my doctor brother hadn't turned me into the type of superficial suburban princess I'd spent my life parodying.

My mother led us to the middle, chose a row, and went in first. My father followed, so I wound up sitting with my dad to my right and Abram to my left. During the long ceremony, my father translated the Hebrew into my ear: "Four sheep, three goats, two cows, and seven ducks."

"Is that my dowry too?" I whispered in his ear.

"Abram is a nice man," he whispered back.

At the start of the cocktail hour, Rabbi Levin and his wife, Esther, rushed over to greet me.

"Rachel Solomon!" Esther said, kissing my cheek. "The big-shot New Yorker. And this must be your handsome husband."

She knew damn well I wasn't married. "This is *my friend*, Abram Silver," I said, taking a flute of champagne from the waiter walking by and downing it.

"Friends is good," Esther said. "Nothing wrong with friends."

"I'm so happy you could come." Arlene took me by the hand and whisked me away. "I'm sorry about Esther. What a *bala-busta*," she said in my ear. "Are you surviving being back in this haunted house? Jeez, Abram is cute. You didn't tell me he was so cute. And a brain surgeon. What's wrong with him? Tell me now."

"He dumped his wife with two kids, he's having too much fun hanging out with my parents, and for the last year and a half, since his father died, he's been living with his mother," I blurted out, snagging more bubbly from a passing waiter.

"Maybe he's worried about her being alone," she said.

"Of course you're a romantic optimist tonight. You look gorgeous," I fawned.

I'd met Arlene when our family moved next door to hers in Highland Park. She was seven years old; I was two years older, and Arlenie looked up to me. She was a fragile, earnest girl. In high school, while Nicky and I drank, smoked, did drugs, and bedded a steady stream of bad boys, Arlenie remained sober while dating what she called "the three Ns: nerds, nebbishes, and nudniks."

After I moved to the big city, I'd spent thousands of hours on late-night phone calls, giving her advice. When she'd met Gary eight months ago, it appeared to confirm all the psychobabble I'd been preaching: good things happen to good people, wait for true love, you never have to settle. I was always so brilliant with other people's love lives.

Gary was six feet tall, a lawyer with dark curly hair and a sweet smile. When he'd proposed on Arlene's twenty-fifth birthday, she'd called me drunk at 3:00 A.M. "He got down on his knees! I can't believe it. Can you believe it's happening to me? Oh fuck, Ricky. I think I'm finally happy."

I wasn't surprised Arlenie was becoming a Mrs. I was stunned that she'd used the word "fuck." It was the first time I'd heard her swear. Now that I was single, Arlenie was with a cool guy, giving me uplifting advice about men. I drank some more. A gaggle of girly girls from my old consecration class spotted me.

"Hey, it's Rachel Solomon," said Sherry Gruber, fake-hugging me hello. "I haven't seen you around lately."

"I moved to New York," I said. Nine years ago, you dolt, I didn't say.

"Oh, that's right. For law school, right?" Sherry asked.

"Photojournalism." I smiled.

"You remember Ari?" She pointed to the skinny nerdball standing by her. I nodded to him. "We've been married six years now. We have three children." She took out pictures to show me before I could stop her.

I grabbed cheese puffs and little hot dog hors d'oeuvres from the waiters going by, washing them down with more bubbly as Julie Asher, a popular cheerleader who'd lived down the block from me, came over. She had three kids too, and was visibly pregnant with her fourth.

"I saw your photographs in *The Forward* and the *Chicago Trib*," Julie said. "I remember you used to take pictures for the yearbook. That's so great."

"Thanks." I felt relieved that somebody here knew what I did. But I hated that it still mattered so much what my old classmates thought of me. Abram came over.

"Your husband is so handsome," Sherry purred, loud enough for Abram to hear.

"Thanks. Yours isn't so bad either," Abram answered with a wink.

"Sorry." I took out a cigarette.

"Wouldn't be so terrible. Would it?" Abram asked within her earshot.

Wow, implying he was interested in marriage in public, amid the married burb brigade, no less. I recalled Elizabeth's calling him "the anti-Matthew." Boy, had she nailed it.

When I introduced Abram to the groom, Gary thought he looked familiar. I figured they'd been on opposite sides of some horrific malpractice litigation. But then my mother came up behind me and said, "You wouldn't believe it. Gary's father had a brain aneurysm three years ago, and guess who saved his life? Abram!" She was glowing. Gary's father came over and greeted Abram with a huge hug. Everyone turned and pointed their fingers at my date, muttering, "That's the doctor who saved his life at Rush." My parents joined in the buzz. After all these years of wanting their approval, I had finally made them really proud of me. Unfortunately it was for choosing the right Jewish doctor escort.

The parent pleasing reached its crescendo when Abram insisted we slow dance to "Sunrise, Sunset," sashaying us right next to my mother and father on the dance floor. They were grinning, looking at us. I grinned back. I must have really been drunk because instead of the revulsion I'd felt during synagogue events my parents used to force me to attend, I was elated. Something I'd done had finally elicited their delight.

When they left at midnight, Abram insisted we stay. We joined in the bunny hop with Rabbi Levin and Esther, then did the bump and the Macarena with Arlenie and Gary. Who knew people still bunny hopped, bumped, and Macarenaed in this day? How corny. But what if Arlenie got a mensch lawyer and I got a mensch doctor? I dared to fantasize, plastered out of my mind and laughing. Worse, I suddenly wondered if I'd become an artistic rebel not for serious political reasons but as a defense against rejection. Perhaps now that social respectability was possible, I could actually do this. As we slow danced to Stevie Wonder's buoyant, hopeful "For Once in My Life," Abram rubbed my back, and I thought, what was so great about Manhattan, anyway? With millions of people crowded into tiny side-by-side apartments, I still managed to be lonely. Working a hundred hours a week, I still could barely afford my rent. The city was loud and dirty.

"You're a terrific dancer," Abram flattered.

"I feel like the prom queen." I hiccuped, about to get up the nerve to ask him if he wanted to get a room for us at the Water Tower hotel. It was only half full; I'd called that afternoon to check.

"Then I'm the king," he said. "Hold your breath and count to ten." I did, and it worked; the hiccups went away. Elizabeth had the right idea. It could be fun, having my very own in-house doctor to take care of me.

"My mother made me try on every expensive dress at the mall, but we couldn't find a new one," I mumbled.

"You look perfect," he said.

He was the one looking perfect. I had to keep reminding myself that he wasn't divorced yet, had deserted two children, and was currently living with his mother. But as my mom had postulated, he could really be a major mensch, wanting to take care of her. Didn't they say that the way a guy treated his mother was the way he'd wind up treating his wife?

On the way out, he gathered up kosher cookies, macaroons, and brownies from the sweets table and put them in two napkins in his pocket. "One for my mom, one for your parents," he said. The gesture was either lovely or pathological; I was too drunk to decide. The groom's father stopped Abram on the way out and said, "Without you, I wouldn't be here tonight," and bear-hugged him again. I felt like Abram deserved to get a blue ribbon for Best All-Star Jewish Wedding Guest.

On the way to my parents' house we talked about Arlenie, Gary, Gary's father's brain operation, and Abram's birthday the next day, gossiping like we were best friends.

"Tomorrow you'll meet my mom, Aunt Sasha, and Uncle Ilya—he's my dad's brother. You would have hit it off with my father. He loved art and photography."

"I'm psyched to meet your family." I lit a cigarette and stared out the window, gleeful and dizzy, as we drove through my old stomping grounds. I felt safe and warm in Abram's sleek Jaguar. I heard the echo of Arlenie saying, "Oh fuck, Ricky. I think I'm finally happy." I pictured what it would be like moving back here. I took a deep breath, ready to ask him about getting a room at the Water Tower. "So I have a surprise for you...," I started to say.

"So Nachamah's coming to the party tomorrow too," Abram said at the same time.

"What?" He'd relayed this like it was important news, but I couldn't focus on why.

"What's your surprise?" he asked me.

"Who's coming?" I asked him.

"Oh, Nachamah and the whole Orthodox group from New Jersey." He turned off the music. "Remember, I told you about her."

I vaguely recalled his mentioning her name. "She's one of your Russian cousins?" I asked.

"Well actually, she's Ilya's wife's cousin," he said.

Oh? That meant she wasn't really a relative of his. "How old is Nachamah?" I asked, having pictured a twelve-year-old.

"She's nineteen," he said. "Turning into a real beauty."

Wait. Why was a nineteen-year-old beauty he wasn't related to flying in from a different state for his birthday?

"You invited her to your party?" I asked. "As your date?" Wasn't nineteen much too young for a thirty-five-year-old? She was even younger than me. I shouldn't have had so much to drink. I was getting everything confused.

"I didn't invite her. My mother told her about the party and she flew in to surprise me," he said. "Though I offered to reimburse her for the ticket."

"So you're *dating* her?" I asked again, coughing up smoke.

"I'm not sure I would call it dating. I've shown her around Chicago a few times. But I've known her for years, since she was a little kid," he said. "You'll like her. She wants to be a photographer, like you."

"Orthodox girls don't fuck," I declared, not quite realizing I'd said it out loud. Then I hiccuped, letting my cigarette fly out the window.

Abram didn't react. Did he know I'd had way too much bubbly? When we pulled up to my parents' driveway, he stopped the car, walked me to the door, and kissed me quickly on the lips.

"That was the best wedding I've ever been to. Don't forget my party tomorrow. At one," he said, gently handing me the now-crumbled cakes from his pocket.

"Okay, thanks, me too." I waved as his car pulled away.

Inside the house, it was quiet. My parents and the visiting relatives were asleep. In the kitchen I ate all the stolen sweets myself, then shut the lights and turned on the burglar alarm. I couldn't be with a guy who wasn't yet divorced, had deserted his children, and was currently living with his mother anyway, I told myself. Not to mention the Orthodox nineteen-year-old he was probably going to marry. In my pink bathroom I threw up all the champagne, cookies, and little hot dogs. Then I called "Northworst" Airlines and booked an earlier Sunday return flight to New York.

I was back in my apartment by noon. I unpacked, unrolling the plain black eyelet-sleeved dress and hanging it back in my closet. I noticed the red light from my machine flashing. I wondered if it was Abram, calling to see why I wasn't at his birthday party. Or Matthew, phoning from LA to say he'd made a terrible mistake and couldn't live without me. I played the message.

"Hi, honey," my mother's voice said. "I found your heart at Neiman Marcus. You accidentally left it in the dressing room. I'm mailing it back to you."

chapter twenty
double mazel
September 8, 2003

"Are you sure the Solomons haven't checked in yet?" I asked the Plaza desk concierge on the phone. "Dr. and Mrs. Joseph Solomon, from Highland Park, Illinois. They reserved a suite."

"No, like I told you when you called five minutes ago, they have not checked in," he sniffed. "When they do, I'll give them the four messages you've already left."

"Thanks," I said, calling Northwest again to make sure their flight had indeed landed, as the airline had told me a half hour earlier.

It was one o'clock on the day of my opening and there were no phones ringing, no texts, faxes, messages, or press calls, no flowers or champagne being delivered—no chaos whatsoever. It was too quiet. A bad sign. The reception at the Soho gallery was scheduled for six o'clock that night. My parents, two brothers, and two sisters-in-law were due at the Plaza by noon. My New Jersey aunts, uncles, and cousins were supposed to be meeting us for lunch by now. Had the airline clerk mistakenly told me the plane had landed when the flight was late? I called the limo driver I'd hired to pick them up at LaGuardia but he didn't answer his phone either. Where was everyone?

I paced around, ran out for cigarettes, then came home and checked my phone messages. I'd somehow missed one, from my mother. Thank God, I bet they'd just landed.

"Elizabeth's been in labor for six hours. No baby yet. Her family is here. My brothers are flying in, meeting us all at the hospital," she told my machine. "We're not going to make it to New York, honey. I'm sorry. I'll call you later."

The "all" apparently referred to Elizabeth's mother and sister, my parents, brothers, second sister-in-law, and all of my New Jersey aunts, uncles, and cousins who had flown all the way to Illinois instead of driving an hour to come to my show— changing their itinerary to be with the baby maker and not me. I had joked that Elizabeth would give birth to the first Solomon grandchild in the middle of my show, a crowd of Jewish doctors surrounding her, in all her glory. But this was worse. Talk about being stood up. My own family was picking her on the biggest day of my life.

I called Nicky and left a subtle message: "Emergency. I'm going psycho. Call me. I need you."

I marched around my apartment, feeling abandoned and re- placed. I called Peter to see if he'd remembered to tell the *News- day* critic to come. I tried Betsy to see if her friends at *The New Yorker* were going to show. I left three messages for Ruth at the *Post*, reminding her that tonight was the night. I tried Jane, who'd promised she'd be coming. I left messages for Andy, Eliot, Hope, and Stanley, even Matthew, in case he was in town. Nobody picked up their cells.

When I came out of the bathroom, I noticed that the light on my answering machine was blinking. There was one message. It was one thirty. If Elizabeth had popped out the baby by now, my parents could still catch a plane from Chicago at three and be here in time. But the voice belonged to Joris. He said the press had been calling the gallery all day. So had an editor from Rizzoli, who was coming to my show and wanted to meet me. He'd loved the photo series I'd taken for *The Jewish Forward* on downtown Hebrews.

I'd shown those Lower East Side pictures to every photo editor at the city's five big dailies. Not one had been the least bit interested. I'd finally given them to *The Forward*, which had offered me thirty dollars a shot. I'd let them print all ten on the conditions that they only got first rights and that the photo credit read "Ricky Solo." So I'd be getting the approval of the Solomon clan while erasing them at the same time.

I played Joris's message five times. How bizarre. I'd displayed my shots of the downtown bag lady, flophouse transvestite, urban gardener, and tattoo artist up front at the gallery, since they were the most up to date and provocative. Ironic how I'd almost left out the portraits of old Jewish Lower East Siders altogether, assuming they were too ethnic and out of fashion. But when Uncle Max promised he was coming, I'd stuck in a row of them last minute. I even took Max's suggestion and titled the pictures by using the subject's profession and location of their work, the way he used to. So there was the Last Kosher Butcher of Broome Street, the One-Eyed Waitress at Ratner's Deli on Delancey, the Pillow Maker of Ludlow, the *Mikveh* Lady of Pitt Street, the Hasidic Wig Seller of Suffolk. Rizzoli couldn't possibly be interested in those kooky old relics, could they?

I pulled a black dress from the closet, the long, low-cut one with eyelet sleeves. It somehow looked just fine on me in New York. I tried Nicky again. Luckily this time she picked up.

"Elizabeth's giving birth at Rush Hospital in Chicago. She's in labor."

"Right now?" she asked. "Nothing like being literally up-staged. It's your worst Freudian nightmare."

"I know. And my whole fucking Jersey *mishpokhe* flew out to welcome the newborn."

"What? They're not coming to your show?" Nicky asked. "That's insane."

"It's the first of the Solomon grandchildren and there hasn't been a new kid in the family for a decade. They were worried the species would die out or something." It was so ridiculous I had to laugh—while smoking and crying at the same time.

"I'll be right there, baby. Be calm. All I have to do is get dressed."

I smoked six cigarettes and listened to Joris's message ten more times. Nicky finally showed up, looking gorgeous in a black minidress. She got me stoned with a thick joint of Jamaican and spewed more verbal abuse on my procreating sister-in-law, and we danced to Natalie Merchant's "Jealousy" over and over until I was okay again.

"It's kind of scary how this Elizabeth chick has taken over your entire family. Like a cross between *Single White Female* and *Rosemary's Baby*."

I often felt like Nicky was the only person who ever got me. I grabbed the hemostat Ben left as a roach clip and squeezed the tips around the joint, handing it to her. "I just can't believe they're all missing my opening."

"Well, you said friends are the family you get to choose." She inhaled a few more times, blowing smoke out the window. "All your friends are coming."

"Stop quoting me back to myself," I said. "So I have news. Joris thinks this editor at Rizzoli might want to publish a book of my downtown portraits."

"Your series from the flophouse?"

"No. The editor liked the old Jews."

"Because *he's* probably an old Jew," she said. "When I

interviewed at MTV, the president turned out to be a schleppy Jewish guy who went to school with my dad in the Midwest."

"That was just your foot in the door. You got the next ten promotions on your own." I put out my cigarette. "What's your title now?"

"Vice president in charge of East Coast documentaries. They're getting me an LA office too. I'll be a total sellout."

"I've been trying to sell out for years," I said. "Nobody was buying."

When we were growing up, Nicky had been both my prettiest and my most political girlfriend. Now she was the most successful too, making two hundred thousand dollars a year and living in a three-thousand-square-foot Tribeca loft. She'd moved there with her latest guy, a broke and volatile nineteen-year-old Turkish translator she'd picked up in Belize. Was it my imagination, or did the most ambitious, successful people have the most trouble with love?

"Ever hear anything about Matthew in LA?" I asked.

"Don't ask me today," she said.

"Tell me," I insisted.

"They shoot the messenger."

"I won't."

"I heard his old girlfriend Alice moved to LA to be with him," she said. "They're getting engaged."

"Damn it all to hell. He didn't want me to move out there, but he wanted her to. I just heard that Abram got engaged to his fucking prepubescent cousin Nachamah in Chicago. Can you believe it? Three months after our big double date." I hit the last of the joint again, deeper this time, feeling like a repeat loser in love.

"Well, both those guys had 'fear of intimacy' written all over them." Nicky took the roach from me and sucked in herself, then put it out.

"*You* fixed me up with Matthew!" I yelled. "And they're having no trouble getting intimate with other women. Just not with me."

"Engaged isn't married or healthy," she said, as if that was supposed to help. "And they were both too old for you, anyway."

"So the control group is sleeping with a foreign teenager who didn't finish high school?"

"Screw you. At least I don't need a man to feel okay about myself."

"Screw you. I don't *need* a man. I *want* one. That's healthy." I lit a cigarette and coughed.

"It just seems like you're always jealous of other people's weddings. You're buying into all this marriage propaganda, like a white dress and a ring would really make you happy." She sneered.

She did have a point. I couldn't wait to get away from my clan. Now that I was finally free, and on the verge of real success, I was dismayed to be single, dateless, and bummed my family wasn't here to suffocate and overfeed me. Nicky had this amazing high-powered job and traveled the world and slept with whomever she felt like.

"I'm not saying there's anything wrong with wanting to be married or have kids," she said. "But just do it for the right reasons."

"Envy and desperation isn't good motivation?"

"Look, any idiot can get married. All you need is another idiot," she said. "But look at what you've done. You're making a name for yourself with your art—which nobody can ever take away. Not your doctor brothers or baby-making sister-in-law or any grandkids. You're the star tonight."

More than a hundred people were already crammed into the Lacey Jones Gallery on Broome and Prince streets. Everyone was hugging and air kissing me, patting me on the back and saying "Bravo." They all came! A critic from the *New York Times* was talking to the Rizzoli editor. Nicky handed me a glass of Merlot as strangers smiled, waved, and came up to congratulate me.

"The old Jews are just stunning. Your best work," Hope Maxwell said.

"Let me get both of you," one of the shutterbugs shouted.

I posed with Hope, honored to be in the same frame as her, hyper and buzzing. I saw my old boss Richard and ran up to kiss him, posing with him too. Instead of me taking pictures of other people, photographers from all the newspapers and local magazines were taking pictures of me. For once I didn't mind being on the other side of the camera.

I stared at my portraits lining the sparse, elegant brick walls. The downtown misfits I'd shot were here too, celebrating with me. Odd that these were the people my parents saw every day growing up, the religious characters they couldn't wait to flee. I recalled the pictures my parents had shown me as a kid—my great-uncle Tudras, the mystic rabbi from Minsk, famous for his long auburn beard. Grandpa Jake, standing in front of his storefront with his "Solomon & Son Furniture" sign. Sitting on the steps of her tenement's fire escape was my grandmother Sophie, the woman I looked like but had never met. "You've brought her back," my mother used to tell me. I'd brought them all back. In some ways they'd been hiding in my inner eyes all along.

When I walked the length of the gallery to shouts and applause, I felt light, like I was floating. Of course my brain knew that my fifteen minutes were almost over. The work was what counted. As my shrink constantly warned me, shows, money, and press coverage were superficial and fleeting. But the truth was, it meant everything to me. I wasn't sure if it was dumb luck, or if I deserved it, or if I had merely desired the acclaim to fill up the hole in my heart so desperately I'd made it happen. All that mattered was that I'd made it here. I felt safe and at home, as if the rows of my crazy urban ancestors were watching over me, like bodyguards, the faces of my past guiding me to my future. Nicky was right—nothing could take this away.

"Ricky, long-distance call for you," Joris called out. "You can take it in the office."

"Okay, thanks." I pushed past the crowd, kissing, hugging, and greeting everyone as I made my way to the back. Who were these people? I didn't even know half of them. How flattering that strangers were crashing my opening.

I picked up the phone and said, "Hello."

"Elizabeth had the baby." It was my mother, calling from the hospital, bringing me back down to earth. "Sidney William Solomon. The first grandchild of the family. Everybody's celebrating."

For an hour I'd actually forgotten who was missing.

"Sidney?" I asked. What kind of an old-fashioned moniker was that? It sounded like an *alter cocker* in Florida.

"Elizabeth named him after my father. Isn't that the most wonderful thing you've ever heard?" my mother asked. "He looks like him too. She had him at six o'clock." It was uncanny, how Elizabeth had even gotten the timing right, along with the Jewish ritual of naming kids after dead relatives. I'd uncovered a meaningful way to honor my parents and their history just as she found a way to totally usurp me.

"Little Sidney is seven pounds, four ounces," my mother went on. "He's so beautiful."

"Mazel tov." I feigned happiness. "That's great, Mom. Thanks for letting me know."

"Listen, we're all going to fly in to see you next week," she said. "The gallery will be open, right? So can we do another party, just for the family? Then we'll all take you out to dinner to celebrate. You'll pick the place. Okay? We'll fly in just for you. Next Friday."

"Okay." I felt flat and deflated, like a balloon with all its air let out.

"Little Sidney has red hair on his head already, just like your brother Ben did," she said, sounding dreamy.

"Cool, Mom. But listen, there's a hundred people here at my opening. I have to go."

———

The next Friday night, one week later, my family finally made it to the gallery.

"Hey, Dad," I waved as he got out of the sedan from the car service.

"He's a grandfather now," Aunt Sally said, getting out of the backseat.

"He's too young to be a grandpa!" Uncle Max got out next, then Uncle Izzy, who patted my father on the back.

Another rented car pulled up, this one carrying Danny, Kim, Aunt Ida, and cousin Eve.

"Hey, how's it going?" I called to them.

"I can't believe you have your own solo show," Danny said.

"Thanks." I blew him a kiss, missing Ben.

"Hello, Grandma," Sally said to my mother. "You're too sexy to be a grandma."

"At least Elizabeth didn't have it in the middle of the opening," Kim joked, hugging me. "I heard you sold four photographs. That's amazing."

I hugged her back. "Joris said if I can get them forty more portraits, Rizzoli is definitely interested in doing a book."

Joris and Nicky had shown up for my second mini-opening, as had Jane and Andy. Instead of thinking of who was missing, I made a list in my head of who'd come to both.

"Did you see her picture and the rave in *The New York Times?*" Nicky asked my family, pulling out the clip from her purse.

Jane took the article and read the pull quote out loud: "'These incredible portraits provide the most honest, vivid record we have of this exotic old world.'"

"I like *Newsday*'s better," Andy jumped in.

Uncle Izzy turned to my father and said, "The baby is a Virgo, like me."

"Sidney William Solomon. Seven pounds, four ounces," Aunt Sally said.

"You weren't kidding about your relatives," Nicky whispered. "They're acting like your family is this dying breed that just got spared from oblivion. Are they giving out birth announcements at the door?"

"Will you join us for dinner so I don't go crazy?" I begged her.

"I'd rather have a root canal," Nicky answered in my ear.

"Are you two next to have babies? You better hurry up, you're not getting any younger," Uncle Izzy said.

"What a week," cooed Aunt Ida.

"Are you going to look at my old Jews or what?" I asked Uncle Max, more than a bit miffed by his neglect. "I even named them the way you suggested."

"I know, I saw them. They're terrific," Max said, patting me on the head. "Rachela, you did good. It's double mazel!"

"Yeah, double mazel," said another male voice behind me. I turned around, shocked to see my brother Ben, in a blue blazer with a rose in his lapel and a cigar in his mouth.

"What are you doing here?"

"How could I miss your first show?" he asked, sweeping me up and spinning me around, the sound of clapping and flashes going off.

"Congratulations on being a father," I said. "I can't believe you came."

"Elizabeth made me come. She wouldn't let me miss it," he said. "We're so proud of you."

After everyone settled in, I sneaked into the back office to have a cigarette and called Elizabeth.

"Did you get my messages?" I asked her. "Did you get the balloons and flowers I sent?"

"It's a boy. I really wanted a boy!" she squealed. She sounded elated. Or was it drugged? "He's perfect. Sidney. He's so beautiful."

I waited for her to say something about my opening or the incredible reviews or my book offer. When she did, it wasn't what I expected.

"You really owe me," she mumbled.

"For what?" I asked. "Letting Ben come to New York today?" She didn't answer.

"For making my mother and father grandparents?"

"You wouldn't have the show or a book if it wasn't for me," she finally threw out.

My jaw opened, and my cigarette dropped to the floor. I picked it up, fuming. First Elizabeth took over my entire family; now she was claiming credit for my success. Weird, since she'd been condescending about my work from day one. I paced while taking a few puffs to calm down, not sure if I was succeeding because of her—or in spite of her.

"Ricky, there you are." My mother rushed in, put out my cigarette, and pulled me toward the gallery. "Come on. Uncle Max is giving a speech."

"I have to go. Max is making a speech about me," I told Elizabeth, hanging up the phone. "I'll fly there soon. I can't wait to meet Sidney."

Eighty-year-old Max, the clan's patriarch, walked to the front of the room and cleared his throat. At last, somebody in the family was eager to attend to the matter at hand: toasting my years of hard work, dedication to my craft, and current good fortune. I hoped he would quote the *Forward* review again, this time to everyone.

"I would like to start by thanking everyone for coming to this happy occasion tonight," Uncle Max said. "This is a very important time for the Solomon family. We've waited so long to continue our legacy. As most of you already know, Joseph and Leah have just welcomed their first grandson into the world..."

part
four

chapter twenty-one
baby love

September 4, 2006

It took three years for Rizzoli to publish my book, *Walking My Father's Old Streets,* under my new alias, Ricky Solo. I wasn't sure if I'd wanted a different identity or just a less ethnic-sounding name. Funny since it wound up consisting of fifty black-and-white portraits of elderly Jews still living on the Lower East Side.

I flew home to see the modern Jewish Illinois branch, excited for my book signing at the Highland Park Borders the next night. I was pleased when my brother Danny picked me up at the airport, assuming he'd want to hear all about my latest career coup. Yet he spent the ride home complaining about the skyrocketing costs of medical malpractice insurance at Rush Hospital, where he was interning, completing the trio of myopic Solomon medicine men. When we arrived home, there were a bunch of cars in my parents' driveway. Who was over? I bet my mother had arranged a little book party to greet me. How sweet.

Alas, in the kitchen I found my parents with Elizabeth's mother, her sister Michelle with her two daughters, and Elizabeth's three tykes. Sid, now three years old, said, "Hi, Aunt Ricky," and waved. On my mother's lap was her beautiful dark-haired two-year-old granddaughter Sophie, named for my mother's late mother. Elizabeth was sitting at the head of the table, her hair cut shorter, like my mother's. In her lap was her brand-new baby, Jacob, named after my father's father. Elizabeth's mission seemed to be to resurrect our entire lost family tree. Of course I'd expected to see her and her three kids, just not the moment I arrived. What were all the Manns from Westchester doing here?

"Hi," I smiled, startled, pretending this was a great surprise. "Nice to see everyone." And it was. The kids were adorable. "Where's Ben?"

"Emergency at the hospital." Elizabeth held up Jake, a three-month-old with chubby cheeks and red hair. "Come on, Jakey, dat's a good boy. Yes!" she said. "Dat's right."

"He's gorgeous," I said.

"I'm playing on Grandpa's computer and you can't stop me," Sid told me before running down to my father's den.

"Well, he told us, didn't he, Jake? Yes he did, didn't he?" Elizabeth cooed.

From the second Sid was born, Elizabeth had become a hyper-smiley, gushy, baby-talking mommy. I'd assumed she'd get over it. Yet she seemed to get sillier and coo more with each birth. Who would have thought?

"Come on, angel face, sweetie pie. Say 'Hi, Auntie Rachel. It's so nice to meet you.' Isn't it? Yes." She held Jake in front of me.

"Hi, honey," I said, kissing his cheek, touching his tiny finger.

"Auntie Rachel flew here on a big airplane," Elizabeth said.

"Yes. For a big reading," I said, proudly putting a stack of my books on the table. I expected everyone to grab them, but the only thing being grabbed was my mother's chef salad, pizza, sliced turkey, and salami. Miffed, I sat down and took a spoonful of tuna fish. Elizabeth made herself a salad. Then she changed her mind, put the lettuce back in the bowl, and took slices of roast beef from the fridge.

My mother must have caught my reaction because she laughed and said, "I know. She's not a Solomon. We always know what we want to eat."

"Yes, we do," agreed my father, who'd just walked in. "Got any pastrami?"

"There's a double-decker from Cohen's Deli with your name on it." Mom took it out of the refrigerator for him.

"Hi, Daddy." I kissed his forehead.

"People from the *Chicago Tribune* and ABC-TV called for you yesterday," he said. "I left the numbers in your room."

"Fantastic. Thanks," I said, about to tell him more about the press when he walked past me.

"There he is! Come here, angel face," my father squealed, taking Jake from Elizabeth. "Come talk to your old grandpa."

"Isn't he delicious?" my mother said, taking Jake from my father.

Nobody seemed to notice my book. In my absence, the Solomons' new dinner game had become Musical Babies, making me miss the diseases.

"While you're home, make sure to get some good pictures of the kids for me," my mother added. "I have a new pink outfit I'll put Sophie in."

"No problem." I was freelancing for the best publications in the country, I'd had an incredible art opening, and my portraits were now in a book that had received rave reviews. Yet I felt like Mom was implying that my purpose on the planet was to capture cutesy scenes of the grandkids given to her by Elizabeth.

"Where's my Sophie?" asked my father, making squeaking noises. She came over and sat on his other knee. "I'm so glad you're both with me now." He patted her head gently. "Grandpa was getting so lonely without you."

"I can get you a copy of my last interview if you want to see it," I offered him.

"I could use some more grandchildren around here," was his response.

Elizabeth took Jake back and bounced him on her knee. "You'd like that, Jake, wouldn't you?" she said.

She'd wanted to name her second son Joseph, after my father. But when my mother explained that Jews don't name children after anyone living, she'd picked Jake, after my grandfather. When I asked her why she'd only used her dad's moniker for her firstborn's middle name, she'd told me, "My dad had such a lousy life, I didn't want to continue the curse." Her kids were the opposite of cursed. In this huge, comfortable house, where everything used to revolve around my mother and her three offspring, everything now centered on the three babies and mommyhood of Elizabeth.

"Hi, Ricky," said Elizabeth's niece Andrea. "I think your book is really cool."

I signed one and handed it to her.

"Really? I can keep it?" she asked, in the voice of someone not used to getting presents.

"Sure." It reminded me of when I'd given Elizabeth my red blazer in my Fifth Avenue apartment, years before.

"You have to always remember you grew up privileged," Elizabeth had told me the first time she'd visited Highland Park. "That warm, loving mother of yours is a miracle. You're very lucky." Had she been plotting to steal my mom ever since? My mother looked so happy to have grandkids, I thought as I sat back down and took some salad, joining my ever-expanding family at the table.

"Congratulations on your book," Pamela Mann told me. "Very impressive."

In jeans and a sky blue sweater, she looked younger and more relaxed than usual.

"Do you really think so?" I couldn't help but ask.

"Yes. You have a ruthless eye," she said, catching mine and nodding. "Don't be afraid of it." She'd been married to a serious photographer; she understood these things.

I wanted to hear more of Pamela's assessment of my work, but just then the baby spit up all over himself, which garnered a round of applause. Pamela got up to get paper towels. Michelle cleaned his face with a washcloth. My mother took my hand and pulled me into the foyer, whispering, "I have a present for you." I basked in her attention, which I'd been longing for since I'd walked in. She handed me a black chenille sweater with a pink trim collar I'd have to cut off or dye.

"Thanks, Mom." I kissed her cheek. "What's going on? A Mann family reunion?"

"I should have warned you. They've been in town for two weeks. The girls drove in with Michelle and their grandmother. They've come over three times already. I'm tired of feeding everyone."

"So why don't they go out to eat?" I asked.

"Well, they don't have a lot of money. And it's very nice that Elizabeth's relatives came all this way to help with the baby," she said. "I want to spend time with my grandchildren. Aren't the kids precious? I could just eat them up."

"You're coming to my book signing tomorrow night, right?"

"Let's see what's happening," she said. I was about to feel hurt that her priority was Elizabeth's kids. But then I realized she was talking about my other sister-in-law, Kim, who'd had another miscarriage.

"Is Kim okay?" I asked, empathizing with the woman who couldn't have children.

"She said she just needs some time alone," my mother said. "She's blue. Dad's sending her to the top fertility guy at Rush. I hope they'll try again."

The living room was overstuffed with a playpen, a crib, a stroller, baby car seats, and cartoon videos. There were pictures of Sid, Sophie, and Jake on the mantel over the fireplace, near the bar, and on the walls. Where was my image? I felt a pang when I couldn't even find the framed copy of my author's photo, which I'd sent home. I felt lucky to have a career that kept me captivated in another city. Imagine how horrible it had to be for Kim to hang out here, in the shadow of Elizabeth's fertility.

"Come eat." Mom led me back to the kitchen, but I wasn't hungry.

I wanted to tell her about my book signing in New York, and the surprisingly nice write-up my book had received in *The New York Times*. I'd brought her six copies.

"Want to take a walk?" I asked, hoping to steal some time alone with her.

"Good idea. Let's all take a walk," Elizabeth jumped in, hijacking my plan, putting Jake into a high-tech stroller.

Pamela Mann escorted Sophie, who was hitting a toy drum, and Michelle held on to Sid, who started singing the annoying Barney song, while Andrea waited outside, whistling. Just what I was in the mood for—the Solomon version of the Von Trapps.

"Isn't he the cutest?" Elizabeth patted Jake on the head as I walked next to her, pushing the stroller for lack of anything better to do with myself.

"I'm the fastest," said Sid, clearly irked by the attention his younger siblings were getting. I chased Sid down the block. Sophie waddled, trying to keep up with us. All the Solomon children were too close in age. Elizabeth was continuing the generational rivalry.

"Okay, Speed Racer," I said, picking up Sophie and spinning her around, then putting her down near the curb.

"Bonsai!" Sid yelled as Jake let out a combination burp, yelp, and giggle.

"Spin more," said Sophie, tugging at my hand so I'd lift her again.

"You got it, baby Sophie," I said, spinning her as she giggled gleefully, keeping her little arms tight around my neck.

She liked me!

But when I put her down she ran right over to Grandma Pamela, who took her hand. Maybe at that age they liked anybody who paid attention to them?

"Make sure you get some pictures of us all before you go," my mother repeated.

"Yes, hurry, since it's the first time in weeks I don't have spit-up on me," Elizabeth joked.

She looked pretty in her light pink dress. "Aren't we feminine today," I said, touching the collar.

"From your mother," she whispered. "She gets me the greatest stuff from Marlene's Designs. Your mom has the best taste of anyone I've ever known."

So the transformation was complete. Elizabeth was wearing the pastel clothes I wouldn't wear, and going to the beauty salon every Saturday with my mother to see Ricardo. She'd become the daughter my mother had always wanted. She even called herself Mrs. Solomon, like my mother. Strange name for a former feminist WASP.

"Have you talked to Kim?" I asked. "Is she okay?"

"She hasn't been coming to your mom's house lately. She's not so great with the kids."

"Kim had three miscarriages while you had three babies," I snapped. "What do you expect?" I was having trouble with it, and I didn't even want children.

"You sound like you think it's my fault," Elizabeth said.

On some level it didn't seem fair to Kim, as if there was a limit to how many babies this generation of Solomons was allotted and Elizabeth had hogged all of them.

After another mile everyone went inside, except Andrea, a sullen and gangly fourteen.

"Come on," she said. "Go another mile with me, Ricky."

I really wanted to go in and make some calls. But Andrea looked so thoroughly alone. "Okay, just one more."

"It's so exciting, having your own gallery show and publishing your pictures in a book," she said. "That's what I want to do."

Andrea was growing on me. "You'll have to come hang out with me in the Village," I said. "Like Elizabeth used to. If you want, I'll show you how I develop pictures in the darkroom my dad made me here."

"My dad isn't around much since the divorce," she mumbled.

"I'm sorry." I put my arm around her. "That must be hard for you."

The sun was going down. As we turned the corner, Andrea pulled out a pack of Marlboros from her backpack. "Do you mind?" she asked. "Want one?"

I shook my head; I was cutting down. Plus I didn't want to encourage her. "It's really a bad habit," I told her. "You have to quit."

"I know. My mother found a pack in my room and told me to stop," she said. "I wish I could come to your book signing, but we're leaving tomorrow. My grandmother is driving. She's so uptight, she's the worst driver."

"Pamela's okay. She hasn't had it so easy," I heard myself say. "Give her a break."

I escaped into my bedroom to call my old Chicago gang. But soon I heard the baby shrieking close by. I went to my brother

Ben's old room next door. It was filled with a changing table and another crib. Elizabeth was changing Jake, cooing and ga-gaing.

"Isn't he gorgeous?" Only a mother could see a screaming kid with a dirty diaper as gorgeous. "Michelle took a ride to the store with Katie. I think she's having a hard time dealing with all the attention being lavished on my kids."

Who could blame her? "That's pretty normal, isn't it?"

"Yeah, probably. Where's Andrea?" she asked.

"Still outside."

"What's she doing out there alone?"

"Having a cigarette," I said.

"Andrea smokes?" Elizabeth raised her voice. "Oh no, that's awful. Michelle's going to freak out. I have to tell her."

"Michelle already knows. She caught her with a pack," I said. "Calm down."

"I'm not going to calm down," Elizabeth said. "It's a disgusting habit."

"You used to drink and toke all the time. What's the difference? That it's the one vice you never had?"

"There's a big difference!" she yelled. "I can't believe you let her have cigarettes."

She picked up Jake, marched down to the kitchen, handed the baby to her mother, and went outside, looking for Andrea. I followed her out the door and onto the front porch, semi-stunned by her overreaction.

"What was I supposed to do?" I asked. "Grab the pack from her hand and break them all?"

"Nicotine is dangerous." She went down the driveway, but Andrea was nowhere in sight. Then she walked back.

"Do you have amnesia?" I asked. "We were dropping acid and giving blow jobs when we were her age."

"That has nothing to do with you smoking in front of her. You're being a bad influence," she scolded.

"What are you talking about? I'm the best role model Andrea could possibly have."

"Oh yeah, how's that? You smoke and drink. You live alone. You're a workaholic who hardly ever visits your family," Elizabeth spit out.

"You gotta be kidding. A Midwest mommy who hasn't had a job in five years is trashing me for being nice to hordes of her relatives who came to town to leech off my mother?" I screamed back. "If you're going to be a self-righteous hypocrite, do it in your own house. Not mine."

"It's your parents' house!" she shouted back. "Not yours. You couldn't wait to leave."

"You've taken it over! My mother's feeding your whole family. Your kids' stuff is everywhere." I felt like there was no longer room for me.

"You haven't been back to visit since last summer. You haven't even spent one minute with your new nephew!" she ranted. "Don't you even care about your own flesh and blood?"

Oh my God. I suddenly recognized that exact tone—from my childhood. Elizabeth not only had my mother's name, hairdresser, and clothes, she was now speaking in the voice of Leah Solomon. She really had converted to our religion—guilt.

"My mom finally figures out that I get to have my own life and now *you're haking* me a *tshaynik*!" I told her.

"I don't know what the hell *haking* a *tshaynik* means," she said.

"It means beating a teakettle."

"What?"

She didn't get how Yiddish worked. "It's like talking nonsense." I was still yelling.

I looked up and noticed that my mother and Pamela were watching us from the kitchen window. It was open, so they could also hear us. They both wore the same horrified expression, appalled by their daughters' lack of constraint. Pamela and my mother had that in common—an irrational fear of what the neighbors would think. They'd been in the kitchen, eating, playing Scrabble, and merrily taking care of their grandkids the whole time, getting along much better than their daughters.

I stormed upstairs and called Nicky in New York to get her take on the fight.

"Well, smoking *is* a terrible habit," she said. "I wish you'd quit. You know it's a sore spot for Elizabeth. Her dad died of emphysema."

"He died of liver problems, from drinking," I said. "She just says emphysema because it's less threatening since she likes to drink."

"It's less threatening to you to blame it on his liver," she said.

"I was just trying to be nice to Andrea."

"Who thinks you're this cool famous New York photographer. Don't you get it? Elizabeth is jealous," Nicky said. "You got a show through her father's old agent. Your work finally made it into *Vision* magazine and galleries where she wanted her work to be, and now your book is getting raves. Her photographs were never published, remember?"

"She has everything she wants. She's married to a successful husband with a new house and three kids," I said. "She just wants to be a doctor's wife and mommy now."

"She still takes pictures all the time. Ben told me at the gallery," Nicky said. "She just doesn't talk about it anymore."

Ben had told her that? I sat down on the bed. Every time I reduced Elizabeth to a female stereotype, she turned, like a kaleidoscope, into someone else.

At six o'clock on Thursday night my mother and father drove me to Borders, where my picture and a stack of books were in the window. The reporter from the *Chicago Tribune* and the ABC camera crew were there. Danny and Kim handed me a dozen roses—surely her idea; my brothers had never brought me flowers before.

"You okay?" I asked. Kim nodded. I said a silent prayer that God would give her the next mini-Solomon. Like my mother, I just wanted peace.

Ben arrived, holding Sidney with one hand and Sophie with the other. I waved, assuming Elizabeth was parking the car. As I signed books, I kept looking toward the door, but she never showed.

chapter twenty-two
trauma center
December 22, 2006

Hating the woman I had accidentally handpicked as my brother's wife seemed moronic. So when Ben and his growing brood flew to New York for the holidays, I decided to end the antagonism between me and Elizabeth by playing the generous, sweet, warm auntie my shrink insisted I really wanted to be. I invited them downtown to the new three-bedroom, three-bath apartment/work space I'd just moved into. I splurged on a bunch of Hanukkah gifts for the kids and promised myself I would not be materialistic, moody, jealous, angry, or stressed out this time.

They were due for an early supper at five o'clock. By seven thirty they had yet to arrive. I hadn't smoked a cigarette in three weeks, but I suddenly craved one. I moved the pictures of me with Sidney, Sophie, and Jake to a shelf that was at eye level, so Elizabeth could see how prominently they were displayed. I took all the blue-and-silver-wrapped presents from the closet, placed them on the table. That was too obvious. I put them back in the closet. When the buzzer finally rang I turned on the foyer lights, waiting by the door. Ben came first, holding Sidney.

"Howdy, Sis!" Ben said.

"Right on time, as usual." I pretended it was a joke as I led them inside.

"Great space. It's so big. Almost as big as our new house."

But your house is in the boonies and mine is in the coolest city in the world, I thought, kissing them both hello.

"I didn't want to come here. I want to go to the zoo," Sid cried, grabbing my hair. "I'm hungry. Where's your food?"

"Kid's got your personality," I told my brother, unclenching Sid's little fist from my tresses.

Elizabeth walked in holding Jake in a car seat and looked around.

"Hey! This is huge," she said. "Must be two thousand square feet. Our house is four thousand."

Yes, your dick is bigger than mine, I didn't say, smiling widely and focusing on what was important. "Where's my Sophie?" I asked as she peeked around the corner.

"Here I am, Aunt Ricky," said my adorable niece, who was wearing a pink dress. Her hair was now cut with long bangs on top, just like mine. I wondered if that was my mother's idea, Elizabeth's, or Ricardo's.

"I'm so glad you're here. I've been waiting for you!"

"I'm so sorry we're late," Sophie told me. "The baby threw up and there was a lot of traffic. I hope we didn't keep you waiting too much."

"No problem, honey." I hugged her hello. My mother had said Sophie was ridiculously mature and well spoken for a three-and-a-half-year-old, a fully formed mini-person. Funny, Elizabeth never apologized for being late or explained why she'd been delayed. It seemed incongruous to hear my mother's politeness coming from the mouth of this amazingly sophisticated little girl. I found it fascinating, especially because my parents said I was precocious and articulate at a young age.

Sid took advantage of the attention I was giving his sister by flinging books across the floor. A biography of Diane Arbus hit the chair. My thick *Andy Warhol Diaries* skipped across the couch. I put the books high up where he couldn't reach as my hardcover Annie Leibovitz landed on the table, nearly knocking over the peanuts.

"Sid, honey—I have something for you." I hoped for a deal: I'll give you presents if you promise not to touch anything. I took the boxes out. Sidney ripped his open, throwing the blue wrapping all over.

"A dinosaur! He loves dinosaurs!" Elizabeth cried.

I glowed. Then Sidney grabbed the Slinky on top of the box. He threw it across the floor, ran to get it. He threw the Slinky again, in awe.

"They always love the cheap thing you grab at the counter," Ben shrugged.

"Jane stopped by our hotel today," Elizabeth said.

"That reminds me, I have a present for you," I told her. I knew she would love the photograph; I couldn't wait to give it to her. "And I have something for Sophie and Jake," I added quietly.

"Why don't you give out gifts after we eat, so they don't get food all over them?" she said.

I felt hurt that they didn't want to open them now. Then again, I wasn't used to eating with three little kids.

"You know, that doctor guy never called Jane back. Poor Jane. She really liked him."

"I'm fixing her up with a friend of Nicky's," I said, hoping we weren't now going to be playing Dueling Jane.

"Are you seeing anyone?" Elizabeth asked.

"I've been dating a bunch of different guys. No one special," I lied.

I'd actually recently fallen for Claudio Vinoly, a thirty-three-year-old art dealer from South America I'd met through Joris. Though Claudio wasn't Jewish, I'd finally found a cool guy who fit me—tall, smart, handsome, age appropriate, into my work. Yet fearful of getting my heart slaughtered again, I was playing it cool for once—not telling anyone, trying not to overanalyze his travel obsession, hoping it didn't mean he was running away from something (as in me.)

I handed Elizabeth the menu from Sammy's Noodle Shop, where she and Ben had insisted we order in from. She circled six dishes and five appetizers. Ben put Sid on his shoulders. Sophie looked at them and started crying. The kids were already competitive with one another.

"I have to feed the baby." Elizabeth picked up Jake.

I worried she'd whip out her breast and I'd have to watch her play Super Mammary Mom of the Millennium. But luckily she went into the extra bedroom. I called in the dinner order. As I hung up, I heard a crash. I came out of the kitchen to find Sid in front of the crystal vase he'd smashed. It had been a present from my mother.

"I'm sorry." Ben swooped him up. "We'll get you a new one."

I wanted to scream and let him pay for dinner tonight. But I was dead set on being the hostess with the mostest and kindly uttered, "Don't worry about it."

I went for the broom. My mother had told me that Ben and Elizabeth had been having trouble with Sid, who'd tested positive for ADD. I hoped he was okay, sweeping the shards into the dustpan and then vacuuming the floor so nobody would get hurt.

"Cute pictures." Ben looked at the photograph of me with his kids that I knew he'd notice. Then he turned to one of him and Elizabeth at their wedding, standing next to Danny and Kim.

"Mom said Kim's pregnant again," I said.

"Yeah," Ben said. "She's five months in."

Please, let Danny and Kim have the next baby, I silently begged God. I put my hand over my heart and Ben nodded, putting his hand over his heart too, as if joining in my silent prayer. It made me feel closer to him.

When the food came, I quickly transferred it into bowls to make ordering in seem less tacky. I placed the bowls on the table, buffet-style, as if I'd at least prepared something, if not cooked it. When Elizabeth brought the baby back, Sophie started crying again.

"She's getting an ear infection. I think the plane made it worse," Elizabeth explained.

"Bummer," I told Sophie. She looked upset, which was upsetting me.

"We can't get decent Chinese in Zion," Ben said, filling his plate with General Tso's chicken.

"Try some moo shu," Elizabeth said, giving him a pancake, ignoring her sobbing daughter.

"Don't cry, Sophie." I walked over to her and crouched down. "Want to open your present now?"

"Yes," she said, sniffling.

Elizabeth shot me a glare.

"What? I waited," I mumbled, handing it to my niece.

Sophie ripped open the pink wrapping around her President Barbie doll and looked overjoyed by my present.

"She's still a little too young for Barbies. She cuts off the hair and eats the shoes," Elizabeth said, putting Jake back into his car seat, where he miraculously fell right asleep.

"I only ate the shoes once," Sophie protested, pulling the doll out of the container.

"Look. She's the president of the United States of America," I sang.

"No ashtrays around. Did you quit smoking again?" Elizabeth asked.

I nodded.

"How long this time?"

"Three weeks."

"I thought the shoes were candy!" Sophie whimpered.

"Your mom said Sophie's just like you were." Elizabeth picked her up and rocked her back and forth. "She cries all the time, like you used to do."

She'd stolen my sibling, re-created two redheaded Solomon boys, called herself by my mother's name, and given her daughter the name of my dead grandmother. She'd already muddled up the Solomons' whole genealogy. Now Elizabeth was giving birth to me?

"I didn't cry a lot. I spoke really young, like Sophie." I defended my childhood, thinking that Sophie and I were both misunderstood prodigies.

"Oh, Ricardo says hi. He did my hair before I left," Elizabeth said. "He came to your mother's house."

I could handle her getting my brother, parents, and all the babies. But now Ricardo was making house calls for her? He'd never once offered to come over when I'd called. Why? Because it was too hard for Elizabeth to schlep to the salon with the baby? I heard another crash and saw that Sid had dropped his glass on the floor. Damn it. I should have used paper cups.

"Jeez. What's wrong with him tonight?" Elizabeth looked embarrassed.

Did that translate to I'm sorry? I was about to lose my composure when Sophie came by and sat quietly at my feet. Was it my imagination or was she trying to stop any fight between me and her mother before it started? I picked her up and rocked her while Elizabeth swept up the broken glass. I couldn't help but wonder what else they were going to break tonight. But then Sophie leaned her head against me as I ran my hand over her pretty long hair and I felt calm, realizing how much I loved her and how little I cared about stemware and vases. Sophie shut her eyes and fell asleep. Ben took a picture of us. My apartment would soon be filled with pictures of me holding Elizabeth's children.

"Sid can't stand it when Sophie cries," Elizabeth said quietly, poking the tofu she'd asked for, obviously not wanting it anymore.

"Yesterday he came up and put a pacifier in her mouth," Ben said. "It was cute."

"He was trying to shut her up," Elizabeth said, plunging into what Ben hadn't eaten of the General Tso's.

I bet Sid and Sophie would turn out like me and Ben—too close in age and thus competitively overlapping forever. Dr. C often reminded me that I was the one who'd introduced my brother to his bride and created the triangle. Yet sometimes it seemed destined, like Elizabeth had to exist to continue where my rivalry with Ben had left off.

"How's Dad doing?" I asked. "Mom said he's having the hip replacement operation January third."

"He really needs it." Ben shook his head. "He used to carry furniture up and down broken tenement stairs for his father."

"Wasn't that just for a few years?" I asked.

"Ten years," Ben said. "From when he was eight years old through high school."

Poor Dad. It was as if his mean father was haunting him from the grave. I felt like I should fly in for his surgery, but I was up to my eyeballs in work that week.

"I think he's afraid to have an operation," Elizabeth said.

"All doctors are afraid of hospitals," Ben explained. "Because we know what goes on."

"Should I fly in?" I asked, feeling scared to think of my father as vulnerable for the first time.

"No, you don't have to," Elizabeth said. "We have a sitter staying over that week so I can go with him and help your mom."

I felt a surge of gratitude that she'd be around to nurse my father, since I couldn't be there.

"So you gonna open my other gifts or what?" I asked.

Elizabeth opened the rest of the presents I'd picked out for Sophie, miniature black jeans and a black leather jacket from Baby Gap.

"Just what we need." Ben held it up.

"A baby Morticia," Elizabeth said.

Was that sarcastic?

Sid went into my office to play a computer game. He was a computer whiz, smart as hell. I peeked in and saw him pushing buttons and yelling the commands. I followed him in, nervous that he'd crash the computer like he'd crashed everything else today.

"Want another present?" I asked, luring him back to the living room. "I have some great dog and cat stickers. You like dogs and cats, right?" I gave them to Sid with a pad so he wouldn't stick them on my walls.

"Spock croaked," he said.

"Really? Your dog died?" I asked Elizabeth. "What happened?"

"Oh, I was running with him and he just gave out."

I didn't even love dogs, but for some reason this made me very sad.

"We got another Lab for the kids," she said.

"It was Spock's time," Sid said robotically, obviously repeating what they'd told him.

I took out the photograph Hope had given me of Elizabeth at three years old, looking just like Sophie. She was eating a butterscotch sundae from room service at the Plaza. Hope explained that after Elizabeth's father had gotten his advance for *Blind Streets* he'd taken his girls to the Plaza for the weekend. It was the happiest time Elizabeth had ever had with her father, Hope said. I'd had the photo matted and put in a silver frame. I handed it to Elizabeth, excited to see her reaction. But I felt slighted when she didn't open it.

By the time they were ready to go, it was almost midnight and the rain had turned into a storm. I helped pack up the kids, their stuff, and the presents, not wanting them to leave. Should I invite them all to stay over? How would I handle it if they broke something else? I grabbed an umbrella. Elizabeth held Jake in his car seat while I walked them outside to get a cab. There weren't any around. The rain was getting heavier; the wind was rustling. When Sophie started whimpering, I picked her up and held her close.

"It's okay, baby," I said.

"We'll go around the corner, find a cab, and swing back." Ben took Sidney by the hand.

"Bonsai!" Sid yelled, jumping into a puddle and splashing.

Elizabeth and I waited under the building's canopy so Jake and Sophie wouldn't get wet.

"Jakey Jake, you okay, sweetie poo?" Elizabeth asked, rocking him.

I held Sophie. She didn't cry that much. Elizabeth was crazy. If Sophie was feeling a little overly sensitive, it was because she was surrounded by too many close-in-age brothers. Having kids three years apart was the healthiest span, all the baby experts wrote. I didn't even have children and I knew this. I'd lived this.

"Hey, *sheyne meydl*," I whispered to Sophie. "Thanks for coming to hang out with me."

"Next time can we do a playdate?"

How cool! Sophie wanted to play with just me! "You're on, kiddo."

The cab honked, and Ben and Sidney waved from the front seat. I held the umbrella over Elizabeth, who got in the backseat with the baby. Ben loaded the equipment and presents into the trunk. I didn't want to let go of Sophie, but I reluctantly handed her over to Elizabeth, who waved good-bye as they drove off.

Up Broadway, the glare of streetlights shined on the slippery pavement. It was dangerous to be out on a night like this. I was worried about them. The wind turned my cheap umbrella inside out and the rain hit my face. I threw the broken contraption in a garbage can in front of my building. My arms felt empty. Noticing a soggy pack of Marlboro Lights in the trash, I looked inside. There were three left but I didn't take one.

Back inside I surveyed the damage—just the vase and the glass. They were good kids, I thought. If I ever had any, I wondered if they would look like Sophie, Sid, or Jake. But I wasn't as selfless as Elizabeth. I didn't want to compromise my career. And I couldn't bear the thought of having to relive every year of my own childhood. I had too much baggage I wasn't ready to unpack. I didn't want bars on my windows. There was too much breakable artwork in low places here.

I felt hurt that Elizabeth had never opened the special framed photograph I'd given her. But trying to be generous, I thought of how beautiful my niece and nephews were. And how happy she was making Ben. I turned on the dishwasher, then called their room at the Parker Meridien. Nobody answered. My mother made us check in the minute we got anywhere. I dialed again. Finally, at one o'clock, Elizabeth picked up.

"You're home okay?" I was relieved to hear her voice. "What a storm."

"Damn cab driver went up Third Avenue," she said. "I told him to take Park."

"Well, I'm just glad you got home okay."

"Where did you get that picture?" she asked.

Oh good, she'd opened it. "Hope found a negative I was able to blow up," I explained. "I've become friends with her lately."

"When I was growing up, Hope was my fantasy mother," Elizabeth said.

Hope and my mom were the same age. So Elizabeth and I had not only swapped lives and cities, we'd switched female role models. If I had an imaginary mother, she'd definitely be a well-known photographer in the Village.

"That's why you fell for Ben at the Plaza that week in New York," I told Elizabeth. "The first guy who got you a butterscotch sundae from room service won your hand."

"I did not. Don't be ridiculous," she said. "Ben and I stayed at the Parker Meridien."

No, I was sure that the first time they'd stayed at the Plaza. That was the whole idea of giving her the Plaza photograph. "So you don't like my present?" I asked, feeling dejected. I'd managed to fail at everything tonight.

"Ricky, you gave me the best present anyone ever has. You gave me Ben."

It really touched me when she spoke so sweetly of my brother. It made me feel as if I'd succeeded at something much more important than Hanukkah gifts.

"Thanks for coming downtown," I said. "It was great to have you over."

"I thought you were mad. We'll get you a new glass and vase."

"Don't worry about it," I said. That was what family was for—to break things that couldn't be replaced and replace things you didn't know were missing. "Sid is just like Ben was."

"Your mother said Ben was a hurricane."

I heard Sophie in the background. "Is she okay?"

"Crying again. She's driving me nuts," Elizabeth said. "Gotta go."

"Love you," I surprised myself by mumbling, quickly slipping it in the way Ben did, before I hung up the phone. It was the first time I'd ever said it to her, and I wasn't sure if she'd heard.

chapter twenty-three
mother's day
October 14, 2007

When my mother found out that Aunt Sally and Uncle Max had both been diagnosed with cancer, she lost it, Elizabeth called to tell me. So I decided to fly home for Mom's sixtieth birthday weekend, hoping to celebrate and console her while getting some time alone without the whole Solomon brigade busting in on us. She promised to pick me up at the airport, so when I walked outside the baggage claim at O'Hare to find Elizabeth there to claim me, I felt slighted. My sister-in-law was sitting in a brand-new gigantic SUV I'd never seen before. It was silver, the shade of my mother's Cadillac.

"There's the famous shutterbug." She smiled.

"Hi." I kissed her cheek automatically; she didn't seem to mind. "Where's Mom?"

"She asked me to come get you," she explained.

"Is she okay?" Leah Solomon was more literal-minded than I was. She never didn't show up when she said she would.

"She wants to stay with Max in New Jersey but they don't want her to visit now. Their insurance covers home care, and there's not enough room."

Boy, it must be bad if the New Jersey branch wasn't welcoming her to visit. I sighed, putting my black bag in the back, filled with three kiddie seats, Shrek, SpongeBob and Dora the Explorer videos and stuffed animals. "What a truck. When did you get it?"

"Ben got it for me. More than six months ago," she said.

Was that a hint I should have flown home to see her gas guzzler sooner?

She pulled out of the space, expertly maneuvering to avoid the car parked to her right, and zipped onto the highway. I'd known her all these years without realizing she was an ace driver. When had that happened? I hardly drove anymore, was barely in automobiles these days, unless you counted quick jaunts uptown in taxis and town cars for art openings. I turned to inspect Elizabeth in the driver's seat. She looked pretty, with silky Ricardo hair and my mother's makeup. But she was a little heavy; she hadn't lost all her baby weight yet. It had taken three pregnancies, but I was pleased to finally be thinner than she was.

I spied the Presidential Barbie I'd sent Sophie on the floor of the backseat, picked her up and brushed her off. "I found the Barbie jet on eBay. I ordered one for Sophie."

"She's still kind of young for Barbie. Your mom says you didn't really like them until you were five. Before that you'd get upset that the snaps and buttons on their outfits were so small," she said. "When you couldn't change their clothes, you'd just switch their heads."

"Mom doesn't know what she's talking about. I always loved Barbie," I sniffed. "And the woman president needs her own private plane."

"Hate to tell you, Sophie's more into pink Tinker Bell and ballerina dolls."

I turned on the radio and heard "I Walk the Line," one of Ben's favorite songs. It was mellow; this one I didn't mind.

"No more Johnny Cash." She laughed, switched stations, and careened into the fast lane.

Good. I wanted to get to my mother sooner. It felt like we were soaring from up high, looking down on all the smaller cars. Elizabeth was a speed demon, supremely confident at the wheel like everyone in my family except me. In Freudian dream analysis, driving a car symbolized being in control of your sexuality, Dr. C once told me, analyzing why—for a feminist—I preferred to be driven. I took out a cigarette and lit it, opening the window.

"I thought you quit smoking." She gave me a horrified look.

"I made it four months, longest I've gone without." My cell phone rang. Noticing the number, I picked up. "Mr. Korones, hi. Yes, of course I've seen the new section of *Vision*."

"You can't smoke in here," Elizabeth hissed.

"Ssh," I told her.

"You want to profile me? Really? With photos of me and my work? Wow, that would be amazing. Monday? This Monday? But my new show isn't until next fall; what's the rush? Really, the possibility of a cover? That much lead time? Okay, I'll get my publicist on it. I'll try her now."

"You have a publicist?" Elizabeth sounded shocked.

"I coordinate all press with Tiki, my publicist at Rizzoli, and Joris's gallery person," I told her. "*Vision's* new editor wants me in their annual young turks of the art world issue. Could be a cover story. Do you know what this would mean for my career?" I took a puff, assuming she'd be awed I could actually wind up gracing the cover of our old magazine.

"I hear the new editor's even dumber than Richard," was all she said.

"I have to find Tiki right away." I dialed Tiki's numbers and left a few frantic messages.

"You used to parody idiots attached to their cells and Black-Berrys," Elizabeth sniffed.

"That's when I was broke and nobody important was calling me." I couldn't wait to tell my mother—who would totally get what a huge deal a *Vision* cover was. She'd be so proud.

"You can't smoke in here," Elizabeth repeated.

I sucked in smoke deeply once more before letting my cigarette fly out the window.

At my parents' house I ran in the front door, screaming hello to my mom. "Where's the birthday girl?" I yelled. Nobody answered. A playpen, two strollers, and rainbow-colored noise books seemed to forever litter the foyer.

"They're in the basement watching a video with the kids," Elizabeth said, sounding like I wasn't supposed to interrupt. She led me to the kitchen. The table was set. She took out cold cuts and lettuce from the fridge, put them down in front of me, then heated a teakettle on the stove. I'd never seen her play matriarch of Mom's kitchen before; it was unnerving.

Well, I was starving. I went to the fridge. Avoiding the plate of lasagna, I pulled out pickles, a tomato, and steamed broccoli, Elizabeth's favorite, which my mother had obviously cooked for her. For Danny she always had the chopped liver he liked. For Kim she got little fruit tarts. You knew you were officially a member of our clan when Mom had your food down. I took out chopped carrots and the bottle of my favorite Caesar salad dressing, but it was almost empty. I searched for the special tuna I liked from Star Deli, but I didn't see any. Had Mom forgotten?

I'd envisioned eating while playing Scrabble and catching up with her. But she was too busy with her grandkids and had obviously appointed Elizabeth the gatekeeper. I shoveled a big salad into my mouth, but she was barely touching her greens.

She sipped herbal tea and nibbled on a cracker. I tried to reach Tiki again, but nobody answered.

"Can't you stop working for one meal?" she asked. "It's really rude."

I stared at Elizabeth, about to ask when Ms. Social Retard had morphed into a Mom-blocking Miss Manners. But she didn't look so hot. Something wrong and weird was in the air, but I couldn't figure out what it was. Aside from my mother's not rushing to serve me a meal in her beloved kitchen like she'd always done before.

"You're not eating," I said. "Are you sick?"

"Morning sickness," she uttered.

Morning sickness? Oh no, was Elizabeth...?

"I'm pregnant again," she told me. "Three months in."

Her news made me crave a cigarette, a joint, *and* lasagna. No wonder she looked a bit heavy! Why couldn't she just gain some damn weight for *no* reason, like most people? I added five slices of cheese and a handful of cashews to my plate, then drowned the mound in the rest of the Caesar dressing and Thousand Island, vaguely aware that my salad now had more calories than the pasta I'd originally wanted.

"Congratulations," I eked out.

Although I was taken aback, the truth was that lately I'd been feeling extremely relieved that I'd picked a baby machine for my brother, as if I'd chosen a surrogate womb to carry the next generation of Solomons so I didn't have to. She'd taken away all the pressure for me to marry and procreate for the wrong reasons, like trying to pretend I was normal or wanting to please my parents. Sometimes it seemed as if Elizabeth and I were a couple who'd split up and I'd negotiated the better deal in the divorce settlement. She got the diamond ring, the big house in the burbs, and all the babies, while I was awarded her dad's agent, a bestselling photography book, and two thousand square feet in Manhattan.

"I've always wanted four kids," she said. "Four is the perfect number."

"So I'm not your rival anymore," I said. "Now you're competing with my mother."

"Me? You're the most competitive person I've ever met."

"You're crazy. I'm not competitive enough. Everything my mother did I couldn't even try. Cooking, sewing, making babies."

"I can see why," Elizabeth said. "Could there be a more impossible role model to live up to?"

"Well, luckily I don't want to re-create my mom's life," I snapped, going back to the fridge to get a diet soda to make up for the eight hundred calories of cheese, cashews, and dressing.

"Why not?" she asked. "Your mother is the only woman we know who got everything. Look at her. She'll be sixty tomorrow and she has a great husband, a beautiful house, three successful kids, grandchildren who adore her, and a party-planning business she loves."

It shocked me to think of my old-fashioned mother, a stay-at-home mom during my childhood, as an embodiment of the feminist ideal. Then again, she worked to put my father through medical school and started her company after we all went to college. Maybe the trick was that women could have it all, just not at the same time. I took out a chunk of orange cheese and a hard-boiled egg, hungry for my special tuna that wasn't there.

"I'm really surprised Mom didn't tell me you're pregnant." I assumed Elizabeth and Ben wanted to tell me themselves.

"We haven't told her yet." Elizabeth crossed her arms, as if to hide her stomach.

Uh-oh. I'd stumbled into an emotional pothole. Or was it a manhole without a cover?

"You've been keeping this secret from her for three months?" I asked. "Why?"

She picked up the knife and stabbed the middle of the thick

cheddar. "She's been in such a bad mood about Max and Sally. And everyone's fussing over baby Hannah. I don't want to steal Kim's thunder. And your mom's mad that Kim and I don't get along."

"So what? You have to tell her." I was appalled. "Didn't Freud say keeping secrets is poisonous to your soul?"

"Oh good, psychobabble." She rolled her eyes. "Just what we need today."

"What's the problem?" I asked, not getting it. "My mom loves her grandkids. She'll be happy to get another one. It's not a big deal."

"You haven't been around in a long time. It's becoming a bigger deal." Elizabeth squinted, flicking slivers off of the cheese she wasn't eating, seeming weary and worried.

"Why?" I chomped on a carrot.

"Your dad spoke to Max and Sally's doctors yesterday. Their prognoses are not good."

"Both?"

"His melanoma is malignant, and her breast cancer is stage four, with metastasis to other organs." Elizabeth dunked her tea bag in and out of her cup.

A doctor's daughter, I instinctively knew the next question was "How long do they have?" I was shocked that nobody in my family had told me that Max and Sally were this ill. Desperately searching for something else to say, I finally tried, "I bet my folks are glad you understand the medical terminology."

"Not really. I screwed up. It was a stupid time for me to ask your parents to be the kids' legal guardians in case anything happens to us."

"I'm sure they'll say yes," I said, puzzled, trying to decipher how this was connected to Max's illness, my mother's not coming to the airport, and the missing tuna.

"They said no. They think they're too old to raise four little kids. My mom's ten years older. They want us to ask Kim and

Danny. But Kim's overwhelmed taking care of one baby. And I'm not having my children raised by someone who hates me. I thought of my sister, but she's divorced, broke, and can barely deal with her own two kids."

Having yet to digest the news about Elizabeth's new fetus or the sick cells of my uncle and aunt, I couldn't wrap my head around the rest of the Mann family's soap operas. Why was she telling me all this now? "So what are you going to do?" I ate all the cheese slivers Elizabeth had sliced.

She poured a few Sweet'N Lows in her tea, then stirred. "I was wondering if you would consider it," she slipped in. "You're the only one everybody would agree to."

"Consider what?"

"Being the kids' legal guardian," she said. "If anything happened to me and Ben."

"Me?" Oh fuck. I choked on the cheese I was chewing, took a swig of diet soda quickly. She had to be kidding. Wasn't she? Yet the serious look on her face showed she wasn't. Had this inane idea been discussed without me? Nothing like putting me in the worst spot I'd ever been in the minute I landed at my old home.

Luckily my BlackBerry went off. Saved by the buzz. But then I looked at it, looked at Elizabeth, and knew I had to let the message go to voice mail.

"You're young; you could afford it. You have that huge three-bedroom apartment," she listed. "The kids all love you."

They did? Since when? "Elizabeth." I paused. "Your kids are great and beautiful and I love them to death. And I'm so flattered that you guys would even consider me. But—"

"I knew you wouldn't say yes." She cut me off. "You don't want kids, let alone mine. Right?" She looked up at me with a mix of hurt, vulnerability, and expectation, waiting for me to jump in and disagree.

"Do I hear my Ricky's voice?" my father called, coming up the stairs slowly, using his cane.

"Hey, Dad." I rushed to hug and kiss him, relieved for the natural escape from Elizabeth's guilt-inducing interrogation. "How's Grandpa doing?"

"We watched Barney," said Sophie, behind him. "And the *Cat in the Hat* twice."

I went to kiss her, but she pushed away. Oh no, don't tell me my precious Sophie was becoming anti-affectionate, like her mother used to be. She didn't remember how much we'd bonded in New York; I was heartbroken. Or was I paranoid that she'd somehow overheard our conversation! How could I be their guardian if Sophie, my favorite, didn't even like me?

"I get Grandpa's computer," said Sid, behind her. "You can't use it. Just me."

"Enough computer games and *Cats in the Hat*." My father looked tired but jolly, Santa Claus leading the elves.

Ben came up next, followed by my mother, in a light pink sweat suit, holding Jake.

"Hi, Mom," I said. "Happy birthday! How are you? Did you get my present?"

"Aunt Ricky, I love the President Barbie you gave me," Sophie jumped in, slowly recalling who I was and that she liked me.

"My Barbie loves you too." I picked her up and spun her around, wondering why my mother hadn't answered me. Was she ignoring me? Did she hate my gift?

"And I saw your house!" Sophie went on. "Sid broke the vase and the glass all over the floor, remember?"

"That's right!" I squealed. "He was a one-man demolition team. And where did you see my house?"

"In Greenwich Village, New York," she said, suddenly my giggly best girlfriend. "Spin me again."

I was so happy she remembered.

"Can we get a President Barbie for baby Hannah?" she asked.

"Don't I get a kiss?" I asked Sid.

"Yuck. No!" he yelled. "Puke."

I kissed him anyway, then hugged my mother. She seemed frazzled and elsewhere. "Are you okay?"

"Fine," she said, obviously very not fine. "Didn't hear you walk in. When did you get here?"

"Just a few minutes ago." I kissed her forehead.

"Did you eat? Are you hungry?"

"We're eating now. Elizabeth put out some food." I held up a forkful of salad.

My mother sat down at the kitchen table, looking at Elizabeth's bare plate. "You're not eating," she said. "I'll warm up the broccoli I made you."

"No, that's okay. I'm not feeling well."

"What's wrong?" my mother asked.

Elizabeth glanced at me, then looked at my mother and blurted out, "I'm pregnant again." When I'd urged her to spill the beans, I hadn't meant in public in the middle of my mother's big birthday weekend.

I patted Ben on the shoulder. "Good work," I said. "Now keep your pants on for a few years, okay?"

"That's great! Mazel tov!" My father kissed Elizabeth on the cheek and Ben on the head. The senior Dr. Solomon was the ringmaster of Barnum and Bailey today.

"When?" Mom asked.

"I'm three months in," Elizabeth answered.

We all turned to my mother, the candy and balloon lady, the bubbly one, awaiting her blessing. Instead she turned and walked upstairs without a word. My father had become emotional and empathetic, my mother cold and absent. All sorts of insane reversals had taken place since I'd last been here. Excusing myself, I followed Mom up to her bedroom.

She was in the walk-in closet, wearing only a beige bra and shiny Givenchy panty hose, pulling an orange dress over her shoulders. I helped push it down past her knees. She turned her back to me and said, "Zip."

"What are you doing?" I zipped.

"Changing," she said. "Danny, Kim, and Hannah will be here at five."

"Did you get the present I sent?"

"The robe is nice," she said.

I thought a thousand-dollar black satin robe from Bergdorf Goodman was more than nice. I was disappointed by her reaction, but I realized, given the bad news about Max and Sally, that nothing would please her now. Plus I'd probably imposed my color preference on her, the way she used to do to me. I should have picked up flowers too, but I'd sent roses for Mother's Day and my parents' anniversary. I worried we weren't doing enough for her birthday, but she'd insisted no party or fancy dinner. I guessed the sudden announcement of Elizabeth's fourth child made her feel misplaced, not in the spotlight on her big day. Was she feeling upstaged by Elizabeth? Angry that Elizabeth had kept the secret for three months?

She went into the bathroom, turned on the light of her makeup mirror, and sat on the stool. I stood behind her, staring at her face in the mirror. Her red hair—dyed and fluffed by Ricardo—was luminous. But with the age spots on her neck and the lines under her big brown eyes, she suddenly looked older than usual, and tired. She took out lip liner and drew a circle around her lips.

"Mom, you probably didn't mean to, but you hurt Elizabeth's feelings," I said softly. "When she announced she was pregnant, you didn't say anything. You just walked upstairs. That was rude. She's overly sensitive now."

Mom filled her lips in with orange-red gloss, dabbed rouge on her cheekbones, and said, "It's my birthday." She sprayed perfume behind her ears. "I can do whatever I want."

"But you were inappropriate."

"You've been inappropriate your whole life," she said. "I can be inappropriate once if I feel like it."

Okay, she had a point. But this was the worst, wildest role reversal yet—me playing a polite suburbanite to my mother's obnoxious, antisocial rebel. Yet if Leah Solomon was blatantly rude to somebody, there had to be a reason.

"I know you've been having a rough time," I said. "I'm so sorry to hear how sick Max and Sally are."

"They've always been like parents to me." She brushed brown mascara on her light lashes. "I'm just not in the mood for all the chaos today."

"You mean too many grandkids too fast?" I asked. "Or am I projecting?"

"You're projecting." She used a little brush on her eyelashes. "I told everyone I didn't want to celebrate my birthday. I need peace and quiet. I don't have the energy right now."

For the first time ever I feared she didn't want me here. "Was it a bad weekend for me to come home? Is that what's wrong?"

"No! What's wrong is you're so selfish and work obsessed, you haven't been home to visit in a whole year! Sending ridiculously overpriced presents doesn't absolve you from your responsibilities or make you part of my family. You used to make fun of expensive gifts I sent you. You did that whole nasty spread about it."

I flashed to the angora sweater series I'd had published in *Paper* magazine. I'd never known it bothered her. "That wasn't because the gifts were expensive. It was because of the mismatch since I'm so urban and they were so suburban," I meekly tried to explain.

"What could be more mindless and superficial than phoning a Bergdorf personal shopper to send me a designer robe? She forgot to take the price tag off," she snapped, teasing her bangs with a comb, not looking at me. "You didn't even send me a real birthday card."

Ouch! She'd totally nailed me. I hadn't.

"I'm glad that your work is going well," she told me. "But you have no idea what's been going on here."

"So tell me," I said. "What's going on?"

"I'm not feeling well. I'm having hot flashes and migraines and haven't slept well in three months. The arthritis in my arms is acting up. I can barely lift the kids anymore."

Did I know she was arthritic and still having menopausal symptoms? I'd never heard her complain of illness before. I'd asked "How are you?" but when she'd said "Fine" I'd never inquired further.

"And I'm really worried about Sid," she said. "He's hyper all the time, and antisocial."

"Mom, he'll be fine. That test said he has a high IQ. Ben was probably dyslexic and had ADD too, they just didn't have a name for it back then. Now he's a big surgeon," I babbled, trying to soothe her. But this clearly wasn't about Sid. Was it partly the sleep deprivation talking? I guessed she was exhausted from being the big matriarch, sick of everybody's either rebelling against her, or wanting her approval, or trying to be her.

She left the bathroom and sat down on the burgundy and gold bedspread by the window. She looked out at the lake in back. The sun was going down, and the blue neon light from my father's bug zappers was strung along the elms and weeping willows. In the lamplight, she looked smaller and more fragile than I'd ever seen her. I had been away too long. I felt guilty about wanting to share all my news about the *Vision* cover story, as if her job was still to be my cheerleader and to take care of me. I wrapped both arms around her shoulders, as if shielding her from a threat I couldn't see.

"My mother had me when she was thirty-eight years old. She died when I was four," she said quietly. There was nobody to take care of us. "My father died before I was out of elementary school. I know what it's like to grow up an orphan."

Losing her parents so young had never left her. I sometimes forgot what she'd been through and how fortunate I was to still have her and my father to come home to at my age. I scratched her back up and down with my nails, the way she used to scratch mine.

"I'm afraid something's wrong with Sid. Jake is jealous of the older two. And now she's having another baby. Ben's a busy surgeon who's never home. If anything happens to Ben and Elizabeth . . . ," she started to say, but tears welled up and she couldn't finish.

"Women have kids much later now. And nothing will happen to Elizabeth or Ben." I scratched up and down.

"I hope not. I have a business to run. I'm too old to raise four babies now. I can't even carry them for long anymore, and your father needs a cane to walk. Elizabeth's mom is ten years older than me. Her father's dead. Her sister drinks and has no husband and no money. Elizabeth and Kim hate each other. With all Kim and Danny have been through, they're not going to raise four of Elizabeth's children. I'm afraid if something happened to me—"

"Elizabeth and Ben are young and strong. And nothing's going to happen to you," I cut her off, suddenly afraid something could. The thought of her not being here when I came home to visit made me panic.

"I'm not going to be around forever. And when I die, my grandkids could be . . ."

"I'm considering being their guardian," I amazed myself by saying.

"You will?" She turned and looked in my eyes.

"I'm *considering* it," I said slowly. "Elizabeth just mentioned the problem."

"Well, you have a big apartment, and your mortgage is almost paid off. You have money in the bank. You're freelance, so you have time," she listed.

So this had been discussed without me. "But I'm sure you'll want your own kids," she continued. "Right? So this would get in the way."

This was clearly not the time to admit that none of my fantasies for the future involved anybody's children. If I had a crystal ball, I hoped it would show a tall man, Manhattan gallery shows, and a lot of cool cameras.

"If I ever do, I would probably only have one child," I answered. "But listen, nothing is going to happen to Ben and Elizabeth."

"But you'll consider it?" she asked again, as if she thought I didn't quite understand what was actually on the table here. Unfortunately, I did.

"Yes. I'll think about it. And I'll talk to my lawyer in New York. Okay?"

"Okay," she said, sounding better. As well she should. I was so glad she didn't want anything special for her birthday. Except to trick me into having her life.

"But you have to come downstairs now," I bargained.

"No, I don't." She stuck out her tongue.

I held out my hand and she took it, following me back down to her kitchen. My father and Ben were leaning on the marble counter, looking perplexed. I knew they were upset because their plates were empty. They hadn't eaten a thing yet. Elizabeth was sitting by the window, her arms still crossed. Even the kids were silent, a courtroom awaiting the verdict.

"Grandma, I'm hungry." Sid ran up to my mother, wrapped his arms around her legs. She leaned down and kissed him.

"Grandma, aren't we going to light the candles on your cake and sing 'Happy Birthday'?" Sophie asked.

"Da! Ma!" Jake joined in, banging on his high-chair tray.

Out the window I saw Danny and Kim's brown SUV pull up the driveway. It seemed everyone here drove trucks filled with babies in car seats. I sure hoped I'd never have to learn to maneuver one of those mammoth vehicles around here—or anywhere.

"Look who just pulled up." My father pointed to the kids.

"It's baby Hannah!" Sophie said joyously, running to the door.

"Thanks," Elizabeth told me quietly.

I wondered if she was thanking me for talking my mother down. She couldn't already know what had just transpired upstairs. I wasn't *that* transparent. Was I?

My mother smiled at me, quickly taking out the lasagna, salmon, chopped liver, and potato salad from the refrigerator, as if nothing had happened. Then she went to the door, greeting Danny, Kim, and their baby, Hannah. To keep up with Elizabeth, Kim had named her beautiful little girl after another of my deceased relatives, my father's mother. It was the ideal way for *shiksas* to please their Hebrew parents-in-law: If you give me your son, I'll resurrect all of your family's dusty monikers.

"Happy birthday." They hugged and kissed Mom, handing her gifts and balloons.

"Good. You're here. We're all here now." She led everyone into the kitchen, and we all crammed around the table, Sid on my father's lap, Sophie on mine. "Everything will be all right. You're just in time to eat."

"Elizabeth has some news to share with everyone," I threw out.

"Did you hear Ricky's going to be featured on the cover of *Vision* magazine?" she said.

chapter twenty-four
big date
November 20, 2007

"Hi, Aunt Ricky. We're here. Can we do a playdate?" Sophie's little voice startled me over the phone on Tuesday morning.

"Hey, honey. Welcome to New York. Sure. Can't wait to see you." I mouthed that I'd be right off to Suzette, who was sitting on the black leather couch in my living room, checking out the new slides I'd handed her. "When are you thinking?"

"Daddy says noon."

Noon? Today? But that was less than an hour from now! When I'd told Sophie I'd spend time with her during their Thanksgiving trip to see Elizabeth's mother in Westchester, I'd pictured making a plan in advance for a quick weekend brunch. Her timing couldn't have been worse. I was in the middle of charming the hell out of Suzette Wong, the spiky-haired *Vision* reporter interviewing me for their cover story. I was late with two big deadlines before Thursday's holiday. Plus I had plans to go out—and in—with Claudio later.

"Wow. That's soon." I stalled, glancing over at Suzette, wondering how much longer I had to be a dancing monkey to get good press. I'd already sacrificed the entire day before and two hours this morning. "Put Daddy on the phone for a sec."

"Listen, if you're too busy with work to keep your promise—" Ben said.

"I'm not too busy," I cut him off, pondering whether I'd actually promised Sophie a playdate or had just thrown out a casual "Sure, let's hang out." But I was afraid that if I said no, I'd hurt her feelings. My mother's Jewish guilt was kicking me in the gut. "See you soon."

Hanging up, I turned to Suzette. "Listen, I'm sorry. An emergency just came up," I told her. "Is there any way we can finish this later?"

"I'm leaving for Paris tonight," she said curtly.

"How about another sit-down after the holiday?" I asked.

"Actually, I have everything I need."

That sounded cold and ominous. Everything she needed to bless me or to trash me? "I'm available by phone and e-mail," I offered. "Oh, and I downloaded Skype on my laptop if you want a video chat while you're away."

"I'm all set." She tossed my slides down on the table, snapped up her briefcase, and stood up. "I just need Hope Maxwell's number."

"Right." I wrote it down for Suzette, saw her to the door. "Okay. Well, thanks so much for your time."

When she was gone I left a message for Claudio asking to switch our early dinner to late drinks. Then I called Ben back to ask what I should do with his daughter when she got here. I had no idea.

He said Elizabeth was afraid Sophie might be nervous being

alone with me in a strange city. I hadn't thought of that. What if she freaked out or threw up or had a tantrum like Sidney often did? I changed from my black pantsuit to jeans, feeling harried, betting I was more anxious than Sophie. After all, I'd never spent a whole day alone with a four-and-a-half-year-old before. The unanswered question of the legal guardianship of Elizabeth and Ben's kids was still unsettled. This could be a good test. If I couldn't handle an hour with my adorable niece, I couldn't even consider raising the whole brood. Right?

Luckily when Ben and Sophie showed up, she seemed fine. In fact, she was jazzed to hang out with me.

"Hey, Aunt Ricky. Nice place," she said, as if she'd never seen it.

In jeans, a Windbreaker, and Nike sneakers, she was dressed like an athletic young mini-Elizabeth. But with her bangs and hair as long as mine, I thought she looked more like me. Giving her a big hug and spin hello, I asked, "When did you get so pretty?"

"Ricardo did my hair before I left," she said, primping.

As Ben took a call from his office on his cell, she checked out the apartment, walking into my bedroom, office, and bathrooms. "You live here all by yourself?"

"Just me."

She leapt into the walk-in closet and called out, "You have so many coats!" It reminded me of the way her mother had once inspected my old place. "No pets?"

"Nope."

She looked amazed that a household could contain just one female, with no father, brothers, cats, or dogs. I waited for her to ask about the square footage. But she was more interested in the old semi-destroyed Barbie dolls on my shelf and took down the frazzled Malibu Francie. "You can go now, Daddy. Just girls."

Ben shrugged, finishing his call. "We're taking the boys to the science museum. I'll come get her around six."

Six? "That's six hours," I blurted. My entire workday would be shot.

"Well, you have my cell number if you freak out playing mommy," Ben razzed me, having obviously read my panicked expression.

"There won't be a problem," I told him.

"No problem," Sophie reiterated, throwing her coat on the couch where the reporter had just been, opening up the book of slides on the table. She was more confident we could handle a whole afternoon together than I was.

"Okay, okay. Just the girls," Ben said as I walked him to the door.

When I came back, I sat down on the couch with Sophie. "What are you in the mood to do?"

"What are my choices?" she asked.

Uh-oh. I didn't know. "Well, let's see, we can go to the playground, to the zoo, to a museum, to a movie, shopping, out to eat, for a walk," I improvised, exhausting my repertoire of potential kiddie activities. I worried it was too many options. But the last thing I wanted to do was go up to Central Park or to the Bronx to see smelly animals. Could I take that one back?

"Let's eat," she said without hesitation. I was relieved.

"Cool. We can get Chinese, Italian, French, or Japanese." Elizabeth bragged that Sophie ate everything, but did Midwest munchkins her age eat sushi? "Or we can go to the dive where your mom and I used to go."

"The dive," she said with glee. "What's a dive?"

"It's a place that's not too fancy." I grabbed my coat and helped her back into hers, then ran to the bathroom to slap on the nicotine patch so I wouldn't be tempted to smoke around her. I made a mental note not to swear or say anything risqué. As I led her out the door, my BlackBerry buzzed. I took it out of my pocket, thinking it was Suzette with some last-minute question, but it wasn't. I left it on the foyer table. Then, on second thought, I slipped it back in my purse.

"I'm pressing 'L,'" Sophie informed me in the elevator. "Last time we were here Sid pressed all the buttons and we stopped at every floor. Dad said it was like the local subway."

When the doors opened, she sprinted across my lobby, waving to the doorman as if they were old friends. Taking her hand as we headed toward the Village Den, I walked on the outside near the street, nervous someone on the crowded avenue would bump into her. "I saw three dogs in your building. Don't you want to get a dog?" she asked. "Daddy says you need two or they get lonely. Mommy likes cats better. Sidney wants a bird, but I hate birds."

At the diner, the owner rushed over. "Ricky. Where've ya been? Is this your daughter?"

"No, it's my niece, Sophie."

It had been only a year since I'd been there. Lately I'd been frequenting uptown hot spots Claudio favored. I'd complained to Dr. C of the inanity of Manhattan's rich restaurant rituals. But she felt it would be emasculating to deny him the pleasure of wining and dining me. Since I never felt sexy *after* a huge meal, Claudio and I compromised. I'd show up at his Fifth Avenue and Sixty-fifth Street penthouse early and jump his bones, then we'd hop in the shower and go be gluttons wherever he wanted, satisfying all appetites. I'd made fun of Ben and Elizabeth's penchant for fine cuisine, dubbing them "a waiter's dream" for ordering so much at chic restaurants. What a hypocrite I'd become, falling for a fancy Upper East Side foodie. Nicky joked I was losing my anarchist credentials.

"This is Sophie," I told everyone proudly, leading her to a booth in the back.

My old waiter, Louie, came by with water and Diet Coke. "What can I get ya, Ricky?"

"You can order anything you want," I reassured Sophie.

"A large Coke, please," she said. I smirked, knowing Elizabeth never let her have sugary soda. When he left, she asked, "How did that man know what you drink?"

"I always get the same thing."

"How did they know your name?" she marveled.

"I tip really well."

"Don't you cook like Mommy?" she asked as Louie brought her Coke.

"Nope. Can't cook worth a darn. What do you usually eat for lunch?"

"Turkey sandwich on whole wheat," she reported. "With apple sauce."

It sounded bland to me, but then again, my favored meal before noon was cigarettes, warm diet soda, and leftover dope. Elizabeth's kids were all slim and athletic; I had to hand it to her for that. "Well, you're on vacation. So order whatever you want."

"Promise not to tell?" she asked, peering over her Coke glass with saucer eyes.

"Swear." I crossed my heart.

In her tiny voice she asked, "Do they have pancakes?"

"Let's ask Louie." I flagged him over, realizing I was about to ruin my usual fat-free yogurt before sex and dinner rule. "I'll have a cheddar cheese omelet and a bagel. Sophie wants to know if you have pancakes."

"You can have them with bananas, blueberries, or chocolate chips," he recited.

She looked up at me with a devilish smile and said, "Chocolate chip pancakes with lots of syrup."

"You want bacon or sausage with that?" he asked.

"Bacon, please," she replied.

This kid definitely had Solomon DNA. She knew exactly what she wanted without hesitation, she was impatient and always on time, and she had a marked preference for fattening junk. I felt like a mad scientist who'd genetically replaced some of her Mann tics with our tribe's traits. My BlackBerry buzzed in my purse. I pulled it out, noticing Claudio's number, but I didn't pick up. "Lot of calls today," I explained.

"Mommy says you're getting rich and famous," Sophie said.

"Really? She said that?" I was pleased. I'd been worried Sophie could sense that Elizabeth and I had been contentious lately, but she seemed oblivious. "What else did Mommy say?"

"You don't have a husband 'cause you're a workhall."

It took me a second to figure out she meant workaholic. I laughed. "Well, I've been struggling for years and it's finally going well. So I don't want to miss my chance."

"For what?" she asked.

"For cool assignments. Tomorrow I'm shooting photographs for *The New York Times Magazine*." I left out that it was crack babies at Harlem Hospital.

"Do you get tired working all the time?" She unwrapped her straw, put it in her Coke, sat up on her knees, and took a sip of her soda.

"Well, I'm lucky that I love what I do."

"Is your house always so quiet?"

"Pretty much." It occurred to me that Sophie was the only member of my family who ever asked me questions about myself and my career. "Why? Is your house always loud?"

"Yeah. Jake cries at night. The dogs bark. Sid smashes toys. Daddy snores, so Mommy makes him sleep in the other room. He sounds like a bulldozer. It scares me and the dogs."

I liked that she was so open, spilling her feelings without hesitation, just like another Solomon—me. "Being in a big family is hard," I told her. "I have two brothers too. Wasn't so much fun." When I finished my soda, I called out, "Louie, another Diet Coke, please." He brought it to the table with another straw.

"Your brothers are Uncle Danny and my daddy, right?"

"Right. I love them a lot, but growing up with three kids close in age was a headache."

"Sometimes I get a headache too," she said. "It stops when you grow up?"

"Yes. It gets a lot better," I said, not sharing that what helped most was moving seven hundred miles away.

When our food came, Sophie ate each of the chocolate chips with her fingers first, then drenched her pancakes in syrup and dug in. "Louie, can I get another Coke please?" she called out.

What a hoot. Though Elizabeth might not want her corrupted by my big-city bad habits.

"Have you decided what you're going to be when you grow up?" I asked.

"A photographer in New York."

"Really? Great choice!" I beamed. "That's fantastic."

"And I'm going to get married and have five babies I breastfeed," she added, finishing her pancakes. "'Cause it's better to feed the babies that way."

"Five babies, huh?" There went my feminist victory. But I bet it was a sign of good self-esteem that she wanted to surpass my mom and hers by having more kids than they did.

"You don't want a husband?" she asked, unwrapping a new straw for her second Coke.

"Not yet."

"Do you want any babies?" she said.

"There's a lot of ways to have a great life." Was I allowed to confess that my clan made me crazy while my career made me joyous? There was nothing I found more enthralling than capturing downtown characters with my camera. And then sitting on my darkroom floor at 3:00 A.M. with my negatives and contact sheets spread out, feeling like everyone was begging me to read the dark, secret stories their eyes were confessing. I couldn't believe my exhilaration when photo editors who'd ignored me suddenly called to say they were blown away by my latest clips. And to finally be able to pay my bills the day they came, to buy whatever I wanted, with money left over to anonymously donate to charities that helped people who deserved it. "Some girls get everything they need from their families, and others get happy through their jobs and friends," I decided on answering.

"Aunt Ricky, can I ask you something?"

Uh-oh. How much more intrusive could she get? Elizabeth told her she'd grow up, get married, and have kids. Could my career focus confuse her or screw up her worldview?

"You can ask me anything."

She moved in closer. "Can you get soda pop whenever you want?"

"Always," I said. "Best thing about getting big."

As we paid at the counter, I checked my BlackBerry and saw I'd missed a call from Suzette. Shit! I phoned her back, but she wasn't in. I tried not to worry as I strolled my neighborhood with my niece, showing Sophie my favorite haunts. "This is West-beth, where this amazing photographer Diane Arbus used to live." I pointed to the apartment complex.

"Is she still there?"

Guessing "She offed herself" wasn't the appropriate answer, I said, "No, she lives somewhere else now."

"What's this?"

"The White Horse Tavern," I told her when we passed by the bar. "It's where your grandpa William used to hang out."

"That's Mommy's daddy? What did he do there?"

Instead of "Drank himself into oblivion," I said, "He'd play with all of his friends."

"Did you know him?"

"I met him once," I told her. "He took very beautiful photographs."

"Just like you," she said.

We picked out cheap magic tricks, lollipops, and glow-in-the-dark Slinkys for her and her brothers at Tah-Poozie on Greenwich Avenue, and then shared a chocolate Tasti D-Lite with sprinkles. At One Fifth Avenue I said, "Your mom took me to a party here and introduced me to all the exciting art people in the city."

"Did you have fun?"

"Yeah, we really did."

At the light, I checked my phone again. In the second I was looking down, Sophie walked ahead of me, and a big scruffy guy with a duffel bag approached her. I ran ahead, my heart racing. "What are you doing?" I yelled at him, and picked her up, freaked out that he was trying to abduct her. But when I saw his face I recognized him as the harmless disabled vet who slept on a Washington Square Park bench. Relieved, I put her down, slipped him a dollar. Then I held Sophie's hand closer, not wanting to frighten her.

"Who's that?"

"He's just a neighbor I know. Don't worry."

"He needs a bath," she said. "Did you give him money 'cause he's poor?"

"Yeah."

For the rest of the way home, I held her hand tight, staying on the street side, carefully monitoring the traffic, not letting Sophie out of my sight. When a bus driving by splashed a puddle, I picked her up again quickly so she wouldn't get wet. Then I zigzagged around a nose-ringed idiot not watching where ashes from her cigarette were falling. I'd never felt so protective of anyone.

How fascinating to retrace the steps of the Village that Elizabeth and I once took with her daughter. If there was a cosmic justification for all the suffering and sour grapes I'd felt with my sister-in-law, surely it was Sophie. What a miraculous gift. Looking back, everything that happened since I'd replaced Elizabeth at *Vision* now seemed destined. If anything did happen to Sophie's parents, I thought—for a minute—I might be able to handle this. Then again, entertaining one kid for a few hours was screwing up my work and love life. I couldn't imagine being responsible for four kids every day.

Walking into my building, I was taken aback to bump into Claudio. "Hey, babe."

"Hey. What are you doing here?" I checked my watch. It was four o'clock. The message I'd left asked if we could switch our plans to eight.

"I was just leaving a note with your doorman. You didn't return my messages."

"I turned my phone off." He looked hotter than usual, in his brown suede jacket, cowboy boots, and tight black jeans that made me want to take them off of him.

He crouched down to be on the level of my niece and asked, "What's your name?"

She hid behind my legs and held my hand tighter.

"This is Sophie, visiting from Illinois. We're having a play-date."

"Oh, your brother and Elizabeth's daughter?"

"Do you know my mommy?" Sophie asked, clinging to my leg.

I'd told him about the condescending psycho sister-in-law who drove me insane.

"I've heard very nice things about her and hope to meet her soon," he said.

No way was that happening anytime in the near future. My family was still hounding me about Matthew and Abram. I wasn't providing any more ammunition. I was about to whisper that I'd see him naked in a few hours when he stood up. "Turns out I have to fly to Barbados tonight. There's an opening Joris needs my help with."

Had he stopped by for a quickie before he left? The thought gave me a thrill.

"Aunt Ricky, I have to go to the bathroom," Sophie said.

I felt awkward, not sure whether to invite him up or not. But he seemed to be making Sophie uncomfortable. "Okay, I'll take a rain check," I said.

"Want to come with me?" he threw out. "It's only three days."

Aside from a brief jaunt to Las Vegas for a hotel opening, we'd never traveled together. I'd have loved to go away with him. But I couldn't postpone my *Times Magazine* shoot tomorrow. Could I? I'd have to get rid of Sophie to rush around packing, find my passport, get cash on the quick. Ben had said I could call him to come get her whenever I wanted.

"I have to go to the bathroom," Sophie repeated.

I patted her head, looking at him, feeling like I could so easily fall right into his arms.

"Now, or I'll have an accident," she insisted.

"Wish I could," I told Claudio. "But I'm hanging out with my niece today. Sorry. Call me when you get back."

"I'll call you later, before I leave." He reached over and kissed me on the lips. Then he stroked my hair, looking at me oddly, like he didn't want to go. Had my blowing him off turned him on? I should have tried playing hard to get a long time ago. But I wasn't playing. As into him as I was, Sophie was more important. Was seeing me with a child altering his perception of me a bit? Maybe it could be altering mine.

"See you later, cutie," he told Sophie, winking at her as he left.

She pulled me into the elevator. When the doors closed, she said, "Who was that guy?"

"That's Claudio."

"Can he be your husband?" she asked.

Did I have any family members not trying to marry me off? "No, he's my friend."

"Where's Barbados?"

"Even farther than Illinois," I told her.

"He talked funny," she said. "Is that where his mommy is?"

This one never stopped talking and asking questions; it was

a little draining. Inside my apartment, I took Sophie into the bathroom, but she said she was a big girl and didn't need my help. When the phone rang, it was my mother. "I hear you have a visitor," she said, sounding gleeful that I'd spent the day with her granddaughter instead of in the darkroom.

"It's Grandma Leah," I told Sophie when she came out.

She rushed to the phone and took it from my hand. "Hi, Grandma. I had the best day. Aunt Ricky took me to this dive where I had chocolate chip pancakes, bacon, and Coke, but don't tell Mom. Every person there knew her name! And we bought magic tricks. And this tall guy who talked funny wanted to take Aunt Ricky on a trip but she told him no 'cause she's too busy with me."

Had I actually done that? After her rapid recap of our play-date, she handed me the phone.

"Why aren't you going away with Claudio?" Mom asked. She was so desperate for me to get married, even a foreign, non-Jewish guy would do.

"I have too much going on right now." My BlackBerry buzzed again. I remembered how hurt my mother was that I'd put my work before my family and let it go to voice mail.

While we were talking, I noticed Sophie checking out the pictures on the shelf. "That's Aunt Kim and Uncle Danny," she said to herself. "This is me and Hannah, my best friend. The next one is Grandpa Joe and Grandma Leah." Then she picked up the one of me and Elizabeth, in contrasting blazers. "Oh boy, look at that. Aunt Ricky's in black, Mommy's in red." Sophie giggled. "Are you girls all done fighting now?" she asked the photograph, cradling us close.

chapter twenty-five
getting the picture
August 9, 2008

Passing the newsstand on my way to the Northworst gate at LaGuardia, I was shocked to find Sienna stupid Miller's face plastered on the September issue of *Vision* instead of mine. I'd been bumped—because the hot blond Hollywood starlet had jumped into bed with yet another leading and very married man. How come when I triangulated I just got heartache but she got the fucking cover?

I masochistically bought the damn rag, depression washing over me as I read my disappointing four-paragraph profile—on page 26—with a small, sucky picture. I flashed to the morning I blew off that reporter Suzette Wong for Sophie, obviously a major faux pas. No wonder the bold print inside screamed: "Nepotism News Flash: How Ricky Solo Manned Up to Storm the Art World." How did they know about my link to William Mann?

In the taxi to Ben and Elizabeth's, I left a message on Dr. C's machine, wishing I could turn around and go home. But I'd promised to take pictures of Nicky's wedding that night. I was meeting her whole entourage at the Chicago Four Seasons at 6:00 P.M. sharp. It seemed inconceivable that she was moving back to Highland Park to wed Kenny Klein—a *heymish* divorced accountant we'd been ignoring since junior high. Even when she was jet-setting around the world, Nicky and I had the same home base. She was the only one who got me, since we were kids. Her leaving New York was more painful than all my other breakups combined.

My plan was to breeze into the Saturday afternoon barbecue Elizabeth was hosting for my dad's birthday, bestow presents, meet her six-month-old, Maxwell, and escape to Nicky's event fast, via car service, without any domestic drama. I was so demoralized I didn't know how I'd make it without the cigarettes or booze I was quitting. Again.

I expected my trip to have a somber undertone, since Elizabeth's latest offspring was named after Uncle Max, who'd died of cancer in January, seven months before. Aunt Sally had passed away a few hours later. My mother, still in mourning, took comfort in the timing, as if Sally saw no point in being in the world one day without her *bashert*. I'd been considering buoying Mom up by announcing I was ready to become the legal guardian of Ben and Elizabeth's kids, in case anything happened to them. But now I felt like an imposter with a career obtained under false pretenses, all my old insecurities and doubts resurfacing. I called my shrink again, who texted me two words: "Feelings misinform." What the hell did that mean?

Paying the driver, I got out at chez Solomon, schlepping my heavy leather suitcase filled with my evening outfit and camera equipment. Two black Labs jumped up to greet me. The bigger one slobbered all over me. As Max used to say, "Nothing's so bad it can't be worse." Walking inside, I passed a new, bigger wooden mezuzah on the doorjamb. In the bathroom I cleaned off the slobber, redid my makeup, and brushed my hair. On my way to the living room, I noticed two menorahs on the shelf in the foyer, next to two Yahrzeit candles. In the hallway, two fat tabbies lay next to the dog crate. I didn't know they had two cats. While I lived alone, they lived like Noah's Ark; even the Stair-Master was paired with a rowing machine.

When I hugged my mom, she asked, "What's wrong?"

"Nothing." I didn't need to concern her with such trivial matters.

"Don't tell me nothing," she said, reading my face.

"*Vision* bumped me from the cover."

"Oh, Lois called to say congratulations on the article. She said there was a cute picture of you. And they mentioned your show next month."

"Really? That's all she said?"

Mom nodded. "We'll pick up a copy on the way home if we can."

Although I hated my puny *Vision* profile, I was annoyed that my parents hadn't rushed out to get a copy.

Looking around, I noticed Sabbath candlesticks on the counter, next to this week's *Forward*. What was going on? "Funny that Elizabeth suddenly has all this Jewish stuff all over," I mumbled.

"It's not sudden," my mother said. "She's been thinking of converting for a while now. We've spoken to Rabbi Levin twice. We think it's wonderful."

Converting? I guessed latching on to the idea of Elizabeth's kids as Yids was a way for Mom to replace the *mishpokhe* she'd just lost.

"She wants us to feel comfortable in her home," Dad piped up.

"How *frum* of her." I used the Yiddish word for pious Orthodoxy, already wishing I could leave. I scanned the living room, which was crammed with kids, pets, and toys. "I'm surprised there's room for guests with the animal stuff and exercise equipment."

"But look how slim Ben is." My mother pointed to him, in the corner with Danny.

I agreed Ben looked good. Relaxed, thinner, content.

"And she's a wonderful mom," my mother rubbed in. "She adores those kids."

As if on cue, Elizabeth came over, holding baby Max, her biggest child, who'd weighed in at nine pounds, eight ounces at birth.

"You couldn't just have the third boy, he had to be most giant male baby in the history of the world," I fawned, touching his arm and kissing his forehead.

"I know." She laughed. "My Max is a huge little guy."

My BlackBerry buzzed. It was my *Times* photo editor, asking about the preliminary head shots of Gloria Steinem I'd taken the week before. At the paper's insistence, I'd tried a digital camera, a Canon 1D. But three of the JPEG's hadn't gone through. I called back to say I'd resend them later, then checked my watch. It was 4:00 P.M. The car was coming at 5:00.

"You just got here and you look like you want to go," Elizabeth scolded.

"Sorry. Crazy weekend with Nicky's wedding. And I'm on deadline for the *Times Magazine*," I said. "Can you believe they bumped me from *Vision*'s cover?"

"Don't you want to meet your new nephew?" Her voice was tinged with the brand of guilt particular to the tribe she hadn't officially converted to yet.

"I just met him. He's adorable," I replied, smiling.

"You looked at him for two seconds," she said, pouting.

"I don't want to be late for Nicky's wedding. The *Vision* piece sucks. And I can't screw up a *Times* assignment on an important social icon. Steinem's a big coup."

"Ha. Some icon. She marries for the first time at sixty-six and then she's surprised when the guy croaks," Elizabeth quipped.

Before I could overreact, Sophie, hiding under the steps, called out, "Hi, Aunt Ricky."

"Hey, sweetheart. How's my pal doing?"

She smiled but didn't get up to hug or kiss me. I knew she needed time to get used to me again, but I felt crushed. My father, still limping from his hip replacement and using a cane, managed to hobble over to Jake, who gurgled, "Pa! Ga! Pa!"

"Did you hear? He said 'Grandpa!'" my father bragged.

I slinked to the kitchen, opening the stove to find a brisket cooking. What was next—my dead zadie's potato kugel? In the fridge were several two-liter Diet Cokes. Everything here was king-size—even the babies and the soda bottles. I found an open bottle of Manishewitz red wine, took out a Barney the Dinosaur mug from the shelf, and poured myself a cupful. So much for sobriety. I craved a cigarette too, remembering a gas station a mile away where I could buy a pack. But I'd glued the nicotine patch to my arm, and Ben insisted that smoking while wearing the patch could cause a nicotine overdose. "Someone's fingers fell off," he'd ominously warned.

Peeking through the doorway, I watched my father playing with Max. Then he kissed Elizabeth on the cheek, which made me wince. I finished the wine and poured myself a bit more. The clock on the microwave said 4:15. The hotel was an hour away. I called the driver to come earlier, at a quarter to five, nervous about the traffic. I went over to Elizabeth and said, "Listen, I have to go soon, so I'll leave the presents for Dad and the kids downstairs."

"You can't go yet." She took my hand. "I need a big favor."

Oh no, now what? I'd already bequeathed her my home state, my eldest brother, my beloved parents. After my lawyer's final okay next week, I was one minute away from signing away my life of fun and freedom to be her children's de facto mommy. What more could this woman possibly want from me?

"For your parents' anniversary, we decided to give them a

framed photograph of the family—with you in it. We need you to take it. Your mom said you have all your cameras here. Did you bring the self-timer and the tripod? We could do it now."

"Now?" Getting everybody together would take too long. I looked at my watch: 4:22.

"It would mean a lot to your mom and be really special. An original Ricky Solo."

Shit. She used flattery, mother guilt, *and* my new moniker. Good ploy. I found my bag, went into the powder room to change into the black dress and heels I'd brought for the wedding. If this horrible day had to be immortalized, I might as well look thinner.

"Okay. Listen up," I announced to everyone when I came out. "I'm going to get one picture of everybody outside on the back lawn. But let's do this quick. Will you help me get the kids together?" I asked Danny.

"Sure," he said, waving Kim and Hannah outside. "By the way, nice piece in *Vision*."

"Nice? The idiot reporter said I only got my show because of William Mann."

"Just in the dumb headline. The article implied that Mann's agent took you on because you have the same ruthless eye as Mann did," he said. "The link gave you gravitas."

Sweet, but I didn't believe him. "I'm trying to figure out which enemy of mine planted that Mann gossip. And I'm still smarting that they bumped me from the cover."

"You're the only one who knows that. It's a good piece. Don't overthink it," he reassured me, helping herd the Solomons out into the Illinois sunshine while I set up my equipment on the overgrown half-yellow grass in the backyard.

Dad came out the side door, walking with a wobble but without his cane. He held the hand of little Jake, who was toddling quickly.

"Everyone's coming," Elizabeth said. She was in a short skirt, a sleeveless blue blouse, and sunglasses. Annoyingly, her legs were thinner than mine. But I was pleased to detect a varicose vein behind her knee, and her stomach didn't look as flat as it used to.

"Hurry up." Mom took Sophie's hand. "Ricky has to get to her friend's wedding."

"Oh, Ricky, I found your third-grade photo," Elizabeth said. "I don't get why you used to cut yourself out of the pictures. You weren't ugly or fat. Your mom's right; you were always pretty."

"Stop going through my old yearbooks. Can't you just leave them in my mom's closet?"

Dr. C found it bizarre that I expected belongings I'd left behind at my parents' house a decade ago to remain untouched. Then again, she didn't have a friend ransacking her childhood, popping out a tribe of mini-people who resembled her and answered to the names of her dead relatives.

Kim joined us, holding her beautiful little daughter, Hannah. Sophie held Hannah's other hand, announcing in an official tone: "Everyone, this is important. Aunt Ricky's taking our picture."

"Cool color scheme," I complimented her on her black summer dress, which I'd bought her.

"My Village outfit," Sophie sang. "Look, Hannah's wearing the one we got her too."

Whenever I gave her presents she sent me a card filled with glitter and stickers with smiley faces. "Sophie writes better thank-you notes than you do," I teased Elizabeth.

Kim laughed, but my mother glared at me.

"Yes. Aunt Ricky loves to take our picture," my mother told the girls, who unlike the grown-up females present, had adored each other from day one, unequivocally.

'Hurry up." I looked at my watch again. It was 4:35. "My car is coming in ten minutes. I have to be at the Four Seasons at six."

"I can't believe Nicky the rebel is moving back here." Ben grinned. Her decision to return scored one for his side.

As everyone gathered, I tried a fifty-millimeter lens to get the sky in the background. With her red hair, orange and yellow flowered sundress, and red lipstick, my mother looked like a Tropicana commercial. All the loud colors and patterns clashed. No wonder my best work was in black and white. Sid ran inside.

"Shit, it's late. Will you get Sidney?"

"Don't swear in front of the kids," Elizabeth scolded. "He probably ran back to his video game. Ben, will you go get him?"

"Hurry," Sophie said. "We need everybody in this picture."

"Why didn't you bring Claudio with you?" Kim asked while we were waiting.

"Because showing up with a rich Venezuelan Catholic lover would freak out the Highland Park kosher crew?" goaded Elizabeth.

"Because I don't need a date," I said, for once keeping my love life to myself.

"Did you hear Abram Silver's already divorcing the young wife?" Elizabeth asked.

"Is this a free photo shoot or a gossip-fest about my exes?" I asked, though I had been happy to note that when Abram tried to friend me on Facebook his profile status was "single." Guess his nineteen-year-old Orthodox almost-cousin wasn't such a godsend after all.

Interestingly, Matthew Wald also made contact after his broken engagement with a chatty e-mail that ended "See you at Nicky's wedding." I'd forgotten Nicky was the one who'd fixed us up. I ignored both men's cyber salutations. Ironic that the minute I didn't need a guy around, they were all over me.

"Claudio's such a sexy name." Kim wouldn't let it go. "Think he could be the one?"

"Right now I'm just having fun." At thirty-two, I no longer felt desperate to figure it out. Indeed, Hope had given me Rilke's

Letters to a Young Poet, where he said that people with artistic temperaments shouldn't marry until they were thirty-five.

"Getting married could be fun. What are you waiting for, Social Security?" Elizabeth needled.

"Oh, good. You name your kid after Max and channel his *alter cocker* voice too," I said.

"What's an *alter cocker*?" she asked.

"An old Jewish kvetcher in Florida," Danny explained.

"What's a kvetcher?" Kim wanted to know.

"What does it sound like?" Danny asked.

"A rutabaga," she answered.

"A ruta what?" Sophie asked.

Ben finally emerged with Sid. I switched the lens to a twenty-four-millimeter. Still no fluid line or symmetry. Kim, in a flowered T-shirt and culottes, stood beside Danny. Mom's orange silk sleeve bled into Jake's striped shirt. The two dogs ran out the door, followed by the cats, like they wanted to be in the shot too. Too many fabrics, colors, and styles. Or did the ragtag mix make the composition interesting? I took a light reading, fixed the meter, set the self-timer for thirty seconds, and looked through the lens.

"Sid, sweetie, you're not in. Move a little to the right," I said, but he didn't. "Come on. I just need one damn picture." I switched the timer to sixty seconds.

"One damn picture," he repeated.

"See what happens when you swear around the kids?" Elizabeth said.

"Yeah, see what happens?" Sid said, rushing up and pulling down my new Nikon.

"Hey. Don't touch my camera." I grabbed it from his hand.

"Don't yell at him!" Elizabeth screamed at me.

"He could break it."

"So? We'll get you another one," Ben said.

"Oh, right. On a Saturday night in *Shnipashuk* we'll find a special-order eight-thousand-dollar Nikon," I said.

"What's *Shnipashuk?*" Kim asked.

"A name Mom made up for God's country," Danny filled her in.

"Why don't you just tell your kids not to touch my equipment?" I asked.

"Kids don't do what you tell them," Elizabeth shouted. "You're such a control freak."

"Me? What are we all doing at your house today?" I asked. "We should be at my mother's, which would be easier for everyone but you."

"We switched your dad's party to Saturday afternoon because you had a wedding tonight and you booked your flight home for tomorrow," she argued.

"If you care about my schedule, why did I have to come an hour out of my way to get here? Since you became a kid factory, you're in control of everything," I blurted.

"You come home once a year and want everything the exact same as last time."

"What are you, the new Solomon guilt-meister?" I asked her. "You're worse than Uncle Max and Aunt Sally combined."

"You were too busy to come to her shiva in Fair Lawn," Elizabeth accused.

Why was she bringing that up? "After two funerals, I couldn't hang out in Jersey all day because I work. Remember what that is? It's the thing some people do to pay their bills."

"You didn't come to my father's memorial service either."

"I would have been there if you'd invited me," I told her, realizing our old arguments had never faded one bit. They merely came back in different incarnations, snowballing unexpectedly while I wasn't paying attention.

"You were invited," she added.

"You sent everybody else invitations, but called me an hour before."

"So what? I was too busy mourning my dad to play Miss Manners," she spat out. "And you've never even apologized for missing all three of my sons' brises!" Elizabeth was really on a roll.

"Oh, I'm sorry. I meant to miss all my deadlines to fly across the country every time one of your boy's penises needed to be nipped."

"Did you hear? She said 'penis'!" Sophie giggled.

"Pee pee," said two-year-old Jake, getting into the act.

"Look what you're doing!" My mother shook her head, hands on her hips.

"Yeah, what's wrong with you? Are you four years old?" my father yelled at me. "Why are you causing a fight for nothing on my birthday?"

"Your birthday is tomorrow," I snapped.

"You're leaving tomorrow! You just got here and you can't wait to leave," Elizabeth poured it on. "Chasing after magazine covers is more important to you than your family. We only rate an hour of your schedule."

"Oh yeah? Well, I'm rearranging my entire life to be your kids' legal guardian!" I surprised myself by shouting. "What do you call that?"

Everyone quieted down. Elizabeth looked confused. "What? When did you decide to say yes?"

"After six shrink sessions and two meetings with my lawyer. I even had baby guards put on all my windows," I admitted. "Do you know how ugly they are? They block the view."

"Are you just doing it to placate your mother?" she asked in a quieter voice.

"No. I'm not placating anyone. I love your kids. You know, I gave up a vacation with Claudio and screwed up the *Vision* article by blowing off the reporter for my playdate with Sophie," I told her.

"Oh, that's why Suzette said you were too busy for her."

"*You* spoke with the reporter?" Now I was the one in shock. "She called you?"

"Yeah. Hope gave her my number."

"*You* were the one who said I only got my show because of my link to your father?"

"No, of course not. I told her Joris was drawn to your photographs for the same reasons he loved Dad's work. And so was I."

"You did?" Elizabeth was comparing my work to her father's— and favorably? Since when? I was floored, and flattered beyond words. "Why didn't you ever tell me that?" I asked. On second thought, by generously connecting me with her father's editors and agents, maybe she had.

"You'll really be their official guardian?" she wanted to know.

"Yes." I nodded. "Not that anything will happen to you or Ben, but…"

"You'd have to learn to cook," my mother piped up.

"I can't get around easy these days," Dad said. "You'd have to come visit us more."

"Are you sure you could handle it?" Ben asked.

"Yes, I'm sure," I said, not sure at all. In fact, me in charge of four Midwestern munchkins seemed like the most disastrous— albeit hilarious—idea I'd ever heard. But it was time to stop chasing after bylines I already had for money I didn't need and make peace with my family, especially its new *yiddishe* mama, Elizabeth. They were always there for me, and I had to start coming through for them, showing up more.

In retrospect, I suddenly regretted not making her father's memorial service. After all, he wound up being related to me, on the same family tree. And the trade-off had never been accidental or one-sided in the least. Elizabeth and I had stolen each other's birthrights, our bloodlines overlapping, her story now part of mine.

"Can we take the picture already?" Sophie called out. "It's hot, and my hair's sweating."

"God forbid we ruin your Ricardo hair," I said, checking my watch. It was five o'clock. The driver—and Nicky—would be waiting for me. But this was more important. I reset my camera. "Everybody smile."

"No damn picture. I hate pictures," Sid screamed and ran to the swing set.

"Oh no. Get him," my mother shouted.

Damn it! Now I'd never get the shot. I had to leave in a minute or I'd be late for Nicky's wedding, and I was on the early flight back tomorrow morning. If I couldn't do this, Elizabeth and Ben would end up hiring an amateur to overpose them all against a red velvet background, and I would be left out. Tears rushed down my cheeks.

"Don't cry, Aunt Ricky," Sophie said. "If you want, I'll come hold you."

How wild to hear my mother's warmth emanating from this mini-Elizabeth, named after the grandmother I'd never met, whose face I only knew from the worn photograph that fascinated me as a child.

"I'm okay, angel," I said, walking up to Elizabeth, touching her elbow. "Look, you're right. My mother would love one shot of all of us. But I need your help." I owed it to my mom to do this. Or was this photograph really for me?

"I know. It's so hard to please her," Elizabeth said under her breath, confiding in me as if we were—and always had been— the very best of friends.

What did that mean? What wasn't pleasing Mom? I thought of the last time she'd said that. Up this close she looked tired, thicker in the middle. "Elizabeth, you're not...?"

"Two months in," she whispered back. "We haven't told any-one yet."

I was flabbergasted. Was this why Sophie wanted five babies? So Elizabeth wasn't just converting. She was emulating my observant female relatives in the old country who didn't use birth control, interpreting "be fruitful and multiply" as a mandate to personally repopulate our religion. How many kids could I get stuck raising, a whole minyan? What would she do next—start wearing a *shaytl* and going to the *mikve*?

"Mazel tov," I said, kissing her cheek.

"Okay. Let's do this," Elizabeth sprung to attention, handing baby Max to Ben. She marched over to the swings. With hands on hips, she reasoned with her stubborn firstborn.

My BlackBerry buzzed. My publicist texted: "*Today Show* loved *Vision* article, wants you on Tuesday. Are we on?" Man, were we on. But I'd answer later. First things first.

"Okay, we're doing this," Elizabeth said, dragging Sid back to the group shot.

"One damn picture," he said calmly, posing.

The entire Solomon gang reassembled. I reset the self-timer, squeezing back into the frame. Elizabeth was on one side of me, my mother on the other. I put my arms around both.

"Say 'love,'" said Sophie, leaning her head against my knee.

"You goofball," Sid shouted. "You're supposed to say 'cheese.'"

"Love works better," Sophie yelled back.

"I forgot how hard it is getting everyone to pose together," I told Mom.

"Now she's driving me crazy trying to get into the picture," my mother said, smiling as the shutter clicked.

about the author

Susan Shapiro is the author of the nonfiction books *Five Men Who Broke My Heart, Lighting Up, Secrets of a Fix-up Fanatic, Only as Good as Your Word,* and the comic novel *Speed Shrinking.* She lives with her husband, a TV/film writer, in Greenwich Village, where she teaches her popular "instant gratification takes too long" writing classes at The New School and private workshops. You can reach her through her Web site www.susanshapiro.net.